SE

by

Michael James

First published in Great Britain in 2009
This edition by Tyne Green

A CIP catalogue record for this book
is available from the British Library.

ISBN 978-0-956 1843-0-6

Printed and bound in Great Britain by
Think Ink, 11-13 Philip Road, Ipswich,
a division of Micropress Printers Limited.

For my children
Nick, Lucy and Tony

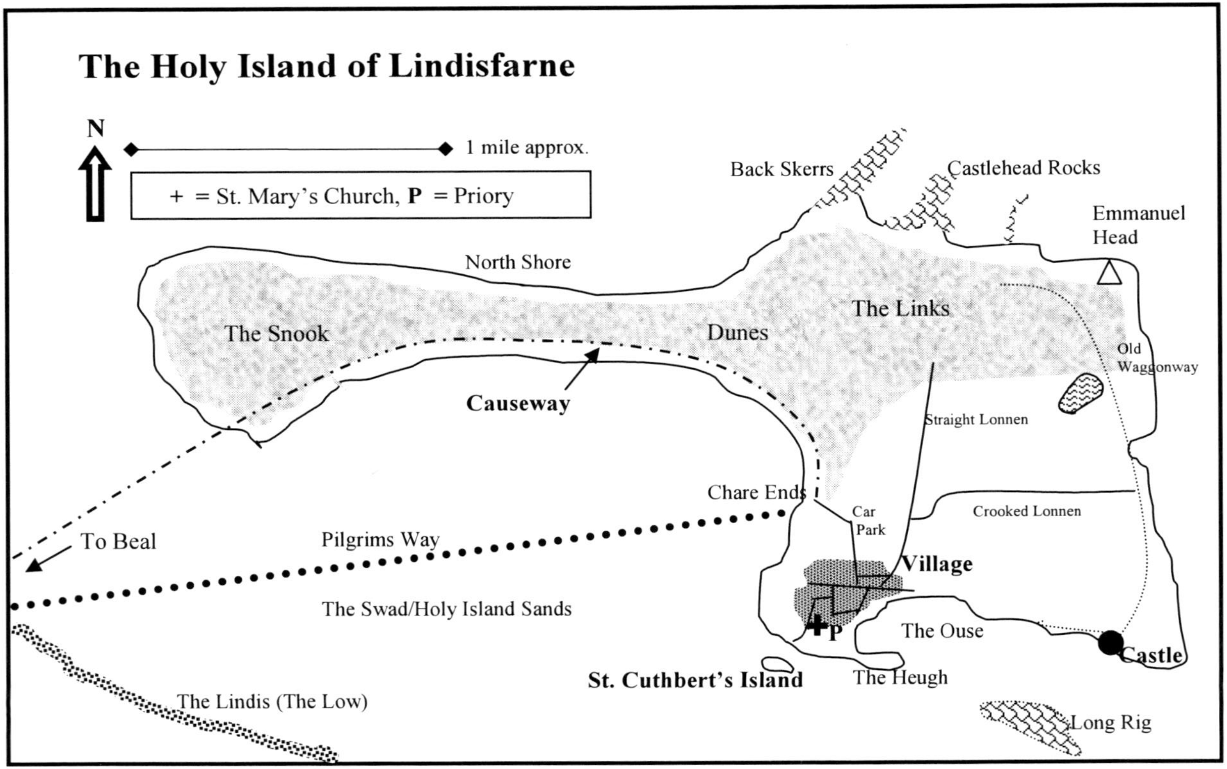
The Holy Island of Lindisfarne
N
1 mile approx.
+ = St. Mary's Church, P = Priory
Back Skerrs
Castlehead Rocks
Emmanuel Head
North Shore
The Links
The Snook
Dunes
Old Waggonway
Causeway
Straight Lonnen
Chare Ends
Car Park
Crooked Lonnen
To Beal
Pilgrims Way
Village
The Swad/Holy Island Sands
P
The Ouse
Castle
St. Cuthbert's Island
The Heugh
Long Rig
The Lindis (The Low)

PROLOGUE

The Holy Island of Lindisfarne, earlier times

Lindisfarne in the autumn months, seen from the Northumbrian shore, appears yellow, almost golden. It is a combination of sunlight, the reflection of sunlight and clouds off water, the marram grass that waves like wheat over the dunes, the sandstone and limestone strata overlain with broken shells and sand on exposed shores and outcrops.

With the Farne Islands to its south, the island forms the eastern tip of the Great Whin Sill, a slab of dolerite, or "whinstone", which traverses the north of England and appears most noticeably along the line of Hadrian's Wall. Like the rest of the Sill, the whinstone of Beblowe Crag and the Heugh—the Lindisfarne Dyke—was created 300 million years ago by an eruption of molten rock bursting through the island's sedimentary strata from the earth's core. It is thought that Stone Age Man dwelt here five thousand years ago, and that the Romans resettled Holy Island village three thousand years after them.

The main body of the tidal island measures two square miles. It is low-lying, no part of it higher than thirty metres above sea level, cut off from the mainland nine or ten hours each day. A century ago, the only means of access was by foot or donkey or pony cart across the Swad at low tide. For decades, the post cart made the trip twice daily. Until the second half of the twentieth century, there were few vehicles on the island. Those that existed were put to work. Hard work; for the goods they carried were not luxury goods.

Formerly called Inis Metcaut or Medcaut ("island of strong winds") and later Insula Sacra, the island has a long history as a holy place, a place where Christian saints have trod since 635 AD. It has nurtured no less than nine of them, some more luminous than others. Aidan, the Irish-Ionian trailblazer, confidant of kings and father of the Celtic Church in England, founder of the monastery and first of sixteen bishops of Lindisfarne. Cuthbert, the beloved shepherd boy from the Lammermuir Hills, initiate of Melrose, reluctant sixth bishop and committed hermit who longed to be nearer his God. And Wilfrid, the stormy and impatient prelate, the truth-seeker whose temporal horizons radiated like a crusader's. Down the ages there have been several churches on the island: the Parish Church; its neighbouring Priory and Benedictine monastery; "St. Cuthbert in the Sea" on an islet west of the Priory; St. Columba's Church near St. Coombs farm; and perhaps, although there are doubts about this one, a chapel on the Heugh, a hill of Whin-grassland overlooking the Ouse, or anchorage.

Lindisfarne's history, however, has not all been conversion and devotion. In 793 AD the Vikings came "like stinging hornets, like ravening wolves", burned the settlement, plundered the church, slaughtered many of the monks, drowned some in the sea and took others away in fetters.

There was bewilderment and outrage at this act of terrorism. But one chronicler, the theologian and teacher Alcuin of York, who was later beatified, chastised the monks for the lax lifestyle that had sent the Vikings in "divine retribution," and took a sideswipe at Cuthbert for allowing such degeneracy to happen. Never before, he wrote in scholarly Latin, had such a terror appeared in "this place more venerable than all in Britain...The pagans," he wrote, "have trampled the bodies of saints in God's temple like shit in the street."

It didn't stop there. In 875 AD, threatened by a second Viking onslaught, the monks wisely took St. Cuthbert's body, St. Aidan's bones, St. Oswald's head and the Lindisfarne Gospels, and fled briefly to Ireland, nearly losing the Gospels at sea. From 883 AD they settled for a century in Chester-le-Street, then moved to Ripon, then back to Lindisfarne and finally, in 1070, to Durham. They built the first Durham Cathedral, a temporary thing of wood and straw, to house St. Cuthbert's coffin. Then, in 1082, they returned to Lindisfarne to create the See and rebuild the ruined Priory in his memory.

In 1326 came another scourge: Scottish borderers pillaged the bakehouse and brewery. In 1537 the Priory was closed, first its church and then the monks' cell being converted into storehouses for the use of successive monarchs. In 1543 an army was assembled to repel the Scots, and ten warships were recorded as lying at anchor in the Ouse. In 1549 the Fort of Beblowe, the present-day Lindisfarne Castle, was open for business, much of its stone coming from the Priory. In 1613 the Earl of Dunbar ransacked what remained of the monks' work, including roofing lead, bells and anything else of value. And over the next few centuries the islanders became wreckers and smugglers, still praying, but now, so legend has it, praying for God to send them ships, to wreck them on the reefs around their island home.

At its peak in the latter half of the nineteenth century, the population of the island totalled nearly 1,000. This era of prosperity was ignited by the herring fishery and by a Dundee company that began to develop the lime trade, first started by the monks, on a commercial scale. In 1860 the "town" contained nine public houses, but the Saturday market held in the village square had ceased to be a hub of local life. It was in this year too, that posts were sunk across the flats to mark the crossing point, called "Pilgrim's Way," to and from the mainland. Most people walked the route, only a few islanders having the luxury of a pony cart. In a sunlit age when wealth was held by those of a certain class or with some business acumen, rather than those who could kick a football, the island was used as a watering place by Northumbrian and Border gentry for shooting and fishing parties. By the late 1950s, the herring fishery had disappeared, the limekilns had long since ceased to function, and the island's economy was beginning to rely on tourism. Today, the tiny streets and squares of the village have names redolent of its early history: Church Lane, Prior Lane, Marygate, Crossgate, St. Cuthbert's Square, Market Place and others.

The island's early history is remembered, and is held as precious, in other ways too.

The Holy Island of Lindisfarne, September 1958

A small boy sees a man, an occasional visitor to Holy Island, standing in front of the statue of St. Aidan near the dark red ruin of the priory. The man, dressed in a flowing garment unfamiliar to the boy, appears to be arguing. This seems odd to the boy, for there is no one else there to argue with. The man gesticulates once or twice, clears his throat, and spits at the foot of the stone statue.

The youngster wonders whether the man's garment is intended to copy the saint's cassock and cowl, but decides not. He knows what a cassock is. He wears a black one himself, beneath his white surplice, in the Church choir. This one doesn't look right. He wonders what brings the man to Holy Island, and why he keeps coming back.

The boy is tall for his age. He is six years old. He has two sisters and a brother, all younger. Because of his extraordinary name, his siblings, or those who have words, and his new schoolmates, have nicknamed him Alph. This is not because he is yet a dominant male, but short for alphabet: his initials are A,B,C,D. His displeasure at the pejorative has caused many a playground battle. In time, he will learn to forgive his parents.

It is a late September evening, the sun beneath the Cheviot, twilight. Alph can see the lights of the Longstone and Inner Farne lighthouses blinking across the sea. They are friends, constant, comforting. He can see them from his bedroom window. His father has told him that the other Farne Islands, five miles distant, shelter Holy Island's anchorage from easterly gales.

The boy Alph, or Alexander to give him his first Christian name, sees the strangely-dressed man walk through the priory grounds and cross Sanctuary Close towards the shore and to a place where some old fishing cobles lie upturned. They are used as work sheds and stores for fishing gear. Lobster creels are stacked beside them. The remains of shellfish used as bait are strewn across the grass.

Alexander follows the man, wondering how and when he will leave the island again. The young boy knows the tide has turned; the bay is filling slowly with seawater.

He sees the man kneel by an upturned coble and greet another small boy, a boy about Alexander's age, dressed as a miniature version of the man himself. It seems the boy has been trying to skim stones in the shallow waters of the bay. Alexander wonders if this is the man's son.

He draws closer and sees the man and boy on their haunches near the roost of an eider or "Cuddy's Duck," one of St. Cuthbert's own, in the lee of the upturned coble. Alexander is scratched by a thistle, but takes no notice.

He sees the man lift the eider duck from her resting place and wring her neck. The man puts the duck under his flowing robe. He takes the boy's hand. Their heads turn sideways, this way and that, to see whether this act has been observed. Apart from Alexander, it has not.

The man and boy move away from the coble and walk along the shore path towards Popple Well, the outlet of an ancient spring and artesian well.

Alexander is quietly but copiously sick behind a stone wall near the Herring Houses. When he looks up, the two figures have disappeared. He sits for a time, shivering, a bad taste in his mouth. As his horror subsides, puzzlement begins to take its place. Why kill and eat an eider duck? The Harvest Festival has just taken place, and there were trestle-tables laden with food.

The following week, there is a headline in the local paper, The Berwick Advertiser. It reads, "Hunger Drove Fasting Muslim to kill Eider: He and Son Eat It Raw." *Beneath the headline is a picture of the strangely dressed man. In his mind, Alexander can still see the man's beard dripping with the Cuddy Duck's blood.*

Alexander asks his father the question that has been puzzling him: why kill and eat an eider duck? His father shakes his head, and says that sometimes the things people do are beyond comprehension. Alexander asks him to read the story of the court case but his father declines, saying, "Enough. This individual was hungry during his fasting month, the month called Ramadan in the Islam religion. He said he had been driven to kill the duck and eat it, but claimed he had done nothing wrong. However, later that evening he made the mistake of trying to steal a vehicle to get off the island. He was caught by the tide and has now been jailed."

Alexander thinks about it. "So he wasn't punished for the duck. The duck didn't matter."

"Not so fast. There are lessons for you here," his father says. "You see that the headline refers to the duck, not the vehicle. Many people will view the killing of the duck as the more heinous act and this man may find it hard to face the criticism that will come his way. I hope so. It is important that people have respect for other living things, and that criticism may be one kind of punishment. But justice as dispensed by courts is sometimes not quite as we would wish it."

Before his mother puts the newspaper in the scuttle with other material to be used in lighting their living room fire, Alexander borrows scissors from a kitchen drawer and cuts the story out. He does this from time to time, collects press cuttings. But even at six, he prefers the City pages.

Some years later he has this one framed. Many years later still, when he has taken retirement and is back living in his childhood home, he places it on the walnut desk in his basement office.

CHAPTER ONE

The Holy Island of Lindisfarne, May 2007

On the morning of fifth May, Mr. Charley Oakley and Mrs. Rebecca Carter Oakley walked under an eggshell blue sky, edged with politically troublesome black, through the dunes of Lindisfarne's panhandle.

They had been married less than a day, and already the marriage was going south.

And Charley didn't know why. Even in his present apathetic state, during those rare intervals when he could bring himself to focus, it flummoxed him.

"After last night, things can only improve," Rebecca said. "At least, I hope so. That was ridiculous."

As was this, she thought. Ten in the morning, and Charley was an apparition wrapped in a cloud of down-market aftershave, last night's beer, and this morning's kippers.

Charley grunted. He couldn't recall last night. Or anything about last night beyond the doorway to the second pub. But one thing was clear enough: sometime during it, the girl he had thought of as the next best thing to Kate Moss had disappeared and Norah Batty had materialised. And in true Norah style, he had been ignored, then criticised, and finally punished with the truckload of baggage—the rugs, towels, plastic tennis set, windbreak, fruit, sandwiches, and cool-box of drinks—he was now hauling.

And God forbid that he should complain. Or as much as hint that she may have overdone things, and turned their beach outing into some kind of *Kon-Tiki* expedition. He knew what that would mean. Each time his lips had tried to form words this morning, he had been handed something else. And while he was buckling at the knees, his new wife was carrying a straw hat and a bottle of sun lotion. 59°F and sun lotion! It was like they were moving house, he brooded, and apart from his small Balham flat, they didn't have one yet. He wished he was back there now. He wished he was back anywhere, through both time *and* space.

Although not usually given to introspection, Charley was beginning to suspect that he may have overdone things himself this year.

"And please watch where you put your feet," Rebecca said, pointing to a couple of small brown birds that had flown in panic from the grass. "Skylarks are nesting here." She knelt to inspect a bright green shrub sprouting innocuous quarter-inch balls. "Pirri-pirri. It's a good thing we came when we did. In a month or two, this stuff would snag you for sure."

For Rebecca, it was difficult even trying to be civil. At least, God knew, she should have taken time to think what she was doing; to think about Charley, and the last few weeks. She could hear her mother's voice now; "giddy," "headstrong," "impulsive," and other words to that effect. She was feeling a mixture of rage, self-loathing and misery, and she wasn't enjoying it one bit. She also knew exactly why. She hadn't recovered from being told that Charley had a habit beyond his nightly visits to the pub, and that she had been the unwitting accessory to breaking it.

Charley's habit was falling in love. Granted, it may not have been as bad a habit as crack cocaine, but the eve of their wedding wasn't the time to have heard about it. When, breathing plumes of alcohol, he had unveiled the news that he'd been falling in love each spring for the last eight years, since he was twenty-two. With a great deal more pride and affection than Rebecca thought warranted, Charley called this annual frolic The Game.

He told her the idea had come out of the blue, like King Harold's arrow, while he was watching a pierrot on Hastings seafront. And it had been such a good one, tailor-made for his work, perfect in every way. A few evenings practice in front of a mirror, and he was good to go.

She had known, of course, that he worked in London's Madame Tussaud's, a venue which produced single young women in droves. She had met him there herself. Even without the schoolgirls, which thankfully he'd had the sense to avoid, there had been, quote, "a smorgasbord" of choice. So much so, he'd told her, that Tussaud's Amsterdam, Hong Kong, even New York, couldn't have produced any better.

Then Charley, with the enthusiasm of an infant bush fire licking at dry tinder, got into the details:

Towards the end of March, he would position himself in a tableau and "watch the croc." He knew where to stand, and which tableaux were popular. He could scan a line without moving an eye, helpfully miming this skill for her benefit, as though she hadn't been a victim herself. Inevitably, he'd snickered, one or two had a closer look…who could this be? Which Royal, or other soap opera star, is this? *Harry? But it's not in a nightclub…it looks lifelike though…*

Then, suspecting that Rebecca was less than impressed, Charley was stung into a defence of his Game. Well, she couldn't have thought she'd been his first conquest, could she? Surely it was obvious there'd been others?…And all that practice. How else did she think he'd become so good at it? It had been a simple idea really, like all the good ones were, but it had needed work to reach that level of excellence. Didn't she appreciate that? Practice, patience, and selectivity, all of which she'd seen for herself. Well, he couldn't lower his standards, could he? He had to wait until someone acceptable came by. Someone, that is, without boyfriend, rings or zits. And only if those criteria were met in full, checked and re-checked, would he feel inclined to offer a smile and wink; all of which she'd seen...

It became, for Rebecca, a depressingly personal flashback. She should have left him there and then, the night before their wedding, and moved on. But all those purchases and bookings; the dress, the hat, the flowers, the shoes, the stag night, the train, the car, the registrar, the fees, the dinky guesthouse near St. Mary's Church. How could she?

Oblivious to her horror, Charley had prattled on. Of course, he explained, the Game wasn't foolproof. If everything went well, it followed a predictable sequence: first, shock that this inanimate being had sprung to life, then relief, then laughter, then "cherry-picking time." But sometimes, reruns were needed. The first recipients of the smile and wink might just be passing through, like Americans on one of their whistle-stop tours. He shrugged what passed for his shoulders; he'd met a few like that. One year, there had been a day-tripper from Calais, then a Chihuahuan groupie following a Stones world tour. (Charley still had wistful feelings about the groupie, but at least had the sense not to say so.) But it was a bad year if he hadn't scored by April Fool's Day. And there'd been only one of those...

To cut a long story short, Charley then fell serially in love. He stayed in love until fall, with a personal best of November, said goodbye, no hard feelings, took the winter off to drink with his pals, and kicked the cycle off again in March. Perfect. Like picking cherries.

What did she think? he asked. Nice one, eh? Nice eight in fact, since he'd started the Game.

Rebecca hadn't replied. She'd gone into the bathroom to get over the shock. Two nights, one day, three hot showers, one cold shower, four meals, a train journey, a wedding, a car journey and a messy pub-crawl later, and she was still getting over the shock.

"Nearly there," she said now, trying to quell her conflicting emotions, keeping her eyes on the dunes and sea. And to think the last novel she'd read had been Ian McEwan's *On Chesil Beach*, a story of stalled communication between newly-weds. She should have paid more attention to it, and especially to Florence, its heroine.

This time, Charley didn't even grunt. He was thinking of March sixteenth, the day this corking girl, six feet tall, blond and brown-eyed, had wandered through the museum. Alone, no rings, a perfect complexion. As sexy as the museum's latest, a scrupulously madeover Kate Moss, reclining on a Barcelona daybed next door. He had gone through the smile and wink routine. Shock, relief and laughter, like ducks in a row. On his next break, Charley took her for coffee.

Rebecca had told him she was over from New Zealand for three months on "a big O.E." She explained it was Kiwi for overseas experience, an extended holiday. For Charley, whatever else it might have been, it was irresistible; a new variation, a hint of the exotic. The timeframe was shorter than ideal, but you never knew; with a free spirit like this, another personal best was possible.

It had taken two or three dates, par for the course. Followed as usual by lunchtime trysts, evening booze-ups, nocturnal frolics and days out in the Birdmobile, his four year-old Mazda. He'd enjoyed showing her off, introducing his latest catch to his pals. So where, to coin a phrase, had it all gone wrong? What had happened since yesterday? Where had his memory gone? A hangover was fine; Charley knew about hangovers, but this was amnesia. It was as though someone yesterday had clicked a switch off in his head and hadn't clicked it back on.

He could just about recall the wedding, and especially the two witnesses, a local couple who had joined them off the train in a beeline for Cushy Butterfield's, the station bar. Charley hadn't liked the name. He preferred homely names like Red Lion or Black Bull, not memorials to mythical north-east trollops. But Rebecca, entranced by their accents ("like my Mom's"), had invited these two along. What could he have done? Tell them his wife-to-be didn't understand British reserve? Geordies, for Pete's sake. Unintelligible, northern, soccer-daft aliens. He had sipped his Brown Ale, picking at his fingernails, worrying if witnesses got speaking parts.

But as far as he knew, the formalities at least had passed quickly. Afterwards, the newlyweds had headed north for their wedding night, with Rebecca floating plans for a day or two in Edinburgh, and then the Highlands. "But Holy Island first," she'd said, trying to salvage something worthwhile from the day, about which serious doubts had already crept in.

Charley had smiled his best lascivious smile. "Anywhere with a bed. The Kama Sutra Kid rides again." That was what this whole deal was about, after all, so did it matter where they went? Holy Island, Scotland, the Gobi Desert for all he cared. He hadn't a clue where Holy Island was. Somewhere north, and north to Charley was a land of striking miners and flat vowels. Rain and gloom and incomprehensible accents, like yesterday.

He hadn't taken to Holy Island, didn't like the place at all. No bustle, no noise, no girls to chat up, no pubs to speak of. But the two there were had pulled him in like magnets.

He had a hazy notion that he'd been asked to leave the first. It might have had to do with throwing beer mats and, although it seemed unlikely, plastic lures. Charley hadn't appreciated that the faux lugworms were giveaways from the sponsors of a fishing tournament, or that the fishermen weren't amused by his cavalier antics. He didn't know what the things were. A quaint local custom, he'd assumed; something fittingly backward.

But if the first pub was a hazy memory, the second was a black hole.

If Charley had been able to find a key to his amnesia, it might have been the memory of a local man giving him a glass of 75° proof Laphroaig malt whisky, and telling him to hold on to the bar while he drank it. He had blithely ignored this advice, thought the guy was joking, took a mouthful, and fell over.

The black hole had lasted until the wake-up call at eight, a clamour loud enough to evacuate the cemetery. He hadn't been too happy about the proximity of the cemetery anyway, and the awakening had been like having Big Ben for a room-mate. He had been shaky ever since, dropping clothes, soap, his shaver; fumbling coffee cups, cereal bowls, butter, toast. A plate of Craster kippers and a pot of marmalade had fallen off the breakfast table and into the landlady's new top-of-the-range Wilton carpet.

Now, feeling no better than when they'd set out, he tried to change hands with the food and drink. Bloody armies have set out with less, he muttered to himself, staggering along tenuous pathways.

"Did you say something, Charley?" Rebecca asked.

"No, no. A bit awkward is all." No offers of help, too much to ask.

"Still feeling crook?"

Charley grunted again. Although the free spirit seemed to have dissolved, her accent remained as pleasing to the ear as ever, even if some of the words were strange. And she did look good in the cut-off jeans and tank top. Maybe, he thought, they could find a nice secluded spot to lie down and strip off. Having got him this far, the Fates, whom he was inclined to blame for the whole sorry mess, could hardly object to some conjugal rights, could they?

He hoped he had performed okay last night, but wasn't sure. He had been curious to know if sex was any different on your honeymoon night...well, it would have to stay a mystery. If this stab at marriage withered on the vine, and UK statistics weren't exactly encouraging, he wasn't about to repeat the exercise just for curiosity's sake.

Stumbling along, only vaguely aware that Kate/Norah was engrossed in botany and biology, pointing out plants and birds here and there, he looked up at the sky. The Fates were ganging up on him there, too. A curtain of clouds was forming along the shoulder of that rounded hill they called the Cheviot. It looked like it was getting heavier. Join the club, Charley thought. His whole life was getting heavier.

Back in Holy Island village, Alexander Beauregard Courtney Deville was drinking coffee in his basement office at Fahr House. He had an important meeting tonight and expected the village to turn out in force. There was the referendum vote to announce, the results of their own truly *local* election, followed by discussion on the next steps down their chosen path. It would be difficult, he thought, to imagine a meeting since the days of the holy saints that had been more important to his homeland.

He felt calm, and thoroughly in control. His only regret was that his wife Nicole was not there to enjoy the day with him, but Nicole had died three years ago. She would have known what this day signified, and if there was such a thing as a heaven above, which was a difficult proposition given that Deville's beliefs fell on the far side of agnosticism, he knew she would be up there cheering him on. There were still days when he felt as if an essential part of him had departed with her and, whatever his beliefs, he never forgot that Nicole had been a devoted Anglican as well as a loving wife and mother. This morning, as he often did, he would visit her grave at St. Mary's, leave some flowers, and try to have a sensible conversation with thin air, grass and a headstone.

Although Alex Deville had lost his wife, he had three children, all of whom were back home and proving to be invaluable aides in what had become his life's work. Beyond genetics, he could take little credit for how they'd turned out. While he had been commuting to and from London and elsewhere, making friends and contacts in the world's financial centres, Nicole had brought them up. In his opinion, which was as biased as the next man's, the results had been outstanding. Max, Sarah and Alistair were three different characters, each with their own interests and skills, who dovetailed perfectly. He loved them all as individuals, but also had a liking for his conceptualisation of them; as the doer, the carer and the thinker.

He knew he was at a loose end, killing time. He had tried reading a newspaper but it had been full of post-election garbage, politicians putting the usual gloss on it, trying to explain against all logic why they didn't have bloodied noses. In one case, a senior Party figure, after a night he may have preferred to forget, had greeted faithful followers at one isolated success with the memorable phrase, *"didn't you all do well?"* Deville wondered where these people got their false optimism from; rentafantasy.com? Then there was the speculation about the impact the results might have on the Handover at Number Ten, and whether the Prime-Minister-in-waiting would assume the throne without opposition. The media seemed to have given up the notion that it could turn into a re-run of the Gunfight at the OK Corral. Two people, they seemed to be concluding, wouldn't constitute much of a gunfight. And even that might be a democratic pipe-dream; the odds were on a coronation rather than a contest. A pity, Deville thought; some corpses littering the street Western-style would have been nice.

In all truth, there wasn't much more he could do today. All those years of planning and work, of salting away those millions, were about to come to fruition. His preparations had been scrutinised until they seemed perfect. Barring the unforeseen, and all anyone could do in that regard was to be flexible, he was as ready as he would ever be. One thing was guaranteed. If the Scots had struggled to raise a 50 percent turnout in their parliamentary election, and the French achieved 85 percent in their presidential election, Lindisfarne would trump them both. Deville expected no less than a 100 percent vote on the main issue, but whether people had bothered with their District Council ballot paper was another matter…

S-Day—'S' for Secession—had arrived. Although he knew already what the vote on the main issue would be, Alex Deville resisted indulging in anything Churchillian. The malt whisky and Havana cigar, both beloved by the great man, would keep until later, until after the vote had been announced and the business of the night was done. He spent a few minutes checking that a money transfer had gone smoothly, then picked up the phone on his walnut desk, dialled a number at the other end of the country, and waited.

"All is well," he said when it was answered. "Everything is in hand."

He listened.

"Unanimous, all but two. I hope entirely so by tonight," he said, and listened once more.

"Midnight, or just after. The cash is in place as of yesterday." He paused. "I should really take something for the cough, if I were you. Or banish the cigarettes," he added, laughing.

Deville listened a final time, grunted what might have been a word of thanks, and replaced the handset.

He sighed. He supposed he should make two or three more calls, make sure more of his friends knew there was nothing to fret about, but he had never been a devotee of the phone. He preferred seeing peoples' expressions and body language.

It would keep, he told himself. He would pick some sea pinks and forget-me-nots, visit Nicole's grave, and then call in at the village hall and see how the preparations were going. He walked up the stairs to the living room, looked out of the window and thought he had better get to it. The weather appeared to be closing in.

Now that they seemed to be reaching whatever destination Rebecca had in mind, Charley could see that the island was bigger than he had first imagined. On the drive north, between eulogies on bits of flora, Rebecca had told him about 150 people lived on it year round, and that it might once have been two islands, joined by a tombolo. He hadn't been able to see how this made sense; some kind of lottery joining islands? "Oh, right," he'd said. Well, it was better than "bullshit" and he had to keep things sweet for the conjugals. But bullshit, he saw now, it had been. On the map, the place looked like nothing more than a battered saucepan, something unearthed from an archaeological dig. They were now some way along the handle, the village behind them in the saucepan's bowl.

Looking back, he thought there were far too many houses for 150 people. He guessed most of them would be second homes, unoccupied much of the year. Price-wise, they would be way beyond the reach of the locals, something the place would have in common with resorts across Britain, like those in Devon or Dorset where he had holidayed as a kid. Not that Charley had much sympathy for distressed locals. He couldn't begin to understand how anyone would make a conscious choice to live here. Some days the tides must make normal life impossible. Give him Balham, or even Peckham, any day.

And Rebecca had said she wanted to explore the place after her swim. Charley couldn't understand that either, but knew she had some kind of personal link with it. Lindisfarne, she'd told him, had been the cradle of Christianity in England's Anglo-Saxon era. Saints by the dozen. Monks, statues, churches, crosses. Ten minutes of it, and his brain had seized up.

He saw with relief that they must be reaching the end of this cross-country marathon; the North Sea shore was appearing below them. "I think somewhere here will do fine," Rebecca said, looking around. "Breathtaking views, aren't they?"

Charley grunted again.

Sea and sand and spiky grass. He felt like a yak.

He was giving up on secluded spots. With the causeway open, there seemed to be a continual stream of cars and coaches along the shore road. As far as he'd been able to tell, visitors seemed to fall into three groups: warring families on days out, anoraks in muddy boots, and pensioners searching for cups of tea. He wondered how many were stranded over the average summer weekend, and where they could stay if they were. He had seen two hotels, a handful of guesthouses, B&B joints. What could they possibly do all day? Wander up and down the main street eating cream teas, looking for saints?

He stumbled onwards for what he hoped would be the last few tortured yards; two steps forward, one step back, one sideways. He gritted his teeth and told himself to live with it, get through it, and treat it like a slow day at work, a minute at a time. One more day, then check the tides and leave the place behind, leave it to its birds and saints and plastic worms. Let Kate/Norah have her swim today, explore, and write her letters home. Tonight, there were always the two pubs. Even now…maybe he could sit it out for the first hour or so until they opened their doors for anti-dehydration treatment.

No such luck.

"This'll do, I think," Rebecca said, laying her hat and suntan lotion carefully in the grass. "Plant the windbreak, Charley. Take your time."

Charley took his bearings. They were at the high point of the dune system, the North Sea stretching to the horizon in front of them, the tidal flats between the island and mainland behind. His spirits lifted when he saw Rebecca stripping to a bikini, but before he could appreciate its minimal glory she had disappeared downhill.

"Come on, Charley, a swim might help," he heard her shout.

Christ, he thought, she'll freeze. He shivered at the sight of a steel-blue sea, shadows flitting over its surface, and croaked something about fixing the windbreak. Swim in that ice bath? He'd be lucky to last five minutes, and his crown jewels would be the first to go. Global warming? he muttered, wiping the tears leaking from his eyes. What a load of bollocks.

Charley began to wrestle the poles into the ground, finally getting the square of canvas into a semblance of the perpendicular. He sat down on a tuft of grass and peered over the top. Rebecca was a hundred yards out, forging parallel to the shore, her long shapely legs kicking in the waves.

As some much-needed oxygen returned to his head, Charley felt a spike of lust pierce his misery. Christ, she looked like Sharon Davies down there, good enough to turn mermaids green with envy. It must be all those days at Bondi Beach. He felt awe and admiration in almost equal parts, awe winning. He held his wife's skimpy top and cut-offs to his face, and breathed in her scent. Then he folded them, rummaged in the cool-box, and slumped back in the sand.

No aspirins. Carting this superabundance of rubbish and he'd forgotten the aspirins. He opened a bottle of beer. He could feel the breeze quickening, grains of sand stinging his face and arms. Then the first raindrop landed smack between his eyes.

Slipping out of her tank top and cut-offs, Rebecca had debated asking Charley to test the water, as she thought chivalry might dictate. One look at him dropping the bits and pieces of picnic gear had persuaded her otherwise. He had already pretty much destroyed the buffet breakfast in the guesthouse. On their way out, Charley bouncing randomly off hall tables, their landlady had asked if they planned to stay another night. Rebecca had the impression the two things weren't unrelated.

After the first icy embrace of the North Sea in May, she was enjoying the exercise and, in truth, the solitude. She was also glad to be out of London and Newcastle, both of which, especially the capital, had come as a big shock after the clean fresh air and streets of Christchurch, with its pretty parks and pleasant pavement cafés.

How could she have lost her bearings quite so comprehensively? Impulsiveness was one thing, recklessness quite another. She had woken up this morning determined to put it behind her, but the first thing she'd seen out of the window was a car with one of those *A Dog is for Life, Not just for Christmas* stickers. Substitute "Marriage" for the first two words and it was the perfect warning. All those doubts, questions, internal dialectics, for nothing. On the plus side, she had told herself, Charley was totally whacky, four-fifths good-looking (okay, a bit insubstantial) and three-fifths intelligent. From the first, with the waxwork trick, he'd made her laugh. She could even live with his habit of humming nursery rhymes. True, it was distracting in bed, but she'd heard worse...

All that garbage had collapsed in the metaphysical courtrooms of Logic and Truth.

Collapsed in the face of accusations like "piker" (from a fellow-New Zealander), "alcoholic," "Good Time Charley," the last of which had been a slip of the tongue from one of his pals, before his stag night. She should have seen it coming. Since puberty, she'd been error-prone in the week before her period and this time, heaven help her, she'd said "Yes." Admittedly, it was before her introduction to the formative years of The Game, but that was a lame excuse. And one of the tedious things was due tomorrow.

She wasn't sure how she'd come to think of marriage as a good idea. Or any sort of idea. Maybe it was simply that she thought she should do the Right Thing, take the moral path, or some pathetic conceit like that. Then there had been the bare-what-passes-for-your-soul session, The Game that dished out Oscars to Best Serial Philanderers. She should never have set foot on the train. Or should have jumped out of the train, pulled the emergency cord, got off at Doncaster; anything but this.

It was all very well telling herself that she'd been doing the touristy bit, and seeing the sights. But had she really needed, in such a feather-brained way, to fall into the arms of the first young stud in England to amuse her? She knew she was becoming more critical by the hour, but the truly disturbing thing was why the criticism had taken six weeks to materialise. She deserved kicking. His face, even accounting for his night on the tiles, looked like contaminated yeast. His sweater was the wrong colour. His behaviour was delinquent. His hair was...well, like a russet scouring pad. It reminded her of a venerable Aussie cartoon character, Ginger Meggs, whom she'd never much liked in any case.

She had begun to wonder, she realised now too late, how Charley had reached the age of thirty anyway, single and unattached. It was as broad a hint as she could have wished, and now she was asking herself whether she could conceivably be dumber than every Sloane female in London, or those who had come across him. The vision of dozens of size fours dodging her husband's clutches, fleeing hell-for-leather along Knightsbridge, totally depressed her. But here she was, the latest in a line of waxwork *suckers*. The *Game*. Talk about inattentive: she hadn't picked up the faintest whiff of stage-management about it.

Rebecca forged through the swell, casting occasional glances shoreward to see if Charley had appeared. She wondered if he knew their marriage hadn't yet been consummated, and whether that was still relevant in this day and age. With a degree of nervousness, she asked herself whether a quickie divorce might be floating out there in her stars, and how it could have got so near, so quickly. Given his hapless fumbling the night before, she had to concede it was possible. But ohmigod, if that was the outcome, it would simply double the embarrassment. Jumping from the train would have been a lot less stressful.

They had slept together before, of course, but not too often, and certainly not after Charley had drunk enough to launch a liner and peppered innocent bystanders with bric-a-brac. And then—oh, joy!—the whisky, and the kiss of life, with the whole village devouring the free impromptu floor show. She shuddered to think how her Mom would react if she ever got to hear of it. Good Time Charley indeed. Mumbling about Kama Sutras and the Joys of Sex, and trying to get her to put her legs over his shoulders. In the dark, and swallowed in a duvet, she'd have had a hard enough time finding them even if she'd tried. She'd had her share of setbacks with men before, but Charley, last night, had broken new ground. His performance had been so woeful that she'd seriously thought of finding another room, if not another guesthouse. And as for being thrown out of the pub, like a couple of ASBOs: well, that was a first. She was unimpressed with the British fad for anti-social behaviour orders to start with, they seemed such a spineless deterrent, but for Charley to join the club, and take her along as a guest…

Five or six weeks ago, she remembered with mortification, there had even been a *giddy* moment when a child had crossed her mind. Well, she was twenty-six, and these instincts were getting harder to subdue. But even so…Charley's child? That wouldn't have been merely inattentive; it would have verged on the immoral. It would have risked foisting some alcohol-fuelled marionette, a sort of *noir* Pinocchio, on an unsuspecting world.

As recently as two days ago, after the "Yes" but before The Game's Grand Unveiling, she had persuaded herself that here was a guy who at least looked and talked like one. Even if she felt vertically *un*challenged (what a country, where people had to hide from their language like prey) next to him. It was better than some girls managed, she'd consoled herself, including the New Sloaners or whatever they called themselves these days. Now, she wished she'd left him wallowing in his size fours. Quite apart from his bared soul and aberrant behaviour, he didn't *fit* here. He was polluting the place.

She would need to give it time to see if a line could be drawn under his Game. You made choices, like *A Dog is for Life*, and had to live with them, after all. But she would make sure, in case it *was* still pertinent, that the marriage stayed unconsummated tonight; for the whole honeymoon, if need be. And if that made her sound like Britney Spears or some other bimbo, too bad. She would need to talk to him about it after her swim. It was only fair, and she was determined not to follow Florence, *On Chesil Beach*'s naïvely expectant heroine, down the road of shattered dreams. But whether Charley would grasp what she was saying was another matter. He was looking and behaving as if his brain had been pickled.

She gave a little grunt as she flipped over and started back. At least the island was everything she'd expected. Their first view of it across the salt marsh and mud flats in a yellow evening light, the tight cluster of houses and the castle prominent on its southern tip, had seemed perfect, like a long-awaited homecoming. She had almost forgotten that Charley was sitting next to her. Rebecca was glad her mother had suggested a visit, even if she would have been less than thrilled by the circumstances.

Her mother had been born on Lindisfarne in the early 1950s and had often talked of a holiday to see how things were "back home", a phrase which after forty years of residence in New Zealand half amused, and half irritated, her father. But marriage, the arrival of Rebecca, her brother Michael, and then their education, had put the idea on hold. One of the things on Rebecca's must-do list for the day was to send a postcard to her parents. She had promised herself to keep a diary of her visit, and paint some watercolours. She thought her mother would appreciate both, so long as the diary was censored.

She had to do something radical about Charley, but wasn't sure, short of surgery, what would work. As a first step, this afternoon, she would take him on a life-affirming dose of culture; the village, the Heritage Centre, the Gospel Garden, St. Cuthbert's Centre, the priory, the Castle, the whole ball of *wax*. The tiki tour, as her pals in Enzed would say. The Castle especially looked like a healthy trek around the anchorage and along the southern shore. Add exhaustion to his hangover and, with luck, Charley would lose interest in consummating anything. Not even Priapic Man, she hoped, would be able to revive himself from that.

The swim had been good therapy, and Rebecca's mind was clearing. Except for the fulmars wheeling above, she had the sea pretty much to herself. The water was clear enough to see sand and rocks and waving seaweed beneath her, and one or two small crabs scuttling around. She flipped on her back and tried floating, but it was becoming too choppy. A cormorant skimmed past, so close she could see its yellowish eyes. She saw it had begun to rain, and wondered if Charley had started heading for the nearest bar.

Charley hadn't. He was lying semi-comatose behind the windbreak, half-empty beer bottle in hand, and when the raindrops started falling in earnest he jerked upright in consternation. He couldn't believe a sky could darken so quickly. He struggled to his feet, peered into the gathering gloom, and began waving to Rebecca. Christ, he thought, in all that water, she won't even notice it's raining. He tore the windbreak out of the sand and hauled it over his head. The sound was deafening, the acoustics like a steel band.

He looked around to see how much more of this torture was heading his way, and was still mulling it over when movement near their rented BMW caught his eye. The car had been a £1400 extravagance, the thick end of a month's wages blown on this...this *Arctic* Kon-Tiki. He vaguely recalled driving it (thank God, the place seemed devoid of breathalyzer-wielding cops) on to the sandy strip-cum-parking area down there.

It looked every inch of an extravagance, he thought, momentarily lost in admiration.

He took it as solid confirmation of his good taste when he saw that three guys in jeans and T-shirts were clustered round, admiring it as well.

Then he saw one of them bend over, pick up a stone and hurl it through the passenger's side window. Charley jumped on top of a clump of marram grass, still with the windbreak.

"Hey!" he shouted, galvanized. "What the hell!...You down there! *Hey!*"

He saw the guy reach over to the other door, spring the catch and begin fumbling under the dash. There was a distant thump as the bonnet released.

Charley swivelled around; Rebecca was still swimming but nearing the beach. He pointed wildly to the car, threw the windbreak aside and began stumbling downhill through the sand and grass. In his haste, he forgot the warning notices about unexploded ordnance, quicksands and pirri-pirri bur posted at points along the road. He hadn't been tuned in to his wife's commentary about the cutting properties of marram grass, the adhesive qualities of the latent burrs, the stinging and scraping of nettles and thistles, the squawks of agitated birds. The marram grass repaid this negligence by slashing his legs. After ten yards he pottered to a halt, heaved and groaned, and bent down to see if he was bleeding. He checked the car. One of them was still tinkering under the bonnet. Charley got his breath back and started down again, each step sinking in the sand, creating small landslides. Not for the first time that morning, he wished he'd gone easy on the refreshments last night.

He stumbled, sat down in a bushy patch of burrs, and yelped as last year's prickly brown remnants punctured him. What was it Rebecca had said? That this stuff came from New Zealand, like her? That it had some kind of Maori alias: biddy-bid, or some such oddity? Well, whatever its name, he might have guessed it would give him trouble. Christ, until recently, he'd barely given New Zealand a thought in his life, and now the place was all over him like a rash.

He finally made it to the foot of the hill, and paused to take stock. The carnappers were all upright, looking at him. What now, for Pete's sake?

Charley knew he was outnumbered and began to wish he hadn't attempted the slalom. He was half-surprised the car was still there; apparently there were no car mechanics present. Their T-shirts had "Bigg M" emblazoned in red. It meant nothing to him except a case of bad spelling, but it didn't look friendly. "M" for Mama? "M" for Mouth? He gulped for breath, and decided on affronted dignity.

"I say, what do you think you're doing? That's a rented car!"

"Save us grief, mon," one of them said, a big coloured lad with a mashed nose, shrapnel embedded in his face, and cornrows tight enough to cause a migraine. "Slammin set a wheels. Got the keys?"

"No way," Charley said. He was drenched, and dizzy with apnoea. And what the hell was slammin? In the macho jargon of the under twenty-fives, was slammin good or bad?

It took thirty seconds, but seemed longer. Charley was stripped of his keys, his wallet, and bundled into the boot. He banged his head on the lid. When he came to in pitch darkness, the car was speeding along what felt like a smooth tarmac surface. He had time to appreciate the suspension his £1400 had bought, pluck out a posse of pirri-pirri needles, and swear once again at the Fates.

He managed to cushion his arms behind his head, and then passed out again.

CHAPTER TWO

Rebecca waded to the beach with the tide still on the ebb, shaking droplets of water from her arms and legs, surveying the dunes. There was no sign of Charley. It would be good to think he was lying down recuperating, giving his brain a chance to struggle to the surface, but that might be too much to hope. She held her face to the rain, ran her hands through her hair and started upwards, rehearsing some remarks she hoped would hit the target.

First, there was to be no more reference to sex in any shape or form until he had enjoyed a week of *sober* exploration of this wonderful island. A new Game, an inoffensive, temperate Game, was needed. Since her swim had given her an appetite, they would sit out the shower, have a sandwich, and then return to the village. They would find a comb for that frightful hair, and start a mutual education at the Gospel Garden. Rebecca hoped the Garden, recreated after winning a silver medal at a recent Chelsea Flower Show, might appeal to the Londoner in Charley. It was a dim hope, but it was something to hold on to.

In the evening they would have dinner in The Ship Inn, which their landlady, doubtless living in fear of Charley's second coming in the dining room, had recommended. It had wooden floors, she'd told them, not expensive carpets. The fresh dressed crab or salmon salads were excellent. There would be drinks with the after-dinner coffee, Rebecca resolved, but none before. They would then return to their lodgings, replete and tired from their day in the sea air, have a good night's sleep, and explore the north end of the island tomorrow.

Okay, that was the plan. Kind, but firm, were the watchwords. She would leave Charley in no doubt that a reconstruction job was expected. Before she had her tucker, if he wasn't already plastered on the stock of beer he'd slipped into the chilly bin, she might go so far as a kiss. One chaste peck on the cheek, with no hint of promise.

It was a good strategy, she told herself, a nice balance of fairness and challenge. And if it failed, she had an easy fallback. If anything resembling soft porn poked its head over the parapet, she would get Charley blotto. Even if the last thing she wanted to see was Charley with another drink in his hand.

That her plan had a serious flaw became clear when she reached the top of the dunes. Down at the car, Charley had gone off the rails again. He seemed to have graduated from throwing things around to being thrown around himself. He was corralled by three youths, one white, one black, one somewhere in between, who were taking turns kicking sundry parts of his anatomy. And he didn't seem to be offering too much resistance.

"Holy mackerel," Rebecca said. She watched in astonishment as Charley was bundled into the trunk and the vehicle, spewing rooster tails of sand, sped away from the village along St. Cuthbert's Way. To her later embarrassment, her next thought was not of Charley. It was, what a waste of time. The best laid plans, gone up in petrol and exhaust fumes.

Ten minutes later, having abandoned the windbreak, rugs, tennis set, sandwiches and chilly bin to what she hoped would be a grateful young family, Rebecca jogged past the public car park on the outskirts of the village, eating an apple. She'd heard her mother talk of hitching lifts quite freely in her youth. It seemed to have gone out of fashion, here as well as in the rest of Britain, during the last forty years.

Was there a police presence on the island? She couldn't recall seeing one. She considered asking someone if they had a mobile, but none of the cars seemed occupied. She thought she could recall a hotel, a redbrick building called The Lindisfarne, near the first junction. It was worth a try.

Rebecca had been trying to keep her spirits up since Charley went into the car trunk. She had a fleeting notion that they may get into the Guinness Book of Records as the World's Shortest Marriage. She couldn't imagine many people would have done worse, except film stars and models and Ulrika Johnson, but it was nothing to be proud of. There was a sliver of comfort in that, as far as she could tell, he hadn't been knifed or shot. She would get to the whatever-it-was hotel as soon as possible and she would *not* panic. She would just have to hope there was a cop somewhere she could stir into action.

"Hell no, honey," said the guy behind the bar, who appeared to be in his early forties, with a face as round as a skillet and a nametag that read Calum Nelson. "Cop? Don't make me laugh. Gone are the days. No Dixons of Dock Green in this country anymore. Barely any cops at all, for that matter. There hasn't been a cop on Holy Island in my time here. Not what you'd call resident. The nearest one's in Berwick. You're talking twelve, fifteen miles."

"Do you think I could use your phone, please?"

"Help yourself. There's a public phone in the hall. Or use this one in reception. 999's a freebie anyway. Kidnapped…in this place. Huh. You'll be lucky to get a cop who knows what it means, let alone gives a toss. Excuse the French." He pointed to his nametag. "Call me Cal, by the way."

What was the saying? Rebecca asked herself. There'll always be an England? She'd heard her mother use it often enough, but it looked like Mom was out of touch in more ways than one. The England she'd seen, the cities anyway, seemed to be suffering every form of social ill imaginable. To think "back home" had clawed its way out of the blitz for this. The people who'd lived through it must wonder what sort of sense to make of it all. Or maybe that didn't go with stiff upper lips.

She felt a sudden, powerful wave of homesickness. My God, talk about a chain of accidents. You meet a guy, think you're in love, get married, and your newly attached other half adds bingeing to his bed-hopping. Not satisfied with that, he starts riots, gets thrown around like a shopping bag, and the next thing you know you're seeking help from strangers.

Rebecca wasn't happy seeking help, especially not from strangers, because it made her feel uneasy and second-class. Indebted. She put it down to childhood warnings from her mother, still relatively new in a new land. And even if she ignored this maternal advice, what chance would she ever get to repay the debt?

She asked the operator to put her through to the desk sergeant, told him that her new husband had been dumped into a car trunk, that she didn't know the model of the car, except it was a BMW, or the year, or the number, but it was blue, and three youths had driven off with him in it. When she ran out of breath, the sergeant told her to slow down. She spent a fraught five minutes explaining it was a rental, they'd only had it a day and no, she wasn't the hirer or a named driver. Yes, her full name was Rebecca Carter Oakley (barely) and no, she wasn't a UK resident, and yes, she only had a temporary address, and no, this number wasn't hers, and no, she had no idea who the perpetrators were, had never seen them before in her life, blah, blah, blah. She could hear her voice rising as she related these answers, and could almost hear the bloke on the other end thinking *hysterical bloody woman.*

All accompanied by visions of Charley, speeding up the boohai, comatose in a car trunk.

Eventually, after a lecture on police force understaffing, she was told they'd send someone. She heard the cop hitting a keyboard, and swearing under his breath.

"What's up?" she asked more calmly.

"Checking the crossing times. Yeah…nothing to stop them there."

Rebecca had researched the same tide tables herself before their journey north; the causeway had opened just before they'd arrived. Today, she remembered it was open until late afternoon.

"You'll put out an APB?" she asked.

She got another homily on current UK policing and the shortcomings of American thrillers and TV crime programmes.

"On what, madam? An all-points bulletin on an unknown car with an unknown number?"

"Hey. It's blue, it's a BMW and it's being driven by a cross-section of your multicultural society. Salt, pepper and sand, right? It's not as if they're on a family outing, you know."

"Madam, you need to go easy on the attitude. We have racist laws here."

"Sorry. I was just making sure you got the picture." *Madam.* Was he winding her up?

"And you can't remember where you rented it?" Undisguised incredulity. If the guy were here in front of her, she'd stuff his mouth with stale bread and cheese. Or did his clients get full English breakfasts these days?

"*No*...well, Newcastle. Not Hertz, or anyone well-known like that. A specialist outfit, I seem to remember. The name began with an 'F.' Far-something, maybe?"

"Farrington's?"

"Yes, that was it. I think Charley...my husband...called it a 3-series."

"Bad move, madam. Top ten stolen car, in its class. Top three in fact, last I heard," the cop said informatively.

"Well, isn't that good to know, *sir*? It was a treat. A *honeymoon* treat."

"Oh yeah. They're a real treat for your friendly neighbourhood car thief. I'll speak to Farrington's. We'll get someone out as soon as we can."

"Fine."

"Where?"

"Where what?"

"Where can we reach you?"

"Here, I guess. This hotel, or the guesthouse where we're staying."

"You have a picture of this husband of yours?"

"No. We had some taken at the registry office. They weren't ready when we left."

"They'll be worth a try I suppose. Give me the name of the place..."

Rebecca dredged the receipt from her pouch, and gave him the details.

"Okay. We'll be in touch."

"Fine. Thank you."

She slammed the phone down in disgust, blushed and said sorry to Calum—call me Cal—Nelson.

"Not much joy?" he asked, busily dusting malt whisky bottles.

"Oh, peachy. He was more interested in addresses than abductions."

"How long since you left England?"

"I didn't. My mother did when she was fifteen, in nineteen sixty-eight."

"I was telling you, things have changed. Not for the better. Had a cop here once, right? Not now. Had a doctor here once. Not now. Missing a part or two. You're lucky you weren't transferred to a call centre in deepest Essex. Or the outer suburbs of Delhi. It's happened. People forever moaning about it, this gone, that gone. Like a stuck needle, believe me."

As with a lot of bartenders, Cal Nelson had a warped view of humanity. He'd spent too many hours in the company of people crying into their beer. Or at him. Everything from failed marriages to the demise of the milk float.

He was silent for a few seconds. "Tell you what…there's a guy in the village who might help. Alex Deville. He knows people the rest of us don't. And he has a whole array of security cameras and such around the place. The house is only a stone's throw," he added. "A coupla hundred yards over there. I'll phone him if you like, tell him what's happened."

Rebecca listened while he gave directions and made the call, wondering if anyone would be able to track the car, how long it might take, and whether she'd ever see Charley again. It was strange how new worries submerged old ones, like a form of Chinese torture. A worry-a-day-keeps-old-worries-at-bay kind of effect. And she was beginning to worry about Charley. Because he'd been in such a disordered state when they left the guesthouse, he didn't even have his mobile.

She told herself not to be stupid, that he'd be returned when they realised their mistake. After all, what was the point in kidnapping someone like Charley? He had no trade-in value. Rebecca found the whole thing difficult to swallow. And it was humiliating. She couldn't imagine even dumb Sloaners losing their husbands on the first day of their honeymoon.

She thanked Cal Nelson and set off in the direction he'd shown her.

George ("Geordie") Halloran, cub reporter for *The Northern Sun*, the north-east's leading regional daily, was in his cubicle in Groat Market, Newcastle, bemoaning the fact he had once again been bypassed when the big stories of the week were breaking. The big stories being the election results, and especially the Scottish election results; No. 10 Downing Street's variation on the theme The King is Dead Long Live the King; some weasel-eyed rapist/murderer who'd collected a token twenty-one years in Edinburgh instead of being strung up by the balls from an electricity pylon; and a wee girl apparently abducted in the Algarve.

Here he was on a Saturday with nothing better to do, reading some of the headline stories of the last week, and trying to see what magic ingredient they contained that he, in his own stuff, failed to conjure up.

He wandered over to the coffee dispenser, reflecting on the wrong turns life seemed to take and whether, in the journalistic firmament, he'd disappeared down a black hole. He worked hard, did his best to impress the old man, kept beavering away to learn the trade, and was handed down the leftovers for his trouble. "Dig up the figures from last time, Geordie," "Try looking at the regional variations, Geordie," "How about a bit of comparative analysis, Geordie." For God's sake, he was a writer, not a bloody statistician.

Given the shambles that the Scottish Secretary, with help from assorted friends and bureaucrats, had created from what should have been a straightforward voting process, he had wondered which banana republic would be first in line to bid for Scotland's election-rigging blueprint. Maybe Robert Mugabe would be interested, although he'd be struggling to raise the cash. What exactly was a quintillion Zimbabwean dollars worth?

The Scottish election had been proof positive of the maxim; what can go wrong, will go wrong. Different ballot papers needing different systems of voting, 140,000-odd of them rejected as invalid, postal voting slips that didn't fit the return envelopes, counting machines that gave up the ghost, counts suspended, a guy running amok with a golf club in a polling station, voting papers being stuck together with scotch tape, one defeated candidate making noises about legal action, a helicopter that couldn't transport ballot boxes because of fog, and a boat on a similar mission breaking down. Short of stationing Keystone Cops in polling booths, it couldn't have been much worse.

And would heads roll? Geordie asked himself. Of course not, such a thing would be unthinkable, not the British way at all. Geordie could just imagine the reaction: No, no, it was all done with the best of intentions, old chap. What? Resign over the disenfranchisement of a measly few thousand voters? My dear fellow, this isn't Florida, you're living in paranoia alley. A vote-rigging plot? Good grief, you people see conspiracies everywhere.

As for the thing at Number Ten, it was blindingly obvious that Prime Ministers went on too long. What was it with them? They seemed to have a sort of take-it-to-the-wire wish that kept them clinging on far past the time when any sensible human would have beaten a dignified retreat. The Americans had one thing right. Reagan and Clinton apart, they may have elected, or been dealt, a succession of dummies in recent times, but at least they knew a different dummy would appear every eight years, and sometimes not even that. Look at Thatcher. Even as a son whose mother would rise from her grave and clip his ears if he voted Tory, Geordie could see the Iron Lady had done *some* good things. Then, several years into her term of office, came the brainstorm, the iniquitous poll tax. Jeezo, talk about losing the plot. She'd lost the paragraphs and punctuation marks.

But if that aberration had been bad enough, the present holder of her former office was positively submerged in them. Apart from Iraq and disintegrating health, education and police services, there were some hard statistics, and Geordie knew all about those. Among them was immigration, of which Britain had the ninth highest total worldwide and, of those nine countries, by far the smallest land area. He had been taken aback to find that Britain had more immigrants than Australia, five times more than South Africa, and ten times more than New Zealand. One result was that today there were on average 1,000 people crammed into each square mile of England; twice as many as Germany, and four times more than France. Excluding the small island of Malta, this gave England pole position as Europe's most crowded country. Then there were asylum applications: the highest in Europe, and higher than the USA. There was the highest rate of teenage pregnancy in the world, including African peoples too destitute or brainwashed to use birth control. There was the £88 million spent the year before on the expenses of 646 MPs, and the hike in their total income of 75 percent in five years. That little self-tribute, Geordie thought, must have registered at least a fraction of a blip on inflation. Then there were the various tax increases, stealth or otherwise, which totalled more than a hundred in the last ten years. There was the budget deficit, legacy of a "prudent" Chancellor, which was likely to double in a year to £60 billion, and the £20 billion spent on "benefits." There was the national debt, according to questionable official figures, of half a trillion pounds and rising. And there was the trillion pound *personal* debt mountain, also rising. There were statistics, in short, that would make Einstein go cross-eyed.

Whatever happened to government by example? Geordie asked himself. It was little wonder, following that sort of lead, that people were up to their ears in hock. Even if you were able to set aside the human misery, he thought they were pretty damning figures. Some were harder to get, some were more verifiable than others, but together they told a story. And what did they say about the PM's much-vaunted legacy? *To my good old buddy-in-waiting, whose patience has transcended every monument known to man, the following bequests…*

And what did you reply if you were, loosely speaking, the good old buddy-in-waiting?

Thank you so much for leaving me the pigswill, even if I had a hand in most of it. And about time too, you dithering Judas. Good luck on the after-dinner circuit, by the way. Or in some cushy United Nations number, whatever takes your fancy.

My day will come, Geordie thought, sipping his fifth cup of coffee. Statistics be damned, see if it doesn't. And when it does, I'll wring every last drop of satisfaction out of it. Then it's bye-bye Newcastle, bye-bye girl of the moment, hello *LA Times*.

Following Cal Nelson's directions, Rebecca had found Fahr House quite easily. From the outside, given its size and solid stone façade, she had felt somewhat intimidated. Things hadn't greatly improved when she got inside, either. She thought on first acquaintance that Alexander Beauregard Courtney Deville would make most people feel crushed. He was an erect six-four, with penetrating blue eyes, an aquiline nose and teeth like Paul Newman's. A no-nonsense guy, she thought, a power-broker, with more than a hint of self-assurance. None of it surprised her. According to Cal Nelson, he had "long ago reached the top of his particular tree in the jungle, the *acme* if you know what I'm saying."

"I remember your mother," Deville said, having heard the gist of Rebecca's misfortune, and ushering her to a seat. "I could believe I'm speaking to her now, even though she was a strip of a girl when she left. She's keeping well?"

"She's fine, thanks."

"She was impulsive herself, I seem to recall, and rather prone to sudden passions. There tended to be things she liked one day, and didn't like the next. You seem to have taken after her in that regard, as well as physically." He smiled, an incongruously engaging smile.

"Well, maybe, but she isn't here now, so it's no real comfort in the circumstances," Rebecca said, trying hard not to seem defensive.

"Of course not, it wouldn't be. She was my first girlfriend, you know. We were fifteen or so at the time." He smiled again. "Perhaps it's as well she left when she did. I was rather self-centred until I left school. I suppose it's a common enough problem at that age, without ever being excusable."

Rebecca gazed around the room. It was impressive, oozing wealth from every ornament and drape and piece of furniture. What looked like ancestral portraits and photos were interspersed with original oils and watercolours on the walls. From the brief description Cal Nelson had given her, it all figured.

"Yes, well, it's water under the bridge now," Deville added. "Let's see what we can do about your young man. Help yourself to coffee, won't you? I'll be five minutes, no more."

In truth, Deville was relieved at the interruption. It gave him a chance to do something useful before tonight's meeting. His visits to the village hall and churchyard, conversations with friends along the way, and more phone calls, had barely occupied an hour. He had reached another loose end, and Rebecca was a welcome diversion. With her family connections to the island, he hoped she might also prove to be a good omen. Also, he remembered her mother rather more fondly than he was saying and was sure, if Mary Carter née Forster were here, she'd be among the first to wish him well for S-Day.

As he left the room, Rebecca carried her coffee to the window, and distractedly watched a flock of gulls fighting over a scrap of mangled carcass outside the dry-stone boundary wall. She noticed a mobile phone mast near some shrubbery. Above it the sun was just discernible, a dull copper orb behind the thickening clouds.

Gazing at the scene, it struck her that nowhere in her first conversation with Alex Deville had any word of commiseration been offered about her loss. Not a "sorry" or "how awful" or any other hackneyed sentiment. She could readily forgive him for that, but wondered if it was also soon enough for him to have heard of Charley's penchant for trashing places, and to be making judgements. She sincerely hoped, if she was going to have to ask for help, that she wouldn't be bracketed with Charley.

Cal Nelson had told her something of Deville's history. Born on the island, in this house, and educated in the village's First School (there *was* still a school, he'd said, twenty-odd pupils then, seven now, "part-time with the tides") and at Berwick High School. Then up to Oxford, graduating with first-class honours: a "rare event for here". Then a merchant bank in the City, up through the ranks to Board level, maybe Chairmanship, and retiring back to Lindisfarne at the venerable age of fifty-two. Returning once again to the house of his birth; this mansion, Fahr House. *Fahr* being Norse for retreat, or so Cal Nelson thought.

She couldn't imagine Deville retreating from anything short of a WMD, but then he'd have had nothing to do with naming the house.

"It's maybe been translated down the years to Farne," Nelson had continued. "'Fahr,' I mean. But 'Farne' is supposed to mean 'land' as well, in Celtic. And the Lindis is a stream, sometimes called the Low. It runs over the flats. So we end up with Lindisfarne meaning 'stream land,' or something. It's as confusing as hell," he'd concluded, as if someone had set out to bamboozle him.

"What about the Holy Island bit?" Rebecca had asked. "Where did that come from? The saints?"

"The monks gave it the name. Holy blood. Spilled by the Vikings."

"Oh." Come to think of it, she could vaguely recall her mother telling her the same thing years ago. She hoped it hadn't been a bedtime story.

"Anyway, retired or not, Alex Deville is loaded," Nelson had continued. "Way beyond Lotto level...*Euro* Lotto level. Bonuses you wouldn't believe. But he's gonna use them. He's got big plans for this place. Stick around a day or so," he added. "You might get the drift."

It was strange that her mother hadn't mentioned him, Rebecca thought. She knew that Deville's merchant bank had offices in London, Hong Kong, Paris and New York. No doubt there were others. It had been a household name even in New Zealand, and the country of her birth didn't exactly count itself among the world's financial centres. But her mother wasn't to have known he would be here now, enjoying early retirement.

Turning from the window, she picked up a daily paper, vaguely conscious that elections had been underway while she was preparing to get married. The mechanics seemed to have caused some trouble in Scotland, she noticed, although she didn't know why. It all looked apathetic anyway, half of them voting, the other half not bothering. There was a picture of a voting paper that appeared similar to those used in Enzed, but which had somehow caused paralysis. And the Scottish National Party had won—or had they? No one seemed too sure. Weren't coalition governments the norm here, like back home? Didn't people who got the most seats and votes win? Maybe the government had decided to ape the brothers Bush in Florida, she thought, which even for Britain seemed to be taking the special relationship a step too far. She wondered why the idea of independence was causing so much trouble. She'd always thought it a virtue, something people were encouraged to be—as she had been herself, not least to come on this holiday. But to read some of this stuff, anyone would think the Scottish electorate had committed hari-kari. Rebecca couldn't begin to figure it out.

She became conscious of movement behind her, and turned to see a guy in a dark Armani suit and a royal blue tie, in his late twenties or perhaps thirty, with cool blue eyes, crew-cut blond hair, and a neck the diameter of a telegraph pole. Muscles that even the Armani couldn't hide. A light-heavyweight, but not one who'd have much time for Marquis of Queensberry niceties. Maybe he'd be into kickboxing, Rebecca thought, or one of the more lethal forms of hand-to-hand combat.

"Hi. I'm Max, Mr. D's private man. I wondered if there's anything you need. A drink? A sandwich? Restroom?"

"No…oh, no. The coffee's fine. Nothing, really."

"Anything at all, just shout. Press this bell, see?"

Private man? Rebecca wondered. Was this a new calling? Another name for a bodyguard? An aide? Something peculiarly British, like Jeeves?

"No, thank you. No, everything's fine," she said. Which it wasn't, of course, but there was no way she wished to prolong a conversation with this fearsome stranger.

"Not quite, huh? Missing husband, for starters." He smiled, showing a flash of dazzlingly white teeth.

"Well, yes, that apart. I meant here. Everything's fine, thanks."

Max Deville shrugged. "Okay, if you say so. The man won't be long."

"Progress," Alex Deville told her as he re-entered the room. "The police seem to know the car, they have the number, and they're looking for it. No stone, they assure me, is to remain unturned. Well, one hopes it shouldn't be beyond them. I've told them you're here now, so at least they shouldn't lose you in the process."

Rebecca looked at her Cartier, a twenty-first birthday present from her parents. "They could be miles away. It's been over an hour."

"It really shouldn't be a problem if they are able to locate the car. The rental company has GPS tracking on their fleet. This would be an excellent time to see if it works."

"Oh." Rebecca noticed that the telephone was ringing, one call after another. Presumably Private Man Max would be dealing with them, unless there were other servants in the house.

"Technology to the rescue, eh? We'll just have to sit tight and hope your significant other is returned before long. With luck, in one piece and before the tide comes in. Four o'clock is the cut-off time today, I believe."

"They can actually track the car?" Satellite technology had never been Rebecca's forte.

"Apparently so, yes. One of these new-fangled gizmos that I'm afraid I know little about, except they can offer some assistance. Still, we have a few of those ourselves. Come, I'll lead the way. We may be a while, so pour a refill of coffee and bring it with you."

Rebecca followed him through a kitchen as big as a tennis court, and finished as far as she could tell in real marble and stainless steel, with a massive central island, a fireplace you could walk into, pots and pans of all sizes, walnut armoires chock full of crystal and chinaware, and Charles Rennie Mackintosh-style chairs. They went down a flight of stairs into a brightly-lit basement.

Her immediate thought was of the film: *Enemy of the State*. A cross between Jon Voigt's high-tech NSA offices and Gene Hackman's converted warehouse. The hum of air-conditioning pervaded the room. A bank of monitors, a wireless CCTV system, three powerful Packard Bell PCs, a huge Sony LCD TV and two more 32-inch Bravias were arrayed along the length of one main wall. A conference table and eight padded chairs, digital map displays of the island and coastline, filing cabinets and wall units were ranked along the other. Four digital phones, a phone/fax, tape machines, printers, flatbed and film scanners and photocopiers were set on desks and tables. A state-of-the-art coffee-making machine occupied one corner. In the centre of the room, a large walnut desk with a framed newspaper cutting on it, and a leather swivel chair, took pride of place. There wasn't a loose cable or scrap of paper or speck of dust in sight.

She felt she had entered some kind of force field removed from normal domestic life. It was like seeing a Sherman tank on a country lane.

"Let's see if we have anything on them here," Deville said, sitting down at a PC alongside the monitors.

"Ohmigod," Rebecca said. "Incredible. What's all this stuff for?"

"A preparation."

"For what?"

"Perhaps you'll see later. I imagine that whatever happens, you'll be here this evening, wouldn't you say?" He pushed buttons, glanced at screens, paused, and zoomed in. "Is that them?"

"Mmm…yes. It looks like… it is. Yes."

"Well, well. A rum-looking bunch, aren't they? Your description did them justice, I think. Quite apart from their abduction of your husband, they look exactly like the kind of individuals that Holy Island would be far better off without. So, we have something here to show the cavalry when they arrive." More buttons punched and twirled, a printer whirring. "This was taken at eight forty-two this morning; you see the caption? It appears that our friends disembarked from a coach. Perhaps they decided that coach travel didn't suit them, and liked the idea of a Beemer instead."

Rebecca slid behind the walnut desk and looked. As colour CCTV pictures went, she couldn't recall seeing any of higher resolution.

"Those bloody people. They've been asked several times to be careful who, or more precisely what, they bring here," he said.

"Who? The coach company?"

"Who else?"

"But I suppose if people pay their money…"

"How long have you been in England?"

"Seven or eight weeks."

"Beware of following the herd. There's far too much woolly thinking these days and, if you'll forgive my saying so, you've just revealed a tendency to fall into the habit. By which I mean, the habit of excusing the inexcusable." Deville lifted the prints, wafted them in the air. "And you met your new husband when?"

"After a week or so here."

"As we were saying earlier, impulsive." He smiled without a trace of indulgence. "And what do you do yourself, back home in New Zealand?"

Rebecca was getting antsy with this ping-pong third degree. "I'm a plant ecologist. No, that's no longer true. I'm trying to be an artist. I paint."

"You graduated in ecology. And decided against using it?"

"It didn't work. Not for me. I tried it for a time at the DOC…the Department of Conservation in New Zealand."

"A somewhat unusual decision for the Green Age, isn't it? I'd have thought a qualification like that would have opened all sorts of doors these days, in both public and private sectors. How long did you persevere?"

"Mmm…a couple of years. I'm twenty-six now." (Why on earth was she telling him all this? You'd think Lady Luck might have dealt her *one* good conversation this morning out of half-a-dozen.) "It wasn't a total waste. It was a conscious choice."

"Where did you graduate?"

"UC in Christchurch. Biosciences. Four years ago. So yes, before you ask, I've been wasting my time painting for two years," Rebecca said with some asperity.

"Really? I'm a Christ Church man myself. Oxford, that is." Ignoring Rebecca's last remark as if it had never been made, Deville looked critically at the prints. "Not too bad, as photographs go. A pathetic trio, aren't they? Those jeans…I suppose we have American penitentiaries to thank. My son Alistair can work on them a little more, and no doubt improve on them. He has software; Photoshop, ImageMixer, digital enhancers and so on. They're quite beyond me, but they're effective editing tools." He put the prints on his desk, scribbled a note, and idly switched one of the TV sets to Sky News. "Plant ecology…now that could be a useful addition to the party. If your stay were to be extended, so to speak."

"Party?" Rebecca had her eyes on the screen, distracted by a news story of another abduction, a three year-old in Portugal, one that shrank Charley's problems into nothingness.

"A figure of speech…I was thinking ahead. Well, maybe we should let it go for now." Deville grinned at her, his face creasing, and his eyebrows lifting. "But if the day should ever come when you work with me, you'll need to stop acting on impulse. I can't tolerate it, personally, and can't think of the last time I heard of an impulse achieving anything good."

So what, Rebecca thought. Find Charley and the question won't arise. I'm out of here. This pile of a house at least.

Charley was in a force field of his own. His captors had decided to find a secluded spot off the main road, somewhere well away from helping hands, and dump him. They'd made an error, and now they knew it. Strangled yells from the boot had brought them to the realisation that he hadn't, as they'd thought, been alone in the dunes; there was a wife somewhere in the background who might notice he was gone. This was a setback; they hadn't bought the time they'd hoped, so they would need to lose the car. The idea was to get rid of carrot top, drive to a supermarket or public car park, and hotwire another set of wheels. Something less flash. The Beemer, with its smashed window like an open wound, was in any case making them nervous. And it made for a hell of a draught.

The trouble was, they had passed a supermarket by the roadside at Berwick but there was nothing now except hamlets and farms. The Scottish Borders. No helping hands, but no cars either. They discussed their options in low voices because Charley was still in the boot and presumed awake. Ten minutes ago he'd been pleading for a drink, like they were Good Samaritans for fuck's sake.

They'd given up on the GPS display, couldn't work the thing. It had blacked out since one of them kicked it. Another flicked through a road map, swearing under his breath. Didn't car rentals give a shit if their customers got lost? Or their cars?

They decided to follow a signpost to Abbey St. Bathans and what looked like an empty stretch of unpronounceable hills, and make a run for Dunbar. It got a bold-case mention on the map, so it must be more than a couple of shacks. They were pissed off at losing a three-quarter tank of fuel, but maybe there'd be a chance to siphon some off. And they had plenty of readies, didn't they, thanks to Dennis Cumming, Prop., at the Post Office back there?

Their spirits lifted as they motored along the byways. One problem solved; the countryside was getting emptier with each passing mile. They pulled up near a place called Monynut Edge, cut the engine, and hauled Charley out.

"Stream down there, you want a drink," one said, looking around, no sign of habitation at all. "Any clue which way is up?"

"What?"

"Where you're at, asshole."

"No idea." It had been a winding road, and Charley had felt like a sardine in a tin. Add a dash of torture to your list of crimes and misdemeanours why don't you, he thought sourly. Bunch of Geordie yobs.

"Way to go. That's south," pointing north, "back to square one."

"Hey, you can't leave me here!" Charley cried. "Get me near a house at least, I—"

"No way, brotha. Take your chances. Bye-bye, walk or die."

They climbed back into the Beemer, gave Charley the finger, and five minutes later were out of sight. Charley sat on a rock and put his head in his heads. It still hurt. His legs had cramped, and he rubbed them until some feeling returned. He looked at his watch. He'd been an hour in the boot. Fifty miles, sixty? But which was south, north, east, west? Could he believe them? Which way to fucking Holy Island, cradle of Christianity? Which way to Rebecca, Sharon Davies of the frozen fucking north?

He scrambled down to the stream, looked suspiciously at the water and a flock of sheep on the hillside, and thought what the hell, it's wet. He threw some over his face, cupped his hands, and drank. It tasted cold and clean. He decided to follow the car. It had gone in the direction the guy had pointed, but Charley was too dazed to question why they were going back south, and in any case he didn't know south from Siberia.

A crisp mid-day light fell on rolling heather hills, scattered conifer plantations, banks of broom and gorse in bloom, patches of bracken and bramble, streams, and gullies. It was a pristine landscape, as stark a demonstration as you could wish of the North-South divide. For Pete's sake, Charley thought, looking around, the big city could do with a bit of this. Move it three hundred miles south, and it would mop up all those new citizens, the multicultural flash flood, like a squeegee. Mustn't cause offence, though. Let's be fair, remember that a fraction of the fault lies with the natives, doing no one any favours by breeding, and living longer.

Whatever, it held no appeal for him; there was too much emptiness and fresh air, and too many bleating animals. He rose and stumbled down the road, in the direction he believed to be south, relying on the well-tried townie-in-the-countryside rule that even a blind pig will find an acorn eventually.

CHAPTER THREE

At six o'clock that evening, the Holy Island village hall was crammed to capacity. Deville had warned Rebecca to expect it. This was to be, in his words, "a meeting of seminal import." And the hall was the only secular venue on the island big enough to contain the whole community.

Except your kitchen, she thought. Or living room.

As they entered, she'd seen a poster outside, a thermometer charting progress towards raising £330,000 for the Village Hall Restoration Fund. They were nearly halfway there. The dilapidated old structure was on its last legs, the floor moving under the weight of people. Rebecca didn't know it, but the building had been shut down and taped up at the end of the 2006 season. While it awaited demolition, Deville had commissioned some remedial work to accommodate meetings during the winter. Apart from a handful of forlorn tourists, the village streets had been deserted as they drove through. Pubs, hotels and shops were closed; honesty boxes the order of the evening.

It had been seven hours now, with not a word of Charley. She had spent twenty minutes of them with Deville's "cavalry," two cops from Berwick. One had been big and round, the other looked as if he'd just left school. *Messrs.* Plod Major and Minor hadn't exactly inspired her with confidence, but at least they hadn't *madam*ed her. She'd been nameless this time, half a pair of victims.

The search was on, Plod Major had assured her, looking at Deville. Rebecca was well aware that more minutes equalled more miles equalled diminishing chances. Deville, too, had seemed impatient. Whatever scheme was afoot, and Rebecca had picked up hints during the afternoon, this guy had blown his chances of getting in on the act. Plod Minor wasn't taking risks. He was silent, acting like a bystander, squinting up her cut-offs, gawping at the room.

Ogling apart, Rebecca had some sympathy for him; he looked as though he was reliving her own earlier reactions. Well, maybe they had a room to match in Buckingham Palace. The prints Deville had run off, enlarged and sharpened, lay on an oak-and-yew coffee table.

Plod Major told them that the three youths who had taken Charley hostage were wanted on another front, the opportunistic theft of £300 from the Post Office till earlier that morning. "It explains why they needed a car in a hurry," he said. "One feigns a dizzy spell, Dennis Cumming goes in back for a glass of water, concerned citizen. Brick through the glass, Cumming runs back in, they flatten him. Nice easy drug money. What you would expect from Newcastle."

"You know they came by coach?" Deville asked.

"Well, we assumed they must have—"

"You assumed. How else do you think they got here? Cruise ship?"

"Well, we—"

"You don't know their names? You haven't asked the coach people?"

Silence. The cavalry viewing each other accusingly. What a pair of posers, Rebecca thought.

Now, several hours later, not knowing quite why she was attending a public meeting in what amounted to little more than a square Nissen hut, Deville was ushering her to a front seat. It was one of those moulded grey things you just knew would become vindictive after twenty minutes or so. Maybe she'd have been better off standing at the back. Like every public meeting she'd ever attended, the front seats were last to fill.

"You'll see a bit of history made here tonight," Deville repeated in a low voice, "although I do realise, as I've said before, that in the circumstances it may not be entirely riveting. I have to leave you now and take my seat," he said, indicating the dais. "My elder son will look after you. He's been looking into those thugs, by the way."

Private Man Max, in Armani suit number two. He turned in his plastic chair, said he had three names to work with, and patted a space next to him. Rebecca said thank you and eased herself down, thinking: was this surreal, or what? Well, Private Man, bodyguard, elder son or whatever, she was stuck with him. It was too late now to hide at the back.

Alex Deville spent a couple of minutes shaking hands with three other men and a woman at the top table. The hubbub of noise faded. He turned, arms wide. "An excellent turnout, ladies and gentlemen. Does anyone know of a friend or relative who is *not* present?"

"Only Dennis at the Post Office," came a voice from the back. "He's had the polis round, been contacting insurers. Took him a while to recover. He said he'd be a bit late."

"Yes, I'd heard about Dennis. I hope you all signed the register as you came in. It will be important to demonstrate community unanimity tonight, or as near unanimity as we can achieve. We have the results of the vote. I'll ask the Clerk to the Council, Mrs. Swan, to read them to you."

A large blonde woman got to her feet. "The result of the public referendum held on Thursday third May in Holy Island Civil Parish, the count having been made and verified, is as follows: those for secession, one hundred and thirty. Those against, three."

She paused for the room to fall silent again. "Elected First Minister of the Althing of Holy Island, Alexander Deville. Elected founding Ministers, Thomas Walker, James Redman, Michael Cromarty and Elizabeth Swan. No dissenters. Those are the results of the public referendum. Thank you."

There was an explosion of applause, whoops, chatter, people shifting in their seats, feet hammering the floorboards, klaxons, football rattles. Rebecca's ears went numb.

One man shouted, "Who the hell were the three?"

Another man: "Stick that where it hurts, yah Whitehall wimps."

A little old lady along the row from Rebecca clapped loudly, and stabbed a knitting needle in a fellow parishioner's cheek. She patted the injured cheek and apologised. Of all the trappings of modern society, Amy Donaldson did not like the causeway, and never had; to her, it was a great grey snake lying across the flats. St. Cuthbert hadn't needed it, had he? St. Aidan? Not a bit of it. They had managed fine without any such thing, just walked or ridden their donkeys or whatever passed for transport in those halcyon pre-motorised days. Twelve centuries later, in her own youth, the crossing had been negotiated at low water on foot or horseback or a rickety flatbed taxi. Across hard-ridged sand. She could remember the sensation yet; tongues bitten, dental fillings detached, babies born prematurely on that bone-rattling journey. Now it was all air-conditioned coaches, exhaust fumes, and city slickers waving out the windows.

Amy was a traditionalist, a splash of local colour (strong, vivid colour) born on Holy Island ten years before the start of the second World War. She had been a pupil at the First School with two dozen friends when Hitler invaded Poland. She'd been married twice, to Holy Island men, her classmates, and wouldn't have dreamed of looking further afield. She had outlived both. Now, she was everyone's favourite granny, a feisty old lady with fine bones, white hair, staunch opinions, and a heart the size of Bamburgh Castle. Alex Deville knew very well: take Amy Donaldson with you, and you take the island.

"Great stuff," she said, waving the knitting, obviously having come prepared for a long night. "Blow it all away."

"I think we may have to edit some of those comments from the public record," Deville said mildly. "It is, I'm sure we all agree, a resounding majority in favour. As of midnight tonight, this island is duly and cordially seceded from the United Kingdom and the European Union. As of midnight tonight, this community will forge its own system of government, institutions and laws, taking what is good from its present framework and repealing what is bad. Before going on, I'll allow five minutes for that historic message to sink in. However, I do ask people to continue to be positive, to recall undertakings I've given before and intend to repeat for the record tonight. Amy, would you please take care where you poke those knitting needles?"

"Of course I will, First Minister. They're just something to do while you talk."

There was laughter, and more applause.

Ohmigod, Rebecca thought, so that's what it's all about. Her knowledge of British history was hazy. Apart from the U.S. Declaration of Independence—and Scottish and Welsh devolution, long and tortured works in progress—she could dredge up only the Rhodesian UDI in 1965 as any sort of yardstick. That fellow Smith, and his white minority rule? I hope it doesn't turn out like that, she thought, or *him* (looking at Deville) like John Howard's "grubby dictator." Holy mackerel, hadn't there been threats, economic sanctions, charges of illegality, treason? These people must be wired to Mars if they were heading down that road. How could they possibly think they'd get away with it? Maybe there was a dope factory here, and they were all having a dream-in. Rebecca caught herself glancing round to see if there were any obvious glue sniffers or nasal deformities, but she gave it up quickly, ashamed at the thought. They all looked excited, but sane.

She remembered with bemusement Alex Deville's suggestion, made during the afternoon and repeated ten minutes ago, that this event would not be "entirely riveting". For goodness' sake, she was *transfixed*.

Somebody else was now on their feet. "Is the timing right, Alex?"

Another: "How do you think the Scottish results will affect us?"

"I believe someone once said that all of life is a matter of perfect timing," Alexander Deville said. "If not, they should have done. We knew about the timing from the outset. I can't guarantee it's perfect, but I do know one thing. We have surprise on our side, and surprising someone is always easier when they've just had a fright."

"Interesting, huh?" Max Deville said. "Don't let on, but I was one of the three who voted against." He grinned. "Just kidding...well, we couldn't have a whitewash, could we? It leaves me two jokers to speak to."

"What happens now?" Rebecca asked, thinking for the first time that day that Charley had gone from her mind, and wondering if she should feel guilty. Wondering also whether Max's "speak to" was a euphemism for some form of summary violence.

"He'll be telling us," Max said. "It's a big night for him. He won't miss any tricks."

"Does anyone know about it...outside?" Rebecca asked.

"There may have been mutterings in Berwick, people going back and forth," Max said. "It's kind of difficult to have a public vote in secret, even one that's mixed up with other so-called elections. But then you have the ostrich syndrome, and you can rely on them for that. Like everything else in that country we left behind tonight...make believe it won't happen, fudge, put your head in the sand, do nothing till it's too late."

"How's he going to let them know? Will they believe it?"

"Who? Berwick?" A shrug. "They don't signify. London? Like I say, he'll be telling us. It's not as if he's unprepared. He's been working for this twenty years or more."

"Yes. He looks like the sort of man who gets what he wants."

"He's human. Toast and coffee for breakfast like the rest of us."

"Why didn't you say you were his son?" Rebecca asked. "When we met? What was all the private man stuff about?"

"Sorry about that," Max replied. "I've become used to it with strangers. Never quite know where they're coming from. Better keeping them off balance."

"Yes," Rebecca said thoughtfully, "I can see you being careful."

"It's what I am," Max said.

"What do you intend to do with those names? The hoodies? Will the names help?"

"Oh, sure. I'll find out where they live. Track them. Bring them back here. String them up by the thumbs. Or worse." He grinned.

The Bigg M boys had found new transport in Dunbar, a garden centre, with people pottering about choosing plants, separated from their cars by brick walls and impenetrable hedges. They'd hit it lucky first time, a four year-old Ford Focus with a nearly full tank. They had time to switch the number plates of the Focus with a third car, and the Beemer's with it, and thought that should confuse the hell out of all these small-time peasants for an hour or two. They decided the T-shirts were, like, too recognisable and would have to go the way of the Beemer, and snatched new gear off a washing line strung across a secluded back yard. Up-market gear too: Timberland, Lacoste, Polo. A washer-woman of taste. Take a bow, cow.

They reached Edinburgh mid-afternoon, parked in a seedy area between the Royal Mile and Cowgate, and ate fish suppers washed down with bottles of Bud. They argued about which pubs to try, and whether to stay the night. Maybe a spot of gay-bashing? Bruisers meet cruisers, *bam*, like so. But where would ginger beers hang out in this place? No problem, they'd find them. The Focus was well stocked with weaponry; a jack, wrenches, and a brand-new set of Ping clubs in the boot. One of them, Shad Bunglawala, cornrows still as tight as waxed cord, demonstrated with a 7-iron, and looked like he was wrestling with an octopus.

Charley was well and truly lost in the Lammermuir Hills, disoriented by trying to follow the arc of the sun, and twice finding himself back near where he'd started. He suspected one of the sheep had bleated a welcome the last time around, and wondered nervously if he was hallucinating or maybe losing his marbles. He'd had more religious moments in the last two hours than in the rest of his life put together.

He was into unknown territory now, with no familiar sheep for a while and only once the sound of a motor in the distance, faint, mocking, receding. For a time, he'd given up on roads. He'd followed one that turned out to be a cul-de-sac, and ended up at some reservoir in the middle of nowhere. Bad move, he realised now. He should have stuck with it; roads at least had the occasional signpost on them. Or vehicle. None that deigned to pick him up though; hell no, that was too much to ask. One driver had almost brained him with an empty bottle of Beck's. Bye-bye helping hands, good neighbours, all that historic crap. He was exhausted, and his mind was a blur. A fog of random images, nothing that made sense.

He kept looking at his watch, its hands speeding towards dusk and darkness. Maybe danger, too? Death? He had already been attacked by a large bird of prey, a hawk that must have mistaken his hair for a fox cub. Somehow, it had taken some kind of offence. He'd steered clear of gloomy conifer stands; God alone knew what was in them. Wild boars? He shivered, feeling the seeds of panic starting to sprout. Just one house or human, please. Christ, how could a life go so totally down the tubes in just one miserable day? It was all Rebecca's fault. Getting married, dragging him up here, what a crock of shit. Nothing that could be laid on him of course; it was her, the Fates, that fucking island, Geordie yobs, Kate Moss and her crummy on-off boyfriend, some venomous mojo he knew nothing about, that had so royally fucked things up.

Once or twice, he found himself thinking of his parents, his home, and his upbringing in Earl's Court. A nice, *safe*, well-to-do life. Well, not so much today, but then, yes. What had happened to it? Twenty-five years ago, there had been familiar things, familiar faces, familiar places. Traffic wardens and mailmen you recognised. Shops that kept their names, and sold the same goods day by day. Teeming with traffic and fellow Brits, even if a few were criminals or parasites or other species of lowlife. Not a trace of any of them when they were needed. Even a fucking waxwork would be a welcome sight.

Then Charley, a thousand feet above sea level, somewhere between Blythe Edge and Scoured Rig, knowing neither from the Cairngorms or Alps, found himself over his ankles and up to his knees in a bog. He had the presence of mind or sheer good luck to fall backwards, turn on his side, and try to get viable purchase against the sucking black ooze.

A kestrel hovered over him, feathering its wings in the air currents. It was incurious, more interested in something moving in the grass, something edible, a vole or field-mouse.

Charley dragged himself to firmer ground, lay gasping like a stranded trout, with flies hatching from the coating of muck on his pants, and trying to catch his breath, a manic laugh bubbling up.

The business of the meeting had moved on. Deville, still at the dais, was running through a shopping list, a pricey one, his audience engrossed. A schoolteacher was already in place: Mrs. (Minister) Swan would continue with her small team at the First School. A doctor was due tomorrow with his wife: a "friend of mine," well qualified, a Holy Islander by birth. There was some bantering as people told themselves not to catch a germ in the next twenty-four hours. A policeman was expected in a few days: a "friend of Max," an ex-RMP.

"Ha!" said Amy in the front row, brandishing the lethal needles. "Now that's what I call a choice. You men had better watch out. See how zero tolerance—"

There was laughter throughout the room, partly at Amy's mock vehemence, and partly, Rebecca felt, with relief from the hard-nosed business of self-determination.

"He does come recommended," Deville said, flashing his son a smile. "Not just by Max."

The search was on for a vet, someone who could look after farm animals as well as domestic pets. "A catch-all kinda guy, then. Is he goin' to be locum for the doc as well?" a man in a blue guernsey asked. There was more laughter, this time not quite so hearty.

The ministry at St. Mary's would go on as normal; the Church was pretty well immune to national boundaries, after all. The vicar hadn't raised any objections, quite the opposite. His vote had been known for weeks. He was known to hold the view that eternal damnation might be too lenient a verdict when it came to the present British government.

"Going back to basics," Amy said. "The great Saints were no lap-dogs either."

People were already volunteering as firemen, or as crew for the new lifeboat. Rebecca learned that in years gone by there had been two lifeboat stations. "And they made a quicker job getting folk off that causeway than now," was one comment she heard. The islanders were thinking of buying a boat, and of asking the RNLI to adopt it. If "that bloody government over there" would allow them.

Where was the money for all this to come from? she wondered, as the shopping list stretched on. And what were the implications for support services? She heard references to negotiations with the RAF, if the British Government didn't veto them, and with the coastguard, the air ambulance service and Fire Service. In the case of the ambulance service, a new helicopter seemed to be looming as a possible requirement. Then there was the maintenance of the pier, the future management of the National Nature Reserve (another negotiation, with English Nature), the priory (with English Heritage) and Lindisfarne Castle (with the National Trust). Rebecca began to appreciate that there was history here; these things were known about, and people were comfortable with what was planned.

Half an hour into it, she got the rest of her answer.

"We need to concentrate on what happens now," Deville said. "Many of these items can be called works in progress, and will be developed further over the next few months, but tonight we should look to the immediate future." He paused. "First, a promise I made. With the result of our referendum pretty much a foregone conclusion, I arranged the transfer yesterday of £100 million from my Zurich account to the new Bank of Holy Island. It may sometimes have been an embarrassment to earn, if earned it was, but it will be put to good use now. The directors of that Bank will be my younger son Alistair, the four elected founding Ministers of the Althing, and myself."

How many more sons...and were there any daughters? Rebecca asked herself. Calum Nelson had told her that Deville's wife Nicole had died some years ago of breast cancer, aged fifty, but had given no details of the family. It was beginning to sound like a dynasty, a miniature Clan Kennedy. And she had never heard £100 million being given away with less ceremony.

"Second, I have drafted a letter to the British Prime Minister, and another to the Queen, who I believe is in America *pro temps*. Also in readiness is a press release, which will be e-mailed tonight to the news desks of Britain's broadcast and print media, plus some international media. I am thinking specifically of key opinion-formers; the *Washington Post, New York Times, Wall Street Journal, CNN* and so on. The core of the letters and press release is the Declaration of Secession which we will all need to sign before we leave. Copies will be delivered to your homes tomorrow.

"Third, some earthworks and construction works will take place during the night. I refer to the demolition of the causeway, the erection of security fencing from Beal Point to the Swab, and the installation of security gates at the Beal road end. Tomorrow morning, Max and his colleagues will man a guard-post at those gates. They will ensure that proper procedures are established quickly. No one in this room need have any concern about the freedom of their movement back and forth, but visitors and absentee householders will be subject to what are now Holy Island's own immigration controls. All guests resident on the island overnight will be advised of the new arrangements tomorrow morning. Most, if they are staying longer, will be welcome to fulfil their original booking. And your own ID cards will all be ready next week. Alistair has almost finished them."

Rebecca felt electric tension in the room, broken by a deep male voice: "Well, that seems to cover it. Here we go."

"What do you think the reaction's gonna be?" asked another.

Ohmigod, just wait till Mom hears this, Rebecca thought, wishing she had a tape recorder with her. Then she realised that the whole thing would be taped anyway. After less than half a day spent in his company, she knew enough of the man to know it would be second nature for Deville to have set it up.

"I hope you'll let Charley back in," she whispered to Max Deville.

"He'll be fine. Provided he doesn't cover his face with anything."

Huh? she wondered, looking at him sideways.

She tuned back into the meeting as Deville was responding to the question from the floor. "...and the first reaction will be disbelief," he was saying. "The second will be anger, condemnation. The third will be to demand our presence in London, accompanied by threats. No doubt the constitutional experts will have a field day. The fourth will be manipulation of the media. By that time, and this is why the Declaration and our own conduct are crucial, it may be too late. We need to keep holding the initiative, the high ground. I hope the media, or those sections of it who have become disenchanted with Westminster, if they were ever enchanted, will be sympathetic. The fifth step might be to send in the troops, but that would be a gamble. I doubt if this government will have the nerve to gamble; by then, the battle will have been won and lost. There will be a stocktaking, a damage limitation, how to compromise the demands of these pesky islanders, bring them back to heel. At that point, *before* that point, we'll have a full-fledged constitution. And we should have an answer to the question, what form does Holy Island take? Autonomous state, crown dependency, republic...?"

Another male voice: "How's this Bank goin' to work? Like a real one? Barclay's, one of those?"

"At present, it is simply a vehicle to facilitate the transfer of funds, bypassing the clearing banks and City of London institutions. In fact, it's a subsidiary of a well-known American bank, although I'd prefer that fact to be treated discreetly. Sooner or later, as far as the people of Holy Island are concerned, it should operate just as any other bank, or as any other bank *should* operate, somewhere to deposit and withdraw funds, invest, negotiate loans, overdrafts, mortgages. Two members of staff are in place, sufficient for the present."

"Haven't seen it. Where is it?"

"In the Post Office, with the Girobank. It seemed convenient."

Laughter. "Is it goin' to be safe? What about those guys this mornin'?

It's a helluva lot of cash to have lyin' around the place."

Amy snorted. "It's not cash. It's electronic money, am I right?"

Deville smiled. "Correct, Amy. It will be safe, safer than in many banks these days, but this raises a point worth repeating. We must continue to think positive, to stress the benefits of, as well as the necessity for, this action. We have declared for secession. We have not declared ourselves cut off from the world. Many things will go on just as they are. Mail and money will come and go. We've talked about supplies, food-stuffs, medicines, transport for the children. You'll still travel to work, to and from the mainland. One million pounds of the total fund has already been earmarked for public transport, including schoolchildren, and for families needing new vehicles, SUVs and the like, to negotiate the flats. For most of you, your livelihoods will remain much as they are but without the coaches that have caused problems of late. A shuttle service using two new Hummer H3s will be in place by next weekend across the sands. You will still need to reach railway stations and airports, Newcastle, Edinburgh, London and so on, for business or holiday purposes.

"The Scottish Parliament was set up in 1999. The Scots have not been cut off from the world. There's an argument for saying that many Scots would have preferred their new Parliament to have affected their lives in more and better ways than it has; indeed, they have just hinted as much. Their lives, however, have so far been largely unchanged. This has relevance for us only in terms of the external world, as we intend our internal world to be much improved. In the case of the Scots, it is possible that their previous Labour administration may purposely have set out to prevent rather than promote change, to tag Devolution a failure and pre-empt a more serious step. For us, that is an irrelevance; we have not placed ourselves in a holding cell and have every intention of promoting change. Whatever reason the Scottish Labour Party had for their lack of initiative or their fealty to London, and that one may rebound on them, only peripheral adjustments have been made."

"Like no smokin' in pubs," someone said. "Like was about to happen everywhere."

It all seems well planned, Rebecca thought, tuning the discussion out. She wondered if £330,000—holy mackerel, they could *add* a zero or two—had been set aside for the hall, and what people who had donated so far would think. Provided they could get past the shock, and maybe a sprinkling of envy.

"Have you a copy of this Declaration?" she asked Max in an undertone.

He reached into an inside pocket, and unfolded a single page in copperplate script:

Declaration of Secession

We the People of The Holy Island of Lindisfarne, in order to promote the general welfare and security of our homeland, ensure domestic tranquillity, regain natural law and proper means of justice, and secure the God-given blessings of Life, Liberty and the pursuit of Happiness to ourselves and our posterity, **Do Hereby Declare that**:

Whereas governments are instituted by the people, deriving their powers from the people, and subsequently become remiss in protecting, or over-zealous in controlling, those to whom they are beholden, it is the inalienable right of the people to alter or abolish such governments and institute new or amended forms of government with the interests of the people at heart; and in particular

Whereas The Holy Island community is historically and contemporaneously a Christian community with a distinctive ethos and way of life that has evolved naturally over the centuries, as exemplified in the Lindisfarne Gospels created in honour of God and Cuthbert, and that this way of life is at risk of destruction at the hands of the present form of government; and

Whereas the lives of Holy Islanders have been lost due to the neglect of the present form of government, notwithstanding the contribution of The Holy Island community to the British involvement in two World Wars and subsequent conflicts; and

Whereas the institutions and actions of the present form of government have ignored the rights and aspirations of The Holy Island community in terms of the closure and run-down of essential services and of the protection of their land and environment from undesirable and damaging developments; and

Whereas the present form of government and integral political parties have effectively censored, by design or apathy, debate and action on issues of cardinal importance to the well-being of indigenous peoples and their progeny; and

Whereas The Holy Island community and their way of life have been threatened by a range of policies instituted by the present form of government, without consultation, and by the inaction or vacillation of the present form of government in the areas of immigration, crime, health and welfare services, education and home ownership; and

Whereas The Holy Island community question the right of any government to impose by force majeure or default the creation of a multinational, multicultural or multireligious dimension on a distinctive unit; and

Whereas the rights of the people of Lindisfarne have been eroded by British membership of the European Union, with especial reference to the diminution of their Human Rights, border security, staple industries and work opportunities; then

We the People of The Holy Island of Lindisfarne, Hereby Secede with Immediate Effect from the United Kingdom of Great Britain and Northern Ireland, from the local government structure thereof, and from the European Union.

12:01 a.m., 6th May, 2007 AD
Annexed are the signatures of resident Holy Islanders named in the current Electoral Roll, (two) abstaining.

CHAPTER FOUR

Rebecca read the Declaration once, not quite believing it, and then read it again, conscious that the meeting was slowly coming to a close. How did 150 people, or 130 electors, get to agree on all this? She knew close-knit families who would have been at each other's throats.

"Neat," she said eventually. "Some phrases sound eerily familiar."

"The American model was a good start. It just needed tweaking. Some people would say they did a bit of borrowing themselves, from the Declaration of Arbroath." Max nodded at his father, moving towards them off the dais. "We seem to have finished here, anyway."

"How many meetings like this have you had? To get to this point, I mean?" Rebecca asked.

"About a dozen?" Max replied. "Some of them smaller. Winter bugs had an impact."

"We have work to do," Deville smiled down at them. "It was a good meeting, I think, by and large. Rebecca, we should see if there's news of your other half. You're welcome to return with us to the house, to meet the rest of the family and some friends. I hope you'll consider staying the night. We have plenty of room, and it'll be company for you."

"Well, I—"

"It'll be easier for all of us," Deville said. "We can call by the guest-house, and pick up your things. Your landlady's still here," he pointed across the room. "I'll have a word. But we need to get on. There are things to do, a race against time, telephones, e-mails and so on." He turned to his son. "Would you stay on, Max, and supervise the signing? Then bring the documents with you? It all seems orderly, and I see Dennis has arrived. Have a last shot at Old John and Walter, and see if they'll make it unanimous, would you? It would be tidier."

"No problem."

"And try to track that Newcastle mob's addresses after you leave. But the documents first, if you don't mind."

"Okay."

The line of people to sign the declaration was moving forward, with not the slightest hint of hesitation or dissent. Rebecca saw resolve on their faces, and satisfaction. She overheard the phrase "a job well done."

Amazing, she thought, a tiny plot of tidal land like this, on the edge of the UK, on the edge of England, of Scotland, hell-bent on creating an obstacle course for all three.

In global terms, she realised, it would be bigger news than anything the recent elections had produced; bigger than a putsch in Africa, somewhere a thousand times Lindisfarne's size. Tonight, in this tottery little hall, a G8 country had had its face slapped by an island the size of a button. It had been told no, thanks but no thanks, your government's a crock. Well, stripped of the formalities, that was what the Declaration was saying, wasn't it? Whatever would the Americans, or the Russians, or the rest of them, think?

At ten o'clock, the sun had disappeared behind the hills and left a landscape shrouded in blue-grey darkness.

Charley, oblivious to his appearance, happily singing a medley of songs from his childhood—*The Grand Old Duke of York, Who's Afraid of the Big Bad Wolf,* songs like that—zeroed erratically in on the lights of The Goblin Ha' Hotel in the village of Gifford, East Lothian. He had passed through the saddle between Hunt Law and Hogs Law, and had fallen at so many fences that he felt like the back-marker in a Grand National. He had jumped countless streams, and stumbled through tufts of grass and clumps of heather the size of Everest. He had crashed and fallen down a steep slope to a road leading to the farm and hamlet of Longyester, crossed without realising it, staggered across pastures, the going easier except for molehills and *cowpats,* and had seen the faint uneven glow of Gifford ahead. He had no idea how far he'd walked. Twenty miles, thirty? This could be the Highlands of Scotland, for Pete's sake.

He staggered into the pub's lounge bar, singing *Humpty Dumpty* in a quivery tenor.

His entrance provoked unanimous horror from the village maidens, and a mixture of scowls, sniggers and outright contempt from the men. Charley was oblivious to them all, his tongue curled and his lips trembling in anticipation. The Bigg M boys had taken most of his worldly goods, and left him with only three pound coins and change in a trouser pocket. He still had it all, *all.* A miracle...okay, not quite a miracle. But definitely the first and only bright spot of his day.

"Go around to the public bar, son," the barman advised, speaking from a twenty-year age advantage. "They might look after you there. No chance here, not the state you're in." He took Charley's arm and pointed the way.

"What?" said Charley. No drink? It was as though his lips had been shaped around a nice juicy plum and a wasp had leapt out and stung him.

"Not to pull punches, son, but this is the lounge and you look and smell like a walking cesspit."

Charley began to cry. He looked down at his mud-caked pants and said, "I've had a bloody awful day."

"Yeah, I can see that all right. It looks like it's been a shocker. Someone might bring you a pint out," the barman said kindly, sitting him down on a bench.

"Bloody hell," Charley groaned, elbows on his knees, head in his hands, the light from the window highlighting the blood-encrusted scratches on his face. He tried not to think about the muscles in his legs. They were in a state far beyond spasm, and seemed close to losing their bearings.

The barman went back inside and called the police station in Haddington. Not to cause trouble for the lad, but he looked as if a wash and a sleep would do him a power of good, and there was no way he would get either here. Hotels these days seemed to have lost the plot when it came to providing succour to weary travellers. They seemed more interested in Health and Safety, Weights and Measures, Licensing Courts, Disability Discrimination Acts, Food Hygiene, Fire Regulations, occupancy rates, the bottom line—and the old Ha' was no exception.

When the cops arrived, Charley was incoherent with disappointment, thirst and exhaustion. He tried his best to tell them he had been kidnapped, but they weren't good listeners. They were in a hurry to get back to Haddington, watch *Match of the Day* before the pubs got out and the Saturday night mayhem started. Picking up a vagrant in Gifford might be a favour to that well-to-do community and their pal the barman (who provided a complimentary pint now and then) but damned if they were going to start a dialogue. They bundled Charley into the back seat, then into a cell, and left him to sleep it off.

Brother, did this guy stink. They spent the five-mile journey swatting a swarm of midges he'd been harbouring about his person, and bitching about having to fumigate the car first thing. God only knew what state the back seat would be in. The cell, they'd leave to the cleaning ladies.

At Fahr House, Rebecca had moved into a well-appointed bedroom complete with TV, coffee machine, and four-poster. Having done what she could to settle in, and having moved both Charley's stuff and her own from the guesthouse, her imagination had gone into overdrive. It seemed as though transferring his things, even after just one night, had cut a connection. Visions of him lying in a ditch, a heap of clothing under a bloodied piece of Beemer carpet, had floated before her eyes. There had been one solitary call from Plod Major, to report *nothing*. Zero, nada, zilch. No trace of Charley, the car or the Bigg M bunch in semi-detached England, Scotland or the planet generally. Just that "Bigg M" stood for Bigg Market, a city centre street in Newcastle with a history of nurturing Geordie gangs. Crucial information when you had a kidnapped husband and the local embodiments of the long arm of the law couldn't find their own hands.

So much for tracking gizmos, she thought scornfully. When it came to finding bits of metal, this one had been less use than a child's magnet.

There was always Max, of course, even if he and his father had more pressing agendas. Not, given all she'd heard, that she could blame them. In any case, it didn't seem as though they proposed to let Charley get in the way of important business.

Deville and friends were crouched over computers in the basement, 500-word letters and press releases copied, pasted and ready to flash to heads of government and the world's media. 12:01 a.m., the script had said. Everyone in the room was watching the clock.

11:59. Get set.

12:00. Go.

You could almost hear the Declaration spread its electronic wings south, then west, then east. North lay Scotland, the last in line. Holyrood, she understood, would get a courtesy call: "Assuming in the interregnum," as someone cheerfully remarked, "that someone's there to pick up the bloody phone." But this would be after the tidings had been delivered to London, Brussels and Washington DC.

12:04. The phones started ringing. As, of course, they would. The world's media was one sector that never slept.

Since her introduction by Deville to the roomful of people ("the latest victim of the rotten state on our borders") Rebecca had stopped feeling like Exhibit A. Charley had taken a back seat and she was taking an interest in what was going on around her. People, Deville's daughter Sarah and younger son Alistair especially, were being friendly, trying to make sure she didn't feel left out, but they had work to do and she was happy to blend into the background. As far as Charley was concerned, she was helpless in any case, so why beat herself up? What could she do? Tramp the Cheviots? Send up a flare? Yell across the water?

And she was learning something of the frustration, the pent-up fury, which had caused these Holy Islanders to take their step into self-inflicted amputation. After what had happened to her today, or rather yesterday, she could relate to it. One middle-aged lady, Mary Selby by name, had taken her aside and regaled her first with the Tale of the Tourist Who Had Pissed on the Priory, then the Saga of the Salmonella Salesman. If the first, outrageous as it was, had been self-explanatory, the second had given new meaning to the phrase "salmon run."

A young Rastafarian rapper, upset that his impromptu performances were not being accorded the acclaim they deserved in the Market Place and the two village pubs ("we have two, dear, The Tavern—the one that's called The Ship now—and the Crown & Anchor"), had decided to get his own back by branching out into the fish trade. He'd acquired his product for no outlay, simply retrieving it from the wheelie-bins of a fish-merchant in Newcastle. He had then, presumably following instructions from one of a host of available cookbooks, contrived to make a salmon pâté out of it. In Mary Selby's words, it had "seemed to taste all right, at first." It was only when Holy Islanders started dropping like flies in his wake, after two sales rounds and over-the-garden-fence consultation, that the penny dropped.

Fortunately, no one had died, although a dozen locals had since developed a strong aversion to fish products and three had converted to strict vegan regimes. It was not known how many visitors had returned home with dyspepsia or diarrhoea, but food takings in the island's pubs, hotels and cafés had gone south for a month or two.

"This lad came from the same festerin' pit as those who took your man and robbed the Post Office, lass," Mary Selby had told her. "That Bigg Market in the toon. Him and his Godless so-called music. His floppy hat and hair. We're goin' to be well rid of them."

Rebecca was growing more sympathetic by the minute as she listened to the telephone calls and the comments of the people around her. In London, a city she thought filthy, she had picked up on a lot of worries about crime, immigration, the influx of people from new EU member countries, the billions squandered in health and education services. Some of the home truths had shocked her, so far removed were they from the Britain her mother had painted throughout her formative years. Of course, everyone knew about political sleaze and psychotic freaks with bombs, but these weren't exclusive to Britain. Nevertheless, other viruses in today's "back home" could have the staunchest teetotaller reaching for the gin bottle. Even accepting that her mother had come to the realisation that the land of her birth was in terminal decline, Rebecca had found outrageous some of the claims that Charley and his mates had made in various pub sessions. Until, that is, she saw them repeated and reinforced in newspaper and magazine articles.

One in six kids leaving school without the three R's. Sky-high divorce rates. Expenditure per head on policing in England doubling since the mid-nineties. Firearms offences (those that were reported) also doubling. Crack cocaine, real and reconditioned handguns, yardie gangsters running riot ("like this was bloody Johannesburg," in one of Charley's more memorable phrases). Traumatised communities in London, Birmingham, Manchester, ("watch this space"). Babies being violated by "guest" fathers, under the noses of social workers. Cops snowed under with paperwork, cops ("real cops, not the traffic pests") gone from the streets. The list had been exhaustive. Listening to it all had certainly exhausted her. So why don't you all emigrate, she had asked impatiently, if things are so bad? She was told: people *are* emigrating, in their hundreds of thousands, buying homes in Australia, Spain, America, France, New Zealand, Bosnia, Bulgaria ("swapping Balkanised Britain for the real McCoykov"), being replaced by the new East European and Fourth World intake. She didn't like to think what the logical outcome of that process would be, except it wasn't going to have a lot to do with green and pleasant lands.

"There's good news, though," Charley had said, grinning. "We have more illicit shagging than any other country in the Western world, too."

"Really?" Rebecca had replied, although she cringed to think of it now. "It's nice of us to be getting married, then. To be setting a good example."

His mates had had a good laugh about that one.

So between her parents, her reading, and Charley and his pals, Rebecca had been well educated in some of the issues being aired in the Fahr House basement. Others, however, those specific to Holy Island, were new to her.

She overheard Deville at one point saying to a journalist, "I imagine if I worked at the Home Office I'd be embarrassed to admit it. I think I'd tell my kids I'd decided on a new career. Peddling timeshares in Tikrit, English dictionaries in Slough, or something wholesome like that."

Rebecca was surprised by this. Even after knowing the man for less than half a day, she didn't feel it was in character. Earlier, both with her and during the meeting, he had been more measured. She didn't imagine for a moment that it was nerves. Maybe he knew the caller well enough to risk flippancy, or was getting into the political swing, delivering sound bites. She shrugged. Whatever he was doing, she was familiar with the sentiment. She'd been all but glutted on the sentiment.

Poor Mom, she thought, not for the first time. Having memories shattered could be just as bad as having dreams shattered. Given her background, her Mom had always been fascinated by what was going on "back home." And, of late, what was going on back home had seemed incomprehensible. The blind obeisance to America, dodgy inconclusive wars, round-eyed kids brushed off as collateral damage, a Cabinet that circumvented parliamentary democracy every chance it got, the ominous rise of the British National Party, the refusal to punish criminals, the release of criminals whose keys to freedom should long since have been thrown away, ladettes, celebs, chavs, tatts ("whatever abomination next, for heaven's sake?"), hip-hop, binge-drinking, junk food, ten year-olds as fat as Zeppelins, TV shows that would offend the sensibilities of the average family budgie, programme-makers and advertisers with the moral fibre of sand eels, "reality" shows with as much reality as silicon boobs, and sybaritic junkies touted as role models. Individually and collectively, her

Mom had strafed them all.

And there was the reverse side of the coin, Rebecca thought, the things that had been lost to everything but her Mom's memories and those of others her age. Picturesque things, proprieties. Everything from French onion men and dray horses to doffing your cap and giving up your seat...did the new technologies, the iPods and CDs, the cell phones and digital cameras, the new drugs and the cloning, make up for all of them?

Her own father wouldn't look at any British TV import, wildlife and history apart, dated later than 1990 and—which had seriously pissed Rebecca off as a teenager—wouldn't allow her to either. That the same embargo had applied to *Neighbours* ("caterwauling music") was no comfort at all.

She well remembered his views on the BBC's slide into the broadcasting gutter: "I used to admire that channel. It had standards. Then it went liberal, now it's nihilistic. Imagine a western news service failing to grasp that Shari'a law abuses women and minorities. Women the world over are beaten, mutilated, raped and oppressed under that so-called holy law. Instead, the BBC seems to enjoy the idea that religious courts should supplant the UK's. I never thought I'd live to see the day. Ludicrous. A western news service? It's a *dis*service."

Her Mom, in the accent she'd never quite lost, had not been slow to join in this condemnation. "Back home," she'd told her daughter, "people used to laugh at a woman called Mary Whitehouse. She was a proud defender of decency, a real thorn in the side of the media. My word, they could do with several dozen of her now."

Alex Deville was beginning to impress Rebecca.

He was taking many of the calls himself, responding succinctly, positively, persuasively. He, or perhaps his son Alistair, had prepared a Q&A briefing note. Copies were scattered on the table, some displayed on pegboards. His fellow "Ministers" were referring to them. It made for consistency and, once they got the hang of it, a growing confidence. It was almost professional. No, she corrected herself, it was better than that. It was real. And, let's face it, there were professionals, not to mention Presidents of the United States, who couldn't string a coherent sentence together without an earphone or autocue.

The calls kept coming, dozens of them, two, three, four at a time.

So far, she thought, except for one Scottish Nationalist MP whom she gathered was friendly with Deville, all media. Given the SNP's success in Scotland, they could well be partying into the small hours. But no word at all from the Whitehall power base. It seemed weird to Rebecca, but it was a weird country. Maybe they thought it was some sort of prank.

And each call was being taken, not one slipping through the slats.

Not a knee-jerk reaction in sight:

"Our annual cost to the government is about £7000 per head, roughly a million each year...with care, investment, we have enough for a century or more, even given inflation..."

"Yes, Alex Deville has provided the wherewithal but this community will be run as a direct democracy...the funds are there in perpetuity. For public, not personal, use. There are things we need to do, but after the first year or so we'll live off the interest."

"Important community services have gone...they'll be replaced..."

"We aim to avoid being engulfed like mainland Britain...make sure it doesn't happen here..."

"Direct democracy? It means no cliques, no inner circles. It means we'll operate on the basis that only the votes of individuals will approve or reject our laws..."

"There'll be safeguards...sunset provisions...simple common sense..."

"The British government? We're waiting to hear...they've not been as quick on the ball as you have...we haven't yet had the courtesy of a response."

"Defence?...negotiation, why not? In conventional terms, against attempts at terrorism, we'll defend ourselves. A nuke would wipe out more than us...Northumberland, Newcastle, Berwickshire..."

"There'll be no elites, no fiat laws...we'll pay more than lip service to the rule of the people. Our Bill of Rights will be followed..."

Rebecca was lost with one or two of the phrases—sunset provisions?—but was getting the gist. She noticed that the calls were being shared out quite evenly between Deville and the other Ministers. They were deferring to him when it came to the "heavies", including *The Times, The Independent, The Guardian* and some foreign press, but were taking their fair share. The exception was Minister James Redman. Had she been asked, Rebecca would have said that Alistair Deville was doing his best to divert calls away from Minister Redman. It was also clear that the Sarah Deville's derrière held much more interest for Minister Redman than any press call. In fact, it wouldn't be too much of an exaggeration to say he was fixated on it. No wonder Deville's beautiful daughter was taking every opportunity to sit down.

Rebecca also wondered why Redman was wearing make-up. It wasn't conventional make-up, as in a subtle application of face cream or rouge. Nor was it less subtle make-up, of the sort you might see on a cross-dresser. It was in-your-face war paint, the slashes of colour vivid red, yellow and green. Rebecca shrugged and put it behind her. For all she knew, it could be a local custom. Or maybe he was expecting more trouble from the Declaration than his colleagues. Or maybe he was just a nutcase. If so, he wouldn't be the first to choose politics as a cover. She continued to listen in:

"Let me give you an example. Your 1689 Bill of Rights says, I quote, 'all grants and promises of fines...of particular persons before conviction are illegal'...where's the conviction in parking fines? Or on-the-spot police penalties? Your 1991 Road Traffic Act doesn't allow access to a court of law for a conviction, the fine is imposed by the local authority. Where does that leave your Bill of Rights?"

"One of your eminent justices is on record as saying, 'parking tickets are not fines.'" Laughter. *"How in the name of all that's holy do these people get to occupy the positions they do?"*

"If you don't mind, we won't comment on the Scottish elections. They voted, good luck to them. It might be foolish for other parties to ignore what the SNP gained, though. That might rebound, don't you think?"

"Okay, well, why shouldn't they be independent? They've been heading that way for decades. Isn't being independent considered laudable any longer?...put yourself in a time machine, go forward fifty years. The world is going to stop? No more change? National boundaries fixed for all time?"

"Sunset provisions? Our constitution...a week or so...sunset provisions will make sure we don't get half-cocked laws. Any that don't work or get reinstated from time to time will be phased out..."

"Of course we're a special case...every place, every person, is a special case...Scotland, Wales, Shetland, Cornwall, wherever. Excuse me, it's not our *government, it's the* British *government. Do we think they'll see it? No, history tells us they won't, but what matters is that* we *do..."*

"Back up a minute. Would anyone returning to Britain after the last twenty years recognise the place?"

"Europe? We should never have been in Europe. You don't force islands to become part of mainlands...different psychologies...Cuba, Jamaica, the 51st state? China and Taiwan? Somehow, it doesn't seem likely..."

Quite definitely, Rebecca thought, no knee-jerks. This was as smooth as it could get. Well-conceived, well-rehearsed, and business-like.

She had found it difficult to believe at first. Disturbing, even. But now?

Geordie Halloran hunched over his keyboard in the offices of *The Northern Sun* in Newcastle city centre and rattled out the Holy Island story, thinking shit, hold the front page; then shit, *what* front page, it's *Sunday*. He just *knew* he had an above-the-fold front page story, his *first*; and furthermore a story that showed every sign of having the legs to run and run. Had his day finally come? Was it to come on a *bloody Bank Holiday Monday,* with half a paper to play with? Or would the old man tell the advertising staff to pull their fingers out, and go ahead as normal? This *was* happening in the North East, their own patch, when all was said and done. For all Geordie's worries, he thanked his lucky stars he had drawn this shift tonight, and as for his girlfriend moaning about it up hill and down dale...well, she would see the error of her ways when his name was up in lights. Not to mention when his salary doubled, and the "cub reporter" tag had been consigned to the dustbin. He was twenty-six years old, for God's sake.

"Sure you can handle this, son?"

Geordie started. It was the dead of night, with only his desk light burning, and this sudden disembodied voice had issued forth. The Editor, gawping over his shoulder, reading his unfinished, his *unpolished,* copy. What had brought the old duffer in? Who the hell had told *him* what was going on?

"I have my spies everywhere," said the Editor, in a stage bass. For God's sake, was he a mind-reader too?

"*No problema,*" Geordie said. "I got the press release and spoke to the guy Deville half an hour ago."

"You're not finished it yet, then?" the Ed. said snidely.

"Ten minutes."

"I'll be waiting. Make sure there are no holes in it."

Fucking A *olé.* A story to die for, being surveyed like a bad road.

He had managed to get through to the Number Ten press office, but got the distinct feeling he had been held in a queue. They were probably brown-nosing *The Times, The Independent, The Telegraph,* blatts like that, the swine. But he was the man on the ground, where it was all happening, wasn't he?

Well, no, not exactly. That was the conundrum. He was and he wasn't.

What to do? He had to get up there, take his mobile and laptop and shaving gear and a change of clothes and become Our Man in Holy Island.

Let me just get this done, he thought, and I'll have a crack at the old so-and-so. His fingers flew over the keys—well, two of them flew, plus a thumb—and he did a quick word count and spell check. Nearly done; what else was there? He had the background, the gist of the press release, the quote from Deville, and the statement from Number Ten. For what it was worth: "...no intention now or in future to allow the piecemeal break-up of the United Kingdom, in Scotland, Holy Island or anywhere else, yada, yada, yada." The sarcastic sods. The arrogant, lofty, sarcastic sods, keeping him in a queue for God's sake.

He knew he shouldn't—a good journalist had to be objective, right?—but he had more than a passing sympathy for those islanders. Good luck to them, he thought, printing it off. He gave the hard copy a quick read, for he knew how words and phrases could come across differently on a screen, almost as if disembodied. He made a small change here, a deletion there. Okay, he thought, good stuff, now let's get to it, go and beard the old man in his den.

An hour later, a battered valise flung together at his flat, Geordie was heading up the A1 in his Renault Clio. He wasn't sure what he was going to do, arriving at this time of night. He just wanted to get to The Action.

He could live with a few corrections; it was what editors were for, *no*? The old man had left Geordie's byline, stood over him while the offending paragraphs were doctored and patted him on the head. He hadn't raised an eyebrow, let alone an objection, when Geordie had floated the field trip. He had just pulled his ear and drummed his fingers on the desk in a quick tattoo.

"Okay, lad. We'll need to update this later for tomorrow. What better place than on the spot? I'll put Bob Cutler on it this end, it fits in with his Scotland stuff. Which is ongoing, don't let's forget, until they sort themselves out in Edinburgh. Make sure you touch base with him first thing in the morning, and don't get shackled in the politics up there."

Bob Cutler, also known as Old Smokey. He'd been with *The Northern Sun* since the year dot, probably ever since the old Viscount had dreamt up Kemsley Newspapers, slumped over his desk puffing roll-ups like a chimney, his lungs at half-mast.

Geordie wasn't sure about Old Smokey sticking his oar in, Old Smokey being at best a geriatric seen-it-all parliamentary affairs guy, but he could see the old man's point. Someone would have to hold the fort, hang around and do the business at base camp while he was at The Sharp End, *si*? Old Smokey might reliably stretch to that, between coughs.

Before locking up his flat and firing up the Clio, Geordie had tried phoning for a room, but without much hope of raising anyone at this time of night. He hoped the hotels and inns, all four of them, weren't full of anoraks and other assorted tourists. Maybe Holy Island would surprise him, and provide some nice local talent for company. Or maybe not. There was always the average British landlady halfway up the stairs, the light of battle in her eyes. And this was Lindisfarne, the Holy Island. It wasn't Bali or the Balearics, was it?

CHAPTER FIVE

The Bigg Market boys had been having a ball in Edinburgh, stowaways in an enclave of half-dressed cuties and androgynous gays, prowling around the top of Leith Walk and Broughton Street. It was territory not unlike their own home turf, a comfort zone.

First, a derelict with a sandwich board, some shit about Scotland and Trident, whatever Trident was, easy meat for the 7-iron. Plywood flyin everywhere. Let's rock, Jock.

Then a tapas joint, a sassy Scots waitress, bits of pizza and chicken legs and marinated olives, ham as thin as toilet paper. But hey, why pay when you can have it for free? Phat, we're cool, safe blood. They scoffed it, walked out, falsetto squeaks behind them, down an alley. No sweat, pet.

Time for a bevvy, the 7-iron and jack and wrench down trouser legs. Not a happy barman, a guy buggin, swipin cloths at all and sundry. Hey, watch what you're at, some a that piss went on me. Beer spilt, glasses overcome by gravity. Whaaaat? Like, you can't *smoke*? What sorta shit is this? But a coupla big lads, looking a bit narky, let's move, let's go. Yawn, yawn, spawn.

Whoa, hold on. A mingin Alsatian bitch trailin along, clamped to the 7-iron. Home, doggie, home, leave the fucken thing alone. Yellow tombstones for teeth. A kick up the arse? No, okay, maybe not the best of moves. Retreat into another bar, a few more beers. Watch the door; hey you, yes you, don't let that fleabag in. Snap the bolt, dolt.

Then a gift from Providence, a ginger beer. Careful with the blood and piss, man. Don't mess the Doc Martens. Lose the 7-iron, Shad my man, chuck it, buddy. The jack, the spanner, over this dyke, see? Ballin, man. Tears for queers.

Hyper, on to a sauna joint. Don't get these hang-outs in the toon, not like this anyroad. Guys goin in, see? Comin out, shifty, lookin right and left, quickly down the steps, slowly back up. Into a huddle, a quick tally of their cash. What's the, like, goin rate? These bitches…what? A tenner? Twenty? Yah think? Go for it, homeboy. Tough cookie, nooky.

Place closing, mumbling farewells, leaving the girls wrecked. What a rip-off. Eighty quid? Near as owt cleaned out, but hey, worth every penny. Left her for dead, shagged her brains out…yeah…b.j. my arse…did her till she choked. No fuss, puss. Up yours, whores.

Back to the Broughton Street bar, a few more beers, a post-mortem while they blew the rest of the Holy Island Post Office loot. Regrets beginning to set in…

Eighty *quid*? Need more cash, guys. A prezzie from a passer-by? Then a doss-house? Or the wheels? Which way to go? Stay till the dust settles, or head for the hills? But hey, no smokin in pubs? For fuck's sake, not real. Give it ten years, they'll be bannin drinkin in pubs.

Then the fucken pubs.

Then the fucken bevvy everywhere.

Seriously disadvantaged by rising inflation, the Bigg Market trio put the finishing touches to their night in Edinburgh with a second robbery-cum-assault. They drifted along Princes Street (too many lights, too many taxis, too many rubberneckers), and hung a left up Lothian Road. A middle-aged man emerged from a lap-dancing bar, the utilitarian façade of the Sheraton Grand Hotel facing them across a fountained square. They pocketed a hundred and thirty pounds and change, retraced their steps to the main drag, and raised a caretaker in a fleapit near Haymarket. All things considered, a slammin night out for The Poet's Society.

It was half past two in the morning when the press calls finally dwindled. Apart from Mary Selby, who increasingly reminded her of Jane Austen's kindly Mrs. Weston, Rebecca thought she might have made a friend or two tonight. She felt she could easily get to like Deville's daughter Sarah, and his younger son Alistair. With Max, they seemed to be the sum total of his offspring. Not quite Clan Kennedy.

The Private Man had delivered the scroll of signatures and left for the far end of the causeway. He had wished Rebecca well, and told her that she wouldn't be seeing much more of him in the near future. But she wasn't to worry; she would "have the errant hubby back before the day's out, trust me." To his father's delight, Max had given him the full electoral complement: Old John and Walter had signed the Declaration. Rebecca wasn't sure whether this had required any muscle from the Private Man, but noticed no one else was asking.

People were going home and Deville was stretching, telling them that they were off to a good start, and the main media players were covered. He promised to get word out as soon as Number Ten woke up to the loss of part of their bailiwick. No one could understand the silence from that quarter. Didn't they have staff there overnight? Or maybe they'd all climbed under their desks and pulled wastebaskets over their heads. Sufficient unto the week, was that it?

Half an hour later, Deville was still closeted in the basement with the four other elected Ministers over glasses of whisky. All of them waiting, laying bets on the timing of the expected call, and seeming to favour 7:00 a.m. but no earlier. They took some wry amusement at the thought of Whitehall press officers up to their necks in follow-up enquiries. Those poor suckers at least would be earning their keep!

One of the calls had been from the cops. Not about Charley, but to say that the Beemer had been found, by conventional means, in a garden centre in Dunbar. It had been the only vehicle left in the parking lot when the owner had closed shop. Rebecca supposed even Plod Major and Minor, if he could tear his thoughts away from her feminine assets, might twig from that which way the gang had headed. But she had given up on Charley for the night, praying he was no worse than asleep somewhere. She would have to hope Max hadn't just been blowing smoke, and that he, or someone, would come up with something tomorrow. She looked at her Cartier. *Today.*

Sarah and Alistair were sitting with her in the enormous living room. She felt like a corner flag on a football pitch.

"You must be worn out," Sarah said, only four inches short of her father but without his nose. From photographs on the mantelpiece, she had a likeness to her mother. Rebecca was reminded of a young Joanna Lumley: she had the eyebrows and the luxuriant hair, except in Sarah's case it was wavy and cut to fall naturally on her shoulders. And her bone structure was finer. Uma Thurman maybe? She seemed every bit as bright too.

"I guess I should be, but I don't feel it. It must have been the swim I had this morning. Yesterday morning...I keep forgetting," she said.

"Or adrenalin," Alistair told her. "You haven't had much R&R so far this holiday."

She had Alistair marked as the cerebral type. She guessed he was about her own age, possibly a year or so younger. He had so little resemblance to his brother that she wouldn't have connected them at all. For a start, he was nearly as tall as his father but with dark, wavy hair rather than a blond marine crop and, unlike Max, he had a neck. And given his role in his father's new Holy Island Bank and Trust, he must have a brain. They all, Max included, had their father's Paul Newman eyes. Except in the case of Alex Deville and his elder son, they were used as weapons.

"Tell me," she said as she sipped a glass of white wine Sarah had pressed on her, "what started all of this? I mean, how come you decided to go it alone?"

Alistair repositioned a stuffed short-eared owl on a perch, which had somehow taken up residence as the centrepiece of the coffee table. "It's a long story," he said. "Look, like most people in what used to be a nice country, we got fed up. A lot of things have been going wrong. Like every empire there's ever been, Mogul, Roman, Napoleonic, Ottoman, Russian, you name it, each comes to the end of its natural life. Decline and fall, all that, and the British version's the latest. If you read what happened to each of them, they have some distinguishing features. Loss of liberties, over-governance, nationalism, inflation, political hypocrisy, overloaded services, collusive wars, structures collapsing, factionalism, rivalries, minorities...take your pick. Tyrannopolis followed by necropolis, as Mumford would have said; the dying throes of a city state and its final cemetery. We thought it would be sensible to look at alternatives."

"Oh please, don't get him started. He has this second degree in urban planning and it's been a pain in the butt from the word go," Sarah said. "It's too late and this could take all night. Especially if my father comes back and chips in."

"What was the first degree in?" Rebecca asked. He must be bright if he had two full-time degrees at, what, twenty-four? Twenty-five?

"Economics. It's had its uses," Alistair said.

"Spot on, though," Rebecca said, thinking of her Mom. "I mean, I don't know much about Britain except second-hand, but what I do know, decline and fall makes sense."

"The two of them overdo it," Sarah said. "I don't mean they're wrong, but people here had simpler ideas. They just thought the UK was cracking up and when someone offered an exit route, they took it. They weren't interested in empires, they were interested in the mess on their doorstep. They thought: so there are worse place on earth, but that doesn't help us here."

"And things happened," Alistair said mildly.

"Yes, there have been...incidents."

"Such as?" Rebecca asked.

Alistair thought about it. "Well, the last one of any consequence before your Charley's kidnapping was Social Services, and an absentee landlord renting a house to some crackheads. Next thing, the kids turn up at school dressed in pyjamas, the house is gutted for firewood, the vernal equinox arrives in force, and the roof blows off. Exit crackheads, headed for the hills. Or back to Social Services and the next absentee landlord."

"It's the sort of thing that's been on the increase," Sarah said. "Nothing too drastic by themselves, not murders or rapes, but they've mounted up. In the last few years, we've had household pets killed, some housebreakings, a stolen motorbike, shoplifting incidents, fights, drugs, drunkenness, and a lot of litter. St. Aidan's statue was defaced with spray paint, and some incomprehensible graffiti appeared on the west wall of St. Mary's."

"All by visitors?" Rebecca asked.

"Day-trippers. Tyneside mostly," Sarah replied.

"There was the YouTube episode as well," Alistair said.

"Oh? Charley watches that stuff," Rebecca said. "What did you do to deserve it here?"

"Five teenagers off a bus had an idea they thought might get them an internet Oscar. They beat up a local kid, with the Priory as a backdrop. Atmospheric, happy-slapping stuff. And what did they get for it? Take a wild guess. Slaps on the wrist from the judge, probably another wannabe social worker. Why can't these people stick to their job descriptions?"

Then there were second homes, an issue that had multiplied in the nineties. Sarah told her it had come to a head when a Durham property developer gazumped a popular young local couple, bidding for an empty cottage that needed modernisation. He hadn't modernised it; he'd taken a short cut, pulled it down, and replaced it with two town houses. They were now being rented out at an exorbitant weekly sum and were standing empty forty weeks of the year.

That was bad enough, but what had sent Holy Islanders into collective orbit was that the young couple had been dragged into survey, legal and mortgage costs by an itinerant building society representative who moonlighted for the selling agents. The two had been left high, dry, and broke when their bid failed.

"An interesting phenomenon, second homes," Alistair said. "Less people, less spending, less of a community. Not just taking houses out of reach but shops and services as well, plus all sorts of useful little support systems for the older folk—"

"It's a hobby-horse," Sarah said, shaking her head. "Or one of them. I warned you."

"And there's more," Alistair said. "The country club, the landfill—"

"More will keep," his sister said firmly. "What's important, Rebecca, is that these are annoyances. Negatives. Micro-issues. Things to put behind us. The thing is, we felt we'd be better off taking charge ourselves. That's the top, middle and bottom line of all this. But now we need to get to bed. I've a feeling tomorrow's going to be an early start."

Rebecca wasn't sorry to say goodnight. She had a cosy bedroom, twice the size of hers at home, but only a quarter the size of the Fahr House kitchen. She tried to say a prayer for Charley, thinking he deserved at least that much. First thing tomorrow, if there was still no word, she would do it properly, visit the church near the Lindisfarne Hotel, and light a candle if they had such things. Well, he *was* a Catholic, wasn't he, albeit comprehensively lapsed? Then...she'd see if she could somehow help Max.

It wasn't the PM who called the next morning. It was too far beneath him, the newly-elected Althing Ministers agreed; he couldn't be expected to dirty his hands on something like this. And Lindisfarne's secession wasn't really sexy, like a desert war or Rose Garden press-call, for instance. It didn't have enough pzazz, or any real potential to resonate down history. *What are* we *to that guy?* Minister Michael Cromarty asked his colleagues rhetorically. *A couple of acres of scrubland, a few dozen voters, somewhere off the north-east coast? Part of the paltry LibDem empire? We aren't worth so much as a passing spin.* They all had a chuckle at this. *Sedition not so pure and simple,* Minister Elizabeth Swan added, in a faux Oxford-male voice. *Where's the nearest under-secretary? Ah, there you are...be a good chap, earn your pension this morning, just bring those muddle-headed islanders back to heel.*

Before Deville switched the speakerphones on, the five Ministers took some pleasure in this mild play-acting. They were all tired, and sick of waiting. They had been stuck overnight in the basement of Fahr House, cat-napping whenever they could.

It was the Home Secretary on the blower, at 7:30 a.m. The Ministers had been near enough with the time, but kicked themselves nonetheless. They felt they'd missed a trick in their guessing game. They might have guessed that whomever they got, he'd be Scottish.

As well as being beamed to everyone in the room, the conversation was being recorded. Deville opted to stir things up from the outset:

AD: If the Prime Minister is otherwise engaged, shouldn't I be talking to the Foreign Secretary? And may I ask which Home Secretary? There have been so many lately, I've lost track.

HS: In the circumstances, you are fortunate to be speaking to any senior member of government at all.

AD: We would expect nothing less. But we are not sure you are the appropriate senior member.

HS: And what would lead you to conclude such a thing?

AD: I should have thought it obvious. You have no jurisdiction.

(*Muttered consultations at the other end of the line.*)

HS: Preposterous. I suggest you don't delude yourself into believing that a silly (*more mutterings*) er, unilateral...letter...alters your constitutional position.

AD: We are not deluded. It has. You'll need to acknowledge that, or this conversation will quickly lead nowhere.

HS: Come, come. Look, you believe the government has time and effort to waste on this nonsense?

AD: I believe they should make time and effort. Be assured the people of Holy Island don't feel inclined to be dismissed as nonsense.

HS: The people of Holy Island seem to have been led down a path that is both ill-advised and illegal. Crazy paving from start to finish, in point of fact.

AD: Speak to your colleagues, Mr. Home Secretary. The people of Holy Island have voted one hundred percent for this course of action, freely and resolutely. They are *de facto* no longer part of the UK. Take that as your starting-point and we will make progress.

HS: I might well ask why on earth you people have...(*more mumbled background noises, a "no, no, no"*)...I will rephrase that. Look, there is no possibility whatsoever that this government will stand by and allow any part of the United Kingdom to opt out, to take the law into its own hands, to embark on a course that runs counter to constitutional realities and common sense. I suggest you impress that on your...colleagues. Hoping to float your boat on the Scottish thing, were you?

AD: My colleagues are here listening. They are as impressed as I, which is to say not at all. More importantly, they know they have the will of the whole community behind them. And the whole community will most certainly be apprised of this conversation before the day is out. In fact, we had already taken the liberty of suggesting the script—

HS: Do that, if you please. Convey to your fellow-islanders the displeasure of their government and their sovereign. And tell them to turn back from this idiocy before they look like kindergarten fools. Bloody Nationalists, now this. (*Vehement cautions in the background.*)

AD: I will convey your message, which is not unexpected, but with three riders. First, you are no longer quote *their* government unquote; second, you seem not to recognise that our fellow-islanders are both serious and in full possession of their faculties; and third, I have your assurance that you have indeed consulted Her Majesty the Queen.

(*More muttered consultations.*)

HS: That remains to be done.

AD: Ah. Then please convey our respects and assure her that we draw a clear distinction between her constitutional role and your government's. I should add that I've written to her to that effect, along with a copy of our Declaration. Including the vote.

HS: Your Declaration. Vote, indeed. Who pray did you get to vote? Half the cemetery? And as a matter of interest, what caused this brainstorm of yours? Or was it just a piece of mischief you thought you could piggyback onto an election?

AD: Good of you to ask. To give you the short version, the main reason this island has declared secession is the imperative of retaining its Christian heritage. Something that was clearly at risk, given the actions of a government that has had no moral, let alone Christian, compass since the day it assumed office. We decided to remove the risk. We are not about to sit back and allow your government's pussyfooting stance on immigration, its misguided views on—

HS: Your so-called heritage is not at risk. I have heard more sense from the Conservative front bench. You are simply avoiding modern-day realities, attempting to put some imaginary clock back, fostering a delusion. King Canute comes to mind.

AD: And so he should. The difference being that he was demonstrating an inability to stop a natural tide. You are demonstrating an inability to stop a human tide.

HS: I am demonstrating no such—

AD: Unless of course, being a Scot, your knowledge of English history is flawed. Perhaps you believe the myth that he was in fact trying to stop the tide. Whichever, you and your colleagues will no longer put Holy Island at risk. You need to face the fact that one part of the country you have misgoverned, in order to reclaim proper government, is going it alone.

HS: That is no fact, sir. That is a fantasy. We shall see how long the fantasy persists. Please don't imagine you will be allowed to dream on. The very idea…the whole thing's outrageous.

AD: On the contrary, please don't think there will be any U-turns from this quarter. I hope the next stage of dialogue between us will be less sterile. Good morning.

HS: Persist in this criminal stupidity and I have my doubts.

Rebecca woke at eight o'clock, washed and dressed, made up the bed, and headed downstairs.

Walking past a bay window on a half landing, something caught her eye and she stood fascinated as a peregrine falcon tracked a flight of rock doves over a copse of stunted trees. The peregrine planed sideways, neck arched as it looked down, and chose its target. A direct hit, a snowstorm of feathers, and the falcon carried its fluttering prey to earth. Rebecca turned away as the gorging began, the predator's yellow eyes seeming to look up at her, carrying the message, "*One step closer, this could be you.*" It had taken the falcon seconds, no more than half a minute, to snuff out a lesser life. She wondered how it must feel to have that bird's confidence in its element.

Her period had started, on time as always. She wished the rest of her time-keeping was as good. Before she'd learned this lesson, she had bad memories of being caught once at college without protection, of being sent somewhere remote to count butterflies and moths, and instead counting the minutes until she could get home. Maybe there was a chemist on the island, but she hadn't seen one. She would speak to Sarah, all girls together. Thank God there was another woman in the house. Having to ask Private Man Max or his father would have been real curl-up-and-die territory.

She entered the living room just as the recording was being played; it seemed, from the comments being made, for the third or fourth time.

"Come in, Rebecca," Deville patted the stuffed owl, pushed a plate towards her. "Help yourself to toast and orange juice, coffee if you prefer. We aim to be transparent," he smiled, "so feel free to listen in. I hope you had a restful night after yesterday's...difficulties."

Conclusions were being drawn; that the Declaration had clearly carried the advantage of surprise; that a British government, as with Rhodesia in 1965, was again falling back on arguments of illegality; that phrases such as "kindergarten fools," "this nonsense," "so-called heritage," and "criminal stupidity" were indicative of a contempt they could put to good use with their fellow-islanders. They were also encouraged by the noises off. A bevy of sycophants and bitten fingernails had clearly surrounded the Home Secretary.

Minister Michael Cromarty, bug-eyed with fatigue, swore that, "yon so-and-so's rude-ass manners will come home to bite him before this is played out." Cromarty was a farmer, one of two remaining on Holy Island, a man who crossed the tidal flats four times a year and then reluctantly. He prided himself on his self-sufficiency. He and his wife grew, gathered or reared most of their food on their own land, or had until "the damn EU stuck their noses in." His Holy Island credentials went back for generations. He was an honest man, conscientious, and generous to those he felt were deserving; a man who ruffled people's feathers but took his family, work and churchgoing seriously. These were recognised as worthy attributes and had ensured his election.

"Sarah," Deville looked at his daughter buttering toast, "would you type us up a verbatim copy this morning? So we can distribute it?"

"Sure," she said. "When you've had enough listening to yourself."

Rebecca smiled to herself; daughters aren't easily overawed.

The four Ministers of Holy Island were yawning, a mix of lack of sleep and release of tension. Deville told them to go home, he would not expect another call from London for a few hours: "In the finest civil service tradition, they'll be taking stock." He warned them to expect a media circus, maybe some circling helicopters, later that morning and asked them to spread the word in the village, to make sure everyone kept the journalists on side. "Courtesy, forbearance, even if provoked." He intended to retire to bed himself when he had checked how Max and "the road crew" were making out.

"You'll be relieved to know that Max has been successful on another front," he confided to Rebecca when they had left. "Earlier this morning, he sent a couple of pals and a Land Rover to Edinburgh to fetch those Bigg Market youths back here."

"*Really*? How did he find out where they were? Was Charley there?"

"They told Max's friends that they'd dumped Charley, alive if not exactly kicking, somewhere near Dunbar. Max tracked them by calling their homes. One of them had phoned a brother to say they'd booked into a bed-and-breakfast place in Edinburgh's West End and wouldn't be returning last night."

"How did he manage to get all that…the phone numbers?"

"Max has talents he doesn't advertise. They mostly date from his time as a Marine commando."

Private Man indeed. The short-eared owl gazed at her benignly. She could swear the thing had winked.

"So we don't know where Charley is now? Maybe the police could help…why not just tell them? Why send people all the way up there?"

"My dear girl, they committed their crimes on this island, and this island is where they'll be tried. *Lex fori,* if you will. I gather they are already the proud owners of criminal records as a result of antisocial behaviour, drug-dealing and mugging senior citizens in our friendly neighbouring state." He chuckled. "It should ruin their day when Max takes them under his wing."

Rebecca could believe it. Nevertheless, she would need to thank him. For the moment, she thanked Deville and asked him to pass the message on to his son.

And what about Charley? There wasn't much she could do, was there? Now that his captors had been caught, a prayer at St. Aidan's was pointless. She would just have to sit it out. If he were okay he would surely phone soon. She didn't like to think how she would feel if he didn't, or if Max phoned to say he *wasn't* okay. She wondered how much her feelings of guilt had to do with her impatience—no, let's be honest, rancour—yesterday. Be sensible, you giddy girl, she heard her mother saying. She had to agree it was good advice. She would give it an hour or so, and then see what happened.

She wandered over to the window, saw sunlight glistening on the tidal flats, the Beal Road in the middle distance. Eventually, Charley had to come back that way. She wondered what he would have to say about his abduction, his interrupted honeymoon, his dose of bad luck. Nothing positive, she was sure, and certainly nothing remotely philosophical. A soothing amnesia would be too much to expect. Charley's thinking, as ever, would be as straight as a plate of spaghetti. It would be her fault or Holy Island's, probably vying for first place. Then the Fates. The Labour government's. The Man in the Moon's. Climate change. Anything that floated into what passed for a mind.

At which point the doorbell rang, and seconds later Alistair came in with a young man who looked almost as weary and wild-eyed as the

Ministers who had just left.

"The first of our journalists, Dad," Alistair said. "*The Northern Sun*. Max brought him over in the FourTrax as soon as the tide was out. He's been held up at the gate for an hour or two. Full marks for initiative, would you say?"

CHAPTER SIX

Charley had been awake in his holding cell since seven o'clock. Day Two of wedded bliss had dawned and he felt as if he'd spent another night in a concrete mixer. Also, the cell stank to high heaven. Charley, unaware that it was all his own work, was tempted to complain. The temptation was short-lived. He was booted for his trouble into a shower cubicle by a cop he couldn't recall seeing before, sporting a gut he surely would have recalled, and told to hang loose while his clothes were washed. He would be fitted up with something while he waited, the cop said, fixing him with eyes that held not one drop of human kindness.

Charley did as he was told, hoping the something wasn't going to be one of those tartan skirts. He knew his knees wouldn't stand up to that sort of examination. It still felt as if his centre of gravity had fallen down there somewhere.

Where the hell was he? Some place in darkest Scotland, as far as he remembered. Had he been arrested? Memories of the night before came floating back, invidious as second-hand smoke. He wrapped a towel around his waist, and peered along the corridor. Not a soul about. Then another cop, a newly pressed and shaved young cop, turned the corner and smiled. Not a cheery smile, not even a friendly smile, more a kind of grimace-smile, but Charley would take any smile at all, even one approaching rictus.

"Good morning," the young rookie flicked some dust or dandruff off his tunic. "You've slept it off, then?"

"I'm not sure—"

"Take a seat until your things are done. Here," he said, throwing a blanket.

Charley wrapped himself and sat. "I was going to say—"

"They won't be long."

"I didn't have anything to sleep off, damn it."

The rookie looked at him suspiciously. What was this guy up to? What other reason could there be? Every overnight visitor he'd ever had on a Sunday morning had needed to sleep it off. The only difference here, this wasn't Jimmy or Mac or one of the regulars, and neither did he look like an improvement on them.

"Oh? So how come you're here, then? You're English, are you?" he asked.

Charley started talking, talked like a high-pressure tap, talked about his wedding, his kidnapping, Bigg M logos, his rented Beemer, his sore head, his lost cash and cards, his ovine buddies, his near disappearance in a swamp, his mystery tour through the hills, and his arrival at the Pub with No Beer.

"Where am I?" he asked, running out of steam.

"Haddington police station, in East Lothian. You've heard of it?"

"No. How far is it—?"

"Hang on a minute, hold your horses," the rookie said. "Did you say Charles Oakley? Something came in about this…"

He disappeared behind his counter. "Here we are…something in from Berwick. You've come from Holy Island, have you?"

"Yes, but—"

"My word, have you guys set the cat among the pigeons? It's been on the news. UDI, for Christ's sake."

"What?"

"You don't know?"

"Know what? We were *visiting* the place. On honeymoon, like I said."

"Oh, boy. Do I have a surprise for you."

"Where's Nor…Rebecca?" Charley asked, thinking puh-lease, no more surprises.

"Huh?" the cop looked at the report on his counter. "Oh…your wife?"

"Yes. My wife."

"According to this, when last heard, she was still down there with a guy called Deville. He's been in the news; oh boy, and how. He's been at the centre of things, in the spotlight you might say." The rookie continued flicking through the report, then turned to the front page of a Sunday paper. "It says here he's the First Minister…ex-banker…multimillionaire. Hey, you don't think the guy…you don't think there'd be any jobs going down there, do you?"

"Oh fuck it," Charley said. "How in merry hell would you expect me to know? I'm the sap who lost his wife, his car, his wallet and the fucking plot in the blink of an eye, and you think I'm your fucking *careers* adviser?"

"Language. I suppose we'd better tell them you're here, then."

"Well, shit, it would be a start. Can you give me this guy's number? Am I allowed a phone call?"

"Hey, you've been watching too many TV programmes. You can make half a dozen if you want, as long as you pay for them. For Christ's sake, you haven't been arrested."

"*Charley*? Oh, thank God. Are you okay? Where *are* you?" Rebecca yelled down the line. She could hear a printer in the Fahr House basement, presumably churning out copies of Sarah's work.

Charley blanched and held the phone away from his ear. "I'm okay.

But Rebecca, don't shout, my head...it hurts. I'm in some place called Eddington, something like that, near Edinburgh I think. Rebecca...I have a problem here. I have no money...those guys took my wallet. I only had three pounds and some of it has gone on this call. I don't know how to—"

How pathetic, she thought, he sounds like an *eleven* year-old. A child, with Charley? Some virus far beyond the merely stupid must have invaded her head while she slept. "Hang on, Charley, give me that number so I can get back to you," she said.

She ran downstairs and asked Deville where Max's friends would be now. When he had consulted his elder son and confirmed the Bigg Market youths had just been picked up, she phoned Charley back and told him to sit tight. Good news, she said cordially, a free ride was on its way. Charley, by this time dressed, said fine, munching a bacon roll the young rookie had sold him, one hand in a trouser pocket flicking his remaining coins. Sixty-two pence; he couldn't remember the last time he'd had only sixty-two pence. Maybe in far-off pocket money days. For Pete's sake, the things you took for granted.

In the living room at Fahr House, Rebecca sank into an armchair and told Deville, Sarah, the short-eared owl and Geordie Halloran that at least the saga of Charley's kidnapping seemed to be over. She thanked Deville and told him she was very grateful, she owed him one.

"You'd like to feel useful until they return?" Deville asked.

Oh, oh, she thought, Little Miss Impulse puts her foot in her mouth again. "Sure, if I can help with something..."

"Help? You can help Sarah deliver copies of the Declaration and the transcript. Nothing major, only a few dozen houses to cover. Then you can have a crack at designing us a flag. You're an artist, you told me? Of course, we have some artists already in the village, so you might have some competition. But think of the kudos, the fame."

You asked for this, she told herself, seeing Sarah trying to stifle a laugh.

"Hey, hang on," Geordie said through a mouthful of toast. "You're saying your husband was kidnapped yesterday? From here?" Geordie had just seen the magic words "Human Interest Story" flash before his eyes.

"Yep."

Geordie was enjoying his introduction to Fahr House, and felt just like an honoured guest. Okay, he'd managed a short interview with Deville, but in particular he was enjoying the lissom forms of Sarah Courtney Deville and Rebecca Carter Oakley strung over their armchairs. Like watching spring flowers fresh with morning dew, he thought, waxing lyrical. It was enough to drive a man to writing poetry. He was tall himself, six feet plus, but those legs, what glorious legs...

"Hey, could I help?" he asked. "Delivering those things?"

"Sure," said Sarah, twenty-five years of age, willowy, shapely and beautiful, winking at Rebecca, twenty-six and likewise.

They spent ten minutes collating and stapling, Geordie telling them about his ride in the Honda FourTrax earlier. It was quite a motor, in his opinion.

"How was the causeway?" Sarah asked.

"There didn't seem to be one any more." Geordie had only once before been to Holy Island on a day trip, and had just a hazy memory of the road across the sands. He recalled there had been a panic when someone was late for the bus; someone else, maybe the driver, shouting, "The tide, the tide." His mother smiling, and telling him they might get to stay the night: "Wouldn't that be nice, darling? An adventure." But the latecomer had turned up.

"We'll take the car, have a look," Sarah said.

They drove out of the village along Berwick Road and Chare Ends, past the parking strip where Charley had left the BMW yesterday.

"Holy moly," Sarah said, "my darling brother's nothing if not thorough."

Where the causeway used to be was now a line of broken asphalt, half covered in mud and sand. Sometime just after midnight, the tide had come in and started putting the finishing touches to the work Max's wrecking crew had begun. But the tide was out now. If there had still been a causeway to cross, Geordie thought it would have opened an hour or so ago. Lumps of what used to be road were littered across the Swad, and only the bridge over the Lindis remained. The Refuge Box near the mainland shore lay in splinters. The poles and Refuge Boxes marking the Pilgrim's Way were still intact, as though proclaiming: *This is how it was. On your pins, folks. Walk it.* Some waders, Geordie didn't know what the birds were called, were having a high old time sifting through the wreckage. A line of cars was waiting on the island shore, the drivers and passengers leaning on open doors and bonnets or wandering about. A vehicle transporter plied its way steadily towards them, sunlight glinting off its windshield.

But it had not all been demolition. The morning sun was also glinting off a mesh fence, ten or twelve feet high, strung along the salt marsh on the far shore. What looked like a portakabin had been placed next to an equally high security gate at the Beal road end.

"It looks like he's done what he was asked to do," Rebecca agreed.

"You can say that again," Sarah said. "Well, if anyone ever had any doubts this was for real, they can put that thought right out of their heads."

They watched as the transporter reversed on to the shore road and lowered its ramp. A young fellow in Wellingtons and denim overalls started directing traffic, ushering the cars aboard.

"It all seems *muy* peaceful," Geordie said.

"Didn't you meet my brother on your way here?"

"I think I might have. There was a blond guy with a crew-cut directing things on the far side. He was good with the coffee while I waited."

"That would be Max. And you're surprised things are peaceful? Would you start an argument with him?" She smiled. It was a bewitchingly mischievous smile, and Geordie felt it to his shoes.

"Ummm...point taken. But what would these cars on this side have been doing? Surely no one could have come across this morning. Are these people going to work somewhere?"

"No. The islanders knew what was happening. They'd have fixed their own transport or lifts in vehicles that could make it over there. These will be overnight visitors. They'd have been told about this arrangement at their hotel or guesthouse."

"Jeezo," Geordie said, "it's almost military."

"That's my brother. With a bit of help from his Dad."

They turned around and headed back towards the village, seeing no one, the only car on the road.

"Could I ask you some questions?" Geordie said.

"You'll need to be snappy. Five minutes and we'll be starting the house-to-house rounds. Off the record, by the way."

"*¡Vale!*...Okay. How's everyone going to get back and forth now?"

"Four-by-fours, SUVs, utes, whatever they're called," Sarah answered. "If you'd been at the meeting last night, you'd have heard a million pounds mentioned for that little lot."

Geordie scribbled on his notepad, thinking: what an idiot, wishing he'd remembered his pocket recorder. "What about medical emergencies? People needing hospital?"

"Just like now. Helicopter. Either the Great North Air Ambulance Twin Squirrel, or RAF Coastal Command from Boulmer. If they don't continue the service, and Boulmer's future is looking dodgy, which is Ministry of Defence stuff and nothing to do with us, Max has his eye on a second-hand Sea King."

"Other services? Police, doctor, school, things like that?"

"You *should* have been here last night, and saved me the trouble. They're all in place, or about to be. We don't have either a policeman or doctor at present, you know. In the words of the song, things can only get better."

"Okay. Now...do you think you're going to get away with it?"

Sarah laughed. "At last, the sixty-four thousand dollar question. One of them anyway. Why not?"

"You really think so?"

"I think so, but we'll have to wait and see. After all, what can they do? Given that everyone is four square behind it and there'll be plenty of funds. Where there's a will there's a way, huh?"

"And where are you going with it?"

"Where it leads. To a small, as far as possible self-sustainable, and self-governing island. It's a nice concept, don't you think, George? If it works."

"You have some reservations?" He liked the way she'd said his name.

"Not about the end result, only about motives. I like the positive side of it, making our own way. I'm not so sure about the bellyaching, although second homes are a bummer. And I hope everyone's commitment holds. There are bound to be setbacks."

"Whose idea was it? How did it come about?"

Sarah hesitated. What line should she give? "Actually, no one local. You'll need to ask my father for details, but it came by accident from a group called the Holy Island Roundtable. They met here in 2001, a para-church group, Generation Xers I think they called themselves, to discuss things like cultural change, post-modernity versus Christianity, their mission and hopes for the future. Some of the things they said and wrote were pretty well incomprehensible, which may have been part of their problem, but it was all innocent stuff. They asked themselves, 'What if we could start again from scratch?' They didn't mean it to, but it set people here, people already fed-up with poor leadership, spin, equivocation, the quick fix and so on, thinking of the answer. Not in religious terms, in everyday terms."

Geordie gave up scribbling halfway through this torrent of words, thinking he would need to follow it up later, stick to something easier for now. But she'd just paused for breath.

"There's more, George. There's the feeling that decency in Britain, in their government anyway, has been sidelined. That too much wool is being pulled over too many eyes, to the point where things are being turned on their head, seen through a looking glass. My father, when you ask him, will give you examples. Social tampering, sophistry, double standards, smoke and mirrors. Take that thing with Shambo, the Hindu bull…in Wales wasn't it? What if a few latter-day Sobek worshippers imported some sacred crocodiles to the Tweed? They'd get to keep them? How nuts do you have to be?" She sighed. "Look at the UK Parliament. How they manage to avoid enacting laws that keep pace with modern society. The internet. Europe. What kind of marriage is it when every so-called treaty throws up red lines and vetoes, when every step you take is cautious or mistrustful? Not exactly built on a solid foundation, is it? Veto the wife's choice of shoes, red line the family holiday? How about their stewardship of funds, their failure to distribute them effectively? My father is no socialist, no distributor of wealth for the sake of it, but he could keep you occupied for as long as you could keep awake on the subject of funding essential services and local councils. On the criteria used to allocate those funds, and making sure how and where they're spent. He would point you to a government that takes on borrowing and debt in the expectation of income, not actual income. Where would an average family be if they thought like that? Maybe a lot of them do, and who can blame them, with the example they're being set? Ask his opinion on the National Audit Office. Why are there piles of garbage on the streets instead of police? Why are teachers and doctors upping sticks and leaving? Why are councils allowed to spend money on jollies when services are falling apart? Why are bodies like the National Trust thinking of buying land the government is bent on developing? Is that good stewardship? It seems more like a recipe for conflict. You could look at immigration policies, or lack of them…but ask my father. He'll give you examples. The simple fact is, we decided on this way out because we thought we could do better ourselves. We'd had enough."

Sarah stopped, looking slightly abashed, as if she'd burnt enough passion in a short car ride. "More than you bargained for?" she asked. "You don't like it?"

Geordie wondered if all this was her father talking, or was it her? But he told her he wasn't there to judge; Lindisfarne might well do better on its own, and he had no problem with that. And he'd have plenty of time to discuss these things with her father…he wasn't aiming to be hauled back to Newcastle on Monday.

"Who did the copperplate?" he asked, to cool things down. "On the Declaration?"

"I did. Was there a problem? It was checked often enough."

"No, not at all. It was nice. Appropriate too, I guess. Okay…here's something else. What about your new Border crossing? What about tourists?" he asked. "You depend on them for a living, *si*? How many of them are going to put up with that palaver, the transporter thing?"

"The Border crossing's essential. It underlines something. Our secession, don't forget, is from the European Union as well as Britain. How many Brits realise, do you think, that when they show their passport it's the EU border they're crossing, not Britain's any more? That a Latvian passport is equally as valid? And take a look at the border problems with Ukraine. Imagine the crush at the gates of Turkey if and when they become EU members. Just another case of politicians forgetting to tell the whole truth? You don't hear them talk about it, do you? And the transporter's only here for a day, to get the overnighters out. In future, there'll be a permanent control point where you saw the portakabin. Most people will be brought to the island by our own transport. Ferried, if you like, by Hummer or boat. Sure, we expect a reduction in tourism. But we can live with that if it means improvements in other ways."

"What did you mean, most people?"

"Some will be turned back. Last question, George. We're here."

"Like who? Who'll be turned back?"

"Like anyone hiding under a helmet. Those hoodies yesterday. Any other full head covering, come to that."

"Jeez."

"What? No pidgin Spanish to help you with that one?" Sarah laughed.

Geordie smiled weakly, and wished he'd stuck to admiring her legs. He'd had one unasked question answered anyway; she was too smart to waste her brain rehashing second-hand opinions.

"Who's going to look after that end of it?" he asked.

"Brother Max. Who else?" Sarah raised her eyebrows.

"Well, yes," Geordie said thoughtfully. "I can see Max looking after it all right."

"Enough for now, George dear. It's time to earn your keep."

Geordie stuck his reporter's pad in a hip pocket, cheerfully accepted a sheaf of stapled papers and got out of the car. One of the first houses he called at was Amy Donaldson's. She asked him who he was, then spotted the girls going in and out of garden gates and invited them all in for a cup of tea. Sarah grinned, told Rebecca this could be interesting, an education for George into "the real Holy Island," and led the way.

Hmmm, Rebecca thought, he already got as much of it in ten minutes as I did in a day.

When Charley had first laid eyes on his travelling companions for the trip back to Lindisfarne, his first reaction was that his bride of two days standing was playing some kind of sick joke on him. He corrected himself when the driver, a guy called Spike, after his hair, told him that his bride of two days standing was working for the First Minister of the newly-created Althing of Holy Island. This wasn't just a sick joke, Charley told himself, this joke was lying on its deathbed receiving the last rites. Kate-turned-bloody-Norah had split again. It was Mata Hari this time. And what the hell was an Althing when it was at home? Some fossilised debating chamber? Some Stone Age Icelandic thing? His body language began sending out ill-conceived and obvious signals, which got him a predictable response: ostracism.

So Charley lolled like a rejected waxwork in the front of the Defender 90, alongside Spike and a fellow-joker called Barney, after Barney Rubble of The Flintstones. His kidnappers were caged up in the back behind a wire partition, a modification probably installed to keep Rottweilers or pit bulls from eating the driver. His only consolation was that the Bigg M trio, disguised in fetching new gear, seemed equally surprised to see him again. From the intermittent exchange of whispers behind the wire, they seemed apprehensive about what his reappearance signified. It was probably the least of their worries. He got the feeling that if (a) they could read, and (b) were given a copy of the *Magna Carta*, they would be busily committing it to memory.

It was, all things considered, the longest and least comfortable road journey of his life. Up to and including yesterday's in the boot of the Beemer. He re-entered Holy Island at about ten thirty, just as Rebecca and the others were starting their deliveries. He was taken straight to Fahr House.

The Bigg M trio seemed to be heading elsewhere. Charley heard mention of a converted fish-house from a menacing guy called Max who seemed to be in charge of security at the gate, and who took time out to read them their rights. Charley hoped it would be the last he saw of them, but given the combination of bad luck and sick jokes he'd experienced of late, he wouldn't bet on it.

The trio were clearly unhappy. In a blissfully unconscious irony, Shad of the shrapnel told Max that kidnap was a serious crime, man. He wanted a lawyer, and if not a lawyer a cop, somebody legal, man, this shit had gone too far already. Max simply took his arm, none too gently, threw him back into the Defender 90, and told Spike to head for the jail. Well, tough. Charley couldn't have cared less if they had all toppled into the sea and drowned. He'd have been there with a pole, pushing them under.

Charley had had enough of hoodies, cops, Devilles, Spikes, Barneys, the fucking Scottish Borders and Holy Island. He was penniless, or near enough, and entirely due to them. After that damn journey, he was seething with resentment. His head was beginning to fill with fantasies of vengeance.

"I'm Alexander Deville," the flint-eyed beanpole at the front door said. "How are you? Your wife won't be long. She's out helping my daughter deliver some things."

"I'm not sure I'll be staying long," Charley said, fingering a pimple on his neck.

"Oh? I should have thought you'd welcome some convalescence."

"Is that possible here? Just as soon as I find a bank, I'm off. Back to London and civilization."

The beanpole pursed his lips. "With or without your wife?"

"With my wife, of course."

Charley was disinclined to start debating love, marriage and his wedding vows with a total stranger, First Minister of some unknowable entity or not. What a fucking fraud.

"Is there a bank anywhere near?" he asked.

"A Girobank, at the Post Office here in the village. A choice of banks in Berwick. Or a Barclay's in Seahouses, somewhat further to the south."

"Barclay's would be best. It's where I have my account. See, the problem is, I've lost my cards. Those yobs…is there a car rental place?"

"No, Mr. Oakley. There is not." Alex Deville was wondering how this young man had been brought up; he had every appearance of respectability, even if a tad dishevelled, but not a word of thanks for his lift from Haddington. It was inexcusable, really. Yet another example of the erosion of British values.

"How do we esc…get off this place?"

"If you ask nicely, I'm sure a vehicle will be provided to take you to the main road. Seahouses, if you prefer. Do you still have a cheque book?"

"In my things. My wife should have them."

"Of course. Do come in, have some coffee or tea while you're waiting. Or something stronger? A beer?" Deville recalled Rebecca mentioning her husband's passion for alcohol.

"Where is she? Somewhere in the village?"

"Yes. She is going door-to-door, so I wouldn't know precisely where at this point in time. I'm not even sure which end they started."

"I'll look for her." Charley threw a hand vaguely over his shoulder.

"As you wish. One point though. If you do leave, with or without her, it would be appreciated if you could build a return visit into your plans. Your erstwhile abductors will need to be brought to trial."

"No way would I ever want to see them again."

"An understandable reaction. But in the interests of justice, you may have little choice."

Charley gave an indeterminate grunt and said he would take a walk around the houses. "With or without her" indeed. What bloody cheek. And he was not about to be sucked into another visit to this part of the world, not if he could help it. If that meant steering clear of those *hypnotic* eyes for an hour or two, he'd be more than happy to *haunt* the bloody village streets. Well, the whole shooting match would get what was coming to them. *What goes around comes around*, he thought, enthusiastically diving into clichés. He hoped there were enough soldiers left in Britain to sort the bastards out. A few of those smart bombs would come in handy. One of them smart enough to do away with this…this bloody *palace*.

He should have taken up the offer of a beer, though. Sixty-two pence wasn't going to buy him one, or even a cup of tea, not in this God-forsaken dump.

He noticed a helicopter heading towards the village from the mainland, from the direction of the huge castle that seemed to jut out into the sea a few miles south. Was that south? He couldn't be sure.

Then a flare spiralled up, bright red, several hundred feet high. For fuck's sake, Charley thought, they weren't taking pot-shots at aircraft now, were they? Was that the coastguard? The RAF? Was this civil *war*?

Charley hadn't seen an earlier flare. He had been too engrossed in extricating himself from Max, Land Rovers and the Bigg Market boys. As he watched, a small parachute seemed to open and the flare began to sink slowly earthwards, leaving a trail of white smoke behind in the slight breeze.

"Damn," said a voice behind him; the beanpole. "They must have been trying to leave without knowing the complexities of the harbour. Oh well, it's by no means the first time. And it should provide bit of entertainment for you on your meanderings. Enjoy the village." He left Charley on the doorstep, and went back inside.

CHAPTER SEVEN

"A reporter, young man? I'm going to be on the telly?" Amy Donaldson asked, pouring them tea from a china pot. "My, my. Seventy-seven and I finally get my fifteen minutes of fame." She winked at Sarah and Rebecca, both relaxing with cups of tea in Amy's living room.

"No, no, Mrs. Donaldson...not the telly. I work for *The Northern Sun*—you know, in Newcastle." Geordie was distracted, trying not to look at Sarah crossing and re-crossing her legs. Was this a deliberate ploy? Sitting in the back seat of the car, he hadn't seen too much of them but now, waving around in the armchair opposite, topped by salmon-pink shorts, they seemed *magnetic*. They made his girlfriend's look like stubs, for God's sake.

"Geordie is good with the questions. Not so hot at Spanish," Rebecca said, coming to his rescue. She was wearing jeans, which was a help, but tight designer jeans couldn't hope to hide the length and perfection of what was moving about underneath. Gorgeous. He was finding this impossible, a kind of heavenly torture, too much for a fellow's flesh and blood to take.

"I like a man who's not afraid to ask questions," Amy said. "I've had two of them, and that Jeremy Thompson's okay as well."

"Could I ask you a few?" Geordie said. He flicked his eyes around the small, tidy room, taking in the willow-pattern china, the small oil paintings in ornate frames, the solid mahogany furniture, and the antique-looking ornaments. Tasteful. Well-kept. After the magnificence of Fahr House, it was a relief to be somewhere normal. This was better, he told himself, as he felt his brain refocusing. Oh Lord, he must remember to phone Bob Cutler.

"Fire away, young man. But I might have a few for you, too."

"Can I take notes?"

"Is there something wrong with your memory? We could be in trouble here, son. I've dumped the useless hearing aid. I persevered with it for a couple of weeks, but couldn't go to the loo. Well, it sounded as if I was about to be drowned by a tidal wave. Now you tell me you can't remember, and I can't hear too well. Some interview this is shaping up to be."

"I'm sure we'll be fine," Geordie said smiling, deciding to jump in, to hell with the notes. "So tell me, do you approve what's happening? The island seceding from the UK?"

"Approve? We should have done it years ago. If we'd had the money. It's taken most of Alex's life."

"*¿Por qué?...*Why?"

"That man Major for a start. A disaster. Spitting Image got *him* right, mushy peas and all. And nothing better since. A lot worse in fact. At least he enjoyed his cricket."

"You believe the UK government has let you down?"

"Don't *you* think so? I'm nearly at the end of my life, young Geordie. You have yours to live. Are you going to enjoy it? Live a long and mainly happy one, like me?"

"Well…I hope so."

"You aren't apprehensive? You're content to paddle along reporting things? You can live with floods of immigrants, Hundred Years' Wars on terror—if you can wage war on an emotion—ten-year so-called life sentences, home release, shifty Chief Constables, rapid—or is it random?—response times, red tape, superbugs, all that garbage? You prefer them to peace and hands-on policing and a proper health service?"

"Could I ask the questions, Mrs. Donaldson?"

Sarah and Rebecca were laughing like drains. Long-legged *sirens*. How was a guy to concentrate with them sprawled about, having a party?

"I was mugged myself, you know," Amy continued. "Right here on this island. Or they tried. Some youths from Alnwick. Do you know what they got? A so-called community care sentence. Ha! If it had happened here, if we'd had our own rules, we'd have put them away so long they'd have forgotten who they were."

"I'm sorry to hear that. It's terrible," Geordie said, correcting himself when he saw the light of battle in Amy's eyes. "I mean your being mugged," he said hurriedly. "Is that when you started thinking things were going wrong?"

"No. Oh, it's all become much too lenient, far beyond tolerant. *Human rights*. These people aren't human, how come they have rights? No, no. My first husband would have told you it all started going to pot when the death penalty stopped. My second would have blamed that idiot Heath and his fanciful European ideas, and then that unctuous glob of oil Baker, the self-regarding idiot who outlawed corporal punishment in schools. The slow descent, drop by numbing drop, to the lowest common denominator, he'd have said. Both fine men, my husbands. No fools. Those Yankees, they'd blame the hippies or Vietnam. Nixon. Watergate. But they were headed downhill before those things. And what did we do? Hitched our wagon to the falling star."

"And you, Mrs. Donaldson? What would you blame?"

"Both. And the rest. The shape of things is drawn, young man. But that country over there, that *UK*, has yet to face the reckoning. It may take time, but it'll be a harsh one. It's an insolvent country, wouldn't you say? Seeping, creeping loss of values. All the way to bankruptcy. It'll spit you out in a heartbeat if you start upsetting minorities. Liberal democracy. That's one thing to blame. Democracy in the wrong hands. You're a writer, so tell me. When was it democracy became synonymous with indulgence?"

"*Que*?" Surreptitiously, Geordie fumbled for his notepad. He had thought this would be just another easy interview with another gentle old lady; bad mistake.

"You're hard of hearing as well? Democracy. I hadn't appreciated until recently that it means those with the least reason and the squeakiest voice get what they want. Like cuckoos in the wrong nest."

"I'm sorry?"

"You don't know about cuckoos? Taking over nests, fattening themselves up on credulity? Is that chair uncomfortable for you?"

"No, no, just getting some help," Geordie said, waving his pad. "Well, I may have heard...But you mentioned Europe. You don't think we should be in Europe?" he asked.

"I don't think *I* should," Amy said. "I can't speak for you. And I don't think most Holy Islanders think *they* should. Scratch a Holy Islander and you'll find a Holy Islander. Not a European, and British a poor second. A Holy Islander. Sitting in no-man's land between England and Scotland. Like Shetlanders, sitting between Norway and Scotland. Heck, we've only been part of Northumberland since the 1840s. Before that, from medieval times, we were a floating appendage of Durham. Part of the Palatinate. No, first and foremost we're Holy Islanders. If we didn't know it, we wouldn't know what we were. Are you getting all this?"

Geordie smiled and nodded. "So you think England is what...a kind of foreign country?"

"Oh, now, you're a *reporter*. You like metaphors, eh? You might say they're foreign to us, we're foreign to them. We're a foreign country called the past: LP Hartley said it first, didn't he? They're a foreign country called the present. And they're welcome to it. And their future. We like the idea of making our own."

"And your own laws, I understand." In truth, Geordie was finding it hard to keep up; this was as bad as Sarah earlier. Modern technologies were all very well, but he should have taken the belts and braces approach, and subscribed years ago to a decent shorthand course.

"Oh, there are plenty of laws to break if you've a mind. We might just get rid of some, too. Ask yourself this, young Geordie. How many times do you come across a Bill or ordinance and you think 'hang on, something screwy here, that's not *moral*?' Or 'what's the *point*?' Or your instincts are telling you, 'oh, no, these aren't the values my parents taught me.' Ha! Gay marriages. They need compassion, those people, not consecration. Then, to add insult to injury, gay adoptions. Gambling free-for-alls. Immigrants getting preferential treatment. Abortions on demand, two hundred thousand of them last year; this is *babies* being killed, not vermin. Corporal punishment outlawed. Teachers and policemen eviscerated. Dickensian old folks' homes. Child abuse. Benefit fraud. Welfare dependency. Home Office fiats to go easy on offenders. Anything the fragments of society want, they get. Catchpenny legislation, but at what long-term price? Nice values, eh? And what do the politicians say about it all? Nothing. Or nothing useful. How can they? They're too scared of upsetting the voters, if anyone's still listening. Or strident *minorities* of the voters, I should say. Talk about liberalism in denial. Prattling on about 'winning hearts and minds'...Bah! It's their own cherished liberalising ideas, half a century of them, piling up. Aye, well, you can see them for yourself, those chickens coming home to roost. You don't need me to tell you."

"You don't think society's become...fairer?" Geordie asked, sipping his tea and trying to write at the same time. "I mean, the government says...You don't think that some of those things were correcting injustices? Prejudices? Not all of them maybe, but—"

"Fairer for whom?" Amy replied sharply. "That government over there, whatever it says, has abdicated its responsibilities to its people. The *majority* of its people. All the main parties have. Look at the laws they *haven't* passed. Something to bring the financial institutions under control. Lending vast sums to people with no hope of paying them back. Something to bring those advertisers to heel: look at the amounts spent plugging bingo, gambling, banks, credit cards, car insurance, home insurance. Wouldn't they be better spent on lower interest rates and premiums? On customer service? How about on flood protection, instead of get-out clauses? Or is it one-way traffic? Hit the punters twice over, as taxpayers and policy-holders? Something to bring that internet under control, YouTube, MyWatch, paedophiles and all. And the BBC. Now there's an organisation that has lost its way, and doesn't even know it. Look at the guff that passes for TV or radio programmes and ask yourself, 'Would I miss them if they weren't here next week?' Graham Norton, Russell Brand, Catherine Tate, Jonathan Ross, people like that? I ask you; are you happy with *your* licence fee going on such garbage? It's like a plumbing leak. You start with a drip or two, a liberalisation here or there, and before you know it you have a wrecked society. Or bathroom."

"Happy or not, Mrs. Donaldson, aren't some of those things to do with freedom of choice? A free society? We can choose what we watch, or say, or write. Some people like one thing, others like something else. *Si*?"

"Haven't you been listening, young man? Who is setting standards these days, and what sort of standards are they? Of course we can't choose what we say or write or watch. Not any more, not in any way that makes sense. *We* can't, but apparently religious screwballs can. On the one hand, we're fed rubbish, someone else's freedom of choice. And on the other, things we should be able to discuss are taboo. Not 'politically correct.' Don't talk to me of freedom, like a limp Liberal Democrat. We know the other side of that coin, don't we? Responsibility, eh? Moral equilibrium. Now, tell me, if people aren't responsible, why should they have freedoms? Why not reduce their freedoms? If kids run amok, why not conscript them? Send *them* to Iraq, Afghanistan? It might be more effective than community care sentences, eh? Make an example of them. Pass a few laws to stop the rot. Is that too rich for your taste?"

"Well, you'd have to say it's radical, Mrs. Donaldson. Although conscription…"

Geordie, flexing fingers that were seriously cramping up, became conscious of the girls, making small signals behind him, grinning.

"My God!" He jumped out of his chair, almost out of his skin. "What's that?"

"That? Why, he's a Vietnamese pot-bellied pig, son. He's a pet. He's called George too. After George Clooney, fine handsome man. He has one, or had one."

"Holy cow."

"Don't let him hear you say that, young feller. He's way more intelligent than a cow, and a lot better looking too."

Geordie had to concede it had a nice friendly face, furry and inquisitive. The pig snuffled at him, pirouetted on its dainty feet, belly nearly on the floor, and walked back out.

"How do you manage to keep him? How much does he weigh?"

"Oh, he's about eight stone now, maybe a bit more. He's no trouble at all. He has his own place outside. Wanders in and out to check I'm okay, and treats the house like his own. My second husband built him a sty. Plenty to eat and drink. Couple of baths a day, and he's always nice and warm. He's in porker heaven."

For the first time he could recall in his budding career as a journalist, Geordie was struck dumb.

"Amy, I think we'd better be going," Sarah said. "I mean, we can leave George here, as you're teaching him so much, but we need to get on delivering these."

"Oh, you have him, dear. He's a bit young for me. And he seems to like your legs." Amy laughed. "He can't be all daft. He seems a nice young man, too. Takes insults in his stride and sticks to his job, even under a bit of pressure. How are things at the causeway, by the way?"

"Oh, Max seems to have everything hunky-dory. The fence and gate are in place."

"That Max. He's something else, that boy."

To cover his blushes, Geordie finished his cup of tea and allowed his notepad to drop on the floor. He scuffled around for a while until he felt his face return to normal and stood up. By then, the girls were out of the door, laughing and waving goodbye. He ran after them, remembering to thank Amy for her time and "a really interesting chat. *Adiós*, Mrs. Donaldson."

"Any time, young *hombre*," she said. "You feel free to come back whenever you want, won't you? But bin the Spanish next time. Please?"

Geordie caught up with the girls at the car.

"Does anyone, anyone at all, have a different view? Anyone on the island, I mean?" he asked Sarah, thinking: at all costs get her mind off the leg business, what a total *embarrassment*.

"Oh, we all have different views. Different reasons, different anecdotes. But if you're asking, does anyone disagree we'd be better off on our own, the answer's 'No.' Look at the vote, George. There's been lots of debate, lots of questions to be answered, but we knew what we were voting for. And believe me, it takes something very powerful to make everyone in this community spit on the same stone." She paused. "Do you really think my legs are nice?"

"Definitely," Rebecca said. "He hasn't been able to take his eyes off them. 'On' and 'stalks' comes to mind."

Geordie supposed he'd just have to get in the back, suffer their giggling, and maintain a stoic dignity. Shit, could he remember everything Mrs. Donaldson had said in there, or read his own scrawl? What absolute, *exclusive* gems she'd given him. But what an idiot, leaving his recorder at Fahr House along with everything else. Well, he wasn't to know he'd be getting such good stuff so soon, was he, from her or from Sarah? He'd just have to check back with them if he wasn't sure of his ground. He climbed into the car with as much dignity as possible, ignoring the looks he was getting.

But he recovered enough to ask Rebecca, in between house calls, about the abduction of her new husband. He got the distinct feeling that this Charley guy wasn't exactly in her good books, and found it hard to believe after only two days of married life. The guy must be a first-class dumbbell, Geordie thought, to get on the wrong side of a drop dead gorgeous girl like this so fast. How the hell had he achieved it? He wondered about probing deeper, and then thought, no, he wasn't aiming to sink to red-top depths, or cause his writing hand more pain. Besides, he liked Rebecca and you didn't dump on your friends, at least those your Editor knew nothing about. He might write it up sometime as a side dish to the main course, how two young newly-weds had been cruelly caught up in an island's bid for independence. An added extra; something Bob Cutler, Old Smokey, didn't need to get involved in. He was looking forward to meeting this Charley, not so much to get his side of the story, as to see what the prize specimen in the village Leek Show looked like. If, like other villages in the north, Holy Island produced enough home-grown stuff to have Leek Shows.

An hour later, after several more conversation pieces along the way, and with Sarah regularly being asked how her Dad was doing, they finished the deliveries. When they got back to Fahr House, Deville told Rebecca her husband had been and gone not half an hour ago. She said she'd head back out and look for him. Geordie invited himself along, which had nothing to do, he told himself, with Deville diverting Sarah downstairs to help her brother Alistair with financial stuff, and some research on second homes. Having learned a hard lesson, he took his pocket recorder out of his gear and stuffed it in his jacket. He told Deville he'd had an instructive morning, meeting Mrs. Donaldson. What a jewel *she*'d turned out to be, he said.

Deville looked at him with interest. "Indeed yes; Amy. A stalwart of this community. One of the very best. I tried to persuade her to stand for election but she wouldn't have it. She tried to tell me she was too old. And you felt you got on well with her?"

"I seemed to. It was difficult to tell."

"Good…incidentally, you should think of staying here, you know, until your assignment is over. There's little point in trying to find a room elsewhere. We have more than enough here and besides, a lot of your professional colleagues have arrived. You'll probably find the place is fully booked."

Geordie thanked him and thought, what a bonus, living under the same roof as those legs for a day or two. Not to mention the rest of her. Or having the inside track handed to him on a plate. He felt so well-disposed towards his fellow-man that he phoned Bob Cutler before they left, and brought him up to speed. Not much joy there, though; he was told to stick with it and get some copy through by six. It didn't sound like Old Smokey was doing anything constructive. He was probably sitting on his backside venting smoke like a fumarole, coughing his lungs out down the phone, and no doubt regaling anyone who'd listen with anecdotes of the Devolution Bill, last week's Scottish Elections, and other prehistoric crap.

The coxswain and crew of the Seahouses lifeboat, the Mersey class *RNLB Grace Darling* and the inshore "D" class inflatable *Martin, John and Ann*, were well used to rescuing people from the waters around Holy Island. Of the twenty-two "shouts" in 2006, thirteen had featured the island, most of them people stuck on the causeway and retrieved by the inshore boat. Two incidents had involved capsized or beached yachts, the latest of them, at the end of July, a yacht aground off Castle Point.

The flare Charley had seen was of a similar nature, except the vessel was a small dinghy with an outboard rather than a yacht. In the sort of manoeuvre accomplished by the uninitiated with consummate ease, the dinghy had hit a shoal, Long Rig, a few hundred metres outside the Ouse, and flipped. The occupants had started panicking, firing flares at all and sundry.

Geordie and Rebecca headed along rows of neat grey stone cottages, some white-rendered, down Fenkle Street and past St. Cuthbert's Square. Wallflowers and red valerian were everywhere, and Geordie noticed two song thrushes, birds he hadn't seen for years and which he took comfort in recognising. The cottages looked well-maintained, with some moss growing in the clay pantiles, flowerpots and window boxes filled with viola, geranium, pansies, and busy lizzie. Rebecca commented how charming it all was, nothing above a couple of stories high except the attic windows of the Manor House Hotel and the looming reddish ruins of the priory ahead of them. Geordie nodded, and wondered what the houses fetched these days. They passed the Crown & Anchor and started down Sanctuary Close. A group of solid-looking stone buildings with red pantile roofs were clustered on the shore, a digger working nearby. No missing husband in sight, although they were both now looking in all directions. Rebecca, with some reserve, gave Geordie a summary of her interrupted honeymoon, and Geordie made her laugh by saying she was doing things back to front.

"How do you reach that conclusion?" Rebecca asked.

"Well, I don't have any personal experience," he said, "but I thought most marriages started off okay and *then* went downhill. Things can't get any worse than this, can they?"

They meandered on companionably towards the jetty. Geordie noticed two graceful obelisks, russet-coloured in the sunlight, rising up on a point of the mainland shore, and remarked that they must be navigation guides for boats entering the harbour. He guessed it was about low tide, not yet noon. He could imagine the problems getting in and out of the place by sea, for there seemed to be reefs everywhere.

They went through another old revolving metal gate and along a path beneath the Heugh, a mass of whinstone that looked to Geordie as if it plunged under the harbour and reappeared as the rock on which the Castle stood, ahead of them across the bay.

"It looks like a difficult harbour," he commented to Rebecca. "You must have to zigzag your way in, literally."

"Umm…" Rebecca was distracted. Where on earth was Charley? she wondered. They had pretty well walked through the village, and had been all over it earlier in the car. There'd been no sign of him, and on this stroll with Geordie she hadn't seen a familiar face to ask.

There were cobles moored in the Ouse, some bobbing gently in shallow water, some high and dry, tilted on their sides. Other old clinker-built boats were dotted above the high-water mark along the shore, upturned and covered with pitch tarpaulin, grass growing around them. They were clearly used for storing gear, with piles of lobster creels and coils of rope scattered nearby. Geordie noticed a far-flung collection of fish boxes piled up by the path: Foyle, Pittenweem, Castlebere, Whitby, Buckie, Whitehaven, all points of the compass except east.

They came to the pier, two neat double-banked rows of lobster pots stacked along it.

As far as Geordie could tell, there had been four people aboard the dinghy. He and Rebecca watched them being winched to an RAF helicopter. The dinghy, minus its outboard, was towed into the Ouse by a sparkling blue-and-orange lifeboat, in the livery of the Royal National Lifeboat Institution, called the *Grace Darling*.

"Bloody idiots," a burly man in a blue guernsey said to them. "Don't know what the hell they're doing half the time. Belay that, *all* the time. Why these people don't have to pass a boating test, like people have to pass a driving test, God only knows. Far too much of yon lifeboat crew's work is caused by know-it-all weekend idiots. They should be made to pay the costs. They just don't understand the sea isn't a kids' playground."

"No sympathy here, then, *si*?" Geordie smiled.

"Bloody right. I was a fisherman and I know what yon sea can do."

"As a matter of interest," Geordie said, "what happens to the lifeboat service when you're an independent island?" He was concerned to see other journalists at the scene—some of the competition, by fair means or foul, had managed the crossing—and more concerned to see TV crews. Inevitable, really. But he consoled himself that he did have the inside track, with lodgings in the First Minister's mansion and Amy, the wonderful Amy. He hoped that she would stay inside and out of sight of these pesky vultures, for the rest of the day. Or that her Vietnamese pot-bellied pig would have them for his tea.

"And who are you?" the man asked.

Geordie told him, and added that Rebecca was also visiting, hoping to meet up with her husband. "I drove up early this morning when I heard the news," he said.

"Aye, right. I'm Trevor Patterson. Pleased to meet you. I saw the lass at the meeting last night. Now, lad, you be careful what you write. As to the lifeboat service, the answer's nothin' but good. The RNLI's the RNLI. Those Seahouses lads, aye mebbe the Eyemouth ones as well, they might have a laugh at us but by God they'll be thinking we're not daft. After what's happened to their fishing industry and the riff-raff they get in yon village each summer, they'll mebbe emigrate here. Anyway, we're thinking of a lifeboat ourselves, and a chopper if need be."

"You used to have a lifeboat here, didn't you?" Geordie drew on some vague memories, boring afternoons spent trawling through the archives back in Groat Market. The city seemed like another world. He had a vision of Bob Cutler blowing smoke rings at his desk, the Editor breathing down his neck wondering where the front-page copy was, and people typing up the usual stories: footballers fighting outside clubs, the five fastest pick-up joints on Newcastle quayside, fat ladies on diet fifteen; all the pap that sold papers and made the world go round.

He could almost conjure up in his imagination the noise of sirens and the smell of traffic fumes floating through the windows of his distant office. Where the condemned, as he was beginning to think of them from the lofty heights of his new assignment, would be plodding through all the mind-numbing day-to-day stuff.

"Oh aye, right up to nineteen sixty-eight," Trevor Patterson said. "And long afore, when this was a proper community and people fished and farmed for a living. Not full of day-trippers like them there. Or that fond bugger prancing about." He pointed to a boat moored at the jetty.

Geordie saw a slightly-built young fellow about his own age with hair that might have been red when dry. It wasn't dry. Every few seconds, the guy was standing up, shaking his head, running his hands through his hair, then kneeling down over the gunwales and ducking it in seawater.

"Charley," Rebecca hissed. "What's he *doing*?"

"You know him? He's been fooling about like that for the best part of fifteen minutes," Trevor Patterson said. "I think he has fleas or lice or something. Either that or he's barking mad."

"Holy mackerel…those louts. Or the cell," Rebecca said.

"The what?"

She waved a hand dismissively and marched off along the pier.

"Don't look at me," Geordie told his new pal. "She married the fond bugger." He was latching on well to the local parlance.

"Aye, right, more fool her."

Geordie gazed after Rebecca and thought discretion was maybe his best option. It went against the grain, but there it was. He had enough interesting insights into the secession of Holy Island, not to mention the pitfalls of holy matrimony, without wasting time or words on prize Leek Show specimens.

Geordie noticed that the airlift was over, the dinghy once more moored in the harbour, the *Grace Darling* steaming southwards back to base. The competition was on the move too.

He turned back to Trevor Patterson. "How many fishing boats operate out of here now?" He couldn't resist the question; he was Geordie Halloran after all, information junkie, lifelong admirer of men who took on the sea for a living.

"Half a dozen. A dozen when my grandpa started out. In the eighteen hundreds, three dozen, he used to tell me. Piles of shellfish all over the village. Used for bait, see? Not much in the way of tourism then."

"Any accidents? Boats lost? Local fishing disasters?"

"Oh, aye. The worst was eighteen seventy-five. Pretty well wiped out one family's menfolk. Rough times, in those days. They can still be bloody rough."

"What do the boats catch now?"

"Lobster, crab. Salmon and sea trout in the season."

"And they still make a living?"

"Oh, aye. If they didn't, they'd jack it in. Like a lot of others afore them have had to do. Government assholes. *Brussels*. Only two good things ever came out of yon place. Beer and bloody sprouts."

Geordie thanked him for talking, and said that it had been good to meet him. He said cheerio, sat on a fish box to dictate some snippets into his recorder, and then headed back to Fahr House and his laptop.

"Hello, Charley," Rebecca had cooled off in her short walk along the jetty. "Great...you got back. I was so worried—"

"I've been *bitten*," Charley said. "Look at this." He pulled up his shirt to show her small red spots on his back and ribs. "This bloody place—"

"You won't have been bitten here, Charley. It would either be those louts who took you or your cell last night." Sweet reason was all it took. She had to be sympathetic. No one could say Charley hadn't been through some trying circumstances.

"It wouldn't have happened if we hadn't come here. Bloody place."

"Oh, Charley, you can't say that. The island's a joy. You couldn't help it if some louts from Newcastle decided to take liberties. They're to blame, not the place. It's a lovely island...I've met some lovely people—"

"Oh, yeah? That lanky string of arrogance up at the stately home? Lovely people, my foot. God rot them." He knelt and ducked his head again, muttering.

"Charley, what is the point of continually washing your hair when the bites are on your body?" Rebecca said, starting to feel a trace of impatience.

"They're *everywhere*. I can feel them hopping about, biting. I'm as itchy as hell. All *over*. Bloody things."

"Maybe if we went back to Fahr House? You could have a proper shower, some shampoo, antiseptic cream. Pine disinfectant or bleach, if you're set on making a good job of it. Or maybe your problem is alcohol poisoning. It brings people out in blotches, so I'm told." Steady girl, she told herself, lightly on the sarcasm, gently, gently.

"That place? No way. I'm not setting foot in that place. Bloody man."

"Charley, I've moved out of the guesthouse. I stayed there last night. He and his family have been very good to me while you've been away. Helpful. Hospitable. There are some exciting things happening here. You'll love it. They're—"

"Committing collective hari-kari is what they're doing. No way. Love it? I hate the bloody awful place. God rot the lot of them."

"Charley, that's childish. And you're beginning to sound like a kaka. They've done nothing wrong to you. That man you seem to dislike so much sent a car to pick you up. He and his son found out where you were. They've been absolutely first class—" She saw she was talking to a man under water.

Rebecca waited while Charley went through his shaking and hand-combing routine.

"You can please yourself. I will not be beholden to that man, or his...*body-builder* son. They can do what they like with their island. We're leaving," he said between shakes. "What's a kaka, anyway?"

"A parrot. I have no intention of leaving, Charley."

"Parrot, is it? Then bloody well stay, why don't you. *I'm* leaving. And soon."

"And how do you propose to do that without transport?"

"I'll bloody swim if I have to. That toffee-nosed asshole offered me a lift anyway."

"Oh, so he's good enough to lend a helping hand but not to get any thanks for it?"

"Bloody right. He owes me one. Him and his bloody island."

Had she been right? Rebecca asked herself. Was it possible that she and Charley could set a new record as The World's Shortest Marriage? Had there been any shorter than forty-eight hours? Or was it more likely that their claim to fame in the Guinness Book of Records would be as The Marriage Made in Hell? How had this happened? She had been enjoying her morning, thinking Charley was safe, listening to Sarah and Geordie, and feisty old Amy with a mind as sharp as a tack, and all the friendly people they had met on their rounds. Now this. How had a harmless, amusing twit she had actually thought she'd loved become this ungrateful, Game-obsessed, drunken, prick-less, foul-mouthed, *flea-bitten* relic in a matter of days? Was it her fault? Was it her period? Was everything being skewed by that? No, no, no. Her mother must *never* hear of this. She could barely bring herself to speak for rage. Light a candle for him? If she'd had a blowtorch handy, she'd have cauterized his mouth.

"Charley, I have never heard such ungrateful *rot* in my life. You, you...*manus*. You need to grow up and get a life. Preferably before you drink yourself to death, although I couldn't care much less. I'll make sure Mr. Deville lays on your transport and that he's properly thanked. Go up to the pub on the corner. Someone will come for you. Can you hear me?"

She sighed and turned away. She was talking to a submariner again.

CHAPTER EIGHT

It was almost twelve thirty. The Ministers, with four hours sleep and lunch under their belts, were gathered again in the Fahr House basement. Rebecca was in her room, nursing her period, which seemed to have intensified since Charley left. She hadn't spoken to him again, simply asking Deville if he would send a vehicle to the Crown & Anchor and get Charley to the bank in Seahouses. After that, her transient husband was on his own, another stupid dream shattered. Deville hadn't been surprised to hear Charley was leaving the island. Or that it probably meant he was leaving Rebecca, as in *finito*. He hadn't even reminded her of the pitfalls of impulsive behaviour, for which she was duly grateful.

She was calming down now, thinking that it might be all for the best, and whether Las Vegas might be a viable next option. Did they have Little White Divorces in Vegas, she wondered, as well as Little White Weddings? Was it possible to arrange them by e-mail?

The Ministers were waiting for a call, but had no idea if and when they'd get one, or from whom. They were hoping it might be the British PM. Meanwhile, they were killing time looking at a photograph Max had sent through on Deville's mobile, and discussing something that had been a big issue during the recent referendum: immigration and second homes.

The photograph was of a newly-erected notice at the security gate, with the Snook of Holy Island, the tip of Charley's blearily-seen panhandle, in the background:

CROSS THE TIDAL FLATS AND YOU
ENTER A CHRISTIAN COMMUNITY

All weaponry and mobile phones are prohibited.
For security reasons, any head coverings that may impede identification must be removed and deposited here.
This includes helmets (therefore motor cycles), balaclavas, hoods, cowls, niqābs etc.
A full list of excluded items is available at Border Control.

BE WARNED
YOU WILL OTHERWISE BE REFUSED ENTRY

"Right on," Michael Cromarty said. "It hits the nail smack, bang on the head. We get to see people's full faces, in person or on camera. No more guns or knives or baseball bats. It should keep some of the creeps out altogether. Beats me why some of them came here anyway. Mobiles glued to their ears."

Deville had a moment wondering whether Christianity or security was the more important, but decided to let it pass. He sent a text to Max, telling him it looked fine, and that he hoped to be over later to see it.

"When in Rome, like the man said. Hell, it's the same as being asked to cover up in some countries, isn't it? Take your damn shoes off, that sort of thing," Jim "Cochise" Redman said.

With a name like Redman, he figured he'd escaped lightly. Truth be told, he quite enjoyed the nickname. Not everyone had an Apache Indian chief, real or imagined, as an ancestor. It had given Cochise an avid interest in the independent status of present-day American Indian reservations and their Tribal Councils, and a certain cachet in the recent referendum. It had pretty much made him an expert on the subject of secession, and he'd had more than a measly glass of beer in The Ship's bar because of that. He looked the part too, muscled from his building work, with thick dark locks and prominent cheekbones. He even had a homemade turkey feather headdress stashed under wraps on top of his bedroom wardrobe, and knew of a mail-order firm that had all sorts of similar things in stock.

Deville looked at his younger son and daughter. "So you two, fire away, tell us what you've unearthed on the thorny question of second homes."

"You've had the earlier articles, *The Telegraph*, *The Guardian*'s attempt at pros and cons," Alistair said. "But a lot of what we've seen isn't relevant to Holy Island. A lot of places have expressed concern about second homes, and others have pointed out what they think are benefits. But they're not always on the same track as us."

"You have examples?" Minister-teacher Elizabeth Swan asked.

"To a point. The issue crops up in planning authority minutes all the time; whether there's a way to reserve or allocate houses for locals. One MP in Bath has suggested people should have to apply for change of use to convert a house to holiday use. Another, Michael Meacher MP, has also been beating the drum. Appledore in North Devon at one point threatened to paint a black spot on holiday homes. They probably got the idea from the Great Plague, felt it had something in common. Porthleven, an old fishing village in Cornwall, has recently been up in arms. Their MP has been proposing new planning and/or taxation controls. A fringe outfit called the Cornwall National Liberation Army, a bedfellow he would probably jump out of a spacecraft to escape, has been making all sorts of waves, including but by no means limited to second homes. We had the Welsh in the '80s, burning them down; direct action in spades. And over the Channel, Breton nationalist groups are just as fed up with Brits in general. Mostly, but not exclusively, southern Brits. Second homes are feeling the backlash there too. In Provence, the Algarve, the Costa del Sol and the rest. It's quite a reputation to be getting."

"Aye, right. And who's saying there are benefits?" Cochise asked.

"It's a global thing, don't forget," Alistair replied. "At least in the U.S. and in many European countries like France, Spain, Italy, Portugal, Croatia, Poland and Hungary. There are places with depopulation problems, and some are saying better some life than no life at all. Communities in the U.S. claim that second homers have come in precisely because they're interested in natural beauty and conservation, if you can call artificial lakes and theme parks natural beauty. Some people argue that second home ownership brings wealth, better services, social cohesion; that it supports local jobs, like builders, plumbers, and so on—"

"*What?* Who are they, for Christ's sake?" Minister-builder Cochise again. Fuckers forever speaking with forked tongues, right down through Wild West history.

"Oh, some wealthier firms of estate agents, or those with wealthier clients. A major London outfit, people like that."

"Yeah, yeah. No vested interests there, then." Great White Fathers? Cochise thought. Fucking great white sharks, more like.

"These people would do themselves a favour if they were to keep their own counsel," said Elizabeth Swan, thinking of her school, once mothballed.

"But then we have the other side of the argument," Sarah said. "Spiralling house prices, out-migration of young people, *cuts* in services, overpopulation in the high season, ghost towns in the low, losses in local culture, social meltdown. The figure that keeps socking us between the eyes is that over half the houses on Holy Island, approaching fifty, are now second or letting homes. It's not a big figure, but it's a big proportion. And growing."

"Right. So what do we do about it?" Michael Cromarty asked. "Apart from anything else, it's *immoral* to have people with homes all over the shop when other folks have none. Take those bloody Beckhams." Michael Cromarty, a lifelong supporter of Newcastle United, had been singularly unimpressed by David Beckham's skills when Manchester United graced the verdant turf of Newcastle's St. James's Park. At one point in 1996, Manchester United had trailed ten points behind Newcastle, yet went on to win the Premiership; then rubbed "Magpie" noses further in it by beating them in the 1999 FA Cup Final. That was their "treble" year, when they'd won every damn trophy worth winning. But almost *every* year was a pain with those highfalutin bastards. Nine out of the last fifteen Premiership titles, the top flight of British soccer. It was sheer bloody greed, Cromarty thought, no other word for it.

"We've been looking at Guernsey," Alistair said. "It's not a wholly parallel case, but it's interesting. Much bigger of course, over 60,000 people and 20,000 households. But they have a system with clear links between immigration and housing, work and environment. It hangs together. They don't have a big second home problem, their problem is population control, keeping people and jobs and services in balance."

"So how do they do it?" Minister Tom Walker, chronically overweight and asthmatic, had been silent, suffering from lack of sleep, but he was by nature taciturn. He had been brought up to speak only when spoken to and was reluctant to change the habit. Of late, though, some doubts had started to creep in. Now that he was a politician, he had begun to suspect he might be labouring under a crippling disadvantage.

"First, they're entitled to restrict immigration," Alistair said. "The European Union's freedom of movement rule doesn't apply. They can export to EU countries, without any tariff barriers, and other EU rules have been waived."

"Nice…for them," Tom Walker said, shifting in his chair, wheezing, and fumbling in a briefcase for his inhaler. "Freedom…of movement. Well, yon place we were a piece of till midnight has that in spades, mainly inward. You should know, boyo, all those degrees and all. Would this be…the first time in history the rats have swum in and sunk the bloody ship?"

Alistair smiled. "It could be. Although you could argue the ship's not quite sunk yet, just floundering. Still, Guernsey has special dispensation. And for good reasons, reasons that might be just as valid for other islands. Except they don't have Guernsey's history or constitution."

"So how…do they do it?" Tom Walker repeated. His last effort had exhausted him and he couldn't think of anything better to say before he nodded off. Not for the first time, he thought the damn inhaler might contain a soporific.

"They divide their housing market into local properties, about ninety percent of the total, and 1,600 open market properties. Anyone can live in an open market property, although they obviously pay a premium, but those properties are subject to strict controls. They can only be occupied by people who qualify. And qualification includes being born in Guernsey, being born to at least one Guernsey parent, sharing a property with a qualified person, or getting a housing licence. Once you're qualified as a local, you're a local for life, even if you live away for a time. Housing licences are for fixed periods, usually as long as the person is employed by a specified employer, and between three and five years. Sometimes longer. The point is, or one point is, it's the *occupation* of houses that's controlled, not the house itself. There are empty houses on Guernsey, not everything in the garden is lovely. Someone whose licence expires can still own a house, but not live in it."

"It sounds as if they have it pretty well sewn up, though," Elizabeth Swan said thoughtfully. "There are bits there we could use."

"Yes. Their system's been going a long time and they've ironed out blips along the way," Sarah said. "Another interesting thing is that there are States Houses, owned by the States of Guernsey. They're the biggest social landlord on the island, and manage about 2,000 properties. But, as Alistair says, they're not happy. They say the operation of their housing market needs"—she waved quotation marks in the air—"'innovative initiatives.' They have some poor housing, some under-occupation."

"Christ, we should have their problems," Cochise said. His kin were still living in wigwams, for fuck's sake.

Alex Deville stirred, thinking: where's the phone call? Young Max hadn't cut the lines by mistake with his grabs and bulldozers, had he? "So, have you two got anything ready on how we might proceed?" he asked.

"We tried to cobble something together," his son said. "It's rough but it's a start. Sarah?"

"Okay," Sarah said. "We have a list of six points. We need to make copies for you, but we think when you've had a look and made suggestions, we could put them, or something like them, to the next public meeting. Here goes:

"One. Like Australia, our immigration policy should be geared towards young people, up to middle age, with good command of the English language. Prospective immigrants are assessed and, if approved, should be given residential and work permits, similar to Guernsey, initially for five years.

"Two. The Althing, in effect the people of Holy Island, should take direct charge of buying and selling houses. We would only need outside agencies if we actively wanted to encourage immigration, and maybe not then. We charge a flat fee of £250, say, to the seller, and we need to work on our Land Register."

She paused, glancing at them under her eyelashes. She and Alistair had done their best, but with this newly elected lot, gung-ho to write their names at the top of a long and glorious roll-call, and join the great Saints in the annals of Holy Island, there was no telling whether it would be good enough. She was encouraged to see a nod or two, a wink from her father.

"Three. We take the Council Tax register and write to householders who are not permanently resident. We offer them two options; either sell to us at the price they originally paid—we might add inflation, but based only on the RPI or bank rate since whenever that was—or they commit to occupying the property for at least twenty-six weeks in any one year. If they take neither option, the house will be compulsorily purchased on a sliding scale of compensation, say, at 100 percent of what they paid for it pre-1990 or 75 percent post-1990. Those figures also need further work, they're cockshies.

"Four. We market the houses released by this process, initially to local people, at a price set by the Althing. If there are no local buyers, we market them more widely, but under the same rules that apply to immigration and the commitment to occupy the property for a minimum of six months.

"Five. No one on this island is allowed to own more than one house. Different generations of a family may own different houses, and houses may be held in trust for children, always provided they are properly maintained.

"Six. Any surplus properties are taken over by the Althing as Althing Houses, similar to States Houses in Guernsey, and used for social purposes like sheltered housing, or for essential workers like the new policeman or doctor." Sarah looked around the room. "How does that sound, as a start?"

"It sounds fine," Cochise said, flipping his locks over his shoulders and thinking yeah, outstanding ass, but the white squaw has brains as well as beauty. "Okay, we need to powwow on it, but it's right on line."

Deville dredged up a smile. "Good job, both of you," he said to the nodding of heads. "Food for thought."

"Anything else you want us to look at?" Alistair asked. "As Sarah said, we have things to follow up, but what else is there?"

"You couldn't get into that high security remote access system they have in Number Ten, could you? It would be nice to know what they're thinking, and how they might be tapping in to us. Or failing that, GCHQ?"

"No. Way beyond me," his son smiled. "You might advertise for an ace hacker. Someone aged ten or so who'd like to earn some pocket money and wouldn't mind a long jail term."

"Just joking. You could press on with how we handle the Exchequer, Revenue and Customs. Job opportunities. Tourism: offering good services, getting the right people. Recycling waste: we need to start researching major British companies that might be willing to help with that. And—"

"Hey," his son said, "I didn't mean you to come up with six points of your own."

"There are more like sixty before this is finished," Deville told him. "I was going to remind you of a hobby of yours. New hi-tech industry, your brainstorming ideas. Get those moving, and it'll be a big step forward. And by the way, when it comes to sustainability, have a look at the Schumacher Society in Massachusetts. They seem to be doing some interesting stuff. And there are areas Max will be working on... but let's see how things are going elsewhere."

He switched on the One O'clock News. A reporter was introducing the top story; the Castle, icon of the island, in the background. Deville was pleased to see the man was smiling.

"Today, the Holy Island of Lindisfarne, a small speck off the north-east Northumbrian coast, seceded from the United Kingdom, achieving in one decisive stroke what others—Scotland, Wales, Cornwall, Shetland come to mind—have compromised on, or toyed with, in the past..."

Deville let the TV burble on, but switched himself off. He had been interviewed earlier but didn't think he appeared at his best on camera. Not photogenic, too gaunt. He'd be receiving junk mail for the next year asking him if he wanted a makeover or TV training, he thought wryly.

He had lost count of the interviews he'd given during the morning. They had blended together in a fuzzy mass. How did we all manage in the days of Pathe News and the wireless? he asked himself. It must have been bliss, too bad those plummy voices and grainy newsreels and people who actually read the news had been consumed in the fires of progress. Holy Island might have seen two or three reporters to cover the story then; now, there were twenty or thirty. Plus their hangers-on and gear. Still, he would use them, by God he would.

It crossed his mind to give Rebecca a shout, to see if she wanted to join the group. Why not? It was always good to have other perspectives. And she had to be hurting; she'd been on a two-day emotional roller-coaster. That trouble-maker she'd somehow managed to...He shrugged, half listening to the end of the report, watching his fellow-islanders being interviewed, thinking it had come across as sympathetic, exactly the right note to start on. His four colleagues seemed pleased, applauding the comments of some of their friends. The best part of it was, not the slightest vestige of a crack had appeared in their unanimity.

He thought he might have a word with his new houseguest. Young George (for some reason, his daughter had forbidden the use of "Geordie") seemed bright enough, and Amy had taken to him...it would be interesting to see if there was a way of syndicating his material more widely. He was just about to call Rebecca when the phone rang.

Deville switched on the recording machine.

If someone had asked Alex Deville to describe the British Prime Minister in a few well-chosen words, he would have said he'd be happy to oblige if he knew which part was real. At least, that was what he would have said in a generous mood. For a cardboard cut-out, the man made a passable warmonger.

But to be fair, he would have given the same answer if he'd been asked to describe the last five Leaders of Her Majesty's Opposition. Was there a production line of these animated zombies in some dark Committee Room? And here was the most recent example on the phone; the PM himself, the man who would walk on water but was likely to drown in sand. No doubt hoping to reinvent himself, in the not too dim and distant future, as a carpetbagging global plenipotentiary. And being affable. Wouldn't you just know it? No doubt having been plugged in to the lunchtime news himself:

PM: Mr. Deville. Good afternoon. How nice to speak to you. Now, you're not seriously proposing to proceed with this farce, are you? As if we didn't have enough problems with the Scots (*a chuckle*).

AD: Good afternoon, Mr. Prime Minister. It is not a proposal, far less a farce. Last night, as I told your esteemed colleague earlier today, it became a fact. Perhaps he told you this, although he appeared not to grasp it.

PM: Well, let me be quite clear, we can't allow it, you know. Speaking constitutionally, you're legless (*ha, ha*). You may stir things up for a while, have some fun, but I've no doubt reality will set in.

AD: I wonder whose reality, Mr. Prime Minister. We have no doubts about ours. Your government, on the other hand, has no great track record in dealing with it. Iraq, for example, drags on. And I see the SNP have tried to encourage you to face it.

PM: (*After a pause.*) We must begin to think of ways out of this. I have no wish to cause you embarrassment, to appear heavy-handed or insensitive to your...feelings. But—

AD: We have no intention of finding a way out of this. We are in this and intend to pursue it. That is the reality. As I suggested to your colleague, take Holy Island's secession as your starting point and we'll make progress. Imagine we are not serious, or will lie down and *wilt*, and you'll find you're confronting brick walls.

PM: Speaking of walls, I see from the news that you have already taken some rather rash steps, if I may say so. Security fencing, the causeway and so on. I believe I even saw a border control gate, of all things. You'll have to put it all back, you know.

AD: I disagree. It is an essential part of what we are about.

PM: No, no, far from it. It is a destruction of a public asset. Criminal damage. And to what end? You are cutting off your nose to—

AD: We have vehicles that will provide a safe public service. It can't have escaped your attention that lives have been put at risk on the causeway as it was. Also, there has been as much construction as demolition. Both were necessary first steps.

PM: We need to talk about this. Face-to-face. We seem to be accomplishing very little by telephone.

AD: Nothing, Mr. Prime Minister. Not very little. Nothing.

PM: Would you agree to visit London? Meet my colleagues?

AD: Neither.

PM: Oh, come, come. That is quite unreasonable. You have occupied an hour of the Cabinet's time this morning and I can tell you there are those of my colleagues who do not intend to have you occupy any more. As if the Scots weren't enough.

AD: Oh? And what are these colleagues suggesting? That they will accept this *fait accompli* for what it is? And by the way, when you say 'Scots', are you forgetting that non-Scots live in Scotland? And may well have used their vote to register their own dissatisfaction with your Holyrood colleagues? Are you suggesting only native Scots could have voted Scottish Nationalist?

PM: Ummm...that's not the issue here. As to a *fait accompli*, certainly not, quite the reverse. Look, let me leave you in no doubt they are of a mind to—(*background noises*)

AD: To what, Mr. Prime Minister? To send in the troops, declare martial law? Sanctions or blockades? Echoes of the Rhodesian solution? A bit draconian, wouldn't you say?

(*Deville was tempted to sow some seeds on consensual secession, primary right theory, plebiscitary theory, all that stuff he'd been boning up on, but decided no, too soon, too complicated, keep it simple, wait and see.*)

PM: As I said, I think we should meet. You will need to arrange—

AD: And what would be the purpose of such a meeting? Other than spin?

(*Voice in the background: "Don't let him ask the questions..."*)

PM: To discuss, explore, *stress* the precariousness of your position.

AD: But you have already done so, as has your Home Secretary. I don't intend to elevate it to the status of face-to-face dialogue. Your Home Secretary has said our secession is illegal. I have said his opinion is irrelevant. This island has *de facto* seceded.

PM: I would advise you to think long and hard about the consequences.

AD: Consequences, Mr. Prime Minister? What would they be? As far as everyone on this island is concerned, we have removed ourselves from the whims of Westminster, Brussels and Strasbourg and will retrieve our culture and forge our own society. We see nothing but benefits in that.

PM: Moments ago, you seemed to have a very clear idea of possible consequences. I repeat, and I hope I am perfectly clear, we can't allow this so-called secession of yours. Which I am advised, from what you said earlier and have said now, might more accurately be termed a revolution. Since you appear set on replacing your government rather than merely rejecting it.

AD: Splitting hairs, Mr. Prime Minister? Muddying the waters? Calling us rebels? Are you saying mere rejection would be acceptable? We are happy with the term secession, as agreed by *all* of our people, and my question is, how do you intend to deal with it?

PM: This is going nowhere. I will—

AD: And I have another question I'd like you to consider. Are you surprised that part of what used to be Britain has taken this course? Are you so out of touch? Now that politics in Britain and America, countries once known for decency and democracy, seems to be a matter of marketing rather than principle, are you surprised that your two governments are held in contempt? Internally as well as externally?

PM: That is three questions. Government, sir, is more complex than you seem to appreciate. I will call you back when you have had time to reflect. Or have someone call you back. Meantime, advise your people that this venture is doomed to failure.

AD: I think not. Good afternoon, Mr. Prime Minister. I should say, incidentally, that we are reasonably content with the first items of news coverage. What did you think?

PM: I'm so glad to hear it. But they do tend to turn around and bite you, these people. I look forward to that. Good afternoon, Mr. Deville.

"Do you think you should meet them?" Elizabeth Swan asked.

"No way," Tom Walker wheezed. The telephone had woken him up. "That would give *them* legitimacy. People...would think we were having second thoughts."

"You're right, Tom. Not now, but maybe eventually." Deville switched off the recorder. "We'll see how it goes first. Strange how there are always hawks and doves. Or perhaps not, perhaps it's just the way of the world. We'll see who looks like edging ahead before we consider any meetings."

"I think that's sensible," Elizabeth Swan said. "And let's ask ourselves again: in their shoes, what would we do? What *could* we do?"

"Bugger all," Cochise said. "At the end of the day, what?"

"Chatter. Run around like headless chickens," Michael Cromarty said. "Gnash their teeth. Look like the dweebs they've always been."

"They might fly up here," Cochise said, with something approaching gleeful anticipation. "They'd just be bloody ignorant enough to try setting Royal Air Force One or whatever down on the Swad or Fenham Flats. That'd be something. Great White Bird falls from the sky, loses Great White Father and troops in the Low. Could solve all our problems at once."

"For pity's sake, Jim," Elizabeth Swan said sternly, as if he were ten years old and back in the little school. "You're talking like something out of a Western B-movie!"

"Dream on, Jim," Deville said. "We'd still have the next bunch to deal with, and recent history suggests they'd be no better, whatever colour they might be. No. They will talk, feel insulted, get angry, haul the constitutional experts in, look at options, then either the hawks or doves will come out to play. But let's not forget, we have several things in our favour. First, everyone is of the same mind, everyone is with us. We need to keep it that way. Second, we're well funded, there's no chance of that causing us problems. Third, others are watching with interest and will lend their support if needed. Fourth, we'll be seen as the underdogs; David and Goliath always was a good story. Fifth, they have other constitutional balls to juggle; their difficulties with Scotland, getting Stormont back off the ground, the loss of many of their local power-bases and foot soldiers, their internal succession issue and its consequent reshuffling. And sixth, we have time. We can use it in the media skirmish that will no doubt ensue, and we can use it to put more distance, more obstacles, between them and us. Physical, political, and psychological."

"Amen to all that," Cochise said.

"But what do you think he'll do?" Elizabeth Swan asked again. "What would you do in his shoes?"

"A blockade," Deville said. "Stop people leaving by road. It wouldn't be the complete solution, of course, there's always the sea, but after a month or so it would be debilitating. He might hope a few of us would get second thoughts. With summer on the way, the tourist providers would suffer. If he does take that route, we may need to give them some help."

"Do you think he will?"

"My guess would be he'll want something more dramatic. He's that sort. Something to demonstrate strength. Prop his ego. Decorate his legacy. And it would be out of character for him to think things through. But these are hypotheses, and early days. For us, the important thing is solidarity. And we should never forget what's posted on that wall," Deville said, pointing to a framed paragraph.

"When any form of Government becomes destructive of these ends (Life, Liberty and the pursuit of Happiness), it is the right of the people to alter or abolish it, institute new Government, laying its foundations on such principles and organizing its powers in such form as shall seem most likely to effect their Safety and Happiness."

Declaration of Independence of the 13 United States, The Fourth of July, 1776.

"Well, you're not Thomas Jefferson, Alex man," Michael Cromarty said, "and we aren't America. But you held up our end all right in that little chat."

"Kind of you to say so, Michael," Deville said.

There were times, he thought witheringly, looking at Jim Redman, when he had serious doubts about the democratic process. If ever a man could go off script, it would be Cochise. But he thanked them all for coming and hoped they'd have no more interruptions today. He asked Sarah if she would type up a transcript and take Rebecca and George on the rounds again. The islanders could read newspapers and listen to TV as well as he, but he had given a solemn undertaking to copy verbatim all conversations with representatives of the British Government. And he would do it. Whatever other priorities he had, Deville was determined that cynicism about politics and politicians should be killed stone dead.

The first few hours could have been a lot worse, he thought. Thank goodness he hadn't had someone less amenable, less airy-fairy, on the other end of the line. God knows, he could have been chewed up and spat out by a Margaret Thatcher or Norman Tebbitt. The British system was truly remarkable, how nine times out of ten the whey kept floating to the top.

He thought of Cochise again and shivered. The idea of *Cochise* running the store? The numbskull would outlaw mobiles, and have smoke signals instead. The drafting of a succession plan was becoming more essential by the day. He couldn't have the whey, or worse, floating to the top in the neonatal State of Holy Island, could he?

CHAPTER NINE

The following Saturday, twelfth May, Our Man in Holy Island was up at seven thirty, fighting a rearguard action to remain in Holy Island. Against all his better instincts, against all he'd been taught of journalism, the place was weaving a powerful spell. Geordie was also very comfortable, seductively so, in a house the like of which he had previously seen only in *The English Home* magazine, and in a bedroom that had everything he imagined a 5-star hotel would provide. It not only gave him the luxury of a four-poster bed, 3-inch deep carpeting, a coffee-making machine, a 32-inch TV, a trouser press and a view of Pilgrim's Way, it even had internet access. The only snag being, it was about a quarter of a mile from Sarah's.

Geordie thought he was winning, with a little help from his friends. The village was quiet this morning, and most of the competition had either gone for the weekend or were chasing after breaking stories elsewhere. They'd been doing it all week. Well, they were welcome to the all-pals-together Stormont tea-party, the Liberal Democrats playing ducks and drakes in Scotland, the absurdity that went by the name of a Labour leadership election, Brussels granting (*granting*!) an "indefinite extension" to dual-labelling. My word, he thought, in ten years time we could still be driving on the left, eating Craster kippers and drinking Somerset cider, who knew where their generosity would end? But it would take a miracle of readjustment, given that most "British" legislation now originated in Brussels and whole swathes of government—agriculture, fisheries (what were left of them), competition policy and so on—had been handed to the EU. Not, of course, that the government would ever tell you so. It would be tantamount to saying they were becoming superfluous, and that they, and civil servants, should be culled. Think of all the heartache that would cause. People would be going about crying into their Belgian beer.

Old Smokey was welcome to the crowning of Monsieur Maggie in Paris too. Probably, between coughs, he'd get Sarkozy mixed up with a brand of jewellery, or Russian vodka.

Geordie felt sure the whole lot wouldn't find anything better than was happening here. The more he thought about it, the more heaven-sent the Lindisfarne story became. It had intrigue, politics, characters, humour, and a matchless *mise en scène*. It was short on sex and violence, but sex and violence, thanks to TV and the tabloids, had become commonplace anyway. If people wanted them, they could read the sports pages, watch the News, or buy *Cosmo*.

As flexibility had been needed on the accommodation front, an assortment of camper vans, tents and other bits of human debris had gone with the departing reporters. It had been a cool, showery week and not everyone had found conditions to their liking. The weekend before, an ITV guy had made a total ass of himself, thrown a tantrum when he hadn't found a hotel room, got plastered, bored the daylights out of The Ship's clientele, and left in a sulk when his bosses told him they'd settle for feed from Tyne Tees TV, their regional channel.

Geordie had completed a great week, and filed the thick end of 20,000 words. The Editor had been delighted, and even Old Smokey had been grudgingly impressed. If Holy Island's secession had been the platform, the bread-and-butter that had once or twice edged up the culinary scale into five-star cordon bleu—as when Max had confiscated a .22 rifle from a corduroyed youth in a Range Rover and bent it U-shaped over his knee—the story of George the Vietnamese pot-bellied pig had been the highlight.

He'd learned a lot about the island during the week too, although it seemed the more he learned, the more surprises were waiting around the corner. He had spent a whole day in the Heritage Centre, buying books, browsing through the Museum of Island Life displays, reading extracts from the Gospels, leafing through anecdotal files, and listening to the video clips of native and adopted Holy Islanders. He had visited the Priory Museum more than once, St. Cuthbert's Centre, St. Aidan's Church, the Open Gate Retreat, and the school. The pubs of course, each evening. The history of the local lifeboat, displayed on a wall opposite the Museum, had drawn him back several times. What stories, mishaps, and crises were hidden in those bald descriptions! If only he had two weeks more, or three, or four, he'd follow up on a few of them…

The Parish Church, St. Mary's, had made him wish he had more faith. He'd almost been able to touch the aura of the place, and certainly other visitors had felt the same. Some of them seemed captivated by it. They wandered through the place as if spellbound, drinking in the very air. What a magical place, to be able to reach so effortlessly into modern souls. What blessed relief *for* the modern souls. And what a blessing for the community, evident most of all in the work of children displayed along the south aisle. *Suffer the little children…*he remembered that one. Geordie had reached the view that the small church put many others to shame. He recalled his reaction to Christchurch Cathedral, which he'd visited with his Mum a year or so before she died. A money machine, as soulful as a bank.

He'd woven many of these things into stories. *En passant*, casual, *causal*, not to give the readership problems over their cornflakes, or collect howls of derision from Old Smokey, but to try to give a flavour of what was going on, and *why*.

In the whole week, he hadn't met a single person who had been hostile. People had talked to him openly. How unusual was that? An incomer welcomed? A journalist treated as human? No one back at Groat Market would believe it. He'd wondered how much of it had to do with Deville, the man who could be taken, albeit erroneously, as his mentor. Sure, the guy had been hospitable and helpful, always available for an interview, but never demanding or meddlesome. Geordie lived in hope that his daughter might have had a hand in his welcome too.

And there had been another unusual thing. All these people weren't singing from the same song sheet; nothing so boring. The cumulative effect was more like a symphony orchestra. Different musicians, different instruments, slow sections, quick sections (he didn't know the musical terms), but coming together, and in a crescendo. People had different takes on the secession, including Deville, Sarah, Amy, Alistair, the Ministers (he hadn't fathomed Cochise's take), Trevor Patterson, shopkeepers, fishermen, landlords, landladies, pub staff and everyone else he'd met, but they were all in concert when it came to the finale. They wanted out for all sorts of reasons, but every last one hoped to build something better.

The Rebecca-Charley piece had been binned. Sarah Deville had made it clear, should she come across a reference to it in *The Northern Sun*, the church magazine or anywhere else, that Geordie would be held guilty of a Gross Abuse of Hospitality. Geordie, who had been feeling downright libidinous every time Sarah appeared in the same room, had decided the whole thing was rubbish anyway. Not worth the paper it would have been printed on.

He'd had daily check-up calls from his girlfriend back in Newcastle, but then she'd never been much more than a diversion. She'd told him last night that she'd be going clubbing with her pals in the big city and he, Geordie, could stick his job, his Vietnamese pig, his crummy French car, and Holy Island, where the sun don't shine.

Geordie was no fool, and had taken this as a fond farewell.

And let's be honest, it hadn't lost him any sleep. Rightly or wrongly, he'd developed a deep liking for Holy Island and, with the exception of Sarah, it consumed all his energies. He wondered if part of this was because he was a northerner himself, born little more than fifty miles down the road, and whether readers of *The Northern Sun* would feel the same way. Some would know it as well as he, or better. Would it strike any chords southwards? Not that the paper had many readers southwards, émigré Geordies apart, but he knew some of his pieces had been picked up and quoted elsewhere. In rare egocentric moments, he had wondered how many of the small stones he had thrown in the pond had had a ripple effect.

In all his conversations and readings, he had come to appreciate just how much the place had its own character. And this in turn had led him down a path he felt intellectually inadequate to walk. On the one hand, people were inclined to admire stubborn individuality, weren't they? How often, in shops or pubs or social clubs, did you overhear phrases like "he's a one-off," or, "there aren't any characters any more"? On the other hand, the history of the world until now had demonstrated a successive breaking-down of barriers: individual, tribal, regional, and national. These days, provided you weren't suppressed in something bigger, nothing less than a global construction would do. Then add to that the blind resolve of governments to enforce conformity in whatever ways they could. The EU, for instance, until you looked closely and saw member states (except Britain, ever the sovereign dupe) blithely doing their own thing. The Italians, jailing people for months without trial. The Portuguese, with as much knowledge of investigative good practice as Inspector Clouseau. The Greeks, with toilets that couldn't cope with paper and playing backgammon on pavements. Decidedly character-forming: stubborn individualism, you might say.

Geordie hadn't heard of any of these countries, except Denmark, throwing the dummy when it came to things European. Maybe it was a mainland, continental, thing. But then you had Ireland, one of their success stories...Or maybe it was the nature of Mediterranean-style diplomacy. Espressos and wine on sun-kissed piazzas and terraces. It just wasn't the same at Westminster; even on its best days the Thames looked sluggish and sullen, and on its worst days Baltic. Maybe these other countries just took the money and went on doing their own thing. He knew there were 70-odd billion pounds in the annual EU budget, and they hadn't been able to balance the books since the mid-nineties. Geordie, all those hours of research at Groat Market behind him, knew as much as he needed to know about EU corruption, fraud, waste, milch cows and skewed "internal" audits—except of course in Britain, who thought it only fair to be transparent with its cock-ups...

Alex Deville would have a view. It was a theme germane to the secession. And if Geordie had ever met anyone in his life qualified to speak globally, it was Deville.

For instance, first thing on Monday morning, Deville had asked him if he was able to farm out his stories to other papers. Geordie had said sorry, no. Deville had then phoned "a pal in the World Bank, a colleague of my brother" to ask if this pal would be very kind and speak to the editor of the *Washington Post*. Deville had smiled at Geordie, reminded him that they were interested in politics in Washington DC and, even if this was only small faraway politics, it was worth a mention. After all, there were secessionist movements in several hundred other places in the world, probably half of which America had ambitions to invade, and over a dozen in America itself. Holy Island could be held up as an unfolding case study.

And so the ripple had spread. Geordie's stories, spell-checked in U.S. English and e-mailed across the pond, had begun to appear under the somewhat inaccurate tag of "Our Special UK Correspondent." It wasn't as good as having your name in lights, but it *was* the *Washington Post*. Well, shit, Geordie thought, who could give a damn about bylines when they were following a trail blazed by Carl Bernstein and Bob Woodward, not forgetting editor Bradlee and all those other determined, and sometimes fearful, newshounds.

Then, yesterday evening, threatened by his own editor with a return to base come Monday, Geordie had received another injection of Deville goodwill. The guy had lifted the phone and told the old man it might be premature to think of recalling Geordie just yet, "Things might start to boil up again this week, you know." The old man, being an inveterate newshound himself, had tried to press Deville for details, but Deville had said, "No, just a feeling, but sooner or later they'll come out of hibernation in Westminster." The two of them had finished by having a laugh about something, all good buddies together, and Geordie had woken up bright and early this morning with every expectation of getting a call to confirm his stay would be prolonged. Hospitable and helpful? The guy was heaven-sent.

So, with luck, he'd spend more salad days in the sunshine and showers, not to mention in the company of Sarah Deville.

Geordie almost gave himself a quiet *¡vale!* but remembered in time that Sarah, Rebecca, Alistair, his friend Amy and, according to Amy, George her Vietnamese potbelly, had banned the further use of phrasebook Spanish.

"How do you manage to write so well when you litter your conversation with that rubbish?" Amy had asked him.

He had mumbled about holidays, but it hadn't gone down too well. In fact, he had been vigorously accused of massacring an inoffensive language. So at Amy's insistence, he had put Spanish on the back burner, at least until he had time to give it some serious attention.

But the Vietnamese potbelly was something else. Now that the two Georges had been properly introduced, George the pig had even allowed George the journalist to take him in his harness for a walk. Amy did this every day, the two of them, little old lady and pet, wandering the village streets and shoreline just as anyone might walk their dog. To the locals, they were nothing short of an institution, but visitors were sometimes taken aback. One or two had been seen crossing the street when Amy and George approached, shielding their eyes as though overcome by a sudden desperate need for the shadier side. Amy had told Geordie she thanked

God every day her little pig hadn't been there when she was mugged; "He'd have been traumatised, poor wee thing." But she had some hilarious tales, including the time George waddled into the Post Office with her and decided that the lettuce in another customer's hand was too good to miss.

"You could've heard the screams in Berwick," Amy said, giving George a pat on his pug nose. "He's a bit short-sighted, but there's nothing wrong with his sense of smell or his hearing. That lettuce smelt delicious but the silly woman nearly deafened him. Went off like a fire alarm, didn't she, pet?"

Geordie learned to his cost that Amy kept a tight grip on George's diet, and was roundly rebuked for offering him a crisp. The miniature pig got plenty of water and the occasional piece of fruit or vegetable as a treat; especially raisins, which he loved. But his main meal was specially formulated, and he managed on a cup of it each day. He was housebroken, had his own patch of grass and litter box, and a repertoire of tricks that included blowing a kiss, jumping over a skipping rope and praying. This *was* Holy Island, after all! He knew very well when he was the centre of attention and had a variety of squeaks, grunts, gurgles and sneezes when he wasn't.

George the pig was about three feet long and eighteen inches high, with blue eyes. Apart from his saddle back, pronounced pot belly and straight tail, he was the archetypal piglet. Only Amy would have had any chance of picking him up though, and she wasn't strong enough. He'd once squealed in alarm when Geordie had tried it, and Amy had gone ballistic.

"*Stop that,* young Geordie. He's not a cat or dog, for heaven's sake. He's vulnerable. He's *prey*. He gets upset if he thinks he's threatened. Don't you ever try to lift him again, you daft so-and-so."

It had taken Geordie the best part of an afternoon to get back into Amy and George's good books.

"He's a barrow," Amy said when she'd calmed down and started talking to him again.

"He's a barrel, all right," Geordie said, relieved all was well.

"*Barrow,* you chump," Amy laughed. "Know what that means? Ha! I bet you wouldn't want to know, my lad, if it was you in the operating theatre." A wink to Sarah and Rebecca. "Neutered, poor little pet, when he was two months old. Well, he may not get all the fun he should out of life, but it's been a big plus. Means he doesn't stink the place out. You can hardly smell him, can you?"

"No, you can't. How old is he now?"

"He's eight. Been full grown for the last three, four years."

Geordie was fascinated.

The little thing could even *trot*. He was as friendly and as inquisitive as a puppy, often poking his snout into Geordie's jacket pocket and, much to Geordie's silent amusement, between Rebecca's legs. He liked nothing better than to have his belly rubbed, and would pester anyone who obliged for ten minutes after they'd stopped.

Encouraged by Amy, with help from Rebecca and a smattering of knowledge from her biosciences course, he put together the sometimes touching, sometimes amusing, always entertaining tale of George the Vietnamese potbelly and his Holy Island home. He wrote the story in Amy's house, consuming cups of tea and fruit cake every ten minutes.

It had an important side effect.

If the Holy Islanders had been in any way short of sympathy before this article hit the front page of *The Northern Sun* and was picked up by other papers, *and* TV and radio, they weren't now. A little white-haired old lady, seventy-seven, twice widowed, victim of a mugging, and her cute little pig?

Only in Britain. Or only in Britain Past.

They became the talking point of every journey to work, every shopping trip, every home, every office, every remaining factory in the land. They became everyone's friends and, if Holy Island had still been part of Britain, national treasures.

Of course, as with other generalisations, there were one or two exceptions.

Alex Deville was delighted by it all. He could hear the gnashing of teeth in London from three hundred miles away. He could not have wished for better publicity if St. Cuthbert himself had descended from heaven, given his blessing to his ain folk, and struck Westminster dumb in the process.

He certainly could not have predicted his houseguest would repay him so handsomely or so quickly. Apart from all else, even if it was only temporary, it had taken some of the heat off Deville.

But there was to be no resting on laurels. Alex Deville was in no doubt that the forces of Westminster, the spin-doctors and ballyhoo-merchants, would be mustering. Okay, they may have had a little diversion while they spent a post-election week rubbishing the Scottish National Party, but their attention would be drifting back. He knew he was in for a PR battle. What could he do, what could Holy Island do, to blunt the barbs?

He had a few ideas to keep the bastards wrong-footed, only one directly involving him. He knew the risks in giving other people free rein, especially if their name was Cochise, but he also knew the rewards.

The vicar. The minister of the Parish Church of St. Mary the Virgin was a good man, a traditional caring pastor. Deville, who couldn't have been accused by his worst enemy of being a church-goer, had nevertheless always been a friend of St. Mary's, and for that matter the other churches, St. Cuthbert's and St. Aidan's. They all knew he was someone to call on for help when bits were falling off the roof or draughts were causing bronchitis epidemics. In return, out of the goodness of his heart and a deep distrust of the current British government, the vicar had offered his support in "our secession bid." It was time to ask for it.

Deville would suggest he went ahead on the cross-denominational front, spoke with his Bishop, and try to put together a visit by religious leaders and/or their representative bodies. As far as Deville was concerned, the vicar could muster as many and varied as he could find in the phone book: the Church of England, Roman Catholic Church, Buddhist Society, Muslim Council, Council of Christians & Jews, spokesmen for the Hindus and Sikhs, Mormons, Hare Krishnas, the whole pot-pourri. Personally, Deville couldn't care less if such a visit happened. It would be nice if it did, but the important thing was to be seen trying, to be seen as a community steeped in Christianity, extending an open-armed Christian welcome. And the minister could be relied upon wholeheartedly to try.

Then there was his friendly Scottish Nationalist MP. It was nearly time to table a Question, and who better? Labour MPs were at sixes and sevens, had been ever since the Devolution Bill in the 1970s, and the Scots Labour contingent at Westminster were clearly worried by the Nationalists. The Opposition, those old pillars of unionism, couldn't be expected to help at the best of times, and were fronted by a man who was ducking and weaving on every issue he faced. Why did these people keep electing greenhorns, especially greenhorns with selective hearing impediments? Weren't two lessons, or was it three, enough? Then there were the Liberals, among them the local MP, a classic case of lack of influence, lack of *power*, getting nobody anywhere. The local upgrading of the A1, the main north-south road link, which had been moribund for decades, was a good example. And he could recall the Liberal MP for Shetland making strangled noises when the Shetlanders decided to "have no truck with a Scottish Assembly" in the same 1970s Devolution debate.

No, the Nationalists would be on something of a high and could be guaranteed to make mischief. Deville, not quite half-joking, had suggested the Question: *Would the Prime Minister agree that the United Kingdom is breaking up faster than the Arctic ice-cap?* And a supplementary: *And would he tell us which is the more important in a global context?* But this had been dismissed, albeit with grim amusement, as not being of the correct format. He would leave it to the Nationalists to concoct something telling on their own. *After* consultation. Deville was in no way tempted to trust a party that embraced a mishmash of views ranging from Reaganomics to Leninism. It was a party he suspected would disintegrate into more conventional factions when their primary goal was achieved, but in times of need any weapon was better than none.

Then there was Geordie. He could do two things with Geordie, both of them today. The young journalist had been up early, doing his daily laundry (this as much as anything had impressed his host), and then taking what had become his regular morning constitutional around the village and harbour. Deville had heard him return, quietly as usual (another point in his favour), a few minutes ago.

"George," he shouted. "Come and have some breakfast. And bring those props of yours."

CHAPTER TEN

"Now, George," Deville said after the bacon and eggs and toast had been demolished, "I have a question. Do you believe there is any element of racism in what we're doing? A trace of xenophobia, perhaps?"

"It had crossed my mind. The hijab dress code reference on the security notice, the list of banned items, hints in other media, things like that. Nothing fearful or irrational, though. As in phobia." In Geordie's view, "phobia" was a word as badly abused as "legend" or "icon."

"Exactly. The niqāb reference to be precise, like other items, has to do with security. And the only thing somewhat to be feared is the direction that country is bent on taking. But it's worrying, isn't it?"

"You want to counter it."

"Exactly. Switch that on," pointing at Geordie's recorder. "Give your writing hand a break."

"On the record?"

"Run it past me first. I may be tempted to curse here or there, and wouldn't want that appearing anywhere."

"Okay." Geordie was once again encouraged. Like most reporters, he was used to concealment and evasion, and met them most days of his working life. For a politician, their absence was a pleasant change, and he was getting used to it with Deville.

"First, I would say I'm not racist, but I am most definitely prejudiced. I am prejudiced first and foremost against British quislings who stand for the British Parliament and then do their damnedest to destroy British values and screw things up for the British people. You see what I meant about being tempted to curse?"

"In high definition," Geordie said. "It might be difficult if you keep going on like that to capture the essence, as opposed to the colour, of what you're saying."

"Point taken. I'll try to do better. I am prejudiced against the European Union's freedom of movement policy and against a flood of immigrants so heavy, and this is by no means the sole fault of the European Union, that it is impossible to absorb them, or provide services to cope with them. Last year, 600,000 people arrived in Britain to work. In the first three months of this year, 680,000 arrived as 'temporary visitors' from the newest EU member states. Unbelievable figures, aren't they? And let no one be fooled, these are guesses in the guise of official statistics; the true count will be higher.

"But this is not the only myth the British government is promoting. In the last decade there have been 1.2 million 'official' immigrants, eight times the decade before, but only a quarter have come from Europe. Even after the EU was extended in 2004, the rest of the world accounted for two-thirds of incomers. That rather disproves, doesn't it, government protestations that nothing can be done, that it is all down to EU policy? The British government, had they wished, had every chance to limit immigration. Clearly, for whatever reason, they did not; they preferred their 'open door' nonsense. And whatever that government claims, however much they cloud the figures, however much they argue that these people make an economic contribution, this is a boom with no policy change or end in sight. Its net *cost* to Britain, when you take into account everything from race relations funding through education and translation services to crime, but excluding less tangible environmental and social costs, is running at £3 billion annually. By that, I mean a £9 billion economic cost against a £6 billion economic benefit. And many of these people will stay on. Last year actual immigrants, those who get citizenship, came in at a net rate of over five hundred a day. We hear that Britain will need ten cities the size of Birmingham to cope with population increase in the next quarter century, over three-quarters of the increase being immigrants and their offspring. Take a moment to think what that will do to the floodplains of England. And is this a reliable prediction? Again, not likely.

"*All* of these statistics will be low, since they've lost count of the legal immigrants, let alone the illegals. And yes, I am certainly prejudiced against some of them, whether they are white, black, brown or sky-blue pink, European, African, Asian or whatever, who seem to feel they are owed something, who ignore British values, who feel state benefits are theirs for the asking, or who set themselves apart or try to change *us*. That is not integration. Why, for example, should there be Associations of Black Police, Muslim Police, or Gay Police? Are they police or these other things? If they don't want to be *British* police, why employ them? Why distinguish them? Are they there to succour their minorities, give talks, act as tokens, or perform as police? Or again, why Muslim schools? Why should British society be expected to accept these people's version of 'integration?'"

Geordie stirred. "But there are schools, for example Cath—"

Deville waved a hand impatiently. "Don't give me Catholic schools. Think of your British history. And what children in those schools are taught and read."

"They exist, though," Geordie said. "So how—?"

"Remember that *all* the people of that country, or this island, if they were anything, were Catholic once. Not least the long line of great saints. But to return to the point, that country, its slave-trading days behind it, its championing of desegregation on the back burner, is in the process of allowing Islamic schools. How do you square that circle? Isn't it, by any other name, segregation? How do you square it with a cohesive society? My problem with this foolishness is threefold. One, quite simply, does separation facilitate cohesion? Two, how does it play for the future? What barriers are being erected for people's children? Three, an Islamic school in Scotland closed because of, quote, a 'lack of fairness' in the way girls were treated. I see you don't look surprised. Well, rest assured it won't happen here. A Muslim child will go to the First School. Like any other child."

"So let them have their churches, but draw the line at that?" Geordie asked.

"Within reason. The Althing isn't about to build churches for loose ends." Deville stood up. "Let's get more comfortable." He walked over to the coffee table, and slid the stuffed owl to a more central spot.

Geordie picked up his recorder and sat in an armchair. Deville refilled his coffee cup.

"When you say it won't happen here, do you mean the integration or the immigrants?" Geordie asked.

"Both. But I mean at the scale it's occurring. A wash of multifarious citizenry hitherto unimagined. How many people, relatively speaking, do you think it would be reasonable for Holy Island to absorb?"

"Into the one hundred and fifty already here?"

"Yes. And you are precisely right when you say 'into.' Not 'on top of", or 'against.' 'Into.'"

"Oh, say…thirty. Forty?"

"Over how long?"

"No idea. Ten or twenty years?"

"That sounds more than reasonable, so far as it goes. But you forget the population here was three times higher a hundred years ago. Why not double it now?"

"Why not?" Geordie felt miffed that his off-the-cuff figures had been shot down. He'd been trying to be constructive, but his brain was semi-engaged, the other half on Sarah Deville. And the tape recorder always tended to make him lazy.

"If work could be found for the breadwinners, Lindisfarne could easily absorb forty people, but four hundred all at once would cause problems. For one thing, the support services those people would expect, which would not have been thought of two centuries ago, are absent. In effect, the difference is like being eased out of a job, as against being summarily fired. One is a hard but bearable process over time; the other is sudden and traumatic. A time for high blood pressure and heart attacks. Not so much belt-tightening as how on earth to provide for one's family."

"Fine, but how relevant is it? You're suggesting time is everything," Geordie said.

"Not everything, but change can be quick or slow. Immigration in Britain, at the scale it is occurring, is so quick as to be overwhelming. Public services can't cope now, where will they be in ten years? Political change is more gradual, it can go unnoticed in a climate of denial and expedience. Look at the creeping loss of UK laws and freedom to the EU. Look at Scotland, at the upward movement of the SNP since they launched themselves in the thirties. At first, they were a laughing-stock, but who's laughing now? Would you care to bet against an independent Scotland in another fifty years? Then what of Wales, who started out if anything more militant but seem to have lost a bit of steam? People have been patting themselves on the back this week with the rebirth of the Northern Ireland Assembly. Have they forgotten the avowed aims of the Republicans? Do they believe they'll disappear? Or that the Ulster border is set in stone for all time? But yes, let us probe further into time and change and impact. Let me give you another analogy. Decimalisation. Not the complete analogy, but it's a start."

"In what way?" Geordie had a fleeting moment delving through half-digested remnants of Modern History.

"What your pal Amy would call a creeping loss of values. A plumbing leak, I believe she calls it? An excellent description it is too. Well, before decimalisation happened, in February 1971, the Tories launched a censure motion which 'regretted the system of decimalisation of the currency.' Brave of them not to mince words, eh? I suppose today, the wishy-washy bastards, they'd table a motion regretting the passing of Britain. Anyway, they were conveniently forgetting that a year before, under the Europhile Heath, they'd wanted to abandon the pound themselves and replace it with a 50p unit. In any event, a charming little chunk of Britishness, a system of currency that had survived several centuries of history, including a Norman invasion, a civil war and two World Wars, finally met its Waterloo in a one-man accident black spot called "Sunny" Jim Callaghan.

"I'm straying," Deville said. "Too many distractions. The point is, decimalisation was gradual. Coins were discarded or replaced over a longish period. Like immigrants then and earlier, the Italians, Indians, West Indians, Chinese, Poles and so on, they came in slowly and were absorbed. And the immigrants by and large had every intention of making new lives for themselves *in* the British system. Most of them had come because they had to. Many were encouraged by the governments of the day. Enoch Powell, as Minister of Health, urged West Indians to come and clean the hospitals, which they did. He then famously changed his tune. But generally, the newcomers liked it. It was an opportunity, or it was better than they'd had before. And they tried to *integrate*. Which is not to say that their kids have tried as hard, or don't feel let down or angry. And I for one don't blame them. The choices, if not quite the sins, of the fathers…

"In any case, although there were hiccups with the new currency, many people now have known nothing else. You included. New coins and notes are accepted as part of the natural course of things. It's a kind of foot-in-the-door syndrome, and it can be applied to a lot of liberalising constructions that have developed in recent years. With little or no forethought or conception of consequences.

"Now, Britain faces the euro, awful name, also the name of a wallaby. New coins, many of them, every value different from today's, as difficult for old folk to grasp as decimal coins once were, and sooner or later, believe it, they will be thrust on the British people. As will a European constitution, a European superstate. Amy's progressive plumbing leak."

"The new stuff didn't destroy the market, though," Geordie said. "Or cause irreparable damage. It was just currency. You could argue it made life simpler. Exchange rates, all that."

"Don't kid yourself," Deville replied. "In one or two recorded cases, it caused suicide, no less. And are you telling me the loss of the halfpenny wasn't inflationary? All that rounding up? And if the new currency didn't change the market out of recognition, plastic, deregulation and demutualisation certainly have since. We have still to reap the consequences of those errors in fiscal management, not to mention hedge funds. Still, I did make the point that decimalisation wasn't the complete analogy. It has overtones. The main ones being an under-supply of mandate along with an over-supply of newcomers, coins or people, infiltrating and eventually becoming the rule. Plus, the level of contempt in which the British people are held by their politicians. They're vain people, politicians, vain by definition. Would *you* presume to be qualified to speak for other people?"

"No. But you have."

Deville laughed. "That's where you're wrong, George. I may have to do it for a while to satisfy people like you, but by God not for long. And when I do hang up those particular boots, I'll make sure the new First Minister is installed by public vote, not by a cabal of his own kind like those undemocratic bastards over there. Who have happily repeated the ploy several times over, and look at the bloody excuses for leadership they've produced."

Geordie shook his head reprovingly, and gestured at his recorder. "Strictly speaking, British PMs are never elected by public vote though, are they? They're kind of packaged with their parties, wouldn't you say? But how long do you aim to stick it out?"

A twitch of the lips. "Again, point, or rather points, taken. As to the last, I can't say, but I hope no more than a year."

"Can't or won't?"

"Can't. I simply don't know. We'll have to wait and see. A year at most."

"If you dislike politicians so much, do you still vote yourself?"

"No. And don't get me wrong, there are still genuine politicians. Iain Duncan Smith, for example, who having been removed from the leadership of the Conservative Party has become an impressive, if rather one-dimensional, social thinker. Or young Boris Johnson; a likeable young man. I hope he succeeds in becoming London's Mayor, indeed I hope he goes much further. But he is probably too free a spirit, and it may be as well for him he stays that way. But to answer your question, I considered voting for the UK Independence Party last time. It would have been halfway logical, wouldn't it? But I was deterred by their front man."

"So your main thrust here is anti-British government, especially their immigration and multicultural ideas? And you don't think the other main parties would offer anything better."

"Recent elections have *told* us they won't. For forty years, ever since that humourless bag of bile Heath cast Enoch Powell into outer darkness for his 'Rivers of Blood' speech, politicians of all colours have been terrified of the word 'immigration.' Not one of the main parties is yet prepared to face up to the issue, or even concede it *is* an issue. They prefer engineered issues, false issues. Some individuals, including the female gerbil who goes by the title Communities Minister or some such thing, think multiculture is a sacred cow. Perhaps she is following her leaders; the bon vivant Jenkins, who set the bandwaggon rolling, or the bungling Blunkett, who in a mercifully short term as Home Secretary not only managed to flood Britain with immigrants and its police with imitations, but also as Education Secretary invented 'citizenship' classes in schools to try to paper over the ever-widening cracks. But the latest polls suggest that the great majority of British people have serious doubts about it all. And with good reason.

"Look at crime, an area in which Alistair tells me it is becoming increasingly difficult to find statistical truths. Well, you wouldn't expect the Home Office or British Crime Survey to expose them to the light of day, would you? What we do know is that handgun crime, for example, has doubled since the Dunblane massacre, and since the British government supposedly outlawed most handguns. That handgun crime appears to be concentrated in young black communities is little comfort: what happens when young Asians or East Europeans alight on crack cocaine or crystal meth, and become marginalised? Street gangs generally seem able to arm themselves at will. It rather makes a mockery of social cohesion, of multicultural Britain, doesn't it?

"And what is the British government's response, to this and other stress fractures in areas like jobs and public services? To 'open door' immigration and its progeny; budgetary chaos, exploding housing lists, so-called sheds with beds, human waste and refuse on city streets, creaking schools, deprivation, sectionalism, violent crime, and prison overcrowding? To the dislocation, as Duncan Smith is starting to call it, of whole segments of urban society, the diametric opposite of cohesion? What is their response? *Diversity*. The country has been built on it, they say, we must nurture and be proud of it. Don't talk to us of time and change and impact. We see no causality between immigration and these phenomena. Sacred cow? They are behaving like ostriches. And have as little appreciation of history. They seem to believe that a dripping tap is the equivalent of a flash flood. History, too, is for spinning."

A distant expression grew in Deville's eyes. "But that might be enough for today. Don't you think? Lots of things to keep you going; second homes, community services, employment opportunities, unwanted land development schemes, all good grist to the mill. Next time, we might look at the theory of majority tyranny. Or tyranny in the name of the majority."

"Hmm? Say again?"

"Cruel, unreasonable or arbitrary use of power, the dictionary says. The instances of cruelty, at least on a domestic front, may not yet be numerous, although Ulster political prisoners and pensioners in old folks' homes may disagree, but I think we could demonstrate the unreasonable and arbitrary."

"Such as?"

"For the moment, George, I don't wish to get into it. Other things...well, one example: new gay adoption laws versus Catholic adoption agencies. When the British government decided on a heady brew of social engineering, political correctness and downright offensiveness to people's faith. One malevolent law piling on top of another. You're familiar with the issue?"

"Not really."

"Do some homework. Especially into the children those agencies look after. We might have a closer look at it sometime." Deville took a last sip of coffee and patted the short-eared owl. "But let me offer you another thought to finish with. Assume this government, like any other, or any business or household, has access to a pot of money. It may be real, borrowed, leveraged, encumbered, or plastic money, but how do you think it's being used?"

"You're the expert. You tell me."

"I'll give you another analogy, a better one this time. If you were head of a household, what would you choose to spend these real or illusory riches on? Your wife, your ageing mother, your kids, or the lodger who needs teaching English?"

He stood up and pushed the stop button on Geordie's recorder. "Now. Come and meet our new policeman," he said.

Geordie stayed in his chair. "One thing before we go?"

"Yes?"

"How important would you say your wealth has been to the secession? Or being able to plan for it?"

"Immensely. We couldn't have contemplated it otherwise. As Adam Smith once suggested, serious wealth provides the basis for a system of liberty. It allows people, and states, should they wish, to make decisions without fear. Or favour."

"You could say, umm...a kind of two-fingers-to-the-world importance, then?"

A thin smile crossed Deville's lips. "You wouldn't be putting words in my mouth, would you?"

Geordie had to smile himself when he was introduced to Daniel Brigham, ex-Royal Military Policeman. Talk about someone putting one over on you.

Brigham was a beautiful milk-chocolate coloured guy in his late twenties, six feet tall, with dark brown eyes, a shaved head, a voice like Paul Robeson's, and movements like a panther's. Geordie was still smiling when he was invited to join the new cop on a visit to Charley Oakley's kidnappers.

"I got here late yesterday, and need to inspect their quarters," he was told. "You find something amusing?"

"No...I'm sorry. You lead the way."

Geordie had heard from Sarah that brother Max, pending the arrival of the new cop, had been looking after the three kidnappers, as well as busily confiscating weapons, mobiles, balaclavas and motor-bike helmets. Apart from the now dysfunctional .22, Max had put together quite a collection of armoury. Everything from a kid's catapult to a knuckleduster, several knives, a poker, a lead sap, an iron bar and a baseball bat. So far, the score was: Border Post 36, Visitors 0. And that was just during the week; more fun items were expected when things livened up later today.

"Whoa. Not so fast," Daniel said. He turned to Deville. "Before you go, answer me a question, sir. What do you aim to do with the guys locked up in there?"

Deville told him they were to be brought to trial within the week. He had informed one of their relatives that they'd be tried within fourteen days of their arrest, and would be represented by qualified barristers. Three members of the Althing would be sworn in as magistrates. Should the prisoners be given a custodial sentence, the time they had spent behind bars so far would be taken into account. He told Daniel he was concerned that any punishment should set a good precedent. He had asked his son Alistair, for purposes of comparison, to research the sort of sentences applied to the crimes of robbery and kidnapping in Britain, Australia and Canada over the last twenty years. He had thought about Iran, North Korea, China but had decided no, not quite fair.

He had a minor concern about the kidnapping charge; a key witness had done a runner.

"What about visiting rights?" Daniel asked. "They're entitled to them?"

"Of course," Deville said. "They have already had visits. One mother and one brother have been here, I suspect more for a day out at the seaside than out of concern for their kin. But there we are; we can only do so much to accommodate the niceties."

What he did not tell Daniel was that the mother had been foolish enough to suggest that she would inform her MP if her son were not released.

Bad, bad move.

Deville had said he would welcome this. It would put Holy Island's new penal regime on the map. He would make sure people knew what her son and his pals were accused of; two serious crimes. They had already been through the hands of so-called British justice, hadn't they? Yet they had managed to avoid proper restitution and cause more havoc elsewhere. He would ensure this message was not lost. The people of Britain would be able to see the Bigg Market Three behind bars, as they should be. Housed in clean, secure accommodation. They would see the prisoners being well fed and treated without being mollycoddled.

What the "criminal fraternity" would think about it was another matter. They might get the impression that their human rights to TVs, videos, DVDs and drugs, "all the trappings of a pampered life", were being put in jeopardy by one interfering mother. Some of them might begin to feel jealous of the amount of space the Holy Island inmates had. They might begin to feel threatened on several fronts. They might conclude such publicity should never have been allowed. They might go on strike or start climbing on roofs.

The woman got the message. Silence was golden.

Deville took his leave. Geordie and Daniel made their way towards the Market Place.

Geordie had heard Deville talking to Rebecca about getting Charley to return for the trial. Rebecca had not seemed keen. She'd been swimming a lot, writing a diary for her mother, and painting a couple of small watercolours. Geordie thought they were great: one of the Castle from across the bay, the other of a group of attractive stone buildings on the shore which he and Daniel were now passing. He also knew Deville had given up trying to get Rebecca to design a flag. She had told him his flag was staring him in the face from the island's Coat of Arms or the pages of that mediaeval masterpiece, the Lindisfarne Gospels. There were the Apostles, their carpet pages, decorative birds' heads, cats, the whole illuminated enchilada. For goodness' sake, what more did he want if he wished to portray Holy Island's Christian heritage and sense of community? Deville had muttered something under his breath. It could have been agreement, or it could have been surrender.

Geordie was impressed by the accommodation in the "jail." It had five four-person cells with an exercise area and gym, and looked like it had been put together by a pro. The interior finish admittedly bore the hallmarks of design houses from *High Noon* or *Birdman of Alcatraz*—strong steel bars, heavy locks, tiled floors, built-in concrete bunk beds, sunk steel furniture—but no one could deny the cells were fit for purpose. They were a heap better than those on Robben Island, which Geordie had visited on holiday a year ago.

The inmates didn't seem to think so. They hadn't daubed shit on the walls in time-honoured tradition, but they'd made use of food leftovers.

"Who you then?" the white guy, David Bell, asked.

"I am Daniel Brigham, policeman. This is George Halloran, journalist with *The Northern Sun*."

"Come to see if our human rights are being pissed on? Fucken right."

"Nothing wrong that I can see. Nice cell," Geordie said.

"Nothing wrong?" Daniel said. "The place was brand spanking new a week ago. They've turned it into a pigsty."

Geordie thought pigsty was a bit over the top, but he wasn't about to argue with an ex-RMP about the military definition of apple-pie order.

"You lot," Daniel said, "clean this place up."

He went backed into the lobby, got some brushes and threw them into the cell. He stripped mattresses and bedclothes off the bunks, threw them out the door, went back to the lobby and grabbed a length of hosepipe. He screwed it onto a tap, turned it on and sprayed a powerful stream of water onto the walls and floor. This was all done so fast, the Bigg Market boys barely had time to blink, let alone get out of the way.

"Get sweeping," Daniel said, *basso profundo*, slates rattling in the rafters. "*Scrub.*"

They got scrubbing. Five minutes later the cell was pristine, if dripping.

Daniel threw the mattresses back onto the bunks, folded the bedclothes on top of them, took the brushes, and locked the three back inside.

"Hey," Shad of the shrapnel said, "you don't 'spect us to stay in here, bro? We'll get fucken pneumonia."

"Aw, shame," Daniel said, "that'll spoil the fun. People here are looking forward to lynching you lot."

Shad turned a corner of one of the mattresses, and started whining, "It's damp, man, innit?...wringin wet...fucken pneumonia."

"So on your feet till it's dry. Listen up. Mess with these walls again and I break one arm each. Next time I come calling, I want to see CLEAN AND TIDY. Are we clear on that?"

Nods, mumbles, sideways looks.

Very impressive, Geordie thought. And not a trace of TV sets or videos or DVDs or drugs. Or of conjugal rights or voting papers, or all the other human rights and home comforts for which British jailbirds had, usually successfully, lobbied. Maybe he could whip up a quick exposé on contrasting methods of internment. He wondered: was the *Washington Post* the morning paper of choice in Lewisburg penitentiary? Did its circulation reach the far-flung cells of Leavenworth or Lompoc? A book buff and filmgoer's familiarity with Woodward and Bernstein was all very well, but he really should get to know more about his new undercover employer.

Meantime, he had more than enough material to keep both his employers happy for another day or two. Some things, political correctness for instance, had in his view received enough of an airing. Like the nanny state, it was too soft a target, especially when it was taken to extremes. But wasn't that part of the problem? Familiarity breeding disinterest? And it was still part and parcel of Amy's plumbing leak, an analogy which had almost unlimited mileage.

He had some doubts, too, about Deville's views on diversity. Wasn't it Walt Whitman who said *"I am large, I contain multitudes"*? In Geordie's mind, diversity meant resilience, contradiction and uncertainty, things that made for revitalisation, but he could see where the First Minister was coming from. Too much of anything, particularly if it was force-fed, could be a bad thing. He shrugged. In any case, his views were immaterial. Even if he preferred Amy's plumbing leak as a reason for Holy Island's secession, he wasn't there to prefer, he was there to report. Maybe the BBC—okay, he wasn't perfect, he had hobby-horses of his own—would do well to resurrect the same principle. Decades ago, the BBC's Director-General had been Lord Reith, a despotic, cranky Scot who had nurtured a passionate dislike of television, but had set exacting standards of broadcasting propriety which his successors, notably Baron Birt, had then set about undermining, discarding or dismantling. Ever since the Reith era, Geordie thought, the BBC had had their own progressive plumbing leak, in spades.

CHAPTER ELEVEN

Sunday, the Sabbath of all days, was the day Jim "Cochise" Redman decided enough was enough: his appearance on national TV was long overdue. Until now, none of these damned journalists had offered him so much as the time of day, far less a powwow.

Without meaning to, he handed the exclusive to Tyne Tees Television, the last remaining bulwark of non-print media on the island. They ran it several times during the morning before giving it wider distribution. Once Alex Deville had intervened, it took on more gravitas than the TV crew had first envisaged. Before things got heavy, they believed they'd shot an eye-catching sequence on the "*Man Goes Mad, Demolishes Home*" theme.

It happened like this: Sunday morning at dawn, Cochise the Minister-builder, adorned with head feathers and moccasins, deerskin waistcoat and leggings, climbed into a bulldozer. Shame it wasn't an Iron Horse, he consoled himself, but it was near enough. It had been left unattended overnight by Max and his pals, who had been using it during the week to smooth out bits of causeway wreckage left sticking up after each tide. They were winning this battle, slowly.

He drove the machine along St. Cuthbert's Way to Chare Ends, past the public car park and the dozen bungalows leading into the village. Coming to a juddering halt close to Amy Donaldson's cottage, he peered through the drizzle and mud-spattered windshield at a mobile home in someone's garden.

Cochise had a chronic hatred of mobile homes of any type. He thought they were among the reasons God had invented hurricanes, tornadoes, and thunder in the clouds. To him, they were tin shacks on wheels cluttering up the countryside, paddling along roads, free and clear of tax surcharges, and causing traffic jams. Overnight camping and caravanning was already outlawed on the island; to Cochise's mind, this was but an aperitif. In his new capacity as a Minister of the Althing of Holy Island, he looked forward to getting rid of every last one. His ancestors had made do with tepees and wikiups, finished tastefully with animal hides or bear grass, truly sustainable materials. When they'd moved on, they rolled their gear up, slung it over the back of a horse, and left. None of this swaying along roads with lines of cars piled up behind them. None of these prissy flowerbeds and calor gas tanks and patio crap either, he thought, preparing to set about his work.

But in truth this was only a secondary motive, an added bonus, for bulldozing the thing to kingdom come. With great care, he unfolded a dog-eared piece of paper and read the words of his namesake, the great chieftain of the Choconen people of the Chiricahua Apache:

"When I was young I walked all over this country, east and west, and saw no other people than the Apaches. After many summers I walked again and found another race of people had come to take it. How is it?"

Well shit, Cochise thought, reading it again, it may be a bit high-flown but it had a ring to it. And it was on the money.

The Tyne Tees crew, who had been among the first to arrive when the secession story broke, had struck it lucky. They'd been staying in the nearby Lindisfarne Hotel, and were alerted by the thunder of Cochise's chariot trundling along the public road. It was an unexpected sound at five thirty in the morning. A cameraman, a sound man, a technician and a reporter threw on their clothes and bundled out of the hotel. They tracked down the source of the racket just as Cochise was calculating his angle of attack. They got it all, including clouds of midges.

"He's done *what*?" Deville yelled, eyes like lasers.

"Don't shout so loud," Amy admonished him. "You'll upset George."

Amy had been woken up by the noise too. She was a light sleeper, lighter as the years rolled by, but the sound of Cochise rumbling back and forth, lining up his sights, would have awakened Rip Van Winkle. She decided that there was no one else available to transmit Cochise's folly to the First Minister. So she collected a traumatised George from his quarters and set off down the road, stopping only for a quick chat with Cochise. She hadn't liked the look of him.

"Did he give any reason for this insanity?" Deville asked her.

"You know what he's like, Alex. He got upset when Billy Rankin took in those Polish workers to help in the café, and then again when he put them up in the caravan. Plus, he doesn't like caravans, never has. Plus, he tried to get off with one of the young lasses staying there and she wouldn't have him."

"For mercy's sake." Deville bent down and tweaked George's ear.

"I gave him a good telling off anyway. This poor wee thing thought the sky had fallen in on him, didn't you pet?"

George gurgled.

"I'll bet he did," Deville said, ruffling the pig's bristles.

"These things are sent to try you, Alex. There's only one thing to do."

"Which is?"

"Throw the so-and-so in jail. Then you'll have the high ground. You'll be able to demonstrate ministerial impartiality. Immediate...what's the phrase?...executive action. No one is bigger than Holy Island's law. That sort of thing."

Deville thought about it. "You're right."

"Plus, thank your lucky stars it wasn't a holiday caravan. Or a second home. And it was empty. Good Lord, at Easter-time, he could have had young Poles strewn about dead all over the place. You'll be able to square things with Billy Rankin. Billy did own the caravan, after all. You can cross his palm with silver, right?"

"Are those Tyne Tees people still about?"

"Oh, yes," Amy said. "They'll be dining out on this one tonight. Not to mention when they get back to Newcastle. I'd start moving on it if I were you."

Deville shuddered. "Yes. I'll need to speak to them right away."

"*After* you have Jim behind bars, Alex."

"I'll get Daniel on it first thing."

"How's he settling in?"

"I think he'll suit us just fine. A good sense of humour and a better sense of authority."

"Good. We'll be getting along, then. Are you ready to go, George?"

The little pig grunted, and let out a small squeal.

"You want to say hello to your pal Geordie? If he's up? Come on then."

Alex Deville got the young journalist out of bed, in the process rousing the rest of the household, thinking that if Tyne Tees TV had already got hold of the story, then Geordie may as well get in on the act too. He phoned Daniel Brigham while Amy and the two Georges were exchanging pleasantries, then showed Amy and her pig out.

"Nice one first thing on a Sunday," Geordie told Deville when he heard the tale. Geordie was full of bonhomie after learning yesterday that his stay on the island had been prolonged. He had spent the whole evening with Sarah, wondering how on earth she managed to pour herself into her jeans, how she got out of them, and whether it was too soon to try his luck.

"Bloody man," Deville groused.

"Democracy, Alex. The voters get what they deserve, as they say. Not unlike they do over there," Geordie said, nodding to the mainland.

"I have enough to do without listening to smart-ass remarks."

"Can I tag along?" Geordie asked, trying to keep a straight face. He thought Cochise's solution to the Scourge of Mobile Homes was the best thing he'd come across since he first met George the Vietnamese potbelly. Geordie hadn't much time for mobile homes himself.

"I suppose it can't do any harm. Or any more harm," Deville said, watching his younger son and daughter, with Rebecca, making their way down the stairs.

"Excellent," Geordie said.

"But don't forget, the bloody man's in jail. As of now."

"Good move," Geordie said.

"Well, I can't take any credit for that. I may have made it there eventually, but your friend Amy was right on the ball," Deville told him.

"She's a cracker, that lady. You should have had her in the Althing," Geordie said.

"Shouldn't I just. Instead of the second coming of an Apache chief." Deville laughed. "Well, you have to see the funny side."

"Good thinking, Dad," Sarah said, grinning. "We'll join you, for some moral support. And because this sounds too good to miss."

"My God," her father said, "this is turning into a caravan all by itself."

Was there any way, Deville wondered, not only to inject some sort of balance into this debacle, but also to turn it to Holy Island's advantage? Then he had another thought. He would need to tell Billy Rankin to be careful what he said to the media.

From Deville's point-of-view, the interview was going well. With Geordie, Sarah and Alistair in tow, he had quickly made it to Billy Rankin's house and engaged the Tyne Tees reporter, a thirty-ish blond bombshell called Angela Dunn, in conversation. Ms. Dunn had needed no second invitation to interview him. Here in front of her, on a metaphorical plate, was the First Minister, presumably about to attempt a whitewash job on one of his colleagues. Lovely, she thought, looking forward to skewering him.

For his part, Deville believed he had his questioner just where he wanted her, slipping like an ebbing tide away from demolished caravans, remnants of which festooned the grass behind her, and into his own carefully calculated version of Remedial Action.

He had borrowed George the Vietnamese potbelly from Amy, to milk Geordie's story, and add a touch of local colour in the damp conditions. Amy was standing nearby, making sure no nasty bits of equipment snagged on her pet and that the Tyne Tees crew didn't upset him. Besides, she was interested in all this media carry-on. Changed days, she thought, from when Holy Island got an artist or a writer in the summer, or a couple of reporters when someone was lost at sea.

"It's a shame," Deville was saying, "I feel sorry for this poor man. I hope you'll treat him with consideration."

That got Angela Dunn's attention. "You what?" she asked. "You're sorry? For whom?"

"For Minister Jim Redman. A man I once described as the salt of the earth, and who was recently elected by unanimous vote to the Althing."

"You're *sorry* for him? But what about the owner of the—?"

"Oh, Billy Rankin will be recompensed, of course. Immediately. One of the first things I'll do this morning. He'll be able to buy a brand new mobile home, the best he can find on the market, so long as he uses it with the interests of the community at heart."

"You're sorry for *Redman*? After what he's done? But...you told me he's in jail."

"And so he is, poor chap. Unfortunately, much more than jail is needed in this sad case. Much, much more. He'll need the services of a doctor and psychiatrist, I'm certain of it."

"Why?" Angela asked, thinking too late that she should have taken a leaf out of the lawyer's lexicon and avoided asking a question to which she didn't know the answer. This was fast turning into something more complex than your average whitewash job.

What an excellent question, and such impeccable timing, Alex Deville thought. Couldn't have wished for better if I'd written the screenplay. He bent to give George a pat on the head.

"Jim is somewhat injured," he said. "Bruising, a bang on his forehead which I hope the doctor will be able to treat. But much more worrying is possible insanity. This incident may well have tipped him over the edge."

"*Insanity*? Are you saying—?"

"The poor fellow has been getting worse. Driven to absolute distraction by immigrant workers and the threat they posed to his livelihood. I use the past tense purposely. There will be no threat under the Althing's jurisdiction."

"But are you seriously suggesting...insanity?" Angela flipped a stray curl from her forehead.

"It seems quite obvious to my colleagues and me, but we are lay people and need to take specialist advice. Jim Redman is a broken man."

"So you're bringing in...a psychiatrist?" Angela felt her voice cracking. Midway through this sentence, she had to clear her throat.

"Bringing one in? No, not at all. One is already here on the island, as a normal part of the Althing's new health service. But yes, it's all very sad. I worry, indeed *all* his friends worry, that suicide may be the inevitable conclusion for Jim."

George the Vietnamese potbelly gurgled. It sounded like sympathy, or agreement, or possibly both. Or maybe he was just amused.

"*Suicide*? Surely not, I mean—"

"Suicide. A distinct possibility. Given his concerns and all he has had to face. We must do all we can to prevent it. It's very sad. Tragic. All his friends here on Holy Island will be rallying round, I have no doubt."

"You think immigration...the threat...may have caused him to—?"

"Suicide is a real danger, and it would be the cruellest of consequences. You'll begin to understand why we feel so strongly about the immigration issue. It has caused extreme distress, to the point of a man's life. I directly blame the British government for this tragedy, for putting the man's life at risk. British governments should beware of taking unreasonable, arbitrary actions. But they've been doing it for years."

"Arbitrary actions?" Angela asked, in some trepidation.

"I speak of the Oxford Dictionary's definitions of tyranny. Old people are turned out of their homes to die in so-called care, having been taken for every penny. Because of arbitrary laws, Catholic adoption agencies are no longer able to look after the neediest children. A thousand children each year are being taken from their birth parents, in order to satisfy the British government's arbitrary adoption targets. Young men are sent to die in the desert for arbitrary reasons. Innocent civilians in those desert lands are cruelly and arbitrarily wiped out, in their hundreds of thousands. Parents, families and friends are left devastated, mourning their crushing and arbitrary losses. The examples are legion. They are examples of majority tyranny, or tyranny in the name of the majority. The British government needs to take a long hard look at itself, its ethics and its meddling legislation. They have undermined the institution of marriage and, not satisfied with that, are now undermining the family, the very bricks and mortar of society. The Religious Hatred Bill, another meddlesome thing seeking to promote harmony, risked making elements of religious faith a criminal offence. Arbitrary standards, from drinking to police response times, are set. Who in their right minds, in the present day, would consider these things priorities? From such follies, the impression rightly takes hold that the British government has no idea what it is doing, that it stumbles along day by day, obsessed with peripheralities, or trying to correct its earlier mistakes. Bit by bit, fundamental freedoms are being removed and relativism is taking over. And Jim Redman has been sucked downwards into this vortex of arbitrary injustice."

Deville talked his way through this catalogue without pausing for breath. He guessed it would make any editing difficult.

"Obsessed, er...peripheralities, did you say?" Angela asked weakly.

"Exactly. What else is there for them to do? Brussels and Strasbourg loom large, don't they? *Excluding* MEPs, the House of Lords and local councils, there are almost 1,000 politicians in London, Edinburgh, Cardiff and Belfast. That is more than their equivalents in the whole of the United States. And two-thirds of them are at Westminster. Where, exactly? You've seen the House of Commons, illuminated almost daily on other TV channels; their workplace is empty much of the time. What does that say about their role? What exactly do these parasites do? Apart from squabbling, partying, spending money on kitchens and curtains, grabbing consultancies, giving hand-outs to family members, joining the so-called celebrity circuit, having sex with their secretaries, voting themselves the best of pension schemes, and hitting the front pages for all the wrong reasons? The answer, given they have handed much of their role to Europe, including the 78 MEPs who represent Britain there, is considerably less than they used to do, and that is assuming what they do is still as useful as before. In the mid-1990s, the EU initiated well under half of all British legislation. Now, 80 percent would be a minimum estimate. So why have all these snouts in the trough? Why not reduce them, halve them? We know the answer, don't we? Because the trough is too rich, too irresistible. And because it would require their vote."

"And…so, what in your opinion should be done?"

"We in the Holy Island of Lindisfarne have done what was needed. We have decided on our own form of government. And we will work at it, without expense accounts or allowances or any other self-serving mechanisms. We do not intend to be caught up in the British government's arrogant and arbitrary contempt for the Christian church, British values, the British people, the institutions of marriage and the family. We do not care to be hauled along as baggage in the truckload of weak and watery obsessions, the drive towards relativism, moral decadence, political correctness, *diversity*, and social cohesion, which eat like cankers into the fabric of British society as a direct result of the present, and previous, British government's policies. In short, we have no wish to remain at the mercy of meddlers who exist in super-fogging contradiction of John Locke's idea that the best government is the least government. What the remaining British people do about it is for them to decide. The ballot box, however, seems an increasingly feeble weapon to deal with such flagrant and chronic abuse of power. No wonder the good people of Britain, by which I mean the oppressed majority, are upset and feel themselves to be voiceless. But that is a feature of socialism, under whatever name it comes. Allow it into a country, and that country's people will inevitably weaken while its leaders increasingly pursue their own agendas. What an irony it would be if the legacy of this PM was to make a disgruntled indigenous working class the only true right-wingers left in Britain. Not something of which his socialist forbears would approve, I think."

When he finished, bending to give George the patient potbelly another pat on his snout, there was a moment's silence while Angela tried to digest all this.

She grasped desperately at one of the straws Deville had chosen to emphasize. "You don't feel diversity is the way forward. It seems to be an important plank of—"

"No, we do not. Garbage tips have diversity, as have more amenable things like Olympic sports. And Olympic bids notwithstanding, we can clearly see which of them the British government, in their facile, nanny-state fashion, is bent on concocting. Until recently, they were bent on adding the removal of competitiveness from school agendas and children's minds to their many arbitrary sophisms. Perhaps they still are, although the Olympic bid appears to have inspired a U-turn. Again. Maybe they forgot, if they ever knew, that competitiveness just as much as diversity created the planet we inhabit. And is an equally, some would say far more potent, element of the human psyche. And maybe they also forgot, if they ever knew, that immigrant societies bring their crime and crime lords with them. The Italians in America, the Yugoslavs in Italy and Germany, the Russians in their former satellites, the Poles here of late, and the British themselves in southern Spain."

Finally, Angela Dunn turned to face the camera, struggling for a coherent sign-off:

"Well...there you have the views of the leader of the new government, er, Althing of Holy Island...And of course...insanity may well explain the headdress...why this man was dressed as an...American Indian...chief. Thank you, Mr. Deville."

"My pleasure. Do call if you need more."

Put that in your pipe and smoke it, Mr. Prime Minister, Deville thought. With luck, set yourself alight and scorch the wife and furnishings, be my guest.

Then: I'll need to call another public meeting this evening, he realised. I have to make sure Cochise is explained, if possible taken out of the frame.

He returned George to Amy and thanked her.

"It was worth every minute of our time, Alex. Wasn't it, George?"

The little pig sat on his hind legs, put his front trotters together, and prayed.

"Quite right, pet," Amy said, "we hope it works, too."

She and George set off down the road.

"Bloody brilliant." Geordie meant it, or almost meant it, and was secretly quite pleased to have some of his own research confirmed. "But bits of it sounded familiar, like echoes from yesteryear. Or was it yester*day*? Weren't they the bits that were supposed to be my exclusive to the *Washington Post*? Tyranny, diversity, and all that?"

"Oh, don't be so precious, George. You know very well that I had to seize the opportunity."

"So I'm sacrificed on the altar of convenience."

"That's telling it like it is, George," Sarah said. "I don't blame you for being upset." She turned to her father. "And I hope you'll be able to justify all that stuff about psychiatrists and suicides. They could ask around and find it's all a load of b.s."

"It most certainly is not. The good medic has a psychiatric qualification. His wife is a pathologist and a midwife. They are the complete package. I told the girl as much. 'A normal part of the Althing's new health service' were the words I used."

"Have they had time to do any actual work? Get their hands dirty? I mean in between receiving all those trophies?" his daughter asked sweetly.

"They're fifty-five, not twenty-five."

"And Cochise? Insane?"

"He will be when I've finished with him," Deville said grimly, marching off.

Unknown to Alex Deville, his interviewer having avoided mention of it, Billy Rankin had already run the media gauntlet. Framed against a trellis hanging with clematis and wallflowers, with red valerian bursting from crevices in the stonework on either side, Billy had in fact been a big help to Deville and, incidentally, to Holy Island's cause.

After going through all the background stuff, how long he'd lived in his house (as if it mattered), what did his wife think (as if she was capable of thought), what had happened to his mobile home (take a look around, you brainless floozy), how he had heard about it (how could he have *failed* to hear about it, bulldozers crashing through his garden at daybreak, this stupid Geordie cow asking all these dumb questions), Billy had applied the final thrust:

"And what do you think of the man who did this, Mr. Rankin?" Angela Dunn had asked. "Do you think it might have been some sort of..." (dramatic pause) "... vendetta?"

"Cochise? Don't be fucking stupid. He's as crazy as a shithouse rat. He's the only guy in this entire village that couldn't dependably hit the Ouse with a piss." Billy thought for a moment. "But, shit, he adds a bit of spice. He's not all fucking bad."

They couldn't use it, of course. They could use very little—well, actually nothing—of Billy Rankin's interview. But it did rather reinforce what Alex Deville had been saying. And post-Alex Deville, they knew the "*Man Goes Mad, Demolishes Home*" theme was pretty much dead in the water. Oh, they'd show the thing, a bit of light entertainment never did anyone any harm, but the real news, the national *and* international news, had a lot more to do with Deville's forthright comments on tyranny, relativism, diversity, EU hegemony, and the Mother of Parliaments.

The Bigg Market Three, to give them their now prevalent title, had received a nasty shock when Cochise, still in full regalia, had been shown into the next cell. They'd spent fully ten minutes debating whether they'd been drugged and airlifted in their sleep to Guantánamo Bay, the Alamo, or Little Bighorn. Not having a history or geography lesson between them, much less a GCSE, the debate had some serious flaws.

Sometime later, they were glad to see the black cop hauling the Red Injun out to meet a tall white geezer in a suit. Maybe the *Injun* was being airlifted back to Little Bighorn. Was this new suit CIA? FBI? They lay on their bunks trying to be as unobtrusive as possible.

They were doubly glad the black cop had been in twice this morning and hadn't given them any hassle. No threats at all, not a word. He had just given their cell a quick once-over, hadn't discovered a particle of foodstuff or speck of dust anywhere, and told them he'd see them soon.

They weren't so glad to see the Injun being returned ten minutes later, looking thoughtful. They began to wonder about the guy when he started banging his head on his cell wall, doing some kind of rain dance. They began to yearn for the peaceful days of yore that had preceded his arrival. They were perplexed when he said, "*Daa go te'e*" to them, hadn't a clue he was asking them nicely in Apache how they were. What the hell *was* this? Fuck's sake, wadda flake.

Then another suit arrived, complete with black bag, stethoscope and what looked like a folding table with wheels. The black cop was giving him a hand getting it all inside. The place was turning into Newcastle Central Station. The Injun, blood trickling down his face, was hauled out of his cell by the cop again, and they all disappeared into an interview room.

"Fuck's sake," Shad said, his cornrows now in disarray. "What gives?"

Shrugs. Eyes rolling jerkily right and left. No answer. But it came fifteen minutes later.

The Injun was wheeled out of the room on a portable gurney, head bandaged, strapped horizontally, minus the headdress, but still with the moccasins, waistcoat and leggings, and apparently asleep. He was trundled back into his cell, the gurney's wheels behaving as erratically as a supermarket trolley's.

"What's up wi' *him*?" the white guy asked, eyeballs like low-wattage lightbulbs.

"He's under doctor's orders," the black cop said. "He had an accident and needed sedating. Nothing for you lot to get involved in."

"Fucken headbanger. He was givin himself some cane."

"He'll be asleep for a while. He'll not trouble you."

"You gonna, like, stick around?"

"I'll be in and out. Why?"

"Just wondered...that fucker might get loose."

"He won't. Now, inspection time." Daniel had a look round their cell, under the mattresses and built-in furnishings. He handed Shad a brush. "Good. Keep it that way," he said. "I'll be back with your grub in a bit."

They felt more comfortable after that. If the black cop's voice booming off the walls didn't wake the fucken Injun up, nothing short of a nuke had any chance at all.

The rain gone and the sun out, Sarah, Rebecca and Geordie had decided to take a break and walk around the shore to the Castle. It was slow going. Sarah insisted they stop whenever they met someone, and ask them to spread the news of the meeting in the village hall later. Sarah told people it wouldn't be a long one, nothing heavy, just to keep people abreast of Cochise's shenanigans. Her father had things to say. And no, it wouldn't conflict with evensong.

Geordie noticed the village was slowly filling up with brand new SUVs. They'd been arriving at a rate of three or four a day for the last week.

Alistair was back at Fahr House, typing up notices to stick in shop windows and pubs. Probably, Geordie thought, in between researching penal codes in far-flung countries of the world. Plus other things like photographic ID cards, income tax models, tourist generation, sustainable refuse disposal and footloose industry. Geordie felt sorry for Alistair, eternally cooped up inside with his computer.

Max was doing his usual thing, out at the security gate coping with the Sunday intake of visitors. But today there hadn't been many. Until now, the weather had militated against it, and those who had braved the conditions had been well wrapped-up. Anoraks and fleeces everywhere, global warming not exactly evident. Besides, he wouldn't have much more to do. It was coming up to eleven and the tide was sweeping in fast.

For Max, the week had been a stroll in the park. He was especially pleased with the two new Hummer H3s. Gear-shifts the size of small bolsters, big, boxy, shiny bodies, they looked the part and acted the part. They could cope in water two feet deep, more if pushed, and could carry five passengers and their luggage in comfort. They would actually improve access to and from the island in terms of negotiable crossing times. Okay, rust was a worry, and they weren't the most environmentally-friendly cars in the world. But they would do the job. He could have them converted to hydrogen, as the Governor of California had done with his. And Max liked the yellow finish; you could see them from miles away.

Post-causeway, even with the Hummers doing frequent round trips, there would be less traffic and people to and from the island. But the people who did get to visit would be quality assured. And Max Deville would make sure they would be stripped of anything that in any way risked that quality being compromised.

The only tricky issue during the week had been with the female arrivals, especially those suspected of smuggling weapons for their men. To resolve it, Max had pulled in two of his friends' wives, big Northumbrian lasses not inclined to take any crap from anorexic Geordie or more foreign weeds. Max had reshuffled work patterns so that husbands and wives took the same shift. For Max, this had been a notable display of humanity. Well, he couldn't have them waving to each other every day as they passed on St. Cuthbert's Way, could he? Even his mates needed to get their leg over from time to time. It was called man management.

CHAPTER TWELVE

Eventually Geordie and the girls escaped the village and strolled towards the Castle, stopping at the minibus turning-point near the coastguard hut and Popple Well. An ice-cream van was parked there, people queuing up, glad of a sunshine break. Sarah was pleased to see them. She said it was evidence that visitors were getting to and from the island, even if the public car park was now the exclusive preserve of SUVs and rusting saloons.

"But no big coachloads any more," Geordie said.

"We'll survive. And we didn't ever get busloads of football fans, thank goodness."

Being a football fan himself, Geordie took mild exception to this, but wisely kept quiet. If anything, he was relieved. Most girls of his acquaintance scoffed at the game before caving in for the sake of romantic peace and harmony. So a moderate wariness about the sport and its followers made Sarah normal. Geordie was all in favour of that. He didn't want any pedestals popping up to spoil the fun.

The girls had not met Daniel Brigham before, but here he was at the turning-point, tucking into a strawberry and vanilla ice-cream cone. It seemed incongruous to Geordie. He had imagined the guy eating a diet of raw meat and iron filings.

"I thought I'd explore a bit," Daniel said, voice coming from somewhere just above his boots. "Get to know the place and meet some people."

"You're welcome to join us," Geordie said. He knew what it was to be friendless in a new place. Like his first week at *The Northern Sun*, the winter before last, he had been about as popular as a flu virus until one of the hacks wanted a cup of tea, or Old Smokey began whining for a packet of smokes.

"No. I can't do that, I'm afraid, much as I'd like to. Things to do over there," Daniel said, pointing to the jail, smiling at Rebecca.

Geordie remembered his manners and introduced him to the girls.

He saw Rebecca looking at the ex-RMP as if he was in the Sale of the Century and she might just buy the whole lot. Well, Geordie thought, he's a major improvement on what she had in tow before. Whatever the guy was, you couldn't see him on a trestle-table in a village Leek Show, with a sign saying "Commended" around his neck. Or worse, "Substandard."

Daniel started up the slope towards Marygate, eating his ice-cream cone. They continued their walk.

"Wow," Rebecca said. "What a dish."

"We'd noticed you were rather taken," Sarah said. "Drooling

wouldn't be too strong a word."

Rebecca blushed. "But his *voice,*" she said. "Imagine that in the church choir."

"The church is small and old. We couldn't risk shaking its foundations."

They laughed. Geordie went so far as to give Sarah a conspiratorial wink.

A lone Northumbrian piper was sitting on one of the seats that hugged the dry-stone wall, a cap in front of him. Geordie threw some change in it. The piper nodded his thanks and finished his piece, then said hello to Sarah, who did the introductions this time round.

"Fine mornin' for a walk, folks," Jeff Elliot said. "There are still people about, see? Yon Castle's keepin' busy."

"It's good to know they haven't been put off," Sarah agreed.

"And they aal look human, lass. Your Max is doin' all right."

"I'll tell him you said so."

"Aye, that'll impress the hell out of him."

Geordie saw grazing land behind the wall, with sheep and lambs in tidily fenced fields. In the distance, north of Rocket Field and Crooked Lonnen, an area where the grazing land became dunes, he knew there had once been a nine-hole golf course. Geordie had done his homework, some of it in the Crown & Anchor looking at old photographs, one of them of a golfer. It was hard to imagine a links on that scrubland today, when people seemed to need country clubs and lush grass before they ventured out to play golf. But perhaps they could resurrect the wee course, he mused, if they fell short of visitors. Geordie didn't play golf, but he had the idea that golfers would journey to all sorts of outlandish places to decimate the turf, and fire small white missiles into the nearest available pond.

They left Jeff the piper to his next number, *Over the Sea to Skye*. If and when they got around to building the tunnel, Geordie thought, *Under the Sea to Skye* wouldn't have quite the same allure. He watched Rebecca kneel to inspect a clump of thrift growing in a crevice, lifting the round pink flowers between her fingers towards the sun. Apparently unaware she was doing it, she was quietly humming the tune.

The sun was shining, sparkling off a calm sea, burnishing the grey walls and roofs of the village buildings. Some lapwings clustered in Rocket Field, redshanks and oyster-catchers poked along the shore, a variety of gulls wheeled above them, eider ducks and a pair of shags paddled in the shallows.

As they walked, Sarah gave Rebecca and Geordie a crash course on "Cuddy's Duck", named after St. Cuthbert, the hard-working shepherd boy with the gift of healing who had tried his best to live alone with God, but was induced to take up office as Bishop of Lindisfarne in 685 AD.

She then launched into the saint himself.

She pointed towards the Heugh, behind which lay the small island named after him, where he had first attempted life as one of "God's front-line soldiers." Because the islet was accessible at low tide, he had thought it too easy a life, so left for Inner Farne. With the help of friends, he built a chapel, a small guesthouse and "fishehouse" near Inner Farne's landing place, still called St. Cuthbert's Cove, and stayed for several years until becoming Bishop. His bishopric was short-lived, lasting only another two years. He took it seriously, travelling far and wide, reaching out to people as far away as Carlisle and Kirkcudbright, healing them, bringing them to the faith. But he became convinced he was terminally ill, resigned office, and took his little boat back to Inner Farne. He died there on 20th March 687 AD in the arms of his fellow-monks, who lit torches to transmit the news to Lindisfarne.

"What a sad story," Rebecca commented. She was distracted, still thinking of the new cop's satiny skin and dark brown eyes. They were not the skin and eyes of a man who would play stupid Games, get blotto and throw rubber lures at unsuspecting tourists. Or get mugged by fleas.

"Oh no," Sarah brought her back to the moment. "It's an uplifting story. Imagine this kid, about sixteen years old, looking after his sheep, seeing a vision of St. Aidan's death, and *finally* deciding to become a monk. It might have been a normal way of life in those days, but it was daunting. Imagine him coming to Lindisfarne for the first time at the age of thirty, facing an internal crisis among the monks, praying through the night, praying in the sea, anywhere, everywhere, talking with people, comforting people—hard cases, peasants, people of pagan beliefs—always caring, courageous and compassionate. Then, eventually deciding that his battle against the forces of evil could only be waged alongside what he believed to be his Creator. As a hermit, without human help.

"He became reclusive not because he was disillusioned with the world, but because he wanted to give his God his undivided attention. For him, it was a *positive* thing. Saint Bede writes that Cuthbert was the first man who dared to live alone on Inner Farne, a place reputed to be overrun with devils. He had a spring for water and grew barley to feed himself. He was a simple man, good with his hands, a loving man, the epitome of sanctity. He fought his good fight, fought many good fights, flung himself on the ground to quell a fire threatening to raze his foster-mother's house, and won most of them. St. Cuthbert is still alive, remembered as the Fire of the North, here and throughout Northumbria. But especially here. How can a few hundred years dim the brilliance of such a life?"

She told Geordie, "If you want to find out more, go back to the Heritage Centre or pick up some more leaflets at St. Mary's. But this is what we mean when we say we're a Christian community. This is what it's about."

Geordie's heart sank. For God's sake, no pedestals? Sarah Deville *normal*? He began to beat himself up for thinking such unalloyed rot. He was a positive heathen by comparison, and only went to church these days to see his pals get married. Or bury his mother.

"And you'll need to visit the Farne Islands, both of you," Sarah pointed across the water. "Geologically, we're supposed to be one of them, but detached. They seem close today, don't they? A few miles, five or six. But imagine a man rowing over there, with no outboard, no engine, and maybe a storm brewing. We take it for granted, it's all so easy now. But it wasn't then. Soon will be a good time to go; all the new life, the chicks and ducklings Cuthbert cared for. And no one interested in Christianity should miss the chance to see where he lived."

"Is he buried here? Or on the Farnes?" Rebecca asked.

"No. In Durham Cathedral. The story goes that in 1537, more than eight centuries after he died, his coffin was opened for the last time there. It was the last of several times, because of all the harrying and hiding, but they found again, as they had before, his body uncorrupted. His ring is still used today by the Bishop of Newcastle each time he ordains a priest." Sarah's eyes were welling with tears. "I think that is what you can truly call a legacy."

To Geordie, even a despondent Geordie, the whole place was taking on the aura of a paradise on earth. Assuming paradise was capable of temporal comparison. If it existed at all, it had to be peopled with the same mix of humanity, minus a few transgressors, that had once occupied the world, hadn't it? But quite possibly, the earliest settlers had thought on similar lines. They, not just Cuthbert, must have considered Lindisfarne a safe place, half island—more so then, before the dunes joined the Snook to the main body of rock—and a refuge from a busier world. After his first visit to the Parish Church of St. Mary the Virgin, with a touch of artistic licence given that the building itself hadn't been constructed until the twelfth century, he had described it in an article to the *Washington Post*—he thought Americans might swallow it, Northumbrians certainly wouldn't—as "a building charged with spirit, a place where saints once worshipped, a haven of tranquillity in a turbulent planet."

Approaching the Castle, Rebecca commented that the mainland from here looked darker, more wooded and more treacherous than the island. She pointed out a view she'd like to paint, and regretted that she had left her things behind. Sarah said there would be other days; why didn't she think of staying longer? She smiled at Rebecca. Did she have to go back so soon? After all, it was possible Daniel might help restore her faith in the opposite sex…?

For the likes of him, Geordie fretted, Sarah Deville was untouchable, *several* pedestals removed. No way José, put her right out of mind. Million dollar legs were all very well, but a battalion of saints was serious rivalry in anyone's language. What had Rod Stewart said after his fling with the juicy Joanna? Having stood her up because he'd "got caught up with some tart"? Geordie couldn't recall the other bit, but was sure it had to do with the lady having too much class. It was the same with Sarah. Good Lord, take the luscious Lumley back in time and she'd look *drab* by comparison.

Then there was all that money, all that *opulence* at Fahr House. He could hear his Mum, dead five years now, shaking a finger and telling him "don't aspire to what you can't reach, George." He didn't agree with the sentiment. No one would get anywhere, job-wise, love-wise, life-wise or any other-wise if they followed that line, but it was resonating with him in Sarah's case.

And there was his job. He thought if he worked at it he would make a good journalist, maybe get a position in future with one of the national dailies, but if he earned ten, twenty, thirty times as much as he did now it would still fall a zillion or two short of Sarah's standards. He couldn't stay on Holy Island for the rest of his working life, could he, however much he liked it? And there was as much chance of Sarah Deville coming to Newcastle as there was of George Dubya taking up residence in Baghdad.

He thought of his flat in the Newcastle suburb of Jesmond; there was a good example of what he meant. It was okay as a pad for him, and had Jesmond Dene on its doorstep, a nice park in which to while away hot summer days, but it wasn't something out of *Ideal Home*. Minimal Swedish furniture and Formica all over the place. A lounge, a kitchen, a bedroom and a bathroom. Was there such a thing as a one-up, one-down in the lexicon of real estate? It certainly didn't aspire to the grandeur of a two-up, two-down. In all truth, it wasn't much better than some bed-sit in Boldon out of a Catherine Cookson novel.

And this thing with Cuthbert. For God's sake, how could he compete against a saint?

Geordie gave himself a shake; this was like opening the lift doors and diving down the shaft unaided. Get over it, he told himself, enjoy the day, the company, and the legs. Nevertheless, he wondered…

"This thing with Cuthbert," he said to Sarah. "I can see what it means. But does your Dad believe it? Would you say he's a Christian? Does he have the same ideas as you?"

"You haven't asked him?"

"I was about to get into it yesterday. Things like politics and tyranny got in the way."

"My father is a humanist, although he wouldn't like the tag. And a realist. Any weapon will do, as long as it's effective. Cuthbert is well documented, not least by Saint Bede, so he is sure Cuthbert existed and was a force for good. And he believes Cuthbert is important to this community in every way from heritage to tourism. At its most basic, to income."

"And God?"

"No. He would say there is no evidence for God. My father is no Christian, or any other sort of religionist. He would say religion defies logic. That every other human endeavour—chemistry, medicine, physics, engineering, you name it—has progressed down the centuries, while theology is stuck in the Dark Ages. He would ask how you would reconcile religious ideology with scientific evidence. How a thinking being can follow a dogma literally to death. He believes God, Allah, Eloah and the rest should be consigned to mythology, alongside older gods...Odin, Zeus and the like. He kind of hopes it might happen, maybe sometime in the next millennium. If the planet has that much time."

"Oh? What does he mean by that? Terrorists?"

"Huh? Who needs terrorists when people like Mr. Bush have their fingers on the buzzer? All that born-again stuff. No, I think he's more concerned with climate change."

"If he's so pessimistic, why bother with the secession? Isn't it all a bit futile? Too little, too late?"

"No. And he's a realist, not a pessimist, George. Live as best you can while you can. Try to leave things in the best shape you can for your children. And this island's heritage is one of his *weapons* in the secession. Cuthbert again, rather than Canterbury or Rome. Those, he gave up on years ago when their leaders, the Anglican one especially, began to bring their churches down around their heads. The present incumbent? The fellow with the hair? Oh, dear...the damage ivory towers can do. And to think one of his predecessors was a fan of this place. My father would say a century or two more of Cuthbert's heritage, given what's going on elsewhere, is a bonus."

"If he thinks that way, how does he explain all this?" Geordie waved a hand at the sea, the birds, the flowers, his paradise on earth.

"He doesn't think it needed a God to create it. He believes it's wonderful, not hallowed."

"And may I ask...and you?"

"I go a long way with him. Not forgetting Cuthbert." She smiled. "I'm my father's daughter."

They walked that day to the Castle, past the remains of the *Lorgresund*, the Norwegian vessel used as part of the "Shetland Bus" in World

War II. They climbed down to the shingle beach to see the disused limekilns, with fulmars nesting on their tops and swallows in their arches, and one of the waggonways that in days gone by had brought the limestone for onward shipment. They even found some "Cuddy's Beads," fossilised Crinoid sea creatures that were once used in rosary strings.

Settling down to some work in his basement office, Alex Deville hadn't been surprised to get a call from one of the leaders of the Muslim faith, or about its content. He'd already had a branch of Hell's Angels kicking up a fuss about the moratorium on motor bikes. The only surprise was that after the Tyne Tees thing he hadn't had a call from anyone at Westminster. As usual when the phone rang, he had switched on the recorder. It was a London number.

Khalid Miah had begun by expressing condolences at Deville's "sad loss of a key colleague at the outset of your campaign." Deville thanked him for his concern, thinking people really should do their homework before opening their mouths. Cochise? Key colleague, my sainted aunt.

The Muslim spokesman had proceeded in a congratulatory vein, saying that by and large he admired Lindisfarne's stance. Many of his people felt a growing repugnance at British society; the decadence, the promiscuity, the alcohol, the gratuitous violence, and the prevalence of shallow values. Some were saying that British law was encouraging crime, that it was too soft, and that they would be better served by Shari'a law. The penalties for criminals might seem harsh, but they stopped crime in its tracks. They were saying, "you'd think twice if you knew you'd be stoned or beheaded, wouldn't you?" The British system seemed to have forgotten that the punishment should fit the crime. Shari'a law was seen as "the perfect system of divine law and order," immutably founded in the Holy Koran and Sunnah, the twin sources of Islamic jurisprudence, the keystones of life in an Islamic state.

Deville agreed with part of this, took the rest with a pinch of salt, and understood that the overall message was genuine enough. He recalled a conversation with young George on the subject earlier in the week. They both knew of placards stuck up on bus shelters in London's East Ham and elsewhere that proclaimed Shari'a law to be "the only option for the UK." And of Muslim clerics, by no means limited to the better-known crackpots, who continued to preach that every Muslim had a duty to establish Shari'a law throughout the world; that every Muslim in the UK had a moral obligation to seek its introduction. This had baffled him at first, as for some reason he had assumed Shari'a law to be civil rather than criminal in nature. But a bit of reading, *et voila,* the more all-embracing it became. He had been wrong. Shari'a, as Mr. Miah had suggested, was a whole way of life. Not one on which Islamists were unanimous; but there again, there was Methodism, Mormonism, Unitarianism, as many "isms" as you would care to imagine…

"And your views are representative, sir?" he asked Mr. Miah.

"Representative?"

"For whom do you speak? Or is this a personal call?"

"Oh, no, I am calling on behalf of a representative body. Muslims in Britain."

Deville could guess the reason for the call, but decided to prolong the exchange, and make a few points he felt were worth putting down as markers. "Well, you are not in Britain here, but I have no doubt you will be calling to make a complaint. I appreciate there are shades of opinion, shall we say from the off-white to the black, in Muslim society as in any other. I assume you are one of a moderate shade. The off-white end, perhaps?"

"Well, if you are wishing to put it like that, moderate of course, yes."

"What concerns me," Deville continued, "is the nature of the complaint I feel sure you are about to air, and why you think it will help to air it. I do not feel that anyone, moderate or otherwise, should believe they have a right to change the laws or customs of a country which they visit, or even one in which they may decide to settle. I say this only to emphasize that, in Holy Island, what is happening in Britain is not acceptable. Would you bear that in mind? I see that kind of meddling as being as bad as the behaviour of émigré Britons in Spain, and on a par with émigré Britons in history. It ruins the reputation of empire building, British or Islamic. So before we get to the reason for your call, am I making myself clear?"

"Of course, of course," Mr. Miah replied. "There is no question of interfering, or trying to influence Holy Island in any way. But you are misunderstanding my motives. You are to be congratulated on the ethical stance you have taken. You see? Some of the views I referred to earlier are the opinions of activists, a small minority in Muslim society."

"That is all the more worrying for Britain," Deville said. "Given that the British government embraces and appeases minorities every chance it gets."

"Oh, but we are believing that the British government's efforts towards the integration of the many strands of society are well-intentioned," Miah said. "If not always successful."

"Let us look at those strands," Deville said. "Forgive the historical object lesson, but Christian monks who lived on Lindisfarne could also be called fundamentalists. This is not to say that all Christian monks have been virtuous, but those we had here did not, to my knowledge, advocate the murder of men, women and children by indiscriminate suicide bombing. Nor, to my knowledge, did they hold such outlandish beliefs as a mass market in virgins. They may have held others, but not those. You, sir, claim to come from the strand of moderation. What beliefs, may I ask, do you represent?"

"Well…of course, that people should co-exist, be tolerant, get along with each other. Moderate Muslims, Mr. Deville, are doing their utmost to bring responsibility into this debate. We have no empire-building ideas, as you call them. You see? I must tell you, we are viewing the extremist subset as not so much Islamists as…ideologues. In any case, I imagine Holy Island is…how to put it?…under their radar. And my people, the moderate people I am speaking for, admire your stance. With one small exception. As for the others, they have been told many times that suicide bombing and mass murder are not theologically justified."

"You know," Deville said, "I feel quite sorry for female jihadists."

"Sorry?"

"Well, what have they to look forward to? I imagine, unless they bat for the other side, that seventy-two virgins will hold little appeal. What is the alternative for them? A parade of Catholic priests?"

Silence. Then Mr. Miah said, "I have told you suicide bombers are not justified. I do not think this is a matter for English jokes."

Probably not, Deville thought, especially when you've had a humour bypass. He felt impatience blossoming. It was like talking to a league of bishops, or MPs. "And why would suicide bombers, or any other radicals, need justification? Why would they need any process of rational thought? Surely, all they need is belief."

"I'm sorry? I am not following."

"I am sure you are not," Deville said. "You are speaking to someone who cares as little for religious moderation as he does for religious fanaticism. Precisely who are moderate Muslims anyway, may I ask? Allow me to make a suggestion, hopefully without seeming too provocative. I believe moderate Muslims are people like moderate Christians, that is, halfway followers, people who choose to ignore the less convenient tenets of their faith. People who decide to bypass the letter of divine law, probably quite sensibly, and go, as it were, à la carte. Would you agree that moderation, aside from coming in a variety of shades, has a fatal flaw? That it implies a belief that people are free to believe what they wish, including being nicely accommodating of other views? And that fundamentalists, on the other hand, believe wholeheartedly, and can at least be said to have commitment to their beliefs?"

"I believe you are being provocative, and this is not really what I am calling about."

"I'm sorry if you think so," Deville said. "But let me make my view clear, so that we have no misunderstandings in future. My view is that the whole genre, Bible, Koran, Torah and all, should be viewed as gruesome fairy tales. Or like the *Iliad*, say, or *Aesop's Fables*, as academic classics to be wondered at and analysed, but not believed. Wouldn't such an approach help towards your desire for co-existence and tolerance? A world of simple shared morality, free of religious conflict? All those centuries of strife, relegated to the history books where they belong? But perhaps the moderate Muslims whom you represent also yearn for a Muslim world, and cannot let go of the dream? I believe such a world *is* theologically justified in your Holy Book. Doesn't the Koran demand it? Your moderate friends may well be uneasy at some of the means, but how much of your à la carte menu do you propose to eat? If you'll forgive my continuing the analogy."

There was some mumbling at the other end of the line, and a fit of coughing. Deville waited.

"I am surprised by your attitude," Mr. Miah said eventually. "I was told that I would be speaking with someone whose beliefs, although different, would be of a religious nature."

"My beliefs start and end with my family and the well-being of this island," Deville said. "Your informant clearly didn't know that. It is a Christian island, sir, and will remain one. That has little to do with me; that is its history and hopefully its future. And so far, it has been Christian in a comparatively literal sense. In fairness to you, I would have to say that in a more global context Christians and Muslims have shown themselves to be equally intolerant, and equally evil, down the centuries. One may hope that the world of Islam might transform itself, preferably from within, into a more benign entity. But I am not holding my breath. Fourteen centuries of received wisdom suggest otherwise. And the Christian world for its part has many times been just as à la carte in the application of its ideology, and just as evil. It is even arguable that Christian beliefs are the more outlandish, but theologians are welcome to that particular debate. However, beliefs apart, that has not applied to Lindisfarne; our saints and people have been fairly tolerant and not too evil. In short, and in a global context, I believe the world would be a better place without either creed. Correction, without any creed. To me, all of them seem based on shady origins, developed with shady interpretations by shady people. And with luck, they will all go the way of Mithraism, preferably without the persecution. This may place your views and mine quite far apart along the spectrum, but perhaps not quite as far apart as those of fundamentalists. Don't you agree?"

"I agree that our views are very different, but not with much else you are saying."

Deville laughed. "Very good, Mr. Miah. Then, if you are clear about my views, we can agree to differ. Now, what were you calling about?"

"Your banning of hijab," Miah said.

The crux, Deville thought, thankfully clear and straightforward. "Hijab dress is not banned, Mr. Miah," he replied. "Specifically, the niqāb and burqa are, along with other forms of headgear that have nothing to do with Islam. You will know as well as I that these two garments have been variously used, not for purposes of modesty, but to conceal identity."

"But your ruling on this, Mr. Deville, is an imposition which will cause great problems for Muslim women, women who believe it to be the true course. It is not something to be taken lightly. Some feel protected by the niqāb, indeed prefer wearing it. Allah has spoken to their hearts. They will be unable to accept this ruling."

"They will have to, I'm afraid, or they will have the easiest of options otherwise. I recall my wife some years ago being without a shoulder covering on a visit to a Cairo mosque. Being conscious of local custom, she turned back. We went for coffee, and very good it was, in a restaurant with splendid views of the River Nile from the top of the Hilton hotel. In the same way, the wearing of any full head covering on Holy Island is non-negotiable. For anyone, I emphasize, from Muslims to Ku Klux Klanners, although I must confess that Santa Claus outfits are causing us some conceptual difficulty. Nevertheless, it is to be our local custom, and people will comply with it or leave. It is a matter of simple security. We are not the West Bank, and do not intend that human life should be pursued in bubbles. People are welcome here, provided they are open about who they are and respect our way of life. That is what I meant when I suggested you should distinguish between Holy Island and Britain."

"This will be difficult for some of our women," Miah said. "I am not sure how many visit your island, not many I think, but you will cause those who do great heart-searching."

Deville's impatience went up another notch. "And where, may I ask," he said, "have your interpretations of dress code come from? Am I right in thinking, from sources similar to those which in the Christian world banned most means of birth control? By which I mean, from human, as distinct from humane, sources? Does your organisation follow the school of thought that concluded in the case of a Buckinghamshire school that wearing the hijab headscarf was sufficient for Islamic requirements? Was that the Muslim Council's conclusion, or yours? I'm fairly sure that it would not have been the Taliban's. These variations must be rather inconvenient, wouldn't you say? But assuming the Buckinghamshire case was properly reported, would it be reasonable to apply its message wider than schools? Or was it a sop to the British government, a token gesture to societal equivalence?"

"No, no, certainly not," Mr. Miah said. "You are misunderstanding me again. My people would say that one of the strengths of Shari'a law is its embrace of variations. Regional variations, local variations. This flexibility is one of its strengths. Indeed, our Islamic experts can differ on the interpretations. Different branches of Islam; Sunni, Shia, ascetic sects like Sufi, radical like Hezbollah, strictly orthodox like Wahhabi, vary somewhat in their reading of the Holy Koran. You see? In the case of Wahhabi, the Saudis have been making an interpretation that has caused misgivings, that has deviated from the mainstream of thought, but Islam has been robust enough, versatile enough, to absorb it, you see? As for the Taliban, well...but the common elements are of far more importance than the variations."

Deville, the reason for the call dealt with, was becoming disinclined to prolong this conversation, and was later to regret continuing it. "But wouldn't you say," he asked mildly, "that this versatility may have offered a cloak for skewed interpretations of your Holy Book?"

"Skewed? But I have said it is a strength, and the common elements are...over-arching."

"Perhaps in that case you should reflect on your 'perfect system of divine law and order.' How can something with variations be perfect? Flexibility is all very well, it may even be a seductive thesis to many people, but it seems to me that Shari'a law is inextricably and in all likelihood fatally enmeshed with religious, political and social mores. I would suggest, to the point of total domination of people's lives. And when it comes to authoritarianism, the history of Stalinism or Maoism might provide some valuable lessons. As might papal edicts, come to that. Look where they have got the world in terms of over-population and AIDS."

"You are clouding the issue," Mr. Miah said. "You will not see reason on the matter of hijab dress, then? You will not try to make accommodation for other people's principles and earnestly held beliefs?"

At which point, Deville's impatience reached the top of the dam. He told Miah that once, as a small boy, he had witnessed a starving Muslim kill and eat raw an eider duck, a bird revered in the name of Holy Island's best loved saint. Was that "making accommodation?" Was such behaviour a consequence of Muslim law or religion, or both?

"An extreme case," Mr. Miah said.

Deville finally lost his patience, and his cool. An image of George, Amy's Vietnamese potbellied pig, floated before his eyes. Followed by recollections of Islamic zealots demanding the removal of the Three Little Pigs from the annals of English literature.

He told Miah, if such a thing were to occur again, he would endeavour to persuade his colleagues that the perpetrator should be fed a diet of pork for the duration of his confinement in Holy Island's jail. Would Mr. Miah agree this would be a "punishment to fit the crime?"

Miah said the transgressor would be forgiven by Allah if he were made under duress to eat pork.

Deville told him in that case, he wouldn't bother trying to persuade his colleagues, or consulting the Koran. He would follow Deuteronomy 13 and have the sick son of a bitch stoned instead.

He felt some satisfaction at having managed to dredge the reference up. Quite magnanimous really, given that Deuteronomy featured in both the Bible and the Torah.

The call had ended soon after.

Afterwards, coffee in hand at his desk in the Fahr House basement, Alex Deville had turned his attention elsewhere. Cochise, the stupid bastard, had at least helped out on one front.

Jim "Cochise" Redman, before his descent into wanton criminality, had been an internet junkie. In particular, he had researched whole swathes of Native American history and culture, boring his colleagues and anyone else who entered the portals of The Ship to the point where they would have grabbed a Lindisfarne version of "beam me up, Scottie" like drowning men.

Cochise had given Deville copies of two constitutions, one of the White Mountain Apache Tribe, the other of the Yavapai-Apache Nation in Verde Valley, both in Arizona.

"Examples of my people's good sense. Always remember, for the Apache, the family is the paramount unit. But I know I'm speaking to the converted here," Cochise had said, apropos of nothing. "*Ii na go dzi na tee.*"

Once he'd researched this statement himself, Deville had hoped Cochise wouldn't "see him later"; once a day was more than enough. He put the documents in a filing cabinet, out of sight and mind, thinking they were just another manifestation of Cochise's crazed obsession.

Then one night, trolling through similar documents for Iceland (independent republic), the Faroes (partly autonomous), the Isle of Man (Crown possession with home rule), the Channel Islands (Crown dependency) and other far-flung autonomies like the Canaries and Balearics, he'd started reading them. And thought, good Lord, for once in his off-the-wall life Cochise had done something useful. Deville discovered the two Apache constitutions contained some interesting facts and similarities. Not least of which was that here were two examples of sovereign nations with defined territories, apparently operating successfully within a federal context.

He had asked himself, could this be a fallback option? Did he need such a thing?

It wasn't as if the Yavapai or White Mountain constitutions were from the Middle Ages. It was only 120 years since Geronimo had surrendered to U.S. troops, 110 since the Fort Apache Reservation had been created. The versions of the constitutions which he had in his hands were 1992 (Yavapai) and 1993 (White Mountain). Reference was made to earlier drafts in the 1930s and 1940s. The federal Indian Reorganization Act had become law in 1934.

Both constitutions encompassed their tribe's area of jurisdiction, requirements for membership (broadly, one-quarter Apache blood), elections to office, Bill of Rights, and powers of the Tribal Council. Their preambles, although different, set out basic aims such as protecting and providing a high standard of living for their people, promoting common welfare, conserving and developing land and natural resources, protecting tribal religion, customs and language, and preserving "the inherent sovereign rights" of an Indian tribe.

Nothing to argue over there, Deville thought, even if he could imagine earlier drafts being argued over tooth and nail by federal negotiators.

Both documents included provisions for such matters as regulating and disposing of land, managing economic affairs, overseeing the use of tribal funds, levying and collecting taxes, enacting laws and ordinances, exercising criminal and civil jurisdiction "to the extent permitted by federal law," negotiating with federal, state and local governments, and establishing judicial and law enforcement procedures. The Yavapai constitution had a section on their tripartite system of government; legislative, judicial and executive. It all seemed good stuff; and some of it, suitably amended, was applicable to his homeland now.

As he worked again on the Holy Island constitution and Bill of Rights, Deville smiled to himself as he saw that the Yavapai-Apache Nation made provision for the removal of a Council member for "drunk and disorderly conduct or its equivalent."

He thought Cochise's conduct could fairly be described as "equivalent."

He also remembered that drunk and disorderly conduct in the Apache Nation, and in every other branch of Native Americans, had been a gift of white interlopers. Along with TB, syphilis and other novelties. More examples of immigrants imposing their unwelcome flaws and addictions on host societies.

At the meeting in the village hall this evening, he believed that he had five things to do. The first was to distribute the draft constitution and give people time to comment. He had a few more hours to work on it. Calls from Westminster, media interest, come what may, he was determined to maintain momentum.

He needed to tell everyone he was considering hiring pollsters to find out how the secession was viewed in Britain. It should be worthwhile if the questions were kept simple, and in Lindisfarne's case there were none of the minority choices that Deville was sure had skewed the pre-election polls in Scotland. He didn't know much about polls, but any rational person could see, with a sample of 1,000 and a 3 percent margin of error, an option that registered only one or two votes would get lost in the mix.

He would have to say something about Cochise, tell them Cochise was now under medical and psychiatric supervision. He could hear the sighs of relief now. There could well be the popping of champagne corks in the Tavern later.

He would need everyone's approval of the new housing policy Alistair and Sarah had been working so hard to get in shape.

And finally, he needed volunteers for jury service in the Bigg Market Three case. From what he'd heard in his walks around the village, and from what Sarah had told him, he wouldn't be short of them. In fact, fights could break out if people were disappointed. He would need to remember to take some sort of container along to draw lots and keep the peace. The village hall wasn't up to taking rough treatment, even if some of his constituents were.

He had included in the draft constitution a proposal that normally six people, selected in turn and by ballot, should comprise a jury. He'd explain that he needed things to be in place earlier for the Bigg Market Three's trial.

Just as he was finishing these notes the phone rang, and he switched on the recorder again. A familiar voice floated down the line: "Good afternoon, Mr. Deville (*ha, ha*). Now there's no cause for provocation, umm? Your wee nation seems to be making waves again..."

Twice or thrice during that conversation, in a voice tinged with sardonic jocularity, the British Prime Minister referred to "your wee nation," "your fledgling domain."

Wee man yourself, Deville thought, letting the words wash over him; be my guest, dig your own damn grave.

CHAPTER THIRTEEN

Evening sunlight filtered through the frosted windows of the village hall. It was filling, not to bursting point as it had been nine nights ago, but sufficiently for a healthy turnout. From Alex Deville's conversation with Sarah and Alistair earlier, Rebecca supposed the lower attendance was because no vote would be needed tonight. There must be some sort of fire regulation that limited how many people the room could take, she thought, but if so it wasn't obvious. Maybe all that stuff had gone out the door with the Declaration.

She said hello to Max, who was manning, or more accurately filling, the entrance.

"Still here?" he winked at her. "You must be getting to like it."

"Love it," she said. "Can't tear myself away."

"We'll have you a Holy Islander yet," he said. "But you need fifty years minimum, before you get to be a local. How's the hubby? No longer lost, but gone forever?"

"It looks that way. There's been no word from him in a week."

"That must be a relief to you," Max smiled. "He's no great loss, if you ask me."

Max's attention fixed on a reporter who was trying to sidle in. The guy looked unshaven, as if he'd been here in the same suit day and night for a week.

"Sorry. Holy Island residents and guests only tonight," Max said, as mild as pasteurised milk.

"Good publicity for you, pal, if I could listen in."

"We'll do our best to get by."

"Don't want Downing Street to get an inside track, eh?"

"Off the record, fuck Downing Street." Max smiled.

"What's *he* doing in there, then?" the hack said, pointing at Geordie seated two rows back from the dais.

"He's a friend of the family. A guest."

All the time, Rebecca noted, with his eyes on the door and the other people coming in. All the time smiling. Eyes like his father's, or worse.

"So I'm barred. Like bikers and hoodies," the reporter sniffed, snide to a fault.

"Not if they have an invitation. You don't. The Ship Inn has an open bar for people at a loose end. It's all paid for. Try there."

"Bribery is it? What do you think I—?"

"Hospitality, my friend. Now move on, please. Folks are trying to get in."

The reporter muttered to himself and turned away. Very impressive, Rebecca thought, echoing Geordie at the jail. She wouldn't have guessed that patience and courtesy would be among Max's strong points. Not that the average journalist would see them as being preferable to impatience and discourtesy. Geordie apart, that was; she had taken a sisterly liking to Geordie.

She was pleased to see Daniel Brigham in the hall. He'd been prowling around shaking hands, introducing himself to people already seated. He made his way back to Max and her, smiling as he approached.

"Good turnout," he said. "Enjoyable, getting to know some of these people." He took Rebecca's hand. "Hi to you too. Come and sit with me?"

No need to ask twice, Rebecca thought, holding the hand. Not in a sisterly way, either. It couldn't be impulse this time, could it? The next bloodletting was three weeks away.

The flow of people was easing, and the hall was now nearly full. Deville looked at his watch, signalled to Max, took a sip of water, and opened the meeting.

He began by holding up a bundle of stapled documents.

"This is your draft constitution and Bill of Rights," he said. "They may not yet be perfect, but I believe we're almost there. In total, there are fifteen pages. Rather a lot, but unavoidably so, I'm afraid. I think I've included all those things we've talked about before, the principle of direct democracy and so on, of which this meeting is a case in point. I would like you all to read them, and let me have comments by Friday. At the latest, please. Sarah and Alistair will pass copies along the rows."

"Aye, Alex," a man's voice said. "But what's aal this with Cochise?"

"What's with Cochise," Amy told him, "is that what might have been a disaster came out as some really good PR." She was picking up all sorts of new jargon from young Geordie, and loved trying it out.

"Jim is in good care, but we'll need to replace him in the Althing," Deville said. "He went a bit over the top this morning and may be having a breakdown of some sort. However, he's in safe hands now. The new doctor is looking after him. He should be up and running in a day or two."

"Jesus Christ, I hope not. Can't you keep him where he is—?"

Laughter rang all around the room, and the walls trembled.

"—one or two of us have caravans as well. Not to mention wor hooses."

More laughter, mixed with *eh*'s?

"Oops, sorry. *Our houses*, not them others. How do you lot know about such things, anyway?" From his seat towards the front, Geordie saw that this was Tom Fender speaking, one of the island's last remaining fishermen.

Deville waited for the noise to subside.

"Jim will be fine, I'm sure. But somehow, for the sake of peace and goodwill, someone has to hold his hand and get the message across that he is not an Apache Indian. Much as he'd like to be. Any volunteers?"

"Hell no," Tom Fender said. "I voted for the eedjit but I don't see meself as yon shrink…the Clare guy. Mebbe it's me needs the shrink."

More laughter.

Someone else, a woman at the back, said, "But we all voted for him, didn't we? All I can say is, it could have been worse. We could have had *him* as First Minister."

Laughter again, including Alex Deville.

"Any chance we'll be seein' you about the place in a headdress, Alex?"

Now the room broke loose in whoops and cheers, with one guy trying to do a war dance in the aisle.

"I'll give it a go," Amy said when things had quieted. "Help him on the road to recovery, I mean. Young Geordie can lend a hand, as well."

Young Geordie turned around to look at her as though shot from a cannon, so fast that he felt dizzy.

"What? How can I…what am I supposed to do about him?"

"Ha! Earn your keep. You're an educated man, aren't you? You have the internet thing on your machine? Well, all Cochise's problems started there. You'd be able to give him better things to do. Point him in a new direction. Websites, isn't it?"

"Thank you, Amy. An excellent idea," Deville said. "A decoy, to take his mind off the plight of the Native Americans."

"Aye, an' give Geordie somethin' to do instead of moonin' around the harbour of a mornin'." Not Amy, some guy at the back that Geordie couldn't see.

Laughter resumed, redoubled, everyone having a great time.

Nice to know I'm the stooge for a whole damn village, Geordie thought. And what's with the "mooning"? There was a nasty hint of the lovesick there…he hadn't given the impression…what was that guy getting at? As for his esteemed host, exactly what kind of deal had he made with the old man? Whatever it was, it wouldn't have included being cyberspace chaperone to a nutcase, would it? Shit, he might as well pack his bags and head back to Newcastle before more mischief was done. *Muchos problemas, muy bien,* he thought grumpily, his promise to Sarah, Rebecca, Alistair, Amy and George the pig forgotten in the pathos of the moment.

"All right," Deville said, restoring order. "But to return to the constitution…is everyone happy? Comments by Friday?"

The meeting went smoothly after that, everyone except Geordie in good humour. Alex Deville succeeded in raising six jury volunteers without damage to the fixtures and fittings. Geordie stirred himself enough to realise that he recognised most of them, including Trevor Patterson and Mary Selby.

Dennis Cumming from the Post Office, a.k.a. the Holy Island Bank and Trust, tried his best to volunteer but was persuaded that he might be seen as biased.

"You canna be on the jury and a witness, you daft bugger," someone told him. "*And* a victim, for Christ's sake."

"Look at your constitution, man." There was obviously a speed-reader somewhere in the room, Geordie thought.

Well, could he be a juryman just for the kidnapping case, then? Dennis asked.

No, he was told; it was a nuisance, but the bias was all-embracing.

"Terrible unfair but true, Dennis," the same man said, laughing his head off. "Not to worry. You'll be able to damn them to hell from the witness box."

They all thought the housing policy, which passed unanimously, was first-rate, and the opinion poll idea okay.

"Just make sure the right questions get asked, Alex."

"Aye, an' the folk who are asked them know where Holy Island is. Not in bloody Anglesey." This was a reference to ITN News, which two nights before had failed a basic Geography test.

Deville ended the meeting by saying he had received a second call from the British PM who, understandably in these de-mob happy times, was heading to America for a swansong. He apologised that there had been no time to produce a transcript of this conversation while the constitution was being prepared.

"You're forgiven, Alex man. You've enough on your plate. What'd the slippery scudder have to say this time round?" Tom Fender asked.

"He gave the first hint of trouble ahead. A ghost of a threat, no more. Two threats. He hinted that unless we had second thoughts, he was considering an option to reinstate the causeway. In his words, that he may be compelled to have machines and people move in."

"The military?" Tom asked.

"His words were 'machines and people competent to get it done.'"

"Trust him to put the machines first," Trevor Patterson commented.

"When I pressed him, he pulled back. And hinted I may be looking at a treason charge."

"Who'll get past the gate to do it? Max'll just need to keep his eyes open, won't he?"

"Well, we always knew there would be teething problems," Deville said. "And if the causeway was the obvious starting-point for us, it will be equally so for them."

"By God, just let him try; it's been an improvement already," Trevor Patterson said.

Nodding heads all round.

"Yes. Well, let's all go home and have some rest," Deville said. "My apologies for interfering with your Sunday. Have a good week, everyone."

Afterwards, Rebecca and Daniel, with Geordie tagging along, headed for The Ship Inn halfway down Marygate. Max waved to them as he turned right towards Chare Ends.

"We don't see much of him," Rebecca commented.

"Honey, Max could be standing right next to you and if he didn't want you to see him, believe me, you wouldn't," Daniel said.

"Oh." Rebecca started telling them about the "Private Man" episode.

"That's Max," Daniel said, opening the bar door for her. "A very self-contained guy."

Geordie rationalised his presence by thinking that a supporting role as gooseberry was entirely in keeping with his new-found status. If he was considered a lemon and prune already, why not make a whole fruit salad of it?

At least he could buy everyone a drink. The *Washington Post* pieces were doubling his salary, or would when the cash was wired. Still a zillion or two short of Sarah's standards but hey, a guy could still have a good time. Even if, as now, he was the party of the spare part.

"My Dad would have liked it here," he told Rebecca and Daniel, when they were settled with pints of Holy Island Bitter in front of them. "He was a sucker for pubs with a bit of character, where the ladies can be comfortable."

The light was flat, dusk approaching night, so they were sitting indoors, in a comfortable, rectangular lounge with a window looking out on Marygate. The room had a stone-faced wall along one side, a hanging ship's wheel, a cast-iron wood burner on a brick plinth, wooden ceiling beams and a polished timber floor. Small circular tables and stools were scattered through the floor area, and historical and seafaring pictures and artefacts hung on walls and from the beams. A brick-and-timber serving area was located at the far end of the room, next to a rear door that led out to a beer garden. The pub had been there for centuries, one of the nine that had existed during the hey-day of the herring fishery.

The last time Rebecca had been in was the night of her wedding. It wasn't a thought to dwell on, especially with Daniel sitting there. She wondered if Charley would recognise the place if he ever saw it again.

Geordie liked both village pubs. On his own, he usually drifted to the Crown & Anchor. In that smaller rough-and-ready bar, its open fireplace hung with old photographs of fishermen and island scenes, he could always guarantee getting one of the four tables on which to write up his notes. Wherever he was seated, the bar was within easy hail. It was more of a hidey-hole, less of a showpiece than the Tavern. And there were a couple of nice lasses behind the bar to have a chat with if he and they were in the mood.

"What do you think of the place so far?" he asked Daniel. "Holy Island, I mean."

"Okay. I've met some nice people, some not so nice. Three of them in the jail."

"I'd like to see the jail," Rebecca said, "sometime when you're not busy."

"Anytime you like."

Geordie told them, "I won't be hanging around in here long. Got stuff to do."

"Don't worry about it, George," said Daniel. "Tell me something."

"What?"

"Do you like what they're doing here?"

"I don't have to like or dislike it. I just have to report it."

"Stow that," the deep voice rumbled. "As a person, do you like it?"

"Yes."

"Well, that makes three of us. I wonder if you'd get the same vote outside."

"It's a hundred percent here," Rebecca said. "That's what counts."

"No," Daniel said. "That won't cut any ice at all."

"It's a good start. And the poll should give them an idea."

Daniel shrugged. "Polls. The only ones they take notice of are the ones they can use."

"Why do you say it won't cut any ice?" asked Geordie.

"Hell, this government can't treat its serving soldiers right. So what price its civilians? Or a cupful of them."

"You need to get used to saying 'British government.' They're over there. We're over here," Rebecca said.

"Yeah…okay. Whatever they're called, they're who I meant."

Geordie livened up, thinking of headlines. "Scepticism of Time-Served Soldier," "Ex-MP Slams Ministry of Defence." He saw Rebecca shaking her head, telling him to ease up. All very well for her, he thought, with her reconditioned love-life in the making.

"They had Max," she said to Daniel, smiling. "And you."

"Max?" Daniel said. "Don't underestimate Max. Max is no joke. I'm trained to deal with guys like Max, and I'd think twice."

"We might talk about that sometime," Geordie said to Daniel. "Your time in the forces. What you did, how you—"

"Nothing to talk about. It's the British way. Don't pay them, don't arm them and don't have enough of them. It's how you guarantee men and women of the Right Stuff. Join the army, see the cock-ups. As ever was, but worse. I've got mates who haven't seen their families for months."

"Why did you leave?"

"Time up. And fed up. Being asked to investigate good officers for no good reasons. Whitehall scumbags. They're not fit to lick those guys' boots."

"You should feel at home here, if that's your opinion. Whereabouts did you serve?"

Daniel grinned. "All over. Do you ever stop? As in, have a nice relaxing time?"

So much for "Ex-MP Slams MoD," Geordie thought. Not his day at all. Still, he brightened, it was no great loss. Every other newspaper had already slammed the MoD, usually with justification, each time a serving soldier or flier was killed. Even the generals were making noises lately.

"I'll tell you when he can stop," Rebecca said, interrupting his thoughts. "Friday night. See the sign?"

They looked where she was pointing, and saw a hand-chalked notice: "This Friday. Live Music. Featuring…"

"I think it could be one of the ex-Lindisfarne guys, the group, you know?" Rebecca said. "We should come along, and get Sarah and Alistair to join us."

Geordie drained his beer, told them to have fun, he had to go. "I may not be here come Friday," he said. "One last question, Daniel?"

"What?"

"Has anyone you've met here given you any problems, colour-wise?"

"Hell, no. No one ever does." Daniel grinned.

Geordie left.

He may have heard Rebecca say something about "she likes you, don't be shy" as he walked out, giving a kind of throaty chuckle. He didn't feel like going back and asking her to repeat it. She couldn't have meant Sarah, could she? He peered through the bow window as he walked up the street, and saw them hunched over the table, heads touching, laughing together. Cosy, huh?

Yeah, that's me, Geordie Halloran, he muttered to himself. I'm the village idiot, all right. What did they all do for a laugh before I started "mooning?" Which of them was the proud wearer of the clown's outfit before me? Cochise? Jeezo, what a testimonial. It was enough to make a guy head for the nearest corner and put on a pointy hat.

Sarah was in the kitchen at Fahr House, preparing some supper for her Dad and Alistair, and for Rebecca and George if they returned in decent time. Maybe they were guzzling fish and chips, or some other natural health food, in the Tavern.

The kitchen had been her refuge since her mother died. The house was her responsibility. She had fought tooth and nail with her Dad against hiring one of the local women to help, and she'd won. The clincher had been when she'd asked, with all the confidential stuff that floated across his desk, did he really think that the local rumour mill would stop grinding just for him?

It was a big house to look after, but her mother had done it and so could she. The only thing she'd conceded was someone to look after the garden. Alistair was hopeless, Max was disinterested, and she was damned if she was going to break her fingernails wielding spades and forks.

As she worked, she was thinking about something unrelated to the leeks and cheeses and milk and bread and wine in front of her. Over the last few days, Sarah Courtney Deville had begun to hope that she might, just might, have found a nice, intelligent, good-looking guy. One who reminded her, let's not kid ourselves, of a curly-haired, non-smoking version of Brad Pitt.

But boy, she had met faster barnacles.

Nice, intelligent, good-looking guys were in seriously short supply on Lindisfarne. For her, it was the main drawback in living on the island. Those there were tended either to drift away in search of work if they were local, or at the next low tide if they were visitors. It was, of course, her fault that the barnacle had clung firmly to its rock. She'd made it worse by going over the top on St. Cuthbert, she knew it. She always did; he was a figure from her bedtime stories when she was a little girl, and had grown into an adult companion. It wasn't too much to say that she loved that saint, for what he'd been and what he'd left behind.

And George—she didn't like the diminutive, never had—would be getting ideas that were totally irrelevant, she knew that too. He'd be beating himself up over all the money she had (she hadn't, it was her Dad's), the mansion she lived in (ditto), probably his own measly job (which she thought he was good at) and the measly flat in Newcastle he'd mentioned once or twice (she could have shown him worse right here).

You could see it all in his eyes when she'd been banging on. A kind of dimming sensation, like the world was being leached of light, the look of someone who'd taken a metaphorical punch in the solar plexus. Well, he had to know what she was all about, and either chance it or walk away.

She didn't want a man who unravelled when things went wrong. The only thing she could do was to give him some encouragement, and hint that Fahr House wasn't the be-all and end-all of her life. But she held back at the thought of leaving Holy Island. That would be a bridge too far, especially now there was so much to do. Maybe she could suggest a job to him. Press Officer to the new Holy Island Althing? She smiled to herself. George a latter-day Alastair Campbell? She somehow didn't see it.

Sarah shrugged. He'd be here a while longer anyway, so she'd see how things developed. Okay…she knew how to get a barnacle off a rock, and if George Halloran didn't get his act together *muy pronto,* Spanish crap and all, there'd be a knife somewhere *he* wouldn't like. Perhaps, she thought, it was time to offer a snippet, something he didn't know. His own bedtime story…something with a hook in it for *The Northern Sun.* Something that would allow her to drop a few hints. If he got back in the next hour or so, bright-eyed and sober…

…And there he was.

"It would have swamped the place," Sarah was telling Geordie. "But the planning people in Berwick were all for it, and thought it would provide jobs for local people. It didn't fool anyone here; it would have meant training and qualifications that people here don't have. The jobs would have stopped at cleaners and handymen, and all the good ones would have been snatched up in a heartbeat by the hotel group staff. And there aren't many young people, young *men,* to provide jobs for. Young men leave here, more's the pity." Good grief, she thought, this was a struggle…and he was usually so quick on the uptake!

Except for the short-eared owl, they were on their own in the living room. To help dilute Geordie's inhibitions, Sarah had poured them glasses of white wine. Her Dad was in his basement, Alistair had gone to bed, and Rebecca hadn't returned from The Ship. She seemed to be getting on really well with Daniel, George had told her. Lucky girl, Sarah had said, smiling. No takers. *Barnacle.*

"But what did this big development consist of?" Geordie asked her now.

Sarah sighed. "It was country club type stuff, including a new hotel. But the problem, or one of them, was landfill. They were going Dutch…" (keep at it, girl) "…reclaiming land, and filling in a section of the eastern shore, probably with garbage from Berwick. We don't need Berwick's garbage, or raw sewage on the beaches."

On the hi-fi, Shania Twain was singing about what fun it was to be a woman. She wasn't saying anything about hard graft. Tammy Wynette might have been a better choice.

"What size of place?" Geordie asked, thinking he was lucky to have come back early and have her all to himself, accusations of "mooning" a dim memory. Sarah wiggled her toes. He shifted in his chair, and gave the owl his undivided attention.

"Sixty bedrooms, some with four-posters like the one you have upstairs, nice romantic stuff," Sarah said, by this time feeling somewhat disheartened. "Plus other things: a restaurant, bars, a gym, conference facilities and so on."

"How would they have filled it, year-round?"

Did this guy have a one-track mind, or what? The only trouble was, Sarah thought, it was totally the wrong track.

"Dear knows," she sighed. "They obviously thought they could market it so it would take off okay. It raised a lot of hackles, not just with the locals. They had people like English Nature, the National Trust, up in arms as well. Not to mention the two hotels already here, the pubs and guesthouses."

"I'll bet. Did any of this have a bearing on the secession campaign?"

Sarah topped up his wine. What else was there to do?

"Oh, yes. It's referred to in the Declaration. Remember the phrase 'undesirable and damaging developments'? There have been others down the years, but this made us realise even more that we had to take things into our own hands. Not leave them for Berwick or Newcastle or some guy from the Environment Department to decide. This particular blight was nearly approved a year ago because the Lord of the Manor was away for a month or two, and our local member had flu. He couldn't make it to a planning meeting. The rest of them nearly passed it over his head."

"As a matter of interest, did they suggest resurrecting the old golf course? I was looking at it myself on our walk this morning."

"They got as far as a pitch and putt for their guests. There was no mention of locals being able to use it, which was another nail in their coffin. They're supposed to do their homework, these people, but sometimes it's hard to tell. Didn't your paper pick the story up?"

"Not that I've seen."

"Oh well, it might be worth a mention in one of your pieces," Sarah said. "In the context of the Declaration, local democracy, the blunders and failures you sometimes get. The empowerment of local people, or in this case the lack of it, that sort of thing. How centralised control can backfire."

She took a breath, and gave it one last try: "And the young guy who fronted all this up was a total jerk. Smooth talker, bespoke suits, couldn't keep his hands to himself, God's gift to women. He wasn't a nice bloke at all. There were times I needed a knight in shining armour. You'd have fitted the bill just fine."

She smiled. She had just described, or so she hoped, George's exact antithesis. And if she'd ever heard an open invitation, that was one in cinemascope.

Geordie shook his head sadly. "It's all you need in a small community, someone like that messing about, taking advantage. And do you think, have these people given up the idea, gone for good…?"

"Sorry, George. I'm going to bed. Sleep well. Goodnight." What did she have to do, for heaven's sake? Lie on the floor stark naked?

She marched out.

Was the thudding sound his imagination? Geordie asked himself. Or was Sarah banging drawers somewhere? And what was the sudden departure all about? It could have been the wine, he supposed. Maybe she'd needed to pay a visit. Jeez, women were hard to understand. It had been nice sitting there, just the two of them, having a pleasant, intelligent conversation about things that mattered to her. She had such a lovely voice, educated, but still with a trace of England's finest accent. He could have sat there all night listening to it, no problem at all.

CHAPTER FOURTEEN

"Rise and shine, you lot. Your big day finally arrived."

It was six o'clock Thursday morning, and Daniel was banging on the cell's steel bars with a baton, unlocking the door, and hauling in a bucket and mops.

The Bigg Market Three were already suffering from sleep deprivation, getting up at ungodly hours each morning. During the week, construction work had started in the field next door, pile-drivers racketing from dawn until dusk. The cop had told them it was to be the new Althing House, complete with debating chamber, committee rooms, library, theatre and coffee bar. It was due for completion in six months.

Shad, their usual spokesman, had been inexplicably jumpy on hearing this. "Why you telling us this shit, man?" he'd said. "Fat lot of help to us. We'll be outta here long before that, yeah? Noise fit to wake the dead. Bastards ruining your beauty sleep."

Now, Shad peered blearily at his fake Breitling, and then at Daniel. "For fuck's sake. The thing don't start till ten."

"People to see. Your counsel. Cell to clean. Beds to make. Latrines. Breakfast. Now out of bed, on your feet."

"What gear you got for us to wear, man?"

"Your own gear. Laundered, pressed and A-okay. You think this is a charity shop? UP." Bedclothes were flung off, and mops dished out.

"Fuck's sake. What a fucken liberty."

"You hope," Daniel said.

They'd met three briefs earlier in the week. One calling himself a solicitor, two calling themselves barristers. Who's to know the difference with these suited ofays? Barrister, solicitor, who gave a toss? Like, are we bovvered?

Compared to the first, their second week had been spent in the fast lane. Monday, they'd had the punk journalist, curly hair askew, as hard to shift as a Tyne fog, asking questions. All manner of shit: how they were being treated, had they had visitors, had they seen a solicitor, did they feel prepared, did they have gang connections. Fuck's sake, it was like being in the dock already. More than five minutes with this guy, he'd do your fucken head in.

Then the briefs Tuesday. One of the "barristers" had said he was from the toon, the other had said local. Yawn, yawn, talk to the hand. More questions. Did they have a problem with only two briefs? Did they know they could have six? As in one per person, one per charge? They'd looked at each other. Did these assholes think they were, like, stupid? Six a them linin their fucken pockets? Away and boil your heids. Two of yah's one too fucken many.

And still with the questions. Did they understand the charges? Fuck's sake, Mickey Mouse could understand the charges. How would they describe the events of May fifth? Got a bus, robbed a Post Office, borrowed a car, kidnapped a doofus, dumped him, went to Edinburgh, had a drink, a shag, like an average day. How did they want to plead? Huh?...Like, surprise, surprise...like, guilty might just cover it. On both counts? Fuck's sake, these stupid questions, just make sure we get off light, man, like a month suspended, in that ball park, yeah? Had they scratched the car, broken a window? Oh shit, that was the biggest worry of all, man, a real pisser, they'd lost a lotta sleep over that one.

Then the guy Deville, a long drink of water with scary eyes, telling them there was to be a jury of six, three magistrates, and dishing out copies of a list of witnesses he'd given to the briefs. Who in hell were these people? Rebecca Carter? Dennis Cumming? A cop from some place called Haddington? A tart from Edinburgh? A Newcastle guy? Fuck's sake, it was like the United Nations already.

Finally, the mother again. Floods a fucken tears. Two hundred quid, "all I could raise dear," returned to Dennis Cumming, Prop. How long did they think they would get? Fuck knows; a month or two...givin the cash back would help, wouldn't it? She'd be at court come Thursday, she'd be there for her boy wouldn't she dear, up and down that awful A1, buses and taxis costing her a fortune, getting through that security gate. More tears.

At least the Injun had gone.

No Charley.

Charley was back in London, though not yet among the waxworks. He was "taking a few days off to recover," drinking with his pals, bitching about The State Of Britain, chatting up the girls, dining out on curries and pizzas and chicken chow mein, laying bets on the FA Cup and EUFA Champions League Finals, swabbing his flea bites, and getting his life back together. Regaling everyone who cared to listen, and many who didn't, with the imperfections of Holy Island. And holy matrimony.

Rebecca had tracked him down to St. Stephens Tavern, near Westminster Bridge. Pub chatter, clinking glasses, chairs scraping, coughing, sneezing, swearing, car horns and a TV in the background. Not one of the haunts he'd dragged her into, but he told her he'd fancied a change of scene. She supposed Westminster made a pleasant change from Marylebone or Balham. In that more rarefied quarter of the capital, the sanctum of a spurned authority beneath the tolling of Big Ben, he might even meet an MP who could beat him for bullshit.

No, he didn't want to press charges; he wanted to draw a line under the whole sorry mess. No, he wasn't coming back to Holy Island, not unless he took up arson or demolition as a hobby. If he never saw the place again in this life, it'd be too soon. As far as he was concerned, the Bigg Market Three could rot in hell. He'd had a bill she wouldn't believe from the car rental people, as if it was his fault he'd been kidnapped and the bloody Beemer vandalised. They were saying he'd opted out of premium cover. No, she must be joking, no *way* was he going to pay it.

No, he didn't mind a divorce, it had been fun, it had been a mistake, let's be friends. Sorry, didn't hear that, the noise in here, say again—?

Not consummated? What the hell was she saying? He'd look like a real Char...a real prat if that got out. No way. No, no, no. What did she mean, *not consummated*? His tackle was fine, in perfect shape, last time he'd looked. No way. For Pete's sake, absolutely not. She could find another fucking excuse.

Rebecca said she may already have one in the making; she'd met someone but wasn't rushing it. Could he wait a few weeks? Well, great, bully for her. No problem, whenever she felt like pulling the plug. But hey, none of this *not consummated* crap, puh-lease, no way. They'd had good times, hadn't they, back in the day? Remember The Game, there was always The Game, eh? Good to go, right? How could she do this, be such a 24-carat bitch?

After this conversation, after she had looked at the stunning view from the Fahr House living room once, pictured Daniel in her mind twice and shaken the sound of Charley's voice out of it completely, she had gone down to the basement and told Deville that Charley would not be appearing at the trial. No, she said firmly, in answer to Deville's horrified response, the trial would have to go ahead without him. After all, she had seen the kidnapping and would be there, so what was the problem? Her ex-husband, even if he was sober, would be a loose cannon. Any defence counsel worth their salt would demolish his character as easily as squashing a fly. There were more protests and complaints from Deville. A key witness, central to the case against, would be missing; he was essential to identifying those youths. Between Deville and Charley, Rebecca had had enough for one day. How about subpoenaing the sheep in the Lammermuirs, she suggested. They'd be as much use as Charley.

The village hall was once again pushing its useful life to the limits, this time in the cause of a landmark event, Holy Island's first trial under its new government. Under the watchful eyes of Max Deville and Daniel

Brigham, the room had been carefully arranged. There were seats for Alex Deville, Michael Cromarty and Elizabeth Swan on the dais, and a couple of tables for the accused and their counsel at the front. Alongside that was another table for the prosecution. A raised platform had been constructed to take an angled row of grey plastic seats and a trellis table for the jury; six good men and women with Trevor Patterson their foreman.

People had begun drifting in, but not too many. It was a working day, so most locals had to forgo the occasion. But if they wished, they could see it on DVD afterwards. On the off-chance of problems and post-mortems, but more as an historical record and prototype, Deville was having the whole thing filmed.

Earlier, he had phoned his pal in the SNP to pass on his congratulations to Scotland's new First Minister, and then taken a second call from Khalid Miah, who had seen in a *Northern Sun* article ("a questionable rag, don't you think?") that one of the accused was Muslim. The "misguided young man from a poor family" had not looked at a mosque for years, much less been in one, but once a Muslim always a Muslim. Islam, of course, did not permit or condone the crimes of which he was accused, but Mr. Miah was hoping his kudum would be fair.

"If you believe," Deville said, "that what Islam permits holds sway over the laws of the host country, you have been living too long in Britain, sir. Once again, this is Holy Island."

He had gone on to say that, in any event, punishment would only come into the equation if the Muslim youth and his pals were found guilty. Was he being asked to prejudge? No, no. Was he being asked to treat the Muslim youth in any way differently? No, no. Then what was the point of this call? Mr. Miah said it could be very damaging to the Muslim community in Britain. Great care was needed, there could be a backlash...the boy's mother was asking for representations to be made.

So it was another case of Christmas and Easter, Deville said. Beg pardon? Miah asked. Another case of Christmas and Easter, Deville had repeated. As in, if shops and schools and local councils and the BBC, to name a few, boycotted all reference to Christian holy days, there could be a backlash on the Muslim community? Well, yes...it was a similar situation. Not that he, Miah, was having anything against Christmas or Easter of course. He was sure Mr. Deville was feeling the same way about Eid-ul-Fitr or Eid-ul-Adhia.

Deville, not caring a fig about Easter or Eid-anything, told Mr. Miah not to bother him again and put the phone down. The man was becoming more of a nuisance than the Hell's Angel who checked in once a week.

He watched the three accused and their counsel make their way in, Daniel Brigham with them. He waited for everyone to be settled and opened proceedings, asking the defendants to rise.

"David Bell, Abu Hashmi and Shadrach Bunglawala, you are here today faced with two criminal charges. The first is robbery. How do you plead?"

The barrister from Newcastle, Adrian Haydon-Flint QC, got to his feet. Six feet tall, impeccably suited, a pink carnation in his buttonhole and slicked-back blond hair, he looked every inch how a Queen's Counsel should look. He looked as if he had travelled by first-class rail ticket that morning to Berwick, and then to Holy Island by chauffeured limousine; which indeed he had. Deville hadn't a clue who could have hired him, at an hourly rate which going by appearances could well run into four figures, and could only surmise that Muslims in Britain might have had a hand in it. They probably had the cash. They were probably funded by the British people, via the Treasury and the gerbilistic Communities Minister.

"Mr. Deville, lady, gentlemen, I must protest these proceedings," Mr. Haydon-Flint said. "They do not sit well with me at all. Civil liberties are in jeopardy here. To wit, this is not a properly constituted court of law—"

"Sit down, sir, or you'll find out about civil liberties," Deville said.

"—as I was saying...court of law and cannot in any way—"

"Sit *down*, sir, or you will be held in contempt."

"I most earnestly protest. This is nothing more than a sham. It is as far from—"

"You are sentenced to seven days in Holy Island jail for contempt of court. A further week will be added for each additional outburst. Mr. Brigham, take him away."

Daniel ushered Mr. Haydon-Flint QC out quickly, before he impaled himself further on his pinstripes.

"David Bell, how do you plead to the charge of robbery?" Deville asked.

Three guilty pleas duly recorded.

The other barrister, Malcolm Grant, dressed in nice subdued tweeds, took steadying breaths. He'd told Geordie and his clients that he was local, but "local" wasn't the whole truth. He had a second home on Holy Island. He had also seen a Big Opportunity looming. At this rate, the Holy Island Althing would be staging a trial a week. It put him in pole position to grab a lot of business. He had already replied to Deville's letter, and had happily undertaken twenty-six weeks residence per year. Twenty-six? He'd have signed up for fifty, not forgetting the annual two weeks holiday in Barbados. Besides, he quite liked the place, and his wife was more relaxed. The sea air seemed to improve her libido.

Next week, he looked forward to representing counsel from Newcastle, provided the silly ass didn't let him down by behaving himself in jail.

Deville had engaged a smart young lady from Alnwick, admitted to the bar from the Middle Temple, to act for the prosecution. He asked Ms. Jane White to call her first witness on the robbery charge. She called Dennis Cumming. Between her and the clerk, who doubled-up as caretaker at the First School, little time was wasted on the preliminaries. Deville was impressed with them both.

"...And do you recognise the three youths in this room?" Ms. White asked.

"Shit, 'course I do. That's them there, the young bastards. They should be—"

"A simple yes or no will suffice, Mr. Cumming. You are quite sure?"

"Tricked me proper, they did, making out they'd taken over ill—"

"Yes or no, Mr. Cumming."

"Fucking yes, of course. That's them."

"Thank you. So you left them alone for a minute or two?"

"Yes."

"And how much did they take while you were elsewhere?"

"The thick end of three hundred quid. They didn't get all the bank stuff though, the bastards. You try to earn a decent living and cokeheads like them carry bricks in, jump you, knock you for six—"

"Mr. Cumming. Please answer the questions I put to you."

"Right. Nothing but fucking grief and evasion from the insurance—"

"*Mr. Cumming*!"

"Aye, right."

Dennis settled down after that, with only the odd outburst when the opportunity arose, and had his fifteen minutes in court. He told his friends in the Ship later that he felt he'd done a good job; honour satisfied, justice served.

Malcolm Grant declined to cross-examine. It all seemed pretty bloody obvious. Not to say pointless.

Ms. White then called Miss Monique "Bubbles" Fraser to the stand, a young girl with plump legs, fishnet stockings and a hairdo of many colours. The accused whispered somewhat urgently to themselves while she was being sworn in, fists were brandished, and Abu Hashmi began vehemently to shake his head.

"...And where are you from, Miss Fraser?" asked Ms. White.

"Edinburgh?" The girl looked around in spacey fashion as if debating how she'd managed to get from there to here.

"Where do you work?"

"In a sauna. Just off Broughton Street," Miss Fraser said with much more assurance, having apparently found her bearings.

"And what are your duties?"

"Huh...?"

"Would it be fair to say that you and the other young ladies who work with you offer services beyond preparing steam baths?"

"Huh? Say again?"

"Let me rephrase that. Do you entertain men in private rooms?"

"Objection." Malcolm Grant felt it was time he said something.

"On what grounds?" Deville asked.

"Er...leading?" On second thought, wishing he hadn't.

"Sustained. Ms. White, please avoid leading the witness. Proceed."

"Miss Fraser, what do you do in this sauna?"

"I entertain men in private rooms." Quick study.

"Thank you. And do you recognise a former client in this room?"

"Yes, him," pointing at Abu Hashmi.

"Why does this man stick in your memory?"

"He raped me and beat me up."

The two dozen people in the audience exploded in chatter, mixed with laughter. Deville heard someone say, "That *would* stick, huh?" He paused for a moment to beat himself up; he'd forgotten the gavel Sarah had given him earlier, neatly presented in a bow and with *Lindisfarne's Inaugural Trial* and the date engraved. He used his knuckles instead. The noise subsided. There was a lingering groan from the accuseds' table as Abu Hashmi took a solid one in the ribs from Shadrach Bunglawala.

"Ms. White," he said, "rape and assault are not among the charges today, and I apologise to Miss Fraser for the rowdy behaviour that greeted her statement. Should Miss Fraser wish to pursue those charges, I'd be happy to send a transcript of the proceedings to the Crown Prosecution Service in Edinburgh. I believe it would fall into their jurisdiction rather than ours. Would you establish her wishes later and focus on the robbery charge, please?"

Deville thought it raised an interesting legal point, though. Could you be held to have raped a prostitute who had voluntarily taken you to a private room? Why not, if she changed her mind? But...would that be before or after money changed hands? Forget it, he told himself, there were no saunas on Holy Island and hopefully never would be. It was an intriguing question nevertheless, and he would have to check it out. One dimwit he wouldn't be checking it out with was counsel for the defence.

"Of course, your honour" Ms. White replied. "Miss Fraser...did this individual say anything to you while he was with you privately?"

"He used a lot of really foul language. F-words, c-words, twat, kaffir bitch. Really gross," she said, fingering a tattoo, possibly Cupid, on her left shoulder.

Deville interjected. "The same would apply to charges of racism, Ms.

White. Should the witness wish to pursue them."

"Yes, your honour...Miss Fraser, did the accused divulge anything about this case? About robbing anyone?"

Malcolm Grant let it pass. They were all as guilty as sin, probably of a whole truckload more than was appearing here.

"Yeah, well, before we got into it, he said they'd taken three hundred quid from a Post Office in Holy Island, so they had plenty. He said he could stretch to fifty-five for me, plus the twenty-five he'd paid at the door. That's like for three quarters of an hour. Two quarters too long for the likes of him, believe me."

"Thank you. When you say 'taken three hundred,' did he give the impression this was a normal withdrawal from the Post Office?"

"Shit, no. He said they'd robbed the place. Left the guy on the floor."

"Thank you, Miss Fraser."

A scuffle broke out at the defendants' table. It came to an abrupt end when Daniel, back from his brief sortie to the jail, stepped in.

Next, a woman from Dunbar was called. She recognised her son's and her husband's clothes—"that's them *there*, this is outrageous, the sons of bitches are wearing them." It didn't take Deville long to decide, in the nicest possible way, that she was irrelevant to the Holy Island Bank and Trust incident. But he undertook to return the items of clothing, or compensate the woman.

Amy, sitting at the front, approved. This was definitely good PR.

"I'll take the cash," the Dunbar woman said. "Wouldnae want the bloody things after they've been on *them*."

Deville dismissed the jury a few minutes later after closing speeches. He asked them to reach a verdict on the robbery charge, and told them they would be hearing the kidnapping case later. They took all of seven minutes, which was just enough time for him to grab a quick cup of coffee from Sarah, staffing the kitchen.

Guilty, guilty and guilty as charged.

Deville looked at his watch. Good going, just an hour so far. He said he would defer sentencing until later. He pressed on, got three guilty pleas to the kidnapping charge and asked Ms. White to open the case for the prosecution.

"Call Rebecca Carter," she said.

Rebecca was nervous but proved by a country mile to be the best witness yet. Daniel was proud of her. He liked honest, clear-headed people who didn't use two words where one would do. He thought she looked stunning in her flowery dress and straw hat.

She answered each question "yes" or "no" except when asked to describe the scene of her husband's abduction. She did this with admirable clarity and without swearing. Daniel almost clapped.

"And what are your married circumstances now?" Ms. White said.

"I'm seeking a divorce."

"Would you say the kidnapping had had an injurious affect on your marriage?"

"Not really. He was a hopeless case anyway."

The courtroom burst into laughter again. Deville rapped on the table, his knuckles going red, thinking he should have taken the opportunity to nip out for the gavel when the jury retired. Or asked Sarah to take a break from the kettle.

Daniel looked around the room and said "Quiet," in a voice that would have registered about 1.5 on the Richter scale. The building shook.

In the hush, Rebecca gave him a brilliant smile, and mouthed "thank you."

A pal of Max's was called to relate some interesting things that had been said on the return journey from Edinburgh to Holy Island. Then the cop from Haddington, who was hoping to grab a quick word with Deville about employment opportunities, confirmed that Charley had told him he'd been kidnapped. This was hearsay of course, but Malcolm Grant had decided that a low profile was overdoing things. He much preferred an invisible one.

A partner from Farrington's, the Newcastle car rental firm, told the court that the BMW had been returned "in a shocking state, scratched, window smashed in, shards of glass all over, filthy inside, mud from boot to bonnet, a top-of-the-range SatNav system ruined." It had been found abandoned in Dunbar. He wrung his hands as though the car had been a three-week old infant found on a doorstep. His partners were of a mind to bring civil proceedings pending today's verdicts on "those hooligans." Best of luck with the damages, Deville thought, looking at the hooligans in their stolen gear. I doubt if they'll make you rich men.

The kidnapping case drew to a close. The jury retired for another seven-minute cup of tea. It would have been five, but Trevor Patterson got into trouble from the others for consulting Sarah on what might constitute an appropriate sentence.

Again guilty, guilty and guilty as charged.

Deville looked at his watch again. Nearly noon. An hour and three-quarters. Time well spent. He consulted his colleagues, which took another minute.

"Would the defendants please rise…

"…David Bell, Abu Hashmi and Shadrach Bunglawala, you have been found guilty on both charges, robbery and kidnapping. Taking into account that most of the money you stole was returned, no permanent injuries to persons were sustained, and the absence and apparent disinterest of one of the victims, I sentence you each to four years in jail. Two per count."

A woman at the back of the hall burst into hysterical tears.

Shad: *"What? Four YEARS? What the fuck…!"*

"Sit *down*. Any more outbursts and you will be held in contempt and your sentences increased. I should add that Holy Island does not and will not operate a system of time off for good behaviour. You will serve four years less the eleven days you have already been in custody. However, should you indulge in *bad* behaviour while imprisoned, your sentences will be extended at this court's discretion. I make no apologies for following the Tasmanian example. Mr. Grant, do I make myself clear?"

Mr. Grant stirred himself from his reverie. He had been dreaming of coming down to breakfast to a panting, naked wife, and then walking the length of the village to his new office. It was a good three hundred yards, and as he was fast approaching forty, with a lot of lunches, dinners and bottles of claret behind him, he felt he needed all the exercise he could get, indoor and out. Alternatively, he might be able to arrange a small conversion, install his office in the house, and play a few holes at Bamburgh Castle Golf Club two mornings a week. Decisions, decisions.

"Yes, your honour, perfectly," he said.

"Then please ensure it is also perfectly clear to your clients…These cases are closed. Mr. Brigham, take them away."

Deville thought the young barrister from Alnwick had done a competent job. She had a propensity to lead, but he would certainly commission her again. In fact, if she wanted it, the job of Prosecutor for Holy Island was hers, say for a six months trial period. As for the defence counsel Grant, he had about as much animation as a bowl of cold porridge. God help anyone in that gentleman's charge who pled not guilty.

He was pleased with the morning's work; it had been another solid step forward. True, it had been a straightforward case, but reliable procedures had been put in place, and the outcome had been entirely satisfactory.

He must remember to thank Max again. Max had done a sterling job tracking these people down and persuading them to attend. He had given up on the second car owner in Dunbar; the chap had just been relieved to have his vehicle back in one piece and had no axe to grind. Deville knew nothing about the Broughton Street tapas bar or queer, but they wouldn't have signified anyway. Quite rightly. They were two of the city of Edinburgh's myriad problems.

On the evening of Friday eighteenth May, The Ship Inn was crowded. The folk singer had attracted half the village and a handful of overnighters. Sarah, Geordie, Rebecca and Daniel had walked over together from Fahr House. They were dressed casually, but Geordie noticed that Daniel's T-shirt had an interesting crest upper left, featuring a green wreath topped by a gold crown against a black background. The creases in his jeans could draw blood, and his black shoes were blinding. Alistair had opted out, engrossed in digital editing of the trial.

Geordie had been born on the wrong side of 1980. He knew a snippet or two, but was too young to know everything about the group Lindisfarne, their *Lady Eleanor* or *Fog on the Tyne*. He wasn't familiar with the songs this guy was performing, which were mainly compositions post-dating the group, but other people obviously knew them well. And the singer was okay; he had a repertoire of folksy ballads with tolerable lyrics. Geordie had always been envious of people who could capture a storyline in a few brief words. He admired most musicians and Rebecca had told him this guy wrote his own stuff.

Since their chat in the Fahr House living room on Sunday evening, Sarah hadn't been paying him a lot of attention. She still smiled and joked, but Geordie didn't like the way some of the chemistry seemed to have leaked out of their relationship. He was nervous about asking her why this was, in case he got an answer he couldn't handle. It would be presumptuous anyway, wouldn't it? It might just be his own hyperactive imagination; Sarah could be thinking everything was hunky-dory. He had given up trying to figure it out; girls were an enigma too far. He'd just gone along trying to interest her in what he was writing and thinking. Sometimes he'd raised a smile, once or twice even a note of approval or humour.

"Someday," he'd told her, "I'll write the definitive book on all this."

"A man's gotta do what a man's gotta do, George," she'd said. "And a woman can only do suitably impressed. Bet you didn't know who said that."

"You? Joan Rivers?"

"Don't spoil it; you were right first time. You know, sometimes you can be quite smart, for someone who spends his life stuck on a rock."

"Rock?" Geordie said, wondering where this was heading.

"Not to worry. I do think there'd be no one better to do it. The book, I mean," Sarah had said. Well, where there was hope, Geordie thought, even confused hope...

In light of this inexplicable cooling-off, Geordie had also fallen back on a tried and tested way of helping him sleep at night. Encouraged by the man himself, he had raided Deville's library and was reading copies of Franz Kafka's *The Trial* and the Holy Koran. As anaesthetics, he would give *The Trial* 8 out of 10, but the Koran had unnerved him somewhat. The unrelieved refusal to live and let live, which seemed to permeate much of it, hadn't been exactly relaxing. Would parts of the Bible cause equal gloom in an objective reader? The Books of Revelations or Daniel? So far he was persevering, but was thinking of moving on to Bob Woodward's *Bush At War*, to check if the famed reporter still had the magic.

Now, between the Lindisfarne guy's songs, Sarah was bemoaning her younger brother's all-work-and-no-play outlook on life. "Fat chance of getting him to join us tonight," she said. "These days, Alistair spends all his time in a computer. He's worse than you, George."

Geordie felt sorry for Alistair. After all, with just a bit of help from his sister, the guy was acting single-handedly as the Althing's executive arm. It was nice that Sarah was speaking to him again, though.

Max, as usual, was at the border control point. He tended to be outside the ambit of Geordie's life anyway. Geordie sometimes wondered if Max came back to Fahr House to shower or shave or sleep. Maybe he had facilities at the security gate. Did the guy eat? Geordie couldn't recall him ever having been present for a meal in the family home.

Slightly to Daniel's embarrassment, Rebecca showed the others a copy of a quotation he had pinned up in the jail:

"Next to the blessings which a nation derives from an excellent constitution are those advantages which result from a well-regulated and energetic plan of Police, conducted and enforced with purity, activity, vigilance and discretion."

Patrick Colquoun, former Lord Provost of Glasgow, 1797.

"Good stuff," Sarah said. "That should educate the prisoners."

"I'm not so sure about the purity," Rebecca replied, "but the rest is good."

An advantage of having dark skin, Geordie thought: no one can tell if you're blushing.

"Do you think the sentences were fair, Daniel?" he asked.

"Good thing it wasn't six years. They'd have had to use two hands."

After an hour, the singer took a break. There was a sudden crush at the bar. Someone put on some old-time rock music; Creedence Clearwater Revival's *Bad Moon Rising*, Roy Orbison's *Only The Lonely*. Sarah told them that the landlord wouldn't live with anything dated post-1980, perhaps a year or two earlier. For him, with the exception of Bruce Springsteen, music had stopped when Elvis died.

Daniel, whose round it was, grimaced at the queue waiting for drinks and said, "Should have got to the trough earlier. I'll try in five minutes."

Rebecca said, "Okay. Let's dance."

Geordie sipped his beer.

Sarah sipped her wine. "Want to dance, barnacle? Ladies' choice."

"What? Barnacle?"

"George, you're so slow you're *stationary*."

Geordie thought long and hard about that one while they were shuffling about. It wasn't difficult to concentrate; conversation was out of the question. Sarah kept rolling her eyes at him, pursing her lips, shaking her head. A glimmer of light began to appear. Geordie groped his way towards it. Was it possible? Did she think—?

The piped music stopped. The singer returned to his stool.

Daniel got the drinks. He and Rebecca locked into a conversation.

Geordie drummed his fingers on the table. "What was that about, the barnacle thing?" he tested the water.

"Don't you think I'm attractive? You think I'm some sort of scrubber?"

"Good Lord, no. *No*. I think you're absolutely lovely. The most beautiful…I mean—"

"You mean I'm out of reach. You mean I'm filthy rich. You mean I live in the lap of luxury. You mean I have this big house, this great family. You mean you're scared, you don't want to deal with your life here and now, with me. You'd rather be in some other time and place with someone easier, less of a challenge, some nice working-class girl. You mean you think you're way beneath me. You *barnacle*. You bloody *idiot*. It's all a load of *crap*."

Geordie grinned. "Well, if you put it like that, it must mean I have the ghost of a chance?"

Sarah burst out laughing.

"You won't know until you try. Until you get off your damned *rock*."

Here it was, ten o'clock at night, and Geordie could swear the sun had just come out.

CHAPTER FIFTEEN

Two hours later, around midnight, the first Berwick Borough Council bulldozer crashed through the security gate and went headfirst into the moat.

Max was quite proud of his moat, and had given it a lot of thought. There was the question of where Holy Island land finished and British land began, and then the question of tides. He could armour the trench all he wanted, but knew that the sea could undo the best of engineering works as easily as it could wreck the best of ships.

There was also the length of the thing, how deep it should be, and how wide. Cost apart, and Max had been brought up to respect money, it would be futile to stretch it for miles from the gate. First, there were no other access points except over fields or farm tracks to Fenham Mill, or along the shore from Goswick Golf Club. Second, he didn't want to make life difficult for the coming and going of the Hummers and other vehicles. Third, if people wanted to come in force to Holy Island, they could come by sea. And fourth, he wasn't going to overcook it. The moat would be needed at most for a year, until things were settled. However they were settled, whether as an independent island or, God forbid, an island again under the limp British flag, it wouldn't be needed longer than that.

Eventually he told the squad operating the grabs and diggers to cut the ditch the length of the fence, about two hundred yards towards Beal Point where the Lindis approached the shore, and a similar distance south towards the Swab. He told them to make it ten feet deep, and angle the sides so it was twenty feet wide across the top and ten at the base. The mixture of sand and rubble was removed by dump truck and spread on an area of the flats, waiting to be sieved and smoothed by the next high tide.

When the diggers had finished, he told his squad to lay heavy plastic sheeting and began organising truckloads of stone from Belford Quarry, eight miles down the road. He had this work carried out at night, paying over the odds for the quarry rock. He thought about clearing up the handful of derelict buildings on the island as a side benefit, but decided against. It wasn't worth the effort. The machines would wake everyone up and cause complaints. His old man had enough on his plate without getting that sort of flak. And Max had no wish to upset the secession applecart.

He was careful not to wreak havoc along any part of the Holy Island shore or damage anything historic. No one could accuse Max Deville of losing sleep over the rape of the planet, but he did have sensibilities. And woe betide anyone who messed with his island.

He then started the squad laying the steel wire and pouring the concrete, hundreds of tons of it. This phase was not yet complete but it was getting there. When it was done, he thought, all he could do was monitor it twice a day to see what action the waves had on it. Except for hundred-year storms, he didn't think there would be anything that couldn't be plugged. And he didn't have to worry about hundred-year storms, did he?

The moat followed the shore almost at high water mark, seaward of the ranks of wartime concrete bunkers that lined the salt marsh on each side of the road. Max had made sure the section just inside the gate was finished first. It looked fine and would weather down to look better.

It had been a good fortnight's work. The moat had been started before the PM's call to his old man on Sunday, but the call had injected urgency.

And it had been an efficient operation. Efficiency was another thing Max Deville had been brought up to respect.

As Sarah had remarked, her darling brother was nothing if not thorough.

As became clear later, the Borough Council of Berwick-upon-Tweed was acting on instructions—"requests"—from the highest office in the land. Plus one of the second highest. It made the requests hard to refuse, even if they'd wanted to, and there were those who felt somewhat hoodwinked and put out by the Declaration. It had stolen part of their constituency.

The local Council was "requested" to proceed because it was felt the army would be seen as overkill. Besides, a lot of the army and the more serviceable bits of their equipment were spreadeagled over Iraq, Afghanistan and other far-flung places. Battalions of them were probably getting ready for Iran or North Korea. All in all, they were too busy to be bothered with a piddling island.

Only the timing of the mission to reinstate the causeway was left to the Council, but with the fatal proviso that an element of surprise was paramount. In the Council's judgement, or the judgement of those few councillors in the know, the early hours of a weekend morning would be perfect. That meant, a Saturday. It could not under any circumstances be the early hours of a Sunday. A Sunday was not to be desecrated on the Holy Island of Lindisfarne.

This decided, the councillors left the detailed planning of the mission in the hands of their staff. With the element of surprise branded indelibly in their brains, their staff planned for darkness, and that it should be more or less low tide when they arrived. In fact, the juxtaposition of these two conditions had militated against an assault earlier in the week, and would do so again in a few days' time.

They hired in vehicles and equipment to supplement their own, and organised a flyover in a coastguard chopper during the week. Nothing was left to chance. Unfortunately, at the time the flyover occurred, it was high tide and the moat wasn't obvious. They had heard rumours, but it all looked very peaceful down there, just like Holy Island should look.

The bulldozer had been put in the vanguard of the convoy to smash through the security gate. It came as a big surprise to the driver when he and his machine disappeared at an intoxicating 60° angle into ten feet of water. Seconds later, he was joined by two equally surprised truck drivers, their vehicles laden with rock.

The driver of the fourth vehicle, another truck, peered through the gloom and decided to climb down and have a closer look. He sized the situation up, started shouting and waving, and stopped the convoy behind him. John Moffat had not been keen to draw this shift. He thought working through the middle of the night was a bloody imposition, and he had sympathy for what the Holy Islanders were doing. Hell, who wouldn't leave Britain if they were given half a chance? His wife had been banging on at him about it for years.

Max came out of the portakabin in a hurry, thinking, Christ alive, this'll need a crane. He walked over to the truck driver dressed in his commando gear, an assault rifle slung over his shoulder, and four guards behind him. He recognised the guy.

"John," he said politely. "Get the hell out of here."

"Jesus," John Moffat said. "We weren't expectin' that."

"You need to move. And take this lot with you." Max indicated the motley collection of diggers, dumpsters and refuse trucks stretching up the Beal road. It was interesting how they had all suddenly taken a liking for headlights.

"Jesus, I'm sorry, man. We'll be leavin' right enough. But you have to do somethin' about them." He pointed at the moat, panic rising in his voice. "Get *them* out, willya. Please."

"We'll look after it." Max gestured to his pals. Two of them had already stripped off their combat jackets and pants, and dived in.

"Those guys could be drownin'. Gettin' eaten by crabs," John Moffat said, peering into the inky water, bubbles bursting on the surface.

"How many down there? Just so we know?" Max asked, rapid fire.

"Three. One each vehicle."

"Whose idea was this?"

"The man at the top, so I've heard."

"Let's be clear. Top of what?"

"That tosspot...the PM. Orders from on high, man."

"You know that for a fact?"

"Hell, yes. Councillors been huddled in corners for days."

"He'd have had trouble finding allies amongst your lot," Max said. The Borough Council of Berwick-upon-Tweed (13 Liberal Democrats from 29 seats, no overall control) didn't number itself among leading New Labour strongholds. There would have been civic unrest if it had.

"Och, there's always some willin'. New Council, same faces. They were likely promised seats in the House of Lords and shit."

"Yeah. Now get moving. They'll be okay," Max said, with a nod towards the moat.

"Aye. A lot of us think you're doin' all right, you know. This was bad medicine from the word go. I hope the bleedin' government pays for it. In more ways than one."

John Moffat turned his truck and started up the road, stopping as he passed other vehicles. They all started turning around.

Shouts of "cheers" and "good luck" floated to Max through the darkness.

He looked to see how the rescue operation was going, and could make out two of the drivers already on dry land, kneeling in the mud, retching.

Max went back inside the portakabin and made two calls, one to his father, the other to the doctor. When he re-emerged, three guys were retching, the latest in the hands of one of Max's pals, well and truly in the throes of a Heimlich manoeuvre. Max breathed a sigh of relief. Local council amateurs.

When his elder son phoned, Alex Deville was having a later than usual night in his basement, working on comments on the new constitution. There were only a couple of dozen and most were points of detail or clarification. The draft Bill of Rights seemed to have been accepted by everyone (Cochise, I salute you, he thought). He was altering the constitution as he went, and drafting letters to everyone who had taken the trouble to write. Next week, he knew he'd have to publish a list of the changes. When the time came to adopt the documents, everyone should know exactly what it was they were voting for.

He wasn't surprised to find that Amy Donaldson had produced the one comment of substance. Both he and Amy were staunch opponents of over-legislation, and Amy's comment demonstrated it. They both liked analogies too.

During one chat, they'd likened British law to the game of golf, which in days gone by had happily bumbled along on the thirteen rules, twelve general and one local to the Leith Links, recorded in 1744. Now, with sub-sections and sub-sub-sections (but not sub-sub-sub-sections), it had upwards of two hundred to grapple with. This was marvellous job security for the good old boys in the R&A, but what had caused the explosion of words? New technologies, pedantry, an exponential increase in golfers and golf "crimes," or a simple inability to leave well enough alone?

Perhaps it was because no one could possibly know all the rules, so they broke them and were duly punished with new ones. Or perhaps it was because those drafted a year or two ago had been misinterpreted, or seemed to lack a certain *je ne sais quoi,* and needed fiddling with some more.

The Highway Code was another case in point. How many drivers over the age of twenty-five knew all there was to know? Deville and Amy had been interested to read of local experiments where the removal of a plethora of traffic control measures had actually reduced accidents. They had wondered how much further accidents would be reduced if drug users and alcoholics were to have their licences revoked for life, with a thousand or two traffic cops to check for compliance.

They had felt that one of the keys to good legislation was that it should be ahead of the game, proactive rather than reactive, and had tried in several ways to feed this principle into the constitution.

One way had been to create "sunset" provisions. Deville had drafted a clause whereby any law, one that might initially have been created for knee-jerk, faddish or conciliatory reasons, should be phased out after three years unless it was reinstated by all Holy Island's voters. Amy was suggesting one year and a simple majority. "Take gay marriages," she wrote. "Why prolong that piece of nonsense or make it harder to repeal?"

She went on to address another worrying issue, the mountain of British legislation that would need to be adopted or discarded. "Why tackle the mountain?" she wrote. "Why not just chip away at it?" She suggested that anyone who disapproved of a particular law should be allowed to put it to the vote. If it got a majority, it stood. If not, it fell. This way, they could hold on to the good bits of the mountain, the bits people wanted to live with. "Maybe it's not so much a mountain as a curate's egg," she added.

Deville liked it. There was a conflict with the sunset rule, but that could be resolved by making the rule applicable only to Holy Island's legislation. And Amy's suggestions combined the principle of direct democracy, which they had also been keen to ensure, with a practical way of ridding the island of iniquitous legislation. The only issue left unresolved was British legislation post-2007. Was it ignored, did it become part of the curate's egg, or should it be dealt with under the sunset rule?

Then he got Max's call.

The opening skirmish at last, he thought, heading up the stairs.

The first thing he saw when he entered the living room was his daughter watching TV in the arms of George Halloran. A smile glinted in the ice-blue eyes. Nice to see they still had most of their clothes on, but the young fellow did strike him as a bit of a slowcoach. Intelligent, a lively inquiring mind (one of their latest chats had been about religious ratiocination, or its absence, and the misty appeal of some futuristic secular world government) but, oh dear, a bit of a slowcoach.

"Work to do, George," he said as Geordie sprang to his feet. "You'll need to get your editor to hold the front page. Or I will."

"Why? What's happened?"

Deville told him.

"Oh, Lord." Geordie looked at his watch. Twelve twenty. "I'll need to phone now. Or hours ago."

"Do it from here. I'll help you if you need help. This is a big one, and given the timing, you can pretty well guarantee exclusivity."

"Right. But it's short notice for the old man. He won't like it."

"Just call him. Then we have to get over there. You'd better take this." He handed Geordie a digital camera. "And button the shirt before we go."

"I'm on it." Geordie buttoned the shirt, and picked up the phone. "To hell with him anyway. He's going to have to wait for this."

"I'll come with you," Sarah said to her Dad. "Make the coffee if nothing else."

"Now that you have him you're going to see he can't escape, is that it?" Deville asked, half listening to Geordie on the phone. He seemed to be making progress.

"Something like that."

"Bright young fellow. Industrious. Tidy. Courteous. Good sense of humour."

Sarah squinted at him. "Yes to all five."

"Took him long enough."

Sarah smiled and nodded.

Deville smiled back at her. The doer, the carer, the thinker, and now the worker. It would be hard to beat that combination.

"You should have been here fifteen minutes ago," Max told Geordie when they arrived at the portakabin, which Geordie thought was already looking as though it had a history. "All the trucks and diggers have gone. You'd have had some good pictures of them winding up the hill," he said. "Like an overfed rattlesnake, all greens and oranges and blacks."

"How about the things in there?" Geordie asked, pointing at the moat. "The vehicles?"

"You won't get much of a picture until we winch them out. The moat's full all the time now. You might get something at low tide, in daylight, but it'll likely be cloudy."

"No time," Geordie said. "I have to get the story to Newcastle inside an hour or two."

"Well, if you need a photo, the best thing you can do is take the shivering wrecks inside the office."

"Huh?"

"The three drivers are in there, recovering. Take their pictures. Get their angle on it."

Geordie tried some shots of the vehicles underwater with a flash, but knew they were no good. All he had was a reflection of the flash.

"Useless," he said, "let's go inside."

He got a nice group shot of the drivers huddled in blankets with steaming cups of coffee and cigarettes. Old Smokey would appreciate it, if no one else did. He spoke to the doctor, who told him they'd get over it. "Fit young chaps. They'll be as good as new by dawn. No drownings, no hypothermia, but it could all have been much worse, you know. If they'd been twenty years older?...a different story. It really doesn't bear thinking about."

The guys themselves were happy to talk, and had no problem with being recorded. No, they didn't blame Max or Holy Island at all. It was those idiots in Berwick, who didn't know their corporate ass from their elbow. It was the old mushroom principle again; the guys who were being asked to do the dirty work hadn't been given a word of warning about the moat. Hell, that thing was deep; someone had done a good job. And, Jesus, it was cold enough to freeze Pegasus...

One of the drivers said, "One of your guys was a hero. Eddie here, trapped in his cab, couldn't budge the door. The guy forced it, took him maybe three minutes under there, dragged Eddie out, the cab filling up, and gave him first aid. Both of them could have drowned, easy. What was that thing called?" (looking at the doctor) "...Yeah, Heimlich. He gave him the Heimlich thing then...what's the other thing?...yeah, cardiopulmonary...Christ, that's a mouthful...yeah, CPR. The guy saved his life, no question."

This peroration was confirmed by them all, especially Eddie, the occupant of the improvised bathysphere.

"So who sent you in the first place?" Geordie asked the one who seemed most forthcoming.

"Idiots in Berwick. Under orders from Number Ten."

This was again confirmed by all of the drivers.

"How many vehicles altogether?"

"Three in there."

"No, in the whole convoy?"

"Two dozen or thereabouts. Mostly on hire."

"How long has this idea been in the pipeline?"

"Dunno. Most of last week, I think."

"Since Monday," another of the drivers said. "I work for the Council. These two don't. The rumours started flying on Monday."

"And were the Council workers happy to do it, to come here?"

"Hell no, no way."

"Neither were the non-Council guys," the first driver said. "But the bosses told us they'd lose contracts and jobs if we didn't. Pressure was brought to bear. Dickheads."

Confirmed by them all once again.

After fifteen minutes, Geordie switched off his recorder and thanked them. He told them that they would see their story in *The Northern Sun* this morning.

"Yeah, we were worried you'd say that," one of them said, laughing. "Just glad to get out of it alive, mate."

Geordie spent another few minutes with the "hero," took his picture and then a group shot of Max with him and the other three border guards. Then he switched his recorder back on.

"Hug then kiss," the guy grinned. "Heimlich then CPR. First time I've done it. It worked fine."

"You feel okay yourself? No after-effects?"

"Yeah, no problem, been in worse spots."

"Have you seen and heard enough, George?" Alex Deville asked.

"A quote from you should do it."

"Okay…fine…" Deville contemplated for a moment then said, "As is customary for the British Prime Minister, he sent other people to do his dirty work. As is also customary, it backfired. We have seen another example of arbitrary tyranny, another example of why the people of Holy Island felt unsafe and powerless in the hands of a heedless British government. I'm sure we are not alone in that sentiment. Recent elections, recent polls on topics such as immigration, have shown as much. We have done something about it. As a result, the people of this island feel happier than they have for decades. And why shouldn't they? They are in responsible hands. Those hands are their own."

"Hmm," Geordie said, "that should flesh it out nicely. I need to get back. Any offers?"

"Two more things, George," said Deville.

"Two…? But I really…what are they?"

"Choice. Ever stop to think how fully it's conditioned? People have no choice in the world they're born into, and most have less impact on it than a pinprick. They are buried by it. They find themselves at the mercy of natural forces or supermarket stockists or, in this case, politicians. Can they be blamed for starving, 'choosing' flyblown meat, or sub-standard MPs? For shying away when things become contaminated or unproductive? Is that choice? Especially, looked at the other way, when you consider that many of them, even if they want better, have neither the means nor opportunity to seek it. This island has been given an improved choice, no more. And they've exercised it."

"And the second?" Geordie asked, looking anxiously at his watch.

"Consequences. Ask your readers what would have been achieved if this invasion hadn't nipped itself in the bud. Ask them if they think the future had been given any thought, as might have been expected from their government. As in the case of Iraq, for example. Or Europe. Concentrate their minds on Amy's plumbing leak, on cause and effect. Would the reinstatement of the causeway have succeeded? No. It would have been demolished again. Or would troops have been deployed to defend it? Consider that trench," he nodded at the moat, "as our miniature version of the English Channel. Having breached it, do they occupy Holy Island against the wishes of its people? Behave like Russians? And for how long? It becomes, for the British government, an indeterminate future. Especially as there is no intention here of succumbing. Do you see parallels? Does the British government believe their every aberration becomes the norm, that people simply absorb it, adapt to it, and move on with it as baggage?"

"I've kind of overdone the plumbing leak thing," Geordie said. "Another snafu, maybe? Situation normal, etcetera..."

"That was part of the point I was making about consequences." Deville grimaced. "Socialists, believe it or not, were once held to be society's planners. Not that it's been a much-loved philosophy, bleeding as it does into the nanny state. And this lot don't know where to stop...well, what would you expect from a bunch of incompetent control freaks? The point is, we're trying to repair Amy's plumbing leak, which shows every sign of worsening. To re-establish prudence, sanity. And with one exception, the people here are sane. Which is more than can be assumed from the British government's actions."

Geordie gave it a few seconds' thought. "Okay. I need to get going."

"Take the FourTrax," Max said. "Bring it back when you're done."

"Great stuff," Geordie said gleefully. "I've had my eye on that thing since I came here."

"Just don't bloody damage it."

"How long till the tide comes in?"

"You've got an hour and a half, safe."

"That should do it," Geordie said. "Be seeing you."

Shit, he thought, what a story. What a *scoop*. Sarah said she'd let him get on with it, she'd see him later. He gave her a kiss, and set off back across the sands. It had always mattered to Geordie that his work should serve the forces of good, and here was an opportunity that had come straight out of the top drawer. And a denial from Number Ten would put the icing on it…

By ten o'clock Saturday morning, the British government was receiving universal blame for the Big Bulldozer Bungle. Geordie's story had been picked up by TV and radio, and wires were humming worldwide. The Editor of *The Northern Sun* told him that he had never been so pleased to work all night. He said the same applied for all the newspaper's staff, the online crew included, who'd been hauled in. Or so he thought, but they had damn well produced the goods anyway. What the wife had had to say about it, though…

"Even Old Sm…Bob Cutler?"

"Very pleased with himself. Got through two packs overnight. He managed to pull a ham-fisted quote out of some lass in Number Ten. On the lines of 'a well-meaning attempt to bring Holy Island back into the fold.' Very poetic. Biblical. I'd give her till noon in her job."

"There'll be some follow-up over the weekend. They need to lift those vehicles out of the water."

"Remember it's Sunday tomorrow. And no, before you ask, I won't be running off a special edition. How are things going otherwise up there? Still happy with your lot?"

"I'm in love."

"Shit. I knew it was too good to last."

Geordie and Sarah returned to the scene at eleven o'clock, taking Rebecca with them. The tide was receding and Geordie hoped to get a usable shot of the vehicles in the moat.

He had spent half an hour with Alex Deville looking at pictures from the various cameras around the island, one of them facing across the flats towards the security gate itself, but they'd been indistinct. He could make out a blur of vehicles winding down the Beal road just after midnight, headlights going on as they stopped, but nothing *The Northern Sun* could use. Nothing that Alistair, however much he played with it, however much he muttered about new software, could tweak into a clear enough focus either. Colour, black and white, sepia, bells and whistles, none of them worked.

"I'm sorry I didn't think of this last night," Deville told him. "I was in too much of a rush to get out there. They're not clear at all, are they?"

"No," Geordie grinned at him. "But given your forgetfulness, I'd have been a lot more upset if they'd been usable."

He was pleased to see that he still had the field pretty much to himself this morning, but knew the competition would be hot-footing it up and down the A1. He wondered what else might have been happening to keep them away. Maybe the England cricket team was on top in the Test. Or had been found at sea, drunk in charge of a pedalo. Or maybe Dubya had mistaken his brain for his breakfast grits.

Max and his pals had the gate back in place, dented but functioning.

"Do you ever sleep?" Geordie asked.

Max looked surprised. "Sure. Most nights, we take shifts."

Of course, Geordie thought, stupid question. "What are you doing about the drowned vehicles?"

"The crane's coming in an hour. Low tide. It'll take a while to set up."

"It'll be fun getting a crane down the road."

"A couple of the guys are going up to help. Good thing we don't need passports heading that way. The police in Berwick know what to expect."

Talk about being a step ahead, Geordie thought, this guy's a whole lap. He was beginning to feel Max would have something tucked up his sleeve to welcome the whole British army. Or whichever bit of it was still in Britain.

He wondered, after last night's debacle and this morning's wholesale denunciation, if the army was still a viable option for the British government. He knew Alex Deville was half expecting it: what else could they do? The deed was done, secession declared, the door to negotiation slammed in their face. Unless they posted a regiment of troops at the newly-christened "Lindisfarne Inn," the former Plough Inn at the Beal road end, economic sanctions were unworkable: and even then, the land and sea, as in the past, could provide food if not the finer things of life. And they'd made a complete dog's breakfast of achieving anything via the civilian route. People on the island were still four square behind their Declaration, a new constitution was on its way, and there was more money in the public purse than their great-grandchildren could spend in their lifetimes.

Find a way through that lot if you can, Geordie thought.

And then there was the media. In between the two recent body-blows to democracy—the poll shambles in Scotland and the miserable non-contest for the leadership of the Labour Party—even the denizens of the fourth estate had been building up a sympathetic head of steam in favour of Lindisfarne's secession. Okay, there were exceptions—right wing relics who still clung to the hope that the Tory Party might cash in on the climate of disillusionment, or simple cyclical drift, and rise again like a reformed and shining Phoenix from the ashes—but for the most part the media were either behind it or were treating it as a deserved slap in the face for the UK government. Geordie would have been amazed if anyone had suggested that he'd been instrumental in building this support, but stories like George the Vietnamese potbelly certainly hadn't hindered it.

He knelt to prize out a shell embedded in the foreshore. So what exactly did a barnacle look like?

If I were the British PM, he thought, what would I do next? Send the bombers in? Try to infiltrate? A bit of destabilisation? But that would mean the long haul. Would they have the stomach for it? Were there any George Smileys left now that the Cold War was history? Probably, since it showed every sign of reviving. Le Carré's master-spy was one of Geordie's favourite fictional characters. Maybe he should keep his eyes peeled for a short fat guy "dressed like a bookie" wandering about.

Deville, he thought, had been justified in drawing a parallel with Iraq, even if it fell short of completeness. The 2003 invasion had given birth to a colourful spectrum of opinion, but there were few people now, retiring Prime Ministers apart, who would argue that the follow-up had been other than woeful. And if the initial certainty of the retiring PM had deteriorated into a kind of strained rationalisation (i.e., a whole new set of excuses), what else was he to do as WMDs disappeared into the simoom and events plummeted to hell? Palpitate, have nightmares, howl at the moon? Submit to psychiatric treatment in some private clinic? Holy Island's miniaturised invasion-by-bulldozer had reeked of the same unhinged logic, but even if successful, what would it have gained? What, as Deville had asked, would have been the aftermath?

"How about a walk while we're waiting?" Sarah asked. "Stretch our legs a bit?"

Geordie looked up at her, slim and lovely against a background of blue sky and ochre sand. He smiled. As if those legs needed stretching.

They started along the shore, Rebecca giving them a lesson on the flora they passed, Sarah chipping in with the fauna. A flock of sanderlings were feeding on the sands, building up their reserves for the long surge to their Arctic breeding grounds. The girls debated whether global warming was delaying their migration. Geordie hadn't a clue; something else he needed to read up on.

"What a view," Rebecca said, looking north. "Nothing but sand, sea and birds. It won't have changed in centuries."

"Come on," Geordie said. "It's empty. Wall-to-wall nothing. It's as flat as an iron. I suppose kids might have a game of football on it if they didn't mind getting wet."

"Oh, Geordie," Rebecca said. "Where's your sense of romance? Adventure? Free spirit?"

She bent down to inspect a cluster of thrift and sea campion, now in full bloom and growing in profusion along the salt marsh.

"Kids don't play football anymore, George," Sarah said. "It's Nintendo. And when they're let out, they don't get beyond the front gate. The chances are, in the old home country, they could get molested or shot or knifed."

"Oh, you see them occasionally having a go," Geordie replied. "When their parents get fed up and boot them into the fresh air. If their parents give a damn about them getting fresh air, and ignore all those lurking dangers and tabloid hype. But didn't there used to be teddy boys, skinheads? Every decade has its downside."

"You don't believe things are getting worse?" Sarah asked. "Just hype, is it? And it's early to be thinking of kids, don't you think? Especially when it took you two weeks to work up to a measly kiss. Barnacle."

She winked at Rebecca, and the two of them started to laugh. Sarah added something about the "long, masterful, irresistible seduction campaign" to which she'd been subjected, which caused more laughter.

All girls together, Geordie thought. Here we go, a limpet for life. Well, no more loose talk or free ammo from me. And she was right, worse was undeniably happening, a healthy chunk of it down to the hip-hop urban culture and the anything-goes cosmos of the internet. Maybe more jails, more Daniels, and better judges would help. Bin the Human Rights Act, the Immigration Regulations, the anti-social behaviour orders, the growing family of community service orders, parole, and all the other misused or feeble penal tools. Keep it simple. Lose a few bad role models in Durham and Low Newton jails, as there didn't seem to be any unisex prisons anymore. Make examples of the parents, if they preferred disinterest to discipline. Unfortunately, the world was running out of places to deport them and their rampant offspring to, but disused oil platforms might come in handy, he thought. And what to do about the broken marriages that politicians and sociologists blamed for many of the problems? A policy of selective sterilisation?

Was he being unfair? Well, you could just imagine the reaction, the horror, the unbridled guff those ideas would generate. Good heavens no, outrageous, we aren't *Nazis* for God's sake, these poor people are disadvantaged, disenfranchised, discombobulated by TV and digital fantasies, it's all to do with inequality, no way, we couldn't possibly...what about their civil liberties, who would pay for it (the usual suspects), would it be *legitimate*? Wouldn't it contravene...? Fuck it. Since when had simplicity been a watchword of social engineering?

And more to the point, he thought, since I'm not the British Prime Minister and never will be, what do *I* do next? Leave the island and Sarah? Go back to Groat Market and Old Smokey?

It didn't bear thinking about.

CHAPTER SIXTEEN

Early that evening Sarah and Geordie were in the living room, watching the news. There was a lengthy report on the bulldozer episode, but no comment from anyone in the British government. As usual, the political correspondent projected the authority of a man with the inside track to Number Ten's deepest thoughts, but on this occasion looked as if he wished he hadn't gone there. The guy kept sniffing and looked fed up, Geordie thought, as if the scales had fallen from his eyes. Or maybe the traffic fumes in Whitehall were getting to him, or his cameraman was having a bad day. Whatever the reason, he had an unhealthy Shrek-like cast to his features.

Earlier in the day, he TV crews had scrambled back to the island, "like seagulls scrapping over the leftovers," Geordie commented smugly to Sarah, to shoot footage of the crane pulling the vehicles out. It made picturesque viewing; in fact, with the expanse of sunlit sand in the background, it could have been a scene from *CSI: Miami*. The real story, however, was done and dusted. With the footage in the can, and eager to answer the siren call of Saturday night clubbing in the city's Bigg Market, the crews had gone again.

Geordie was restless, coming down from last night's high.

"I think that owl is watching us," he said to Sarah.

She grinned. "It's one of my father's spies."

"I wondered. Think we could duck behind the sofa while I grab a kiss?"

They spent a pleasant five minutes rolling around on plush carpeting. Geordie had heard of deep pile before, but you could lose the family heirlooms in this stuff.

"How about The Ship later?" he asked, coming up for breath.

"Your lucky pub?"

"You bet."

"When I've made dinner. Rebecca and Daniel may join us again, maybe even Alistair. Rebecca tells me Daniel's been having a lovely day with an unhappy barrister. His partners as well as his family seem to have deserted him; no visitors at all. And Daniel's other charges seem to be in withdrawal. They're not talking to him or each other. They seem to have had a falling out."

"How about your Dad? Give him a break?"

"It's worth a try."

Sarah told him that she'd asked Rebecca if she thought she might stay on Holy Island if the thing with Daniel worked out.

Oh no, Geordie thought, don't ask me anything like that yet. I don't have an answer, and if I had it would be about work and money and a whole string of bridges to cross. You wouldn't like it at all. A barnacle would be about the nicest thing you'd call me.

"What did she say?" he asked.

Sarah laughed. "She didn't. She just said if she did decide to stay and her Mom decided to pay a visit, we were never on pain of death to mention Charley. The ring's been dumped, he's a non-person, and their marriage is a non-event. She's dumped the surname too; it's back to Carter again."

"Did you ever meet Charley?"

"No, I never had the pleasure."

"I saw him once briefly. Except for his hair and twitching, I've forgotten him already. He was that kind of guy. Waxwork just about summed him up."

"Well, you can't say that about Daniel."

"No, you can't."

Alex Deville was in his favourite spot, in the basement with Alistair, calling some far-flung friends to update them on progress. When Sarah and Geordie suggested a visit to the Tavern later, they both agreed. Geordie, newshound as ever, asked them what had been on the agenda to talk about this evening.

"We think we may have registered more than a blip on the radar of public opinion," Deville said. "I've been speaking to some pollsters and they agree. To paraphrase a certain lady, they *would* say that, of course. They're planning to go ahead Tuesday."

"What size of sample?" Geordie asked.

"We're thinking a minimum of 2,000 across Britain, roughly pro rata with regional populations, half male, half female, all registered voters."

"And the questions?"

"We should have a finished version tomorrow. I'll let you see them. But nothing so detailed that it's going to turn people off halfway through. I'd rather have a bigger cohort and a smaller questionnaire than vice versa."

"Okay. But I'm not sure you get better accuracy with bigger numbers."

"That's what I've been hearing. We'll see. We've also been looking at some other UK experiences. Not of secession, because there aren't many of those, perhaps with the exception of the Principality of Sealand, but of Community Companies."

"Oh? What are they?"

"They're Scottish, in a word. Or those Alistair has been researching are. Places like Assynt, Eigg, Gigha, Knoydart, North Harris. Most notably South Uist."

"Oh yeah, the buy-out." Geordie recalled a figure of £4.5 million being reported. Loose change for the future father-in-law. *Aaaaaah*...no, he told himself, don't even begin to go there. Talk about getting ahead of the game...all those damn bridges to cross.

"The community buy-out. Not that it's relevant in itself, except as a wholly laudable marker, but some of the approaches to history and culture, management and development issues, are. And the environment has similarities. More rocks and hills, I grant you."

"Why isn't the buy-out relevant?"

"For several reasons. For them, ownership is a halfway house. They are still at the mercy of the British and Scottish governments and, for education and other services, the Highland Council. And our history is thankfully less one-sided, less despotic. For the moment though, suffice to say it's irrelevant because most of these models were created under Scottish legislation, their Land Reform (Scotland) Act of 2003. Among other things, it requires so-called Crofting Community Bodies to be set up. We aren't in Scotland and we don't have crofts on Holy Island. Although in times gone by we had an approximation. When people were either freemen or stallengers, and common land was shared."

"Really? Crofts?"

"Oh, yes. But I'm going back over two centuries, before the Enclosure Act," Deville smiled. "If you're interested in history, speak to Amy, she's the local expert. I can only tell you that administratively, down the years, this area has been something of a *terra infirma*. Did you know there was a period in the early twelfth century, about twenty years, when Northumberland was Scottish but Bamburgh Castle and 'New' Castle were not? Or that the region was gifted to Scotland in 1139 and taken back in 1157?"

"No, I didn't. That must have needed some fleet-footed government."

"Sow anomalies, reap problems, George. It's interesting, isn't it, to think of Holy Island's history over the last millennium and try to speculate what changes there might be over the next millennium? Provided human life is still here to enjoy them."

"You're saying it puts in context what you're doing. That change is normal, part of life."

"Exactly. Some types of change, anyway. So why not secession?"

"Amy did mention once that the island had only become an official part of Northumberland in the mid-eighteen hundreds."

"And did she also tell you that the Kingdom of Northumbria, Bernicia if you include Durham, was virtually independent in its time?"

"No, she was kind of concentrating on the here and now. Drawing some parallels," Geordie said.

"Well, this was a few hundred years before the nineteenth century, admittedly. But as we were saying, things change. They changed after the Norman invasion of 1066. Twenty-odd years later, Northumberland was cut adrift. Too many troublemakers, too much rebellion. Durham became a kind of buffer zone between the 'civilized' south and the 'uncivilized' north. In 1300, a steward of the Lord Bishop of Durham claimed that his master had equal status with the Lord King of England. He wasn't far wrong. The Lord Bishops post-1066 had their own parliament, army, laws, court system, currency and taxes. In fact, full powers over the Palatinate of Durham weren't returned to the British Crown until 1836."

"So in effect you're recycling history. Applying some of its lessons here, scaled down."

"Not exactly, George, but close. Durham is Durham. Northumbria as a concept has disappeared, except in tourist fluff and one or two institutions: the police force, and a university. And it's unrecognised by the European Parliament or the British government. Also, as you suggest, we are, or were, just a small part of it. But I am saying that history tells us governments change, sometimes by agreement or treaty, sometimes by warfare or rebellion, sometimes by accident or default, sometimes through the kind auspices of the Boundary Commission." Deville smiled. "I'm saying we live and work in a region of above average flux. Amy will give you all the follow-up reading you need, if you've a mind to pursue it. A word of warning though, people have been known to get severe mental indigestion once she starts educating them. She is not a lady who leaves stones unturned."

"Mmm...I may chance it. So how do the Scottish cases help you?"

"As I was saying, they aren't parallel situations. But before you came in, we were looking at development and management options for the Althing. The Scottish cases have done the same. As far as development goes, we need some new initiatives. As far as management goes, the Deville family can't do everything, even if we wanted to. And we don't. I can't speak for my family, but as I've told you before, a painless exit clause—from politics, not the island—is an imperative."

Deville explained that the Lindisfarne Community Development Trust, a principal "stakeholder" in the Althing's economic planning, had begun to consider small high-tech industries, the development of shellfish farming and sea angling, and the construction of a hostel or lodge to attract "a serious type of tourist." It would be important in future, he said, that tourism, on which 75 percent of the islanders to some degree relied, should be seen as a full-time career rather than a fill-in or holiday job. Alistair was doing the research.

"The Trustees are voluntary," Alistair said. "They have other jobs. They need someone for the donkey work. To get them thinking, pump-prime ideas if you like."

Deville added that the Trust was looking to focus tourism marketing on cultural, historical and ornithological attractions, and to give St. Aidan's Winery, its Lindisfarne Mead and other products, a further shot in the arm "when the new craft centre is open next year." Blue eyes glinting, he said he had ambitions for a Lindisfarne Malt. He believed an increase was possible in jobs such as rangers and guides. In the longer term, they would be looking at other options, especially in the aquaculture sector. Activities like seaweed processing.

"Did you know we used seaweed as a fertilizer in the past?"

"No. That must have kept the tourists at bay," Geordie said.

"Not at all. A clean, fresh, natural, iodine smell. There are a lot worse today from industrial or manufactured fertilizers. In any case, there weren't so many tourists then. And those who came were quite familiar with manure. Not like you pampered city folk today," Deville said, with a flash of Paul Newman teeth.

"How long has this Trust been operating?"

"It was formed in 1996. The Heritage Centre, which is owned by the people of the island, was opened in 2000. The Trust has done a sterling job to date, not least in managing several low rental, affordable housing units for young Islanders, trying to keep them here and counter the second home trend. But as we know, circumstances have changed and the possibilities need to be looked at afresh. We are a small island community, George. We don't need to think big. However, we do need to depend less on tourism, even if improved in quality, to make our way. Our GDP, if you will, needs a broader base. As the quote in the Heritage Centre says, we are 'an island distant from the sources of wealth and power.' A couple of dozen permanent jobs, additional to those under Max's wing, would be a major benefit.

"One or two may even appeal to you," Deville added with a smile.

"With respect, I'm not into nepotism," Geordie said. "But thanks for the thought."

"Nepotism? Are we being sensitive? I have no intention of dishing out jobs, never have, never will. But you may find my daughter has an unnerving habit of getting her own way."

"Sorry, I got confused. What about this Sealand thing you mentioned? Where's Sealand anyway? Someone couldn't make up their mind?"

"Full marks, George, for sidestepping your way out of that one. Sealand was a bit before your time. It was taken over by a former pirate radio operator in 1967, and it received a lot of publicity in the late sixties and subsequently. Letters in the newspapers, and airings in the UK,

American and German courts. Sealand is a former Maunsell sea fort, otherwise called Rough Towers, six miles off East Anglia. It was claimed to be a micro-nation by the family and friends who occupied it. In fact, they held it to be a hereditary constitutional monarchy."

"Letters? How did they sign themselves? 'Undecided of Sealand'? 'Lost in *Terra Infirma*'? You could have a field day with the permutations. It's a joke, right?"

"You'd be surprised. It still exists today, forty years on. Officially, it has up to ten residents but the main family is no longer permanently there. In 2006, a fire all but destroyed its top platform and there have been disputes of sovereignty between its main players in the past. But it is no joke. A lot of government time and effort has been expended on its status, as well as attempts to get rid of it. All to no avail. Some of the legal rulings made over the years are interesting. But it's a very different case from Holy Island. For one thing, it is man-made, a floating pontoon with two hollow towers joined by a platform. It was intentionally scuppered offshore Harwich by its former occupants, the Royal Navy. So drawing comparisons could be dangerous."

"I'll be careful not to mention it in the same breath."

"If I may give you a nudge, George, I wasn't altogether dismissing it. A closer look at Sealand might be more than entertaining for you."

"Dad, I'm going to start dinner," Sarah said. "Don't take too long with this. You're doing too much, *talking* too much, and we *are* going to the pub."

"Point taken," her father said, shuffling a ream of papers. "We'll all go and freshen up. Here, George, some reading for you. The State of Sealand."

George looked at the piece of paper in front of him. Stripped to the essentials, it read:

1967 Fort occupied by Bates family. Sealand declared a sovereign entity.

1968 Royal Navy attempt to remove family thwarted. UK court ruling: Sealand outside the limit of UK territorial waters (then 3 miles).

1975 Constitution, flag, passports, currency etc. introduced.

1978 Administrative Court of Cologne in Germany held that Sealand was not a sovereign state, that the requirements for statehood *,** ("a territory, people and a government") had not been satisfactorily met:
"…The life of a community is lacking…(The duty of a state) does not merely consist of the promotion of a loose association aimed at the furtherance of common hobbies and interests. Rather it

must be aimed at the maintenance of an essentially permanent form of communal life in the sense of sharing a common destiny...The common purpose of this association is limited to a small part of their lives, namely their commercial and tax affairs. This degree of common interest cannot be regarded as sufficient for the recognition of a 'people' within the meaning of international law."

1987 UK extended its territorial waters to 12 nautical miles. Sealand extended its own a day earlier. Sealand now deemed by UK courts to be part of Essex.

1990 A U.S. Admin. Court ruled that Sealand was not a valid nation.

1991 This decision was upheld on appeal by a U.S. Federal Court.

1998 (or thereabouts) Documents available under the 30-year expiry of confidentiality show that the UK government drafted plans to take Sealand by force but *such plans were not implemented due to the potential for loss of life, and/or the creation of a legal and public relations disaster*. Note: It seems to be government policy to refrain from comment or action except when forced.

2005 The Times suggests (unconfirmed elsewhere) that UK government and courts eventually concede that Sealand "is outside British territorial waters...and not part of the UK."

2007 Plans to "transfer ownership." Note: a principality cannot be sold.

* **The Montevideo Convention** asserts that a State requires:

- A defined territory
- Permanent population
- Government, and
- The capacity to enter into relationships with other sovereign states.

** The two commonest schools of thought for the creation of "statehood" are constitutive and declaratory theories. In the former, a state exists solely via recognition by other states: either "diplomatic" recognition or recognition of existence. In the latter, an entity becomes a state as soon as it meets the minimal criteria for statehood. Recognition is purely "declaratory."
(See Helmut Kohl/Croatia and Slovenia.) Aruba (Betico Croes) et al: of interest. Also alpha. list of 15 former USSR republics; Eritrea (!), Panama, Coconut Grove, Staten Island case studies.

Holy cow, Geordie said to himself having read it twice. There's stuff here, if it's correct, they can actually *use*. And it helps with the thorny question of what the government might do. Answer: sit tight with their thumbs in their mouths.

I have to check this out, he thought. But where? The internet? The Home Office? The Groat Market archives? I have to concentrate, *work*, put dreams of Sarah on hold until I've dug a bit deeper. And stop being a smart-ass, if possible.

And yes, there was something at the back of his mind about one of the references. Hadn't the then German Chancellor incurred the wrath of other nations by "prematurely" recognising Croatia and Slovenia when Yugoslavia was breaking apart? When would that have been: sometime in the early '90s? And where was the "alphabetical list"?

He had a shower, forgot he had his watch on, panicked, tried to dry it on a heater, got the room too hot, and made it just in time for dinner. Sarah, aware of the document he'd seen, smiled and said he was forgiven. Geordie melted in an instant; just like most other resolutions, his latest one was dead in the water at the first hurdle. They had fillets of plaice, new potatoes, home-grown vegetables. All local produce, and delicious. Someone's been reading my mind, he thought; the futility of sanctions.

Alex Deville was in his suit, appropriate wear for a First Minister. The others—Alistair, Sarah, Geordie, Rebecca and Daniel—were in jeans and sweaters. It was a cool, showery evening. As they arrived at The Ship, they met Amy Donaldson coming out, brandishing a brown paper bag.

"I forgot my Guinness earlier," she said.

"Are you blushing, Amy?" Geordie asked, abandoning his resolution for the second time in an hour. "Caught in the act?"

"Less of your cheek, you young whippersnapper. When you reach my age, you need all the help you can get to have a good night's sleep."

"Would you like to join us, Amy?" Alex Deville asked. "Provided I undertake to keep this young man respectful of his elders and betters?"

"No, no. I need to get back to the other George. The one that's already respectful."

"Oh, come on, Amy, please," Sarah said. "He'll be fine for half an hour. We'd like some different company. Too much of the Deville household can get boring. I'm sick of them. You should have heard them earlier."

"Okay, half an hour. I can't refuse the First Minister's daughter."

They went in, got a table and a round of drinks. Alex Deville was collared at the bar, surrounded by locals. Geordie heard them laughing, asking questions, congratulating him on the media coverage, and Max's handling of "The Four B's: Botched Berwick Bulldozer Business." Geordie wished he'd thought of that one; it was up there with the best of tabloid headlines. He'd seen this camaraderie with the First Minister before, but not in such numbers. For all his riches and a lurking iconoclasm, Alex Deville was a popular guy, and one of them. Also, to be fair, he was more into reconstruction than destruction.

After ten minutes or so, Deville extricated himself.

"We were talking earlier of some Northumbrian history," he said to Amy. "George is eager to have the benefit of your fund of knowledge."

"Really? As in teacher-pupil? That should put him in his place."

Geordie flicked his eyes to Sarah, saw her grin, and raised them heavenwards. "Well," he said, "sometime soon, I'd appreciate it if..."

"You can come to my library when it opens."

"Library?"

"Down at the new Althing House. Alex has asked me to be the inaugural librarian," Amy told him with some pride.

"Oh? When does the job start?" Geordie asked.

"When it opens. When else? About six months."

"Well...I'm not sure...I mean, I was thinking of sooner."

"Claro. Pues, cuanto antes te empezar, antes te pondrás en camino."

"Come again?"

Amy grinned. "I was agreeing with you. Suggesting, in your second favourite language, that the sooner you begin, the sooner you'll be on your way."

"You were?...well, actually Amy, while the story's hot would be better. It might help people—"

"George, history is history. It's not going to go away anytime soon. You youngsters are too impatient. Look at poor Rebecca here. Got impatient, got married, and got her heart broken in the space of a day."

Rebecca laughed. "Not the last bit, please, but *that*'s history."

"Aye, and with a bit of luck it'll teach you something."

Daniel's deep voice broke in. "Maybe we could all use some lessons."

"Ah, now Daniel," Amy said, "what would you need lessons in? I've been meaning to tell you, by the way, how well you handled those people at the trial."

"You should know about your home."

For God's sake, Geordie thought, he's been here five minutes, and it's home already. Lucky guy. Oh, that life could be such a piece of cake for the rest of us.

"If that's your thinking, young man, unlike some ditherers we know," (looking at Geordie) "I'd be happy to oblige. I'll come to the jail. We can start there. And those idiots you have locked up might learn something too, once they've had a piece of my mind."

"I'll look forward to it, ma'am. Especially the last bit."

"The name's Amy."

Daniel nodded. "Amy."

"Good."

"I was thinking, Amy. How things are different on an island."

"Very true. But what do you have in mind?"

"Take shopping. Medicines, hardware, things like that. You don't have them."

"We do the same as other folks do, only a bit more so. We plan ahead. Some things you need daily, some weekly, some once or twice in a lifetime. Like husbands, Rebecca? Eh?"

Rebecca looked somewhat abashed, smiled, and gave a little "umph" sound.

"But they're not here," Daniel ploughed on. "Only a half-dozen shops selling crisps and cards and crafts. Sweets, souvenirs, books, knick-knacks. Mom-and-pop stuff. How do you get meat, vegetables, eggs, bread, and hardware? How about haircuts?"

It was the longest speech Geordie had heard Daniel make. Total verbal diarrhoea. The worry of it all must be keeping him awake at night. Geordie, having asked the same questions *ad nauseam* two weeks ago, could almost have given the answers. But he enjoyed listening to Amy's thought processes.

"We grow them or make them or have them delivered. Or tootle over to Berwick or down to Newcastle for them. If you want a buzz cut, someone here will run the clippers over you. I'll do it myself, if you can pluck up the courage."

Daniel laughed. "Yeah, mine doesn't take much. But how are they delivered? There's no road."

"Have you been going hungry, son? You come to my place for a meal."

"No. I brought stuff with me. Rebecca has cooked for us once or twice, and Sarah."

"There you are," Amy said. "It's simple. You go and get it. Or the small stuff can still be delivered, with the right vehicle. Or they can offload it for Max's boys. The bigger stuff, we still have a harbour. And Max has ideas to roll steel tracks over the Swad, as you see at county shows or golf tournaments. But that's after things have settled down. The causeway demolition was only ever a temporary thing. It'll be back, sooner or later. I live in hope we'll never see it again, but I'm kind of expecting to be outvoted. Right, Alex?"

"We'll see," Deville said. "But so far, no complaints. People here knew of its removal well in advance, Daniel. Suppliers were told in confidence a few days before. We had to make an immediate point, something compelling. It was a similar thing with ID cards. No one here needs them, everyone knows everyone else, but they were useful psychology."

Daniel knew all about striking the first blow, and a bit about psychology. He nodded.

"The thing is, lad," Amy said, "we pull together, help each other. If someone needs something, and someone else is going over, they fetch it. It's what used to happen in the old days, when there were four, five times the people there are now."

"And people with no vehicle, who went by bus?" Daniel asked.

"That was one of the things we planned for. One of the promises Alex gave. Transport to be laid on, as for the kids to Lowick and Longridge Towers schools, assuming they're still allowed to attend. The same price as the bus, and free for the school runs. Sometimes the kids will still need to board, when the tides are against them, but that's nothing new. Two weeks have gone by and it's working fine. No complaints, except from the tour companies."

"It has to be less convenient."

"Ha!—you youngsters and your *convenience*. It's all too easy. You should have had the life of a fishing family fifty, sixty years ago. You'd have built a bit of character then, my word. It's nothing to do with convenience. That causeway's only been here since nineteen fifty-four, raised up a bit three years ago. We made do with ponies and carts before that. The Postmaster and two innkeepers hired them out. Most people used *Shanks's* pony. It's to do with resourcefulness, hard work, pulling together, and getting things done. You need to understand that an island, *this* island, preserves its mental as well as its physical characteristics. You see the land and buildings, but you don't see the ethos and spirit. Sometimes, they just need a bit of reawakening."

"And what's the ethos?" Geordie asked.

"You should know that by now, George," said Amy severely. "Cuthbert. Community. Heritage, in a word. Being different, fashioning lives differently. Some things other islands have—independence, relative isolation, a quality of intrigue, of challenge—but in our case, always Cuthbert. As a shorthand for the saints. *Holy* Island. It doesn't mean we're saints, or God knows act like them, but it's what we're called. What we *are*. And fundamentally, the weaknesses of British governments apart, it's why we seceded."

"Hold on a minute, Amy," Geordie said. "I need to write all that down."

"Cheeky young whippersnapper. There was nothing new in it for you, anyway."

Geordie laughed. "Has there ever been a time when the island's been completely cut off?" he asked. "Abnormal tides, high winds, days at a time? Or in wartime?"

"One occasion comes to mind, in the winter of nineteen forty-seven, and me a young lass. Ah, mind, those were good days. But it was snow of all things that blocked us off for a while. It closed the roads. I remember places in Dorset, they had to use flame-throwers."

"What happened?"

"Eh, George, you're one for the questions. You should give me notice of some of them, you have me thinking of ethos now, and whether I gave you a proper answer. But as to that one, the lifeboat got us out of it. We had one then. The boys went up to Berwick and got the stuff folk needed. Got more than they bargained for, too. They had to bring back a coffin."

"A coffin?"

"As in box. Poor chap had died away from home, a businessman in Berwick. But he was a Holy Islander, so he needed to be brought back for burial at St. Mary's."

Geordie smiled. "I can't somehow see the European Union allowing that these days."

"Exactly. Who needs them?" Amy said. "Now, don't run away with the idea we're turning the clock back. Nostalgia is a seductive thing. An unreal thing, a dream. All those village cricket matches and picnic sandwiches I used to enjoy at Warenford or Bamburgh when I was a girl…oh, don't get me wrong. There was child abuse then, and wars here and there, and drugs, fights fuelled by alcohol, flick knives, keeping up with the Jones's, and strange new pop music. The boys used to smoke Woodbines. A penny each, imagine? And I do mean an old penny, less than half of the present one. But those days are gone, the days of black-and-white TV and spirit stoves, of men letting ladies go first, of being home by eleven after dances, and fathers peering through the curtains. It's re-educating ourselves as islanders, more like. That's the ten-year plan, correct, Alex? It's thinking how do we combine what was good then with what's good now. You know my cottage, George. The furniture has been there since I was a girl, good solid stuff. But I like my electric blanket too, and I've had it only ten years. It's a new addition. See what I mean? And that's where I'm off to now."

"I couldn't have put it better myself, Amy," Alex Deville said. "And I mean any of it." He glanced out of the window. "The rain's off. I'll walk you home while we have a chance of staying dry."

The five younger people spent another fifteen or twenty minutes in The Ship Inn. Other customers began to disperse. Rebecca and Daniel said they would take a walk around by the jail. Sarah, Geordie and Alistair said their goodbyes to the remaining locals and one or two visitors, and set out up Marygate to Fahr House. Crossing the Berwick Road, they heard a helicopter to the north and looked towards the Links, but could see nothing.

Geordie was anxious to get onto the internet, and begin researching Scottish islands, Sealands, former German Chancellors, former Yugoslavias, and USSR republics.

But when they got home, Alex Deville got in the way of those good intentions.

He'd gone. Vanished like a wisp of smoke.

CHAPTER SEVENTEEN

"Odd," Sarah said. "He must have stayed for a chat at Amy's."

On receiving no answer when they came in, they'd started in the basement. Then the living room, followed by the kitchen, then Alistair had tried his Dad's bedroom.

"No sign of him having been back," Alistair said. "The clothes he was wearing this afternoon are still on his bed."

They agreed that must be it, he was chewing the fat with Amy. It made sense to Geordie. If Amy wasn't the power behind the throne, she was certainly some of the brains and vitality. It was ten thirty-five. After ten minutes and a cup of coffee, Alistair said he'd walk around to meet him. He shrugged into a windcheater and left.

"This isn't like him, George," Sarah said, sinking into one of the living room chairs. "He likes talking to people, but not when they've said they're turning in. He likes to be in bed himself by eleven, get up at four or five. You know the old saying, early to bed..."

"Could he have gone to see someone else? One of the other Ministers?"

"Not at this time of night. So I'm getting worried." Sarah looked at him. "I'm going to call Max."

"Why not wait for Alistair? He should only be a few minutes."

"Mmm...I'm not sure. Dad left the pub some time before us, you know. He should have been back just after ten."

Sarah was beginning to feel a draught in the pit of her stomach, much as she had felt the day her mother died. She tried to suppress it, and told herself not to be silly, while she ran her fingers through her hair. Not even the hoot of a barn owl near St. Coombs Farm, a sound she loved, could give her any solace. She got up and went over to Geordie, gave him a kiss, sat down again, and jammed her hands into her hip pockets.

"He wouldn't have had any reason to have the chopper lift him off somewhere, would he?" Geordie asked. "At this time of night?"

"Chopper? Oh, Lord...of course. There was a helicopter, wasn't there?"

"On our way back. It seemed to be over the car park."

Sarah shot up from her chair. "Oh, my goodness...the helicopter. I have to phone Max. We've been wasting *time*." She punched the speed-dialling key on her mobile, trying to stay calm and think at the same time.

"Honey..." Geordie began.

She waved him off with a hand.

I was just going to say no need for panic, he muttered to himself.

There could be an easy explanation, *no*? Imagine Amy, pulling that stunt on him in such impeccable Spanish. Well, it had sounded impeccable. Had one of the vowels been wrong? She'd kept that one well up her sleeve, the old vixen. He found it hard to believe any harm had come to Deville, the man was immune.

"No," Sarah was saying. "He left before…less than half an hour…about three-quarters of an hour now…yes…you saw it?…okay…" (a longer pause) "…See you soon." She switched off and turned to Geordie. "He's on his way."

"I just hope your Dad and Alistair don't walk through the door ten seconds from now."

"Max knows it's something urgent."

"How?"

"He just does. Like I do. Something's screwy. Believe me."

"We'll get some more coffee going," Geordie said.

"The brandy bottle, George. Then coffee, black. Prime the brain."

"Huh?…Right, okay."

He poured shots of brandy into two balloon glasses.

"There's Alistair now," Sarah said.

Geordie picked up a third balloon.

"No sign of him," Alistair said, throwing his jacket off. "The lights are out at Amy's, and I didn't want to rouse her. He's nowhere to be seen in the village. Something's wrong. Give me that glass, George." He knocked it back. "What do we do now? I knew this thing was going too well. We had an island full of false senses of security. Bulldozers, I ask you."

Sarah told him she'd phoned big brother.

"Good idea. He might have a clue where to start. I don't," Alistair said.

"The phone," Geordie said. "The cameras. The recorder downstairs."

"Bloody brilliant, George," Alistair nodded, stressed into swearing. He picked up the house phone, punched 1471, and listened. "No good. Nothing since we went out."

"Couldn't he have gone somewhere else?" Geordie asked. "I mean, has this sort of thing *never* happened before?"

"No way. He'd have said something," the two of them said in stereo.

"He doesn't like surprises and he doesn't like surprising us," Alistair said. "There's too much at stake for that kind of thing. He does things with forethought, logic, one step at a time. This is worrying."

"Okay," Geordie said. "I think I'm beginning to get infected too."

Sarah smiled. It was a poor effort, but it was a smile. "Join the club."

Two minutes later they heard the front door and looked at each other. Deville? Max? Rebecca?

Big brother. Coming up to eleven o'clock.

"It must be open season for kidnapping around here. The chopper set down on the car park," Max said, shrugging off his combat jacket.

"*Kidnapping*?...What do you mean? The public car park?" Sarah asked.

"Yep. I got a glimpse, but couldn't make it out. I thought it was an emergency, but I should've known better. It came in low over the sea, and was here fifteen minutes. Ten five until ten twenty. The flats cleared of water at half nine. I sent one of the guys over to have a look, but it'd gone when he turned the corner."

Sarah looked stunned. "But how could they have got back to a helicopter with him from here? Without—"

"I know how *I'd* have done it. Knocked him out and carried him. It doesn't matter now. They're up and away."

Max filled a coffee cup and frowned at the stuffed owl as if it was to blame.

"Phone? Answering machine?" he asked.

"Nothing. We've tried," Alistair said.

"Okay. Basement."

"Are we sure we're not jumping to conclusions?" Geordie asked as they went down the stairs. "I mean, is there no other explanation...?"

"Hell, no," Max said. "Sorry, George, but stow that. Those cameras, Alistair. Try the car park first. Go back to three minutes after ten or so."

His brother sat at the console, and punched a few buttons.

Max jotted some notes. "Timeline, please," he said. "When did he leave the pub?"

"A minute or two after ten," Geordie said.

"And you?"

"Nearly twenty past."

"And you heard the chopper on your way?"

"Yeah. We'd been out a couple of minutes, walking up the road."

"It figures. So he was lifted at five to quarter past."

"Here," Alistair interrupted. "I've got them."

He had colour CCTV pictures of the helicopter landing, two figures jumping out, ducking beneath the vanes, running towards Chare Ends.

The digital display showed 10:04:40...41...42. Seconds ticking, continuous reel.

"Two plus the pilot," Max muttered under his breath, watching the rotor blades slow down. "Standard low skid gear."

"What?" Sarah asked, beating Geordie to it.

"Easy to get in and out of it. Now, where would they have got one of those? Newcastle?" Max shrugged. "They've blanked out the registration, see? Duct tape or something. Switch to the house cameras, Alistair."

"What type is it? Do you know?" Geordie asked, beating Sarah to it.

"Bell 206. JetRanger. See the markings behind the cabin? Designed for two crew, three pax. Good choice."

"In what way?" Geordie again.

"Range and speed. Reliability. Size. There are better helos, but not a lot this size."

"Who uses them?"

"Hell, everybody. Emergency services, law enforcement, homeland security, military, oil companies, you name it. It's one of the commonest helos in the world. All over the place." He jotted something on a piece of paper.

"How far can they go?" Sarah asked.

Max looked at his watch, then at them. "They've had the best part of an hour. This wee machine could be over Montrose, Whitby or Dumfries by now. Give it another two hours, depending on fuel, it could be past Bristol, Norwich, or Wick."

Sarah groaned, and put her hands to her face.

"You said depending on fuel?" Geordie said.

"Yep. Four people, no baggage. They'd have a range of near enough four fifty miles, if they go easy. If they fuelled up at Newcastle, reduce that by the loose change. God forbid, not Boulmer. Brunton?...no...it had to be Woolsington." He wrote something else down. "From here, they could go four hundred miles, as near as dammit. Pretty much as the crow flies. With the wind, more. Against, less...there they are."

Sarah began to shake, and took hold of Geordie's hand. Her father was walking towards the front door, two figures in the shrubbery. As Deville passed, they jumped him together. No shots, no knives, no blackjacks. One took him in what looked like a judo hold and threw him over, the other sat on his back, pulled a handkerchief out of a plastic bag and pressed it around Deville's nose and mouth. Moments later, he went limp. By the digital read-out, it had taken under half a minute.

10:09:36...37...38.

"Chloroform," Max said. "Or similar. Christ alive, I told him we should have had dogs."

Sarah had seen enough, and put her face in Geordie's shoulder.

The smaller of the two put the handkerchief back in the plastic bag and threw it in the bushes. The other shook his head impatiently and gesticulated. The smaller one scrabbled in the bushes, retrieved the bag and put it in his pocket. Then the bigger of the two got Deville in a fireman's lift, they both had a look around, slits for eyes, and disappeared out of camera range in the direction of the car park.

Max smiled grimly. "Well, they wouldn't have made it onto the island any other way in that gear. One of them has a bit of body strength, and he's in charge."

They had been wearing scarves and balaclavas, pulling the scarves up and the balaclavas down just before they emerged from the chopper. There was little chance of either being identified, and none whatever by people who didn't know them.

Max grunted. "Impressions? Age? Colour?"

Alistair and Geordie looked at each other.

"I don't know," Alistair said. "There was a glimpse getting out of the chopper, before..."

"I have no idea," Geordie said. "Our age group, I think. One was in good shape, the boss man of the pair, as you say. I'd reckon he had four or five inches on the other. They both moved easily enough, didn't they?"

"Yeah. Back to the car park cameras, Alistair," Max said, making notes again.

10:14:21...22...23.

"There. The bigger one's still carrying him," Max added. "It can't have been easy, over the dykes...What the hell? What's got them acting like that?"

"It looks like they're ducking, trying to avoid something," Geordie said, watching the two weaving and gyrating. The smaller one making a run for the chopper, the other labouring with Deville.

"The last time I saw that behaviour, people were under assault," Max said.

"Birds, maybe? Bats? One of them wasn't hanging around for the other," Geordie said.

"Nah, it's more than that. Something's got them spooked."

Geordie squeezed his arm around Sarah, saw the two guys bending below the rotor wash, hoisting Deville hurriedly aboard through the rear door. One climbed up to haul him into a seat. The other got in, and pulled the door shut.

"Weird, but what the hell. They're up and away, the lucky sods," Max continued, thinking aloud. "If they'd had to look for him, or come inside the house...this all worked out just fine for them. Christ alive, he landed in their laps." Max banged a fist on the desk. "So they knew what he looked like, where the house was, and took the short cut by the water tower. They knew all they needed to know. They didn't have to bother with the alarm system to get him, or even ring the damn bell. They must have seen or heard him coming. I wonder what they had in mind if he'd been in the house. It could have been one of you that answered.

"The pilot's white, you notice that?" he added. "Short sleeves. I can't make out much more in there, except he's wearing aviator shades. Huh," peering at the screen, jotting. "The shorter one is white as well. His hands give it away, not that it's much to go on."

Sarah shuddered and raised her head. Geordie stood up, to get her another glass of brandy, but she held on to his arm.

10:17:33…34…35.

They watched the chopper's blades gain momentum, the machine shuddering as the force increased. It seemed to take a long time. Surely there should be people coming out of the houses to see what was going on?

10:19:56. Lift-off.

"The wind's from the south tonight," Max said. "I wonder if George and Phyllis in the end house were roused; the sound would have carried quite easily. They must've heard *some*thing over the TV. Even more so if they were in bed. Can we get better definition on any of that?" he asked Alistair.

"Not really. We can zoom in and sharpen it. But we could do that until the cows come home, and we still wouldn't get their faces."

"Okay, back to the car park, Ali. Let's see if the pilot got out. Fast forward if you can."

They watched fifteen minutes of the recording, condensed to one or two.

"That answers that," Max said. "He didn't move. First light, we need to get out there and see if they left anything behind. And speak to the folks in the bungalows as well. In fact, I may go out with a torch now and have a look," he added, half talking to himself again. "No. The recording machine first."

If things had not been so fraught, Geordie would have given himself a pat on the back. He'd just out-thought a commando. Well, not quite out-thought. But matched him, *no*?

Max played back the last two conversations his father had recorded. The first was ITN News, then *The Independent*, both earlier in the day. Max grimaced and pointed to a rack of tapes stacked in a wall unit. "We need to go through that lot, and see who he's upset the most. What we do know is, they started off north. Those pictures and what we heard at the gate tell us that." He looked at Sarah. "Don't worry, sis. That's half the bloody UK we can rule out."

"It's a start," Geordie said. "If they kept going that way."

"Comedian."

They heard a shout from the hallway.

"Is anybody home? Where are you all?"

It was Rebecca.

Geordie watched her coming down the stairs, thinking for the first time since his arrival that he'd been asking questions not as a journalist, but as a concerned participant. It felt strange but good. He could help the family here, and look after Sarah. By morning, they would have the world's media buzzing round their heads, none of them half as slick at coping with that as Deville. Max would have to do it, or take the first onslaught anyway. Meantime, as a reporter...Oh, no. It was Sunday, bloody Sunday tomorrow. *Again*. Oh *shit*. What to do? Got to phone the old man anyway, I can't let this slip.

If I were a bookie, he mused, how would I lay the odds on this one? The British government, evens...that guy Khalid Miah, 3 to 1...friends and family of the Bigg Market Three, 75 to 1 (too short, how would those ratbags lay their hands on a chopper?)...Berwick Borough Council, 100 to 1...friends of that Newcastle barrister, Haydon-Flint, say 50 to 1... oh yeah, Charley the Prize Leek, about on a par with Haydon-Flint's lot... any Holy Islander, 1,000 to 1...well, wackos would have to be shorter, Cochise 500 to 1...George the Vietnamese potbelly, 1,000,000 to 1...Screw it.

He put his arm around Sarah as she told Rebecca the news. Then it was Rebecca's turn to put her arms around Sarah. Geordie killed some time, jotted down his odds, and heard Max coming up behind him.

"You wouldn't have a gambling problem, would you, George?"

"Hell, no. I was just—"

"Gotta protect little sister," Max grinned. "Who's he?" pointing at the list.

"Him? Oh, he's some Muslim spokesman down in England. He phoned twice that I know of. I think your Dad may have pissed him off. He certainly blew him off."

"Interesting," Max said. "It could even be useful. I'd have Cochise at longer odds, though. The last time I heard, he had a tomahawk, not a chopper." He grinned. "I see your hubbie's in the frame, Rebecca."

"Ex. No way. At ten o'clock? Charley would have been in a pub."

"Are you cool if I put this over the wires?" Geordie asked Max. "Not the list, your Dad? The facts?"

"May as well," Max shrugged. "I'm gonna need a crash course in the media. Take care of Sarah for now, huh? We'll listen to the recordings later. Rebecca," he said, turning to her, "is Daniel still up?"

"He was when I left."

Max took out his mobile. "Daniel?...sorry to disturb...someone lifted my father a while ago...you did?...yeah, that was it...I need your help to run a grid...okay...the public car park...okay...see you in five." He ended the call, shrugged into his combat jacket, and looked at his watch. "I'll be back in forty minutes," he said. "Twelve thirty. Probably with Daniel, so it might be an idea to make another brew of coffee. Try not to worry too much, you guys. There are things we can do. And he's not dead. There's a reason. They'll want something."

"Always look on the bright side of life," Sarah told him with a strained laugh.

"Right," he said, smiling, Paul Newman teeth just like his father's. Then he left, taking the stairs three at a time.

With a neck like that, Geordie thought, it's not a tailor he needs, it's an ostler. The teeth and eyes might be the same, but there's not a vestige of his father's languid charm. On the other hand, the guy was...smart. Well, awesome wouldn't be wide of the mark. If anything untoward happened to his father, or if he was faced with a serious crime of any sort against his family, Geordie was sure that Max wasn't the type to wring his hands. He would think about it, plan a response, and then probably rotate someone's head 180° out of true north.

"But who could have *wanted* to do such a thing?" Rebecca asked them.

Geordie pushed over his list. "If you have any ideas, join the sweep. So far, there are only two runners with any chance at all. He did mention being threatened with treason—"

"I don't think so," Alistair said. "They'd have gone about it differently. I hope."

Geordie phoned Newcastle and roused the old man out of bed. He wasn't happy about it, he was quite disgruntled in fact, until he heard the reason for the call.

"For heaven's sake, can't you people organise things better up there?" he said testily. "As in during the bloody week?"

Geordie asked if he could get the bare facts out over the wire services, and heard more muttered imprecations down the line.

"Just make sure you get some credit. And more important, that this paper gets some credit. Bloody stupid timing," he said, as though Geordie and the kidnappers had been in cahoots. "What is that? Three bloody Sundays in a row?"

Geordie went upstairs, got his laptop and list of numbers, and sent a 250-word e-mail to every wire service he knew. And the *Post*.

"George Halloran in Holy Island, exclusive from *The Northern Sun*."

He sent a copy to the Editor. With luck, that should keep him from cutting his throat shaving. Or overdosing on the Valium, Ritalin or whatever he needed to stay in one piece.

Max and Daniel returned from their car park reconnaissance, exactly as Max had said, at half past twelve. Sarah looked at her brother expectantly.

"There's nothing," Max said, shaking his head. "We had a look at the village end too, in case the wind had blown anything. A fence and a gate have been damaged. Otherwise, no joy. There was no sign of what might have been upsetting them out there, either."

They took their jackets off and Max went over to the wall units, lifting the rack of tapes down. He put them on the table and sat near the recorder. "Now, George, let's listen to this lot. Which days were these chats with the PM and the Miah guy? Can you remember?"

Geordie told him, as near as he could. "There may be others in there, though. I wasn't privy to all of the conversations."

"No, you wouldn't be. No one would. But we'll start with these."

They spent two hours with the tapes, checking them against a list of incoming calls.

Sarah was sitting on Geordie's lap through most of it, intent, and almost oblivious to the continued haunting calls of the barn owl outside. After twenty minutes Geordie's legs had gone to sleep, but what the hell, he thought. She did get up to pour coffee once or twice, which only made him impatient to have her back. After he'd flexed his thigh muscles, and checked that he still had motive power. At times, he forgot why they were listening to tapes.

At one point, Alistair said "Hold on. Whoa!"

"What's up, Ali?" Max asked.

"What the PM was saying. That stuff about 'wee nations' and 'fledgling domains.' Crikey, I bet Dad would have been thinking about using those things as evidence of recognition. The PM couldn't have had anybody—"

"Focus, brother. We're looking for grudges, not fucking recognition," Max said.

"Okay, okay, fine. It could be important, though, later."

After they had listened and skipped through all they could find, the vast majority being press calls, Max stood up and stretched.

"So, George. Nothing much to change in those odds of yours. I would shorten the odds on Miah, that's all. Make him very short indeed."

"And the press would only do it as a stunt," Geordie said, trying to pre-empt an obvious question. "Not worth including."

Max gave him a look that would have stripped paint. "What?"

"The press, kidnap someone. You know…as a put-up job. Stage a kidnap, as a scoop."

"Christ alive, get real. That's as bad as the birds and bats you were on about earlier."

"Well, it's been done before now, to sell papers," Geordie said in self-defence. "Anyway, they aren't on the list. The press, I mean. If you notice."

"I had noticed," Max said.

"What list would that be?" Daniel's voice, rattling the coffee cups.

Geordie showed him, glad to take a rest from Max.

"I wouldn't argue with any of that," Daniel said.

"No," Max said. "Who do we know who might help us get to Miah? Anyone in the Royal Military Police, your outfit? The Metropolitan Police? MI5?"

"Well, the RMP's 32 Special Investigations Branch could get to him easily enough. They're based at Bulford, just north of Salisbury, so they're only an hour or so from London. Miah was phoning from London, wasn't he? And there's a guy at Bulford, John Vaughan, who owes me a favour. But MI5…?"

"Trickier," Max said.

"Yes," Daniel said. "And I don't know anyone well enough in the Met. who might help."

"God Almighty," Geordie said, cottoning on. "It's only a list I was playing around—"

"Don't worry about the damn list, George," Max said. "If we didn't like it, we wouldn't be giving it a second glance. Lower your odds on Miah, that's all. In fact, I'd make him an odds-on favourite. Humiliation, or reacting to it, is a mindset for these people. He's the only one of that lot," nodding towards the tapes, "who would make any sense."

"Just so we're clear," Daniel said, looking at Max, Sarah, and Alistair. "There's no one local it could be? You're sure?" All of them shook their heads.

"No," Sarah said.

"He wouldn't have staged this himself? For publicity? Or to put some blame on Westminster, or wrong-foot them?" Daniel asked.

"Oh, please. He's not Machiavelli. And he would have said something," Alistair said.

"Okay, just asking. And the people who voted against secession in the first place?"

"No, they're squared," Max said. "A guesthouse and a café. There aren't any problems there any more. They were just worried about their takings."

"And he's been retired how long?"

"Two years past Christmas," Alistair said. "It's not to do with his work either. He has friends and supporters in that fraternity, not enemies."

"Fraternity?" Geordie asked.

"The financial sector. The City. It's the last thing they'd want."

What *is* all this, Geordie wondered; supporters? Fraternity? Is it the Isle of Wight next? The Scilly Isles? Shetland? Was there some nationwide plan afoot he hadn't heard about?

"Do you know any of them?" Daniel asked. "Anyone with an inside track to Whitehall?"

"I'll think about it," Alistair said.

Exactly how I'd have done it, mate, Geordie thought. Buy time, fast.

"Okay." Daniel looked at Max. "First, we find out exactly where in London Mr. Miah lives and works. Then we see if we can rattle his bones."

"Right." Max looked around. "You guys get off to bed. And thanks for the help. First thing, George, I'll need you here. I wish it wasn't so, but it is."

"How soon?"

"You tell me. It's your pals who'll be clamouring. The old man will want them treated with Holy Island courtesy. We'll see if I can manage it."

"See you at six, then," Geordie said. Then he added, "Some of them, the 24/7 channels and stations, will be onto it earlier. They'll have the thing I sent through any time now. So if you want some sleep, I'd put the answering machine on with a message saying you'll be available at six. Say you're doing some investigating meantime, whatever sounds sensible. Otherwise, you'll be up all night. But don't unplug the phones. They'll use what I sent until then. Unless, of course, they get something from another source, the kidnappers for instance."

"What joy," Max sighed. "Well, I suppose some coverage might help. You never know."

They prepared a carefully-worded holding message, which Max dictated into the machine, and agreed it was all they could do until morning.

On the way up the stairs, Sarah said to Geordie in a very low voice, "I think I'd like company tonight. Okay?"

He nodded. It was all he could muster. His tongue was stuck on the roof of his mouth.

CHAPTER EIGHTEEN

By 6:00 a.m., Max and Geordie were both in the basement, Max shaved and shining, and looking almost benign in one of his Armani suits. He was engrossed in reading a Q&A briefing that Geordie had spent the last half hour preparing.

Geordie had shaved, but was rather less shining and a lot less well-dressed. He had left Sarah in bed, stretching, blowing kisses, and telling him she'd be down as soon as she could. He was to make sure he held her big brother's hand as well as he'd held hers...well, not exactly, but he knew what she meant. He nearly climbed back in with her, and when she saw him thinking about it, she told him no, get going, there would be other nights.

But after zero sleep, he did feel remarkably fresh, even if sartorially disadvantaged.

By the time the clock reached 6:20, he felt their basement world was taking on a more balanced state. Max was getting as frazzled as Max could get, a faint crease or two appearing in his attire and on his face. He was having to take a sip of coffee here and there, and deep breaths. But, as Geordie freely acknowledged, the phone calls were incessant, and Max was dealing with them. More than that, he was dealing with them with panache.

"How did my father cope with all this crap?" he asked Geordie in a brief intermission. "It's like dealing with ten courts martial at once."

The answering machine had been stuffed with call-back entreaties, but they hadn't had to bother much with those. The people who'd left them were queuing up to talk. Geordie said he'd give Sarah a shout, and see if she could hold some of the calls while Max was talking.

"Good idea. We should have thought of that twenty minutes ago."

I did, but she needs her beauty sleep, Geordie told him silently.

But he took his hat off to Max, with genuine admiration. Each call was being answered, and in cases where the caller had given up waiting, the call was meticulously returned. The ex-Marine was polite, measured, and making clear distinctions between fact and speculation. Yes, he was Alex Deville's eldest son. The best he could do at this stage was to give them a timetable of what had occurred the night before. Also, as far as was known "from eye witness accounts," that a Bell JetRanger helicopter was involved, carrying two people and a pilot.

All of this, of course, had been embedded in Geordie's e-mail, but there was no way the competition take that source as reliable. Better to get it from the horse's mouth and try for a new angle, if there was such a thing.

But the questions, after a while, became repetitive:

"Do you have descriptions?" This was something Max was asked by almost every caller. One, Angela Dunn of Tyne Tees TV, asked it three times, plus every other question she could dream up short of asking Max for a date. Angela had fallen big time for his voice on the answerphone.

None that would help, Max told them all patiently. The kidnappers had been seen from a distance; he only knew that two people in their twenties or thirties had overpowered his father.

"They were young, then?"

Not too young. Where you are, school kids commit murder these days.

"Was your father badly hurt?"

Max thought not. And he certainly hadn't been killed; the "eyewitnesses" had seen him being carried to the helicopter.

"Why didn't they stop it taking off? Or stop them loading him into it in the first place?"

They'd been too far away (a euphemism for watching it all on CCTV an hour later). Had they been nearer, the kidnappers would have had a taste of Holy Island retribution, which may have been more painful for them than it had been for his father.

"Who do you think was behind it?"

He was trying to find out. He would call or e-mail everyone when he knew. "Your support, publicity, might help nail these people," Max said to several callers, when he got the chance. "There could be a press conference at some point. You should try to get here or send someone." Angela was the one caller who expressed real enthusiasm for this suggestion.

"Are you able to go after the perpetrators yourselves? Or will you be seeking help from your neighbours in the UK?"

Max, with a nod to Geordie who had forewarned him of this potential minefield, said he was sure he and his friends would get by without that kind of help.

"Do you think the British government might be involved in any way?"

At this stage, no one was being ruled out, Max said. If he was asked to choose, the important thing to him was to get his father back, not who had been involved. That would come out in the wash. However, it followed closely on the heels of one abortive attempt by the British government to attack Holy Island, so it was always possible they'd reviewed their tactics, and tried something else.

"Has your father made any enemies that you know of?"

The Declaration may have upset some people outside Holy Island, but he hoped not enough to warrant kidnapping.

"How will the secession go, without him fronting it?"

There were a lot of able people on the island. In that respect, nothing had changed. His father would expect nothing to change.

"How soon do you expect a result? To catch these people?"

He couldn't say. He told them to keep checking, he'd do his best to inform everyone. If he happened to be involved elsewhere, his sister Sarah or brother Alistair would help.

While this was going on, Geordie tried to concentrate. It was difficult, because Sarah joined them halfway through and blew him kisses at various points, such as Max's replies to questions like the last. Geordie hoped the night had meant more than a distraction to her. She certainly seemed more at peace, to have re-gathered herself this morning. He had tried to convince her that Max was right, her father had been taken captive for a purpose, and there would be more Acts to this drama.

The phone rang again. Max picked it up.

The Home Secretary.

Max had been recording all the other calls, with Geordie listening on an extension. For this one, Max switched on the loudspeaker. A dying murmur of conversation was discernible at the other end:

HS: Good morning, Mr. Deville. My condolences on your loss, which I sincerely trust will be only temporary. Of course, forgive me for pointing this out, but it may never have happened if…

MD: It is not a loss, sir. It is a crime. If you wish this to continue, please call a spade a spade.

HS: (*After a pause*) Some help is on the way. You will be receiving CID people, senior people, from Newcastle shortly. You should expect them within the next hour or so.

MD: No, sir. They may arrive, but they will not be received. They will be turned back at our security gate.

(*Muttered consultations.*)

HS: This is preposterous. I will instruct them to use force if necessary. This has gone quite far…

MD: Then they'll be turned back with force.

HS: …enough. You will *allow* these people to do their jobs.

MD: They have no jobs here. If they are your representatives, they will be representing a prime suspect.

HS: *What*? You *dare* to allege the UK government is in some way involved in this?

MD: I'm alleging nothing, sir. Like your insult with the bulldozer and its accompanying crew, you are still not taking us seriously. Take Lockerbie. At the time it happened, Libya was not in the frame, but would you have allowed their people access to the crime scene? I am saying that the possibility of loose cannons in your government can't be dismissed. That being so, your people are *personae non gratae* here. When the case is resolved, they'll be welcome as…tourists.

(*More muttered consultations.*)

HS: What have you been telling the press? Rest assured, if you use that line you may have cause…

MD: The facts. You'll hear and read about them. As you haven't had the courtesy to ask me yourself, and have no special interest in Holy Island, you'll have to rely on that source. I don't believe there's anything more I can usefully add. Good morning, sir.

Max put the phone down and switched the recorder off, squawking sounds coming across the airwaves. He turned to Geordie. "Well, he wasn't asking questions, but it was a good briefing note you prepared. Politicians. I'm not sure which is worse, them or talking heads. Or are they one and the same thing?"

"I thought you did a great job," Geordie said. "How about you, Sarah?"

"Abso-fucking-lutely," she said.

Max chuckled. "Language, sis," he said, taking a breath.

"Yes, but mine was a one-off. Unlike some people we know."

With anyone else, Geordie thought, it was possible that this sibling banter could have been taken as a release of tension. But not in this case. Max might be a man who emitted energy like sheet lightning, but he was as far from tension as he was from wringing his hands. The call had been an interesting contrast in styles, with the disembodied Voice of Authority at the other end, somehow trying to project conviction, and somehow failing. Had there been a Cabinet meeting in progress? Ministers sipping coffee, munching their McVitie's—or was it Bonne Mamans these days?—looking at each other, eavesdropping, mumbling rejection or disbelief? Had any of these people, at any point in their favoured lives, set foot in Holy Island? Or for that matter, short of security-cocooned PMs and Defence Secretaries, in Basra or Helmand? Or were their deliberations on those places as disembodied as the Voice? How was it that reality could be ignored so blithely? Did they think the world outside Whitehall was composed entirely of docile dupes? And—the scepticism of the journalist—*could* it be that the British government had somehow been involved in this affair? Was it his imagination, or had there been an echo of Hamlet's mother in those uvular protests?

Half an hour later, by nine o'clock, it had all calmed down. None of it had brought them any nearer to what might have happened to Alex Deville, but it had cleared the undergrowth. And Deville himself had never underplayed the importance of keeping the media onside. That in itself,

Geordie thought, was some evidence of continuity.

Max picked up the handset and speed-dialled.

"Now for something just as useful, and I hope a damn sight more productive." He looked at Geordie. "That's all I can do with the media. We have to get going, contact some friends of Daniel's in the RMP facility down at Bulford…Daniel?"

Well, so what was the difference? Geordie asked himself. Other nations had to call on outside help if criminals jumped borders, didn't they? And if the powers-that-be weren't of a mind to be helpful, or worse, weren't to be trusted, you turned to friends, to personal contacts. It happened all the time. Official channels sometimes just got in the way. It seemed to be in the nature of things, and those things were the same the world over.

While Max was on the phone, Geordie switched the TV on to see where Deville's abduction rated in the news stories of the day, and whether any of the calls were bearing fruit.

The talking heads, Max's other bêtes noires, had for some time been assembling in TV and radio station canteens, tucking into breakfast and reading the papers. They were in demand.

Sunday or not, the talking heads had been seduced from the warm embrace of wives or mistresses by the lure of filthy lucre. And Personal Exposure of course, without which their world would slow down and stop. Their bacon and eggs demolished, with *This Week/Day in Parliament* or whichever programme had called on their services waiting in the wings, they sank their teeth into the latest bulletin from Our Man in Holy Island and shook it like terriers with a rat. They had been here before, and knew the form. Everything was admissible; gravitas (indispensable), speculation, hints, innuendoes, nudges, winks, nods, allegories, similes, you name it. Everything but boring. Boring was the burst pipe, the guarantee that the flow of filthy lucre would be abruptly cut off.

Flicking through the channels, Geordie had found one that seemed promising. In the studio of *Westminster Week*, fetchingly framed against shots of a Bell JetRanger helicopter, one domesticated talking head, the Labour knight Sir Tim Bremner, was saying it was a popular machine with governments and law enforcement agencies. Sir Tim was a security expert of some repute, so Geordie, Max and Sarah watched with interest to see whether any useful insights emerged.

"Government and other agencies among others?" Sir Tim's interviewer asked.

"Yes, but you can't blame the oil companies this time. Or the emergency services."

"So you'd rule out anyone other than governments and their agencies?" Sir Tim's questioner, a hard-eyed anchorman called Mark Thompson, had a reputation for easing his victims into their interview before moving stealthily into a demolition job. Especially, since he was a closet right wing Tory, victims who were Labour knights or peers.

"No, I wouldn't go as far as that," Sir Tim said. "That would be premature. They would be an obvious choice, but helicopters can be chartered. Private individuals can charter them, anyone with the wherewithal. It's not cheap, but entirely possible."

"But you'd agree that this was a well-planned operation?"

"Most definitely. Well executed, too. Clandestine. Quick. In and out with no difficulty, with great stealth in fact, barely seen but for a few rabbits." Sir Tim smiled engagingly.

"You don't say? There are still rabbits on Lindisfarne? I'd have thought myxomatosis would have decimated them long ago."

"No, no, just a dumbing-down effect for the rabbit species, much as TV has been for the human species. Present company excluded, that is. Anyway, the point isn't really germane."

"You didn't mean to let them out of the hat?" Mark Thompson gave a little chuckle.

"The reference to rabbits was an FOS. A figure of speech. A distraction. I think we should forget the rabbits. Put them behind us, move on," Sir Tim said.

"Good call. And the element of surprise? How important was that?"

"Absolutely crucial. A surprise Saturday evening attack, almost Sunday in point of fact, devout islanders preparing for their weekly worship…" (*at which point Max and Sarah started laughing: at ten twenty on a Saturday night*?) "…and with their guard down…" (*at which point Max abruptly stopped laughing*) "…and there was nothing amateurish about it at all. The whole thing has the whiff of some kind of agency involvement," Sir Tim opined.

"Agency involvement? Are you saying a government agency—?"

"Now, please don't put words in my mouth."

"Remind me, Sir Tim, who brought whiffs and agency involvements into the frame?"

"A whiff, only a whiff, but the idea has to be taken seriously. Or perhaps this abduction was the work of a terrorist cell. There are plenty of those. Breeding like rabbits, you might say. But that aside, there are certain agencies which can't be ruled out. Not at this stage."

"And who would be the likely candidates? What would terrorist cells have to gain?"

"Well, perhaps we should put that aside for the present," Sir Tim

Bremner said. "I was thinking on other lines. Not to name names, but the British PM has received a bloody nose from the bulldozer affair, and he'd have to be smarting, wouldn't he? Quite understandable. Wouldn't you be smarting after such a cock...calamitous result, eh? He may well have called on his advisers to have another think. A second bite at the cherry, as it were. Recovery of control and dignity, that sort of thing. But, oh dear, rather draconian."

"Not to say illegal?"

"Oh, most definitely. Criminal, in point of fact. Always assuming that's what happened."

"And where do you think this helicopter might have gone?"

"It's very difficult to say. The thing has disappeared into thin air, which is not an easy proposition. No blips on anyone's radar, so far."

"You've checked?" Thompson asked sharply, the camera zooming in to his face.

"Well, now be reasonable, my dear fellow. One can't be expected to phone every heliport in the land, or see every light in the sky. The question, if one might make so bold, is this: Who has heliports and helipads in abundance? Tucked away in all sorts of places? All sorts of nooks and crannies, the length and breadth? Why, the British military and air forces, of course. The Ministry of Defence. Absolutely swimming in the things."

"And equally so for foreign governments?"

"Well, of course, foreign governments have them too, but to turn your question on its head, what would *they* have to gain? Norway? Germany? France? Places like that...?"

A map of Europe replaced the JetRanger pictures on screen.

"...No, it's out of the question," Sir Tim said, looking at the map in some perplexity. "If the PM is behind this, he wouldn't want the chap held somewhere in darkest Europe, would he? Where those bureaucrats could find him? Or the human rights people? No, no, the PM is cleverer than that. Good heavens, your average rookie *spook* is cleverer than that. No, he'd want him somewhere under the old wing, back here in old Blighty, don't you think?"

"You're the expert. So take us through what you think happened."

"Well, conventional wisdom has it that the JetRanger would have come in over the sea, and departed likewise. That it would have banked north or south a few miles out, over this cluster of...what are these blobs called?" (standing up, peering) "...the Farne Islands. Then, steering clear of built-up areas, it would have tracked the coastline some way out to sea, until it was ready to swoop in and land," Sir Tim's forefinger descended firmly on the city of York.

"York? Why York? Where do they get these people from?" Max asked bale-

fully, waving at the screen. "It's like watching a third-rate comedy duo. It would have been nice to think a so-called expert might have come up with a theory. Or some sort of inside track."

"No, they won't be too happy about it in York," Geordie said.

"...So let's be clear," Mark Thompson continued, "you're saying that this operation may have had some government input?"

"Well, one is drawn in that direction," Sir Tim replied. "I mean...this secession thing. Cleverly engineered, while Westminster eyes were OTB...off the ball, you understand...the elections, the Labour leadership thing. Perhaps decisions were made rather too hastily. Like Iraq, many observers would have you believe. And as with Saddam, the aim would have been to cut this chap Deville's...the snake's head off. Then what happens to the snake, eh?"

There was a fraught silence, until Thompson filled the void. "What does happen to headless snakes?"

"What indeed, what indeed? Good question. Do they die or grow another? Look at Iraq. Several thousand, *countless* snakes...Would David, sorry, *Sir* David Attenborough, be anywhere near the studio? Perhaps he could tell us, ha, ha," Sir Tim whinnied nervously.

"And perhaps you should leave the animal kingdom alone," Mark Thompson said.

"Absolutely. The whole thing is...moot. But moving on, the crucial question is, where can these blighters have gone? And what are they after? What next, hmm?"

"You think they and the helicopter may now be somewhere in Britain?"

"Well, not quite Britain. Received wisdom has it that Bonnie Scotland as a destination is out. O-U-T, out," Sir Tim said.

"Why would that be?"

"My dear fellow, you're not being serious? Good God no, it's inconceivable. Whitehall is already up to here with those unruly—hrrmph—rascals. And let's not forget our history. The Border Reivers...nothing but trouble up there. Steeped in it. The whole place has wallowed in it for centuries. Quite the way of life..."

"So where do you think they might be?" Mark Thompson asked.

"Well, that remains to be seen. As I said, no blips. But the perpetrators will be in touch."

"Oh? And when do you think that will happen?"

"I would say normally, in cases like this, within twenty-four hours or so."

"And snakes aside, have you any explanation for their motive in abducting this man?"

"Well, of course, those people…their mini-secessionist play up there might speak to motive. It has to be the front-runner, surely?"

"*Mini*-secessionist play? You don't approve?"

"Well, of course, they're a small place, and the PM has had his nose put severely out of joint by the thing."

"As well as bloodied? Don't you think he rather deserves it?"

"I'm sorry?" Sir Tim removed a handkerchief from his pocket and wiped his lips.

"Bloodied. As with the bulldozer. Perhaps with justification."

"Ah, yes, I see what you're getting at. Too many noses. But that apart, this chap Deville may well have upset other groups along the way. The secession…well, his stance throughout has been rooted in Christian heritage. But, as we know, not all the world is Christian. Only one third in fact, at the last count," Sir Tim said, waving vaguely at the map of Europe.

"So what do you conclude from that?" Thompson asked.

"Conclude? Well, I conclude that it's conceivable that one such group, for the sake of argument a non-Christian or terrorist group, may have found, let us say, a commonality of interest with the British government," Sir Tim said.

"So we're back to a terrorist group? And a marriage of convenience?"

"Well…the chances are…possibly. As to marriage, I couldn't have put it better myself."

"Really. And do you think anyone else might be caught up in this marital strife?"

"It's possible members of his family…his colleagues in this new parliament thing. Code red or orange for them, eh? As they say OTP. Over the pond, if you will. Severe, anyway."

"And what of the statements Mr. Deville's son has been making?"

"What of them?" Sir Tim wiped his brow.

"What do you think of them?"

"Well, one has some sympathy, of course. I mean, the young fellow has been thrown into the deep end, hasn't he? But he seems…capable. Formidable, one could say. However, I'm not sure he'll have the resources to follow this up. Not as thoroughly as it should be. Where is his intelligence to come from? His information? That's absolutely critical, you know…"

"Jesus wept." Max stood up as if ready to put a boot through the set.

"A marriage of convenience sounds just about feasible," Geordie said thoughtfully.

"Speculation." Max was now so disenchanted he was dismissing everything.

"…But he can't seek help from Britain, can he? If what you've been suggesting proves correct?" Mark Thompson was asking. "Even if he would want to deal with the British government, after all those bulldozers and bloodied noses. In his shoes, would you?"

"Well, no, he seems stuck with it," Sir Tim replied evasively. "His hand has been dealt, hasn't it? One can only wish him luck. Seems to play with a straight bat, though, eh?"

"As you say." Mark Thompson sighed, thinking: more clichés per square inch than a Parliamentary debate. "Well, thank you very much, Sir Tim. Very helpful."

"Always a pleasure to talk," Sir Tim said, rubbing his palms together.

In the Fahr House basement, Max sat down again with a growl of thanksgiving.

The TV picture segued from the studio into plug-in aerial footage of the Angel of the North, a descent over Gateshead, the Tyne bridges in the background, panning towards the MetroCentre, then back to the present and the hustle and bustle of shoppers. The day was breezy, with overcoats billowing, people struggling to keep their hair out of their eyes, and empty crisp packets, paper bags, and burger wraps dancing across the tarmac.

Cut to a youngish couple, early thirties, the man speaking to a roving reporter.

"You're asking us, how do we feel? The fellow's been taken from his kids. How do you expect us to feel? Okay, the kids are grown up, but so what? He comes across as a good guy. It seems like we have terrorists on every doorstep these days."

Next, a woman with plastic shopping bags.

"I hope yon wee island doesn't lose the plot without him. I've had holidays up there. That picture of the son they showed…well, he looks mean enough to cope, doesn't he? That boy could chew bricks and swaller them. But you watch, the government'll be behind all this."

By mid-morning, everyone interviewed in Gateshead's MetroCentre, or further afield, was aware that terrorists or government agents had captured Holy Island's First Minister.

Everyone was equally sure the British PM had had a hand in it.

Television, the modern-day Picture Bible, had given the Word.

CHAPTER NINETEEN

As was only to be expected, all of Holy Island, or at least the resident part, was concerned and outraged at Alex Deville's abduction. No sooner had the media calls and *Westminster Week* subsided than Max, Sarah and Alistair were besieged with callers at Fahr House. Alistair had finally emerged to meet the day, and was now diligently making up for his absence by welcoming people and showing them into the living room. Following Max's phone call, Daniel too had arrived and was having a quiet cup of coffee with Rebecca in the kitchen.

Among the first of the visitors was Amy, out for her morning constitutional with George the Vietnamese potbelly.

"This is a dreadful thing, Sarah," she said. "You must be worried sick."

"Not a word about him so far. Or from him," Sarah said.

"And no idea who's behind it. I wonder what they'll want?" Amy asked.

"Not money," Max said. "They could have tried that years ago."

"Politics," Amy said. "Ha! To think it's supposed to be the art of government.

"Black art maybe. You should have heard the garbage we've just heard," Sarah smiled.

"Oh, that? I switched that off. Got more sense out of George here. Didn't I pet?"

George the pig grunted.

"What can you do about it, Max?" Amy asked.

"Get him back."

"Aye, easier said than done. But how?"

"Sooner or later, they'll be in touch. As the TV oracle said." Max grimaced.

"But what a worry meantime. And to think it happened just after he left my house. He should have come in, and had a cup of tea."

"It wouldn't have mattered, Amy. It could've happened anywhere, anytime in the last two weeks. It's just as well you were out of the way," Max said.

"You'll let me know as soon as you hear something?"

"Of course." Max gave George a pat on the rump as they passed by. George pirouetted daintily and licked his hand.

The other Ministers of the Althing arrived; Elizabeth Swan, Michael Cromarty and Tom Walker together. Cochise, in his Sunday best but without the headgear, knocked on the door a few minutes later, apparently recovered. Then he spoilt it by starting to talk of forked tongues and smoke signals, caravans and shamans, until someone suggested he wasn't making a lot of sense. He sat down with a cup of tea, offended, looking fixedly at Sarah's legs. It reminded Geordie that he and Amy had yet to try therapy on him. He appeared to be in dire need of it.

Trevor Patterson and Mary Selby came along, joined at the gate by Dennis Cumming, who had left his better half in charge of the Post Office shop.

"Lightning doesn't strike twice, right." It wasn't a wholly convincing suggestion, given that Dennis inflected it as a question. "Kidnapping, I mean," he added.

Then George and Agnes Emery arrived from their bungalow next to the car park, with neighbours Cal Nelson from The Lindisfarne Hotel, and Billy Rankin of mobile home fame. Billy wasn't too impressed at seeing Cochise flopped in a chair, muttered, and hurried off to the kitchen. The Emery's were mortified, and confessed to Max that they hadn't heard "the dratted chopper," because their hearing these days wasn't all it should be. They felt they should have done more to stop "this awful thing." Max told them not to worry about it. If they'd tried, one or both of them could have joined his old man. Or worse.

"I was out there too, last night," Michael Cromarty said.

"What? When?" Max asked.

"That bloody fox. He's been after my chickens lately. I took a couple of shots at him last night across the field, just afore that chopper took off. Couldn't get a clear view, missed the bastard. But I thought nowt of the chopper, figured it was just those TV folk or some such."

Max started laughing. "Well, that explains something," he said. "We wondered why that pair were taking evasive action."

"Might have had better luck if I'd had a shot at them," Michael Cromarty grumbled. "Never saw them, or what they were doing."

"Just as well," Max said. "You could've got the wrong guy."

"No way," Michael Cromarty said, offended. "I may be some kinda politico now, but I can still bloody aim straight. The damn fox ducked into a hedge, was all."

As the minutes ticked by, Geordie became quite impressed with Minister Cromarty, whom he had only talked with once or twice before. The guy was no Deville, far from it, but he had qualities. And foremost among them were an ability to listen, a no-nonsense attitude, and common sense. Maybe Deville's yen for political retirement wasn't such a pipe-dream after all, if he got back in one piece and had the chance to pursue it. It had bothered Geordie somewhat that Alex Deville was such a dominant presence in island politics, but once things settled down, if they settled down, Michael Cromarty might provide a safe pair of hands. And Max and Alistair...well, okay, and maybe Sarah—how was he to think straight about Sarah?—would still be there to help. Alistair may even have political ambitions himself.

Cromarty certainly wasn't wasting his breath bemoaning Deville's disappearance, or wondering whether it could have been avoided. He took it as a starting-point. The question was, what to do about it? He and Max had a short, and as far as Geordie could tell, practical discussion on what might be expected from the kidnappers, and where and when it might materialise.

"Not a letter," Cromarty said. "Not if they took a chopper wherever. Unless they have someone helping on the inside here, and I'd have by God heard about it if they had. E-mail, maybe, or text if they have a number? Maybe straight to the TV people."

He and Max agreed that sooner or later they'd hear from somewhere, by some electronic means. Cromarty's instinct was for Scotland. "Somewhere unpopulated. Either that, or somewhere so bloody populated they'll hide in the mix. Bloody urban jungles."

He was happy for Max, with Geordie's help, to deal with the media. "Not my scene." He read Geordie's list of odds without comment, and at one point had a brief *tête-à-tête* with Max and Daniel in a corner of the palatial room.

Geordie would have liked to listen in, but Sarah was holding on to his hand.

The pollsters phoned to ask if they should continue drafting questions for the poll. In their opinion it should still proceed. After checking with Alistair what this was all about, Max put them on hold, telling them to wait until things had calmed down. He said his father would want the spotlight to be on the secession, not himself.

"After that lot," he gestured at the TV, "everyone in Britain will know about Holy Island and the secession. But whether they'll know it from Narnia is another question."

There were other visitors, many seemingly inclined to sit in the Fahr House living room drinking tea until Alex Deville reappeared. All of them speculating when that might be, and not daring to voice any worse scenario. Max told them they had all be better going to church and praying. He had been tied up since dawn with press calls, but now there were things to do which might help find his father. He didn't like to chase people off but hoped they would spread the word that he was busy.

"Right," Michael Cromarty said. "You heard the man. Bugger off, the lot of you."

They took the hint and drifted away into a light rain. Max, Sarah, Alistair and Geordie breathed sighs of relief, and headed downstairs. Daniel and Rebecca followed them.

"Just about now," Daniel said, pouring them all cups of coffee, "Mr. Miah should be receiving some visitors." It was eleven o'clock, and Daniel was right.

Mr. Miah was standing at his front door three hundred miles away in Southwark, looking at two gentlemen in shoulder- and thigh-hugging grey suits. And cool grey eyes to match. They could be twins, he thought. Then, in unison, they flashed two authentic-looking badges. One identified its holder as John Vaughan, the other as Milan Petrov.

"We work for the British government," John Vaughan explained. "This is purely a routine call, sir. We've been asked to help in the disappearance of a Mr. Alex Deville from Holy Island. If we may have five minutes of your time?"

Mr. Miah let them in. He couldn't for the moment think of a life-preserving alternative.

Perched at an MFI breakfast table, his guests told him their task was straightforward; to follow up on phone calls Mr. Deville had received over the last two weeks. It was tedious work, they sighed, but necessary for purposes of elimination. They understood Mr. Miah might have spoken with Mr. Deville on the phone recently. Was that the case?

"Well, yes, that is so."

"And did you have any particular reason to speak to anyone else about these calls?" Milan Petrov asked.

"No, not exactly."

"How about inexactly?" John Vaughan asked. "Have you spoken to anyone in normal everyday conversation?"

"Well, yes, but briefly. Nothing of consequence."

"Who?" Petrov asked.

"Only two people. A colleague and one of his sons. You must please understand, I have many contacts with whom I talk. I am proud to do so, as a representative of my people."

"Of course. But you've spoken only with these two, in normal everyday conversation, about your talks with Mr. Deville?" Vaughan this time, like a ping-pong game.

"Yes, that is correct."

"And did you feel insulted—no, too strong a word—a trifle miffed, at Mr. Deville?"

At this point, Mr. Miah realised the calls must have been recorded. Or Deville had told someone of them. In some detail.

"Well, yes, I am feeling somewhat aggrieved. But—how to put it?—it is water under the bridge. Please understand, all this is several days ago, Wednesday or Thursday, and I have made many phone calls since. Phone calls are a normal feature of my work. You see?"

"Of course. You and Mr. Deville discussed some of the finer points of Shari'a law, didn't you? Crime and punishment, for example?" Petrov asked.

"Yes…Mr. Deville, you see, was expressing some views on this subject. In British terms, more right wing than mainstream."

"Who was the colleague you spoke with about it?"

Thrown by the directness of the question, Mr. Miah in quick succession gave the name Iqbal Khan, and Mr. Khan's occupation, workplace and home address. With each answer, his eyes moved right. Vaughan and Petrov took this as a baseline; that these answers were true.

"Do you know where Mr. Khan is now?" John Vaughan asked.

"No. He will be at home, I think."

"How old is he?"

"Pardon?"

"How old is Mr. Khan?"

"Well, we are of an age. In fact, we have found that we arrived in Britain at more or less the same time, as young men."

Eyes right again, no problem with that one.

"And how would you describe Mr. Khan's beliefs?" Milan Petrov asked.

"In what way?"

A shrug. "For example, would you say he was a moderate, law-abiding citizen?"

"Law-abiding citizen, most definitely, yes. He has never, to my knowledge, been receiving so much as a parking ticket."

"And moderate?" Petrov asked.

"Well…by no means a rabble-rouser. Not at all. An educated man. A devout man, yes."

"A faithful Islamist? A believer in Shari'a law?"

"Moderately so, but not to the extremes, of course. The world has moved on…mostly."

"Sure. But tell us, please, which of your sons did you speak with about these calls?"

At this point, Mr. Miah felt an icy hand creep up his back. He decided on equivocation. Or at least postponement:

Mr. Deville had put the phone down on him, you know. It really wasn't cricket. He had expressed some disappointment a couple of times to his son, in passing. But it had been a mere—how to put it?—bagatelle. He wasn't playing games with his name, of course. Miah…mere. All too easily confused. Mr.Miah tried hard not to give a nervous giggle.

His two visitors listened patiently to this, in silence.

"To which of your sons did you speak?" Vaughan repeated Petrov's question.

"Ah…Mujaahid."

Petrov scribbled a note.

"And is Mujaahid acquainted with Mr. Khan?

"Indeed, yes. Mr. Khan is a family friend of long-standing."

"A little more than a colleague, then?" Vaughan suggested.

"Yes."

Then the dreaded question, asked very quietly and mildly by John Vaughan.

"And how would you describe your son's, Mujaahid's, beliefs?"

"Ah…similar to the family friend's. A nice young man, moderate, devout."

"Similar?" A gentle lifting of the eyebrows.

"Well, you know young people these days," Mr. Miah said. "They are…how to put it?…finding their path, all part of growing up. A natural process. You see?"

"What age is Mujaahid?"

"Ah…twenty-eight."

"What height is he?"

"Height?…ah…six feet one. Upstanding…a good son in all respects."

"And of course you think Mujaahid was aptly named," Petrov said.

"Named? Pardon?" Mr. Miah's eyes now flickered wildly, moving up and left.

"Mujaahid. Doesn't that mean a fighter? A fighter in the way of Allah?"

"Ah…his mother thought it a nice name."

"Does Mujaahid?" A disarming smile, which reached no higher than Petrov's lips.

"He has not been saying otherwise. Nor would he. Such a thing would be unthinkable in a son."

"Has Mujaahid taken any holidays in recent years?" John Vaughan asked.

"In what sense? He has been to Brighton, Bournemouth once or twice."

"In the sense of Pakistan, say. Or a near neighbour."

"Oh, no, nowhere abroad, no, no."

"No unexplained absences? No family weddings in the Orient?"

"No, no, absolutely not. One or two nights away, never unexplained."

"And never longer?"

"Well, public holidays…three nights? But never longer than that, no, no."

"And his friends? Do you know them all?" Petrov asked.

"His close friends, of course. Well, one can't be poking into every aspect of a young man's life, can one? He has his work, interests…"

"Moderation is not the guaranteed mindset, then? Not in one and all of your son's acquaintances?"

"Mindset? But how can it ever be guaranteed?…But, no, no, there is no reason whatever to believe he may have been, ah…led astray. Absolutely not. A fine young man."

"Where is he now?" Both Vaughan and Petrov, mirror images, looking around the room, and through the door into the living room.

"A short break. Only two nights, with an uncle in Kensington."

To his unbounded relief, Mr. Miah's two visitors began to make moves to depart. But before they left, they asked: could they trouble him for the uncle's address? A number they could call? It was tedious, but their instructions were: leave no loose ends. They smiled at Mr. Miah sympathetically. It had every chance of spoiling their Sunday.

Vaughan and Petrov got an address and telephone number. They thanked Mr. Miah for his time and trouble. They would get out of his hair, and hoped he would enjoy the rest of the weekend with his family. Those that remained in Southwark, at least.

On their way back to their car, John Vaughan phoned Daniel on his mobile to say that they were popping over to Kensington. They would touch base again in an hour. As they drove, they kept the radio on to listen in to news bulletins, so they could hear what other people were saying. It gave them some amusement.

They called Daniel back at twelve thirty, heading towards the M25, two men trained among other things in kinesics, the reading of body language, verbal mannerisms, all the unconscious little jerks and quirks that humans are apt to display in social intercourse. It was one of the more esoteric areas of interrogation in which John Vaughan and Milan Petrov had been tutored, but it meant they were as near perfect as possible in the art of recognising lies.

And they enjoyed it. They had honed their skills on each other as well as witnesses and suspects, and made it a little gambling game. Somewhere in normal conversation, they took turns at throwing in a random lie. If the other spotted it, his reward was a free meal. If he didn't, his only penalty was the cost of a pint of beer.

The only downside was, as their proficiency had increased, so the free meals had escalated from their humble beginnings in Wiltshire's country pubs. The last had been at London's Ritz Hotel. They were thinking that they might have pushed their little game to its natural limits. Well, when it came down to it, where else was there to go? New York's Waldorf Astoria was kind of out of the question, Raffles in Singapore even more so.

"Was our boy there?" Daniel asked. "In Kensington?"

"Three guesses," John Vaughan said. "He hasn't been there since yesterday noon. There's an involvement there, but we don't think it's primary. The Miahs would've needed help; it wouldn't sit right otherwise. No way could they afford a chopper; the houses are full of kit furniture. Miah Senior was a head-to-toe Primark advertisement. He's not a bad guy, just a puffball. And he's worried. Our best guess is, the son caught a train north from King's Cross, maybe with a pal, then picked up the chopper. It was likely laid on ready for them. His uncle thought he'd gone back to Southwark; we didn't tell him otherwise. He'll be speaking to Miah Senior anyway, so he'll know soon enough that nephew has done a runner. Let them sweat. You have to try the airports up north, Daniel, and see whatever flight plan they filed."

"Done it. We think they filed to Glasgow, but they didn't arrive. Could be anywhere."

"Well, Miah Senior knew his son was into it in some way," Vaughan said. "He was blinking, shifting his stance, crossing his arms, licking his lips, looking past us all the time. No two ways about it, he'll be sitting on the toilet yet. We both saw it."

"This other one, the colleague, he's not worth following up?" Daniel asked.

"Wrong age group. He's sixty-ish, the same as Miah. We'll do it if you want, though."

"The only thing we're thinking here, Max and me, is the off-chance of Whitehall input. The son, Mujaahid, he wouldn't be likely to know anyone, would he? But the colleague might, if not Miah Senior himself. Assuming the uncle's an innocent party."

There was a silence. Then:

"Yes, well, that could be. Input…yeah, those Whitehall drones are just stupid enough. You can rule out Miah Senior, though, as well as the uncle. We got the idea Miah was telling the truth when he said he'd spoken only to this so-called colleague and his son. But yes, if you put it like that, the colleague could be worth a look. We'll try him. He lives in Watford. Give us till two, lunchtime or so, all right? The traffic's building something cruel down here."

"Thanks for all the help, you guys. It's much appreciated."

"Don't mention it. Do you think we might be in line for a Holy Island DSO?"

CHAPTER TWENTY

Max and Daniel were packing, a process which in their case was quite unrecognisable from the normal holiday chore. In double quick time, things were disappearing from the Fahr House basement's table into two haversacks. Boots and rolled-up items of clothing were the first to go, followed by a lap-top, knives, ropes, binoculars, cable ties, tape, wire cutters and an assortment of stuff Geordie didn't recognise. Some sort of weaponry? he wondered. Gun parts? It was all very neat anyway, very efficient and matter-of-fact. It positively shouted service training and discipline.

At one point, Max handed the phone to Alistair, saying, "Yours."

"Hello…yes, sir, good of you to call…no, I think all we can do in that respect is being done…my father would appreciate it…no, not necessary, Max is handling it…we did see, yes…" (subdued laughter) "…no, we've heard nothing…well, if there's anything you can do in that direction…thank you…it *has* damaged the model but hopefully only temporarily…and how is everything going your end?" (long pause) "…yes, sir…goodbye."

Alistair replaced the phone and started wiping surfaces, putting tapes back in chronological order. All very neat and methodical too.

What sort of model are we talking here? Geordie wondered. What was that about? Someone from the Scilly Isles? Or the City? Whoever, it was clear that journalists-cum-house-guests-cum-sister's-boyfriends weren't going to be let in on the secret.

Then Max was phoning around for a helicopter, something faster and bigger than a Bell JetRanger. He decided on an AugustaWestland Grand, an Italian twin-turbine with a cruise speed of 180 mph and a range of over 500 miles, built to carry six people plus crew. It must be expensive, Geordie thought, as Max flipped a platinum card between his fingers.

It was obviously not a common aircraft, either. There were none stationed at Newcastle, or so Max commented in an aside, but he seemed to be making progress elsewhere. Geordie heard him confirm that he wanted it today, and that four o'clock would be fine. An open-ended charter; the pilot would be put up at Fahr House, and the onward flight plan filed when it was known.

He could land on the lawn. Max gave the co-ordinates off the top of his head.

"Isn't it a bit early for all this?" Sarah asked.

"No. If it's here, we can leave there and then."

"But you don't know where."

"We will. England, Wales, Scotland or wherever, it's almost certainly inside four hundred miles. They'd have done it in one hop. Why take extra risks?"

"You know best."

"Don't worry, sis. As soon as we know where, we'll have him back in a matter of hours. Ali and you and George can look after the damn media."

"Okay," Geordie said. "In that case, we'll get some fresh air." He had already sent a piece that morning to the *Washington Post*, and needed something else to happen before he filed for *The Northern Sun*'s Monday edition. Keeping these balls in the air was getting to be a royal pain, especially since one of them hadn't sent him any payment yet. But on the plus side, the *Post* didn't phone each day to tell him to do what he was already doing.

Max grinned. "Well, you won't get any from those buggers. Hot air, yes; fresh, no."

"I'm surprised *some* of them aren't here by now."

"Why should they come here? They're being hand-fed by satellite."

Geordie couldn't argue with that. He'd had the same thought. Good to know he was getting along with the brother-in-law to be. No, no, wait...Max? The guy had his points, but as a brother-in-law...Jeezo, miss an anniversary, and the next one would be in a wheelchair.

Geordie and Sarah walked hand-in-hand, Rebecca with them, along Crossgate to Market Place, its Celtic cross glistening in sunshine after the morning showers, to the priory museum. Whenever Geordie passed it, he thought what a neat, tasteful conversion it was.

"We'll have the Lindisfarne Gospels in there sooner or later," Sarah said. "Dad doesn't think the British Library is quite their natural home." She laughed. Geordie was relieved to see her vivacity was back, more or less in full flow. Maybe her elder brother's get-up-and-go attitude was to thank for it, or maybe no news *was* good news, although Geordie had never subscribed to that old saw.

On their way through the churchyard, Sarah pointed out a weathered stone lying at the church's eastern end.

"The Petting Stone," she told them.

"What's it for?" Geordie asked. He had missed it on his earlier rambles. It sounded interesting; Holy Island was full of strange little quirks like that.

"You may find out one day," Sarah said. "If you get lucky."

She wouldn't say more. "Don't pester, George."

Petting Stone? Did people lie on it, as in full public view? Or did they christen their pets there? If you weren't too picky, it did have the look of some sort of font. Or maybe it was as well not to know. That went against the grain as well. It wasn't his day. Again.

They meandered through the northern gate of St. Mary's churchyard and hung over the wall to look beyond the remains of Jenny Bell's Well to St. Cuthbert's Island, Hobthrush as was, with its ruined chapel and tall wooden cross.

"We've only had mains water for a dozen years or so," Sarah said. "My Dad had a mouthful or two from the well down there. He says it gave him a taste for Laphroaig, if nothing else. It's a bit too near the sea and the seaweed."

Low tide had been at midday and the islet was accessible, but they opted not to walk over the mud, rocks and mussel-beds. After Sarah's history lesson the previous Sunday, Geordie had made a point of visiting it to see where the saint had attempted his first retreat. Traces of a tiny chapel, "St Cuthbert in the Sea", had been visible, the wooden cross marking the spot where the altar once stood. Carcasses of seabirds had littered the islet, and clumps of thrift that might have been there in St. Cuthbert's time flowered in the grass above high tide mark.

Someone had placed four small white stones beneath the cross and marked them in black ink: "Freedom," "Fellowship," "Family," "Finance." Geordie could see St. Cuthbert agreeing with the first three, although he might have substituted "Father" for "Family," but the last had struck an incongruous note. If whoever had done it had been looking for F's, they might have chosen "Frugality" instead. Finally, Geordie had turned away disappointed. Bad enough that modern-day graffiti was out of place below the wooden cross, but the writer could have chosen his or her words more carefully.

Today as then, some eider ducks were preening themselves on the rocks. A pair of arctic terns darted through the air above them. Sarah pointed out grey seals in the distance, basking on the sandbanks. They could make out some movement, as squabbles broke out over territory. Either that, or the bulls were making their presence felt. Geordie had seen those guys in action; throwing your weight around were the *mots justes*.

They made their way downhill to the shingle beach below the Heugh, heading for the path beyond the sheds of Trinity House. He noticed an older couple walking a parallel path along the shore to their right, bladderwrack popping beneath their feet like bubble-wrap.

As they walked, Rebecca was trying as usual to educate him in the art of plant identification, occasionally jotting notes in a pad. She'd seen the month of May described in the Heritage Centre as "the month of greening up," and asked him whether it wasn't a nice turn of phrase, one in use long before the idea had become a corporate and political football. Geordie nodded. He knew she was still writing a daily diary to her mother in New Zealand: in part, she conceded, to assuage some guilt about her ill-starred marriage. But she knew her plants, that much had always been clear. Throughout their walk, and as they climbed the Heugh, she kept feeding Geordie names of flowers he had never heard of, and certainly couldn't recall ever having seen in Jesmond Dene.

"Why don't you paint some of them?"

She looked at him in astonishment. "I do. Where do you think I go most mornings?"

In the monastic garden behind St. Mary's, they had seen a quaintly old-fashioned display including rosemary, flowering currant, iris, lady's mantle and marigold. Some had been flowering, some budding, others waiting for high summer. Elsewhere there were patches of grass-of-parnassus (not yet showing itself), sea centaury, herb-robert nestling in rocks, the bright yellow of rockrose showing on steep-sided slopes. Rebecca told Geordie she would treat him one day to a lesson in the Gospel Garden. She was quite relieved now to think it had never been polluted by Charley.

The primroses and cowslips they occasionally encountered were like long-lost friends, flowers Geordie vaguely remembered from childhood, from country walks in north Durham. He hadn't seen or thought about them in fifteen years. If he'd been asked, he would have guessed they'd disappeared, blitzed by pesticides or construction companies. Rebecca was identifying every plant they saw. Apart from being an obsession, Geordie wondered, was it a useful talent? He supposed it was, given that so much of the natural world was under threat.

Apart from the older couple they had seen, not many others were about, no locals he recognised. They must be at Sunday lunch, or The Ship, or both, he assumed. He wouldn't say no to either himself; it had been a tiring night and he was thirsty.

The last of the showers had drifted out to sea and everything was washed clean. If he bent close, encouraged by Rebecca, he could breathe in the scents of the different flowers. At least he now knew sea pinks when he saw them. Even to a crass townie like him, the small pink clusters on their long stalks, clinging for dear life to all sorts of unlikely footholds, had become a favourite.

They stopped near the old coastguard station at the war memorial, which was fashioned out of pink sandstone by the same architect who had restored the Castle in the early years of the twentieth century. There were views south towards the Farnes, the hulking mass of Bamburgh Castle; west to the mainland, the two slender navigation obelisks prominent, the smooth hump of the Cheviot on the far horizon; and east across the harbour, the mound called Beblowe Crag on the far point, Lindisfarne Castle perched on its top.

"Fort Osborne," Sarah said, pointing to a ruin along the Heugh. "It was built to repel the Dutch in the last part of the seventeenth century. That one, its twin," nodding towards the Castle, "was built two centuries earlier to repel the Scots. It's been all go here, people forever trying to gatecrash the party."

They walked through the Whin-grassland towards the ruined re-doubt at the south-east end of the crag; sea campion, thrift and buttercups growing in profusion along the top. They sat for a while on a new seat dedicated to a young soldier killed in Afghanistan in 2006.

"No one complains about the loss of lives commemorated there," Sarah said, pointing back to the war memorial. "But this one seems so sad."

"Maybe it has to do with the passage of time," Geordie said.

"Or necessity. Or trust. Or lack of. There'll be others everywhere. *Iraq*. Outrageous."

They turned back along the top of the Heugh towards the village, past clusters of spent daffodils, a blaze of wallflowers, and some bluebells on the banks facing Sanctuary Close.

Beneath them was the string of old upturned boats, reminders of the long-lost herring fishery; with anchors, pallets, floats, lobster pots, carts, fish boxes, nets, ropes, and tackle scattered between them, behind and in front. All apparently haphazard, all spoken for. Imagine this stuff in Byker, Geordie thought; it'd be stripped and gone inside an hour. He could smell the heady mix of algae, diesel, fish offal and seaweed wafting up from the Ouse, the salty tang of the North Sea beyond. Diesel apart, it would have smelt much the same a century ago. Maybe more powerful. A *lot* more powerful, he corrected himself, given the bait and shells and entrails that would have been strewn about the place.

"The Herring Houses," Sarah pointed to an attractive group of stone buildings Geordie had passed several times before. "Where the fish were cleaned and smoked. They're holiday homes now, but maybe not for long."

Geordie had been intrigued over the last few days to see "House for Sale" signs popping up like mushrooms in the village. Eleven of them at the last count. No doubt people who wouldn't or couldn't commit to twenty-six weeks, he thought.

In principle, he had no problem at all with the new rule. He could just about understand, if not condone, the ownership of more than one house by one family: who'd want to spend all their time in a city if they had the means to escape two or three days a week? But he felt that this phenomenon, like many others, had been allowed to go way too far. In particular, he felt that the disenfranchisement of young people, young *local* people, from the housing market, amounted to criminal abandonment on the part of politicians. Where were they to live? In rented property? Tents? Cardboard boxes? God help them if they thought caravans were the way to go. Apart from being prey to Cochise, caravans had a bad habit of devaluing. After a few years, they would simply be back at square one, with nothing to show for it. By 2050, would there be any worthwhile, *working* people left in rural and coastal areas? Apart from anything else, you'd think the politicians would have more sense. These were their future voters, when all was said and done. If anyone by the year 2050 bothered to vote any more.

And there was another thing; the council tax. Why on earth were owners of second homes awarded tax rebates? In Geordie's view, the whole approach should be reversed. Make these people, who had demonstrated an ability to own more than one home, who had exercised a freedom of choice to the detriment of those with less choice, pay double the norm. Treble. Quadruple. Or maybe the economy would plummet, interest rates go sky high. It would just be what they deserved, he thought. Any penalty, accidental or otherwise, would be welcome in bringing the playing field back to a semblance of level.

He would be interested to see what would happen on Holy Island under the new regime. Would the "Houses for Sale" stand empty and rot, or would they be bought by people who would and could commit to twenty-six weeks? Sarah had told him that the first two had been snapped up by returning Holy Islanders. One young family in their late twenties, and one middle-aged family in their late forties, both fed up with life in London and Leeds respectively, had seen a window of enterprise and opportunity opening.

Good luck to them, Geordie thought. A reversal of fortunes, for them and for the island. Not to mention a dose of homespun justice.

They left the Herring Houses and walked along the path to the pier, past the fishermen's huts (cow parsley, Rebecca said, some foxgloves coming through, see?) alongside a rock-strewn beach. Several fishermen in blue Aran sweaters (the older ones), T-shirts (the younger ones) and jeans (endemic), were working on their boats.

"They'll be going out at first light," Sarah said, her eyes clouding over a little. "Life goes on, huh? You should come down and have a look, George. It's a nice sight at dawn, with the sun coming up over the Castle."

It was a nice sight now, Geordie thought. Timeless. A Holy Island postcard that, apart from the jeans, might have looked much the same a century ago. But with more activity. Again, a *lot* more. He had read that in the latter half of the nineteenth century, as many as fourteen hundred herring barrels had been stacked "in piles and rows" along the shore.

"I'd need company," he said.

"You're on. If it's a fine morning. Bring a camera."

One of the fishermen, Tom Fender, who had been vocal at the last public meeting, lifted his head and threw a cigarette over the gunwale.

"Sarah," he shouted, "any word of your Dad?"

"No. Still waiting."

"Max need any help?"

"He seems to be keeping on top of it."

"Aye, Max'll get him back for you. That the new boyfriend yonder?"

"Yes. His name's George."

"Met him afore. A'right, George? Look after yon lass. She's a good 'un," Tom said.

"That's me told," Geordie said, turning to Rebecca.

"You're in trouble. I've got knights in shining armour everywhere," Sarah smiled.

"I wonder if I'll pass scrutiny with them all," Geordie said.

"The nights I've tossed and turned lately, wondering the same thing," Sarah said.

They turned back from the pier and retraced their steps towards Popple Well, bladderwrack and kelp waving in the shallows to their right. The jail and the growing foundations of the new Althing House were on their left.

"Better water from there," Sarah said, pointing at two rusted iron standpipes. "Further away from the salt." She nodded up the hill to a row of properties facing them, running along Sandham Lane from what used to be the Iron Rails pub. "More holiday homes. They have good views, don't they? Some of the best here. It's a pity they're ninety percent wasted."

Looking along the path to the Castle, their route of a few days ago, Geordie could see Jeff Elliot on his bench playing his pipes, the ancient staithes behind him rearing like massive thorns from the rocks. Relics of the limestone jetty, Trevor Patterson had told him.

The strains of *The Water of Tyne* drifted to them along the shore.

"Nice relaxing job, huh?" he said. "And a nice place to do it."

"You need to know music for that kind of life, George," Rebecca said. "You don't qualify."

"Oh, come on, that was just one group. Pub quizzes, I can cope with."

"Well, there's an idea," Sarah said. "They may not have a quiz going at Sunday lunchtime in The Ship, but they'll have beer."

My heroine, Geordie thought. What a girl.

It seemed unusually quiet when they walked into The Ship's lounge, nobody speaking. Then they saw what the punters were looking at.

Alex Deville on the television.

CHAPTER TWENTY-ONE

They wasted no time getting out. No one had noticed them anyway. The pull of the television screen had been too compelling. Visitors were glued to it as firmly as residents.

Geordie took one look and said, "You don't want to see this, not here." He pulled Sarah back. "Max'll have it," he said. "Let's go."

They ran up Marygate past the Heritage Centre and Gospel Garden, past the Post Office and the guesthouse where Rebecca had spent the only night of her marriage, and made it back to Fahr House in less than five minutes. Max, Alistair and Daniel had the same sequence on the big screen. It was less than fifteen seconds long. They were running and re-running it, Alistair freezing it every few seconds, as if hoping something would show that had not been there before. It showed a barren landscape of angular fragments of rock, possibly a cliff-top, an impression of space, maybe the sea below. Gulls gliding on the wind. No background noise. No animals. No trees. Solitary clumps of greenery.

"Tundra," Max said. "Moonscape. I'm beginning to wonder...have they skipped Britain? It looks like you'd imagine Iceland would look."

Alex Deville stood, mouth taped, eyes blazing, ramrod straight, looking at the camera, and then at the shorter of two other subjects. One on each side of him, two people in jalabiyas, keffiyehs bound with agals, the cloth wrapped round their foreheads and lower faces, only the eyes showing. The smaller one had rocks in each hand. The other wielded a sabre, curved from hilt to tip with a single edge, and no pommel.

At the bottom of the picture, a slogan blazoned:

"And slay them wherever ye catch them, and turn them out from where they have turned you out." Qur'ān, 2:191.

Geordie was pleased to recognise it. All that bedtime reading...but they must have been spoilt for choice. No wonder sleep had eluded him; he'd even tried reading it, as advised in the preface, aloud. And maybe it was better in Arabic, almost certainly it would be...

But was the message relevant, or bombast? Who had Deville "turned out"? Muslim women? That had to be the connection, or someone was fooling around. But hoodies or bikers weren't likely to quote the Koran, even if they'd heard of it. It had to be connected with Miah.

Alistair ran the clip to the end. Not a word had been spoken in it.

"Blessed are the war-makers," Max muttered. "Select the bits that suit, why don't you?"

"All religions do it," Daniel said. "Another got us slavery and apartheid."

"Can we all please focus on what we're seeing, Daniel?" Max pointed at Alistair. "You're as bad as him and his fucking recognition."

Sarah clutched Geordie's arm. "This is...they're taunting us. That could be anywhere."

Max looked up again. "It's a bit of staged nonsense, sis. Add a bit of jungle or marble and it'd be a Bollywood musical. And it was about time we heard from them. We got this video clip on the mobile ten minutes ago. Ali's been playing with it but it hasn't helped much. 3GP format, he tells me. A lot of use that is, too."

"It's on TV in the village. In The Ship," Geordie said. He found himself agreeing with Max again. It did look staged, almost burlesque. It just didn't ring true. "Could either of them be a woman?" he asked.

"Not unless they've had a sex change from last night," Max said. "Look at the hands, George. TV...the old man won't like that, not if it's those toxic PC liberals in the BBC."

"It was on Tyne Tees, when we saw it," Sarah said. "But it'll be everywhere. He'll know about it. He'll have assumed that's what it was for...he doesn't exactly look scared."

"Fuck scared. He's weighing up the odds. You can see it. Why does he keep looking at the guy on his left? The one with the stones?"

"And how come both of them are in the picture?" Geordie asked.

"Good question. The camera's propped up, or there's a third party. Maybe the pilot."

"There's no camera movement anyway," Geordie said.

"No. But it wouldn't prove anything if there was," Max said.

"Where do you think it can be?" Sarah asked. After Max's Bollywood comment, she seemed more relaxed, curiosity replacing concern.

"God knows. Somewhere with rocky slopes and sea. Nothing there but what you see. Interesting pose...*very* staged, hmm? Amateurish, like a home video. And they're telling us, 'First instalment, to be continued.'"

"Can I look again?" Rebecca asked. "On a small screen? Better clarity?"

"Why?" Max asked.

"Just bear with me...there might be something there."

"Well, hell, you can't see any less than we have. Do it, Ali."

Alistair switched the mobile to an infrared connection.

"Can you zoom in?" Rebecca said.

"On what?" Max asked.

"Those white flowers in the rocks."

"Jesus wept," Max muttered. "It's nature study."

Alistair zeroed in, the picture retaining good definition.

"More," Rebecca said.

White flowers with yellow centres, dark green elliptical leaves with a deep purple tinge, hairy stems.

"That's *cerastium nigrescens*. Holy mackerel...how lucky is that?"

"What's lucky?" Max asked sharply.

"Because we know where your Dad is," Rebecca said.

"We what?"

"Because that little plant only grows in one place in the world. It's known as Shetland mouse-ear chickweed, a wonderful hardy little herb related to the Arctic mouse-ear. That's your tundra for you, Max, natural debris from serpentine rock. But what may look like a lunar landscape to you is paradise on earth to a botanist. Some of the rarest plants in Britain grow there. Edmonston's chickweed, Shetland mouse-ear, is the rarest."

"Let me get this straight. You said one place in the world?" Max said.

"Well, two to be precise," Rebecca said. "What we're looking at are pictures taken at one of two sites on the planet. But they're within spitting distance. One is a National Nature Reserve called the...Ness?...no, the *Keen* of Hamar. The other is a Site of Special Scientific Interest at...I think it's called the Hill of Colvadale, three, four miles away. The plant's been struggling to establish itself there, though."

"*Where* are these places? Shetland?"

"Yes. Right at the northern point of Unst. About as far as you can get in Britain, I think."

"Christ alive," Max said. "How sure are you?"

"Absolutely one hundred percent about the plant. Not so sure about my geography."

"Believe her," Geordie said. "I've been getting tuition in it all for days." It certainly answered a question he had asked himself earlier. "Useful talent" lay in a nether region between slight and insult.

"Jesus wept. Kiss her for me, will you Daniel?"

"Happy to oblige." Daniel obliged, and looked like he was enjoying it.

Rebecca broke away, looked at Sarah and laughed. "The first time I met your Dad, he told me my degree might come in handy. Little did we know."

"Handy? Fucking A. Where is this place, Ali?" Max said. "Bring it up on an Ordnance Survey map, will you? Or multimap dot com whatever."

Thirty seconds later they had the location.

Keen of Hamar, a site 1200 by 400 metres at its widest, just east of the settlement of Baltasound, Unst. The airstrip at Lat. 60°45′N, Long. 00°51′W. The Hill of Colvadale a mile south of the airfield.

"How far do you reckon from the airfield to the Keen place?" Max asked.

"By road, I'd say three miles into the Reserve," Alistair said. "You'd need to go around the Sound, wouldn't you? It looks like a scattered settlement."

"What's in the place?" Max asked.

Alistair clicked a few more times.

"Hotel...umm...two dozen rooms it says here, pinelog cabins...boat haven...Junior High School and sports centre...Post Office, shops, church, even a brewery. The hotel looks to be quite close to the Keen of Hamar, on the north side of the Sound, east out of the village. Hey, it says the Sound used to be the centre of the northern herring fishing industry. Ten to one some of the older Holy Islanders will have been there." He clicked back to the map, and then a few more times to bring up and zoom in on a satellite picture.

"Job for you this afternoon. Find one of them," Max said, watching the images.

"When you've left," Alistair nodded, switching between them. "We'll have enough to do until then."

"That looks like buildings, habitation nearby." Max pointed at the screen.

"There's nothing much in the Reserve," Alistair said. "Maybe those are crofts, or were at one time. One may be connected to the Reserve...it has a parking symbol there. Baltasound village looks...well, it's dispersed, isn't it? Those nearest crofts, Hamar, Little Hamar, stretch up to the Keen. Look, there's an RAF or NATO radar base at a place called Saxa Vord at the north end of the island. Maybe five or six miles." He clicked to print the map, and then back to the text. "It says here, mothballed in 2005...it's been one of those big golf-ball things."

"Okay. Run me off those pages as well, huh?" Max asked. "And the satellite image."

"Will do."

Max retrieved the map and turned to Sarah. "They've taken the old man out there for the shoot. Maybe from the village. They've been trying to do a UBL in the fucking hills. Well, it just came back and bit them. Look at the contours on the map, the background, and then the video. It's been taken there." He jabbed a forefinger, looked at Rebecca. "Bloody brilliant."

"Your language, dearest, is getting worse by the minute," Sarah said.

Max ploughed on regardless. "And they must have had help with that location. Can you imagine some jerk from Southwark doing it himself? Now all we need's the helo. Showtime, Daniel," Max looked at the wall clock. "Three o'clock. Let's see where it's got to."

When Geordie got a minute to ask, Daniel told him that the visit to Miah's colleague, Iqbal Khan, had been inconclusive. Vaughan and Petrov had left with the impression that Khan had talked about it to one or two people, as Miah himself had done, but so far he wasn't telling. They had asked Daniel if he wanted the guy "put under some pressure." Or maybe a return visit to Miah? Daniel had said leave it, see how things panned out; you could get unwelcome side effects if you scared sixty year-olds out of their socks twice in as many hours.

Now here they were with a location and two or more targets. Geordie could see the anticipation growing in Max and Daniel's eyes.

Max was told the chopper was on time, due in an hour. He took Sarah and Geordie aside when he and Daniel had finished packing. "Not to worry, sis," he said. "We might wait until dark when we arrive, which up there could be nearly midnight. But in seven or eight hours, we'll have him safe. Don't let her lose sight of that, George. Take it as a given."

"He could be killed by then," Sarah said.

"Nah. Not those guys. They were on that hill trying to make a point, trying to give the impression of a threat. There's no immediate danger, they'll be cooking up another video, trying to get the old man to say something. God help them if they try anything more than words. They'll know soon enough the difference between virtual reality and the real thing."

"Don't do anything rash. And don't let them catch you."

Max looked at her and laughed. "As if."

The real public protest began, as fate would have it, in Jarrow.

"Well, there you go," Geordie said. "Payback time."

He was sitting in the living room with Sarah and Rebecca. Alistair was manning the front door again, diplomatically turning away people who had come to commiserate.

Geordie had drafted another Q&A briefing note. Max was in the basement answering press calls: "But only for the next hour, George. Then it's over to you. Poacher turned gamekeeper, okay?"

"Payback for what?" Sarah asked, bringing Geordie back to the present.

"All those history and biology lessons I've been getting."

Geordie nodded at the TV. Apart from paybacks, he thought it would be good to follow Max's orders, and take Sarah's mind off her father's plight. A chance to escape, if only for a few minutes. It was what storytellers were for, *no*?

"Jarrow, my home town. Your turn for a history lesson, girls," Geordie said.

Sky News was covering the insurgency minute-to-minute, placard-by-placard.

By half past three that Sunday, an angry crowd had gathered in the streets of the South Tyneside town. Unlike Berwick sixty miles north, Jarrow was both a Labour stronghold and a place with a glorious history of civic unrest. Not so much New Labour, however: ingrained leanings, if they ever die, die hard. A couple of days ago, Geordie had been interested to see that the prefix "New" had been removed from their website. No great loss, he'd thought, even if it may only be temporary. His town's founding fathers would have been spinning in their graves since the birth of New Labour, trying to figure out which way was left.

As they watched the scenes unfold, he began to talk of Jarrow's links with Lindisfarne. He told Sarah and Rebecca that it had been the home of St. Bede, chronicler of St. Cuthbert, who had left the town only twice in his lifetime. In 794 AD, it had been the second target of the Vikings in England, one year after they plundered Holy Island.

That got their attention.

Geordie told them that the Jarrow Crusade to London in 1936 had been a protest against unemployment, a bid for respect not just for its own citizens, but for British people anywhere who couldn't find work to support their families. Along the route to London, local inhabitants came out and provided the two hundred marchers with food and shelter. When they reached their destination, Prime Minister Baldwin refused to meet them. He sent "Red Ellen" Wilkinson, Labour MP and champion of the crusade, away with a flea in her ear. Three years later, she wrote the book *The Town That Was Murdered.*

"The Labour big shots didn't listen. *Plus ça change,*" Geordie said. He didn't know the Spanish.

"So multilingual, darling," Sarah said.

He ignored it. "Not only that, they also condemned the march, with the unions clinging to their apron strings. But it was a landmark in *their* political history."

As they watched the TV pictures, placards began appearing like flowers in the field: "PM Out," "Free Deville," "Home Rule for Holy Island." Some didn't quite hit the mark, relics from previous marches: "Free Speech, Not Double-Speak," "Not In Our Name," "I Love My Country, Not My Government." There was even a "Ban the Bomb." Which dusty attic would that have come from? Geordie asked himself: these days, the sentiment was pretty well passé without Farsi or Urdu sub-titles. Nevertheless, it was clear what they were all about.

One was generic. "Whitehall Wankers" could have been used any-time, anywhere. But they saw a uniformed policeman point first at it then at the TV cameras, talking to its bearer, clearly advising that while the sentiment was in, the language was out.

Geordie's heart filled with pride. His town, warts and all. Well, people scoffed at Jarrow, a music-hall joke, but to him it had been a good place to be brought up. His mother had been a girl there, granddaughter of a Jarrow marcher herself. His father had never been forgiven for coming from the other side of the tracks at Wallsend. Geordie had enjoyed the happiest of childhoods in Jarrow, learned values there that would be with him until the day he died. He remembered Amy probing him on the subject; she'd been right. And what were they starting here, he wondered, those bloody-minded townsfolk of mine? Geordie recognised some of them, started telling the girls a name or two, apologised—stupid to introduce people they would never meet. Although Sarah...good Lord, no. Much too soon.

But bloody-minded townsfolk was on the button, he thought. In the recent local election, totally against the grain, South Tyneside Council had somehow increased its number of (New) Labour councillors by one.

On the screen, a reporter from Sky News, armed with a microphone, began darting about like Martin Brundle on the grid, interviewing everyone who didn't see his mike first.

Geordie hoped the old man down at Groat Market had followed suit; that Old Smokey had been sent into the fray. Give the old sod some Jarrow ozone to breathe, not to mention a welcome break for his co-workers. Geordie had phoned the old man earlier, saying another front-page story was brewing for tomorrow. No, not the video, something else, he couldn't say right now. He had suffered entreaties, threats, and then dog's abuse, but had told the old man to have faith. Or if not faith, a bit of *patience*. The Editor said, "Faith? You've been in that bloody place too long." They hadn't parted on the best of terms.

As Sarah, Rebecca and Geordie watched, increasingly engrossed, the certainty grew that this was a spontaneous demonstration, for there was no sign of any organisers. But Geordie saw it was growing in numbers by the minute. Obviously the town's pubs had been showing the video clip. There wasn't any soccer to get in the way, was there? Not even darts or snooker or bowls or rugby or any of the other sporting leftovers to which the BBC had been reduced. Well, what did you expect from an outfit whose newsreaders were keener on flaunting their assets and counting hits on their website than reading the news? Bloody drama queens, and not just the women. At least Sky News still had a hard edge to its coverage...

Geordie dragged himself off this hobby-horse and back to the moment. Sarah and Rebecca had begun cheering the people on the Jarrow streets.

So tell us exactly what it is you're protesting about, the Martin Brundle look-alike was saying, scooting from person to person in the crowd.

"What the government's been dishin' out to that wee place. What else?"

"Get a grip, son. Whitehall's behind all this. Bulldozers then kidnapping. What next, for hell's sake? Tanks? They think it's Chechnya?"

"Those people in London, of course, who else? They've been falling over themselves to accommodate other cultures at the expense of ours."

"Holy Island's deein' what we'd aal like tuh dee. Yon lot in London need stringin' up for this. Chicken marsala the national meal, my arse. Empty-headed gits..."

Then the Martin Brundle look-alike to camera, trying to hide a smile: *"The pitfalls of live feed. Heartfelt, nevertheless."*

"...I've been up there many a time. Nice, friendly people. Good luck to them. That poor man's doing his best. Let him get on with it, if he gets back safe. Oh, I hope to God he does."

"The so-and-sos won't be spinnin' their way outta this one. The wicket doesn't look like it's takin' turn this time."

Reporter to camera again: *"The resentment these people are feeling is clear, and it seems to be unanimous. No doubt about whose side they're on, and it certainly isn't the British government's. We could find no one with a different view, or no one that was prepared to speak about it. Now, for the moment, back to the studio."*

"I remember now," Geordie said, snapping his fingers.

Sarah and Rebecca looked at him. "What?" Sarah asked.

"Alderman David Riley was a leader of the Jarrow Crusade. You may not know it, but there was a song written about him. *Marshall Riley's Army,* it was called. Unless I miss my guess, a guy called Alan Hull of that well-known folk group Lindisfarne wrote it."

He beat a hasty retreat before he had a short-eared owl thrown at him.

CHAPTER TWENTY-TWO

Daniel had called by the jail with Rebecca to tell his charges that he'd be away overnight. He told them they would be looked after by Minister Michael Cromarty and a friend, Trevor Patterson, both of whom he was sure they'd remember from the trial. Mrs. Patterson had kindly offered to cook their dinner. Daniel didn't tell them that Rebecca, brown almond eyes beseeching, had been instrumental in getting them fed at all. He wasn't getting much more than nods and grunts from any of them these days. Even Haydon-Flint, the Newcastle QC jailed for contempt, seemed to have caught the habit from the Bigg Market Three, and had sunk into a deep depression. It would teach one idiot to hold his tongue, Daniel thought. There was no proper upbringing, no discipline, in people these days.

Haydon-Flint had asked for a book to read; he had read the stuff in his brief case several times over. After consulting Amy, who had considered a Rev. David Adam book but felt it might be "too pure for a lawyer, even if the vicar would have disagreed," Daniel gave him *Lindisfarne, The Cradle Island* by Magnus Magnusson. Plus a copy of the Lindisfarne Gospels.

"Nice pictures for you to look at," Daniel had said, his voice making the man flinch, and sinking him further into his Slough of Despond.

The AugustaWestland had arrived right on time, rattling branches, and whisking may and lilac blossom across the lawn. The pilot had been closeted with Max for half an hour, getting instructions, and filing a flight plan. They had learned that Baltasound Airport was operating on a care-and-maintenance basis, the oil companies and then the Shetland inter-island service having pulled out. So they phoned Sumburgh and Tingwall Airports to put things in place, and made sure there was fuel available to get them back. They were told it was "chust a lovely Voar day here. Nae wind at aa ta speak of, du kens."

"Probably means no more than a Force 7," the pilot said, grinning.

"What's Voar?" Max asked. He hadn't expected language problems.

"Springtime. Sowing and planting, all that."

The pilot was okay about the mission and said that he fully understood what was needed; of course he could see the importance of getting Mr. Deville back. He would do whatever it took to help. They were paying his company good money, and the aircraft was theirs as long as they needed it. He was a Canadian, and not too interested in British politics. Money talked.

They prepared for lift-off at 4:45 p.m., watched by Sarah, Alistair, Geordie, Rebecca, Amy, George the pig, the Ministers (including Cochise, resplendent in a red, white and black headdress) and half the village.

Fishing rods? Geordie asked himself, as Daniel carried two spinning rods aboard. What was that about? They're hoping to get in a spot of fishing?

"Where are they off to, Alistair?" Mary Selby asked as the helicopter lifted.

"West. We think we may have a hint as to where Dad's been taken," Alistair said. "But no more than a hint."

"Oh, I hope so. But…they're going the wrong way," Mary said.

"Steering clear of Boulmer. Avoiding some traffic out of there."

"Oh. Right. If you say so."

Sarah put her arm through his. "Little white lies, dearest? Tut, tut."

"We don't want to let any cats out of bags," her younger brother said. "She'll be on the phone to Tyne Tees telling them Dad's in the Lake District or Ireland. Over to you, George, to get us out of that one. Little white lies or not."

"No worries. It's both a pleasure *and* a duty. We have to protect tomorrow's exclusive, haven't we?" Geordie said.

He then got down to his new role and found life on the other side seriously boring. There were hardly any calls left to answer; Max had done all the hard work. Those that came in were mostly about Jarrow, and while he could give them some background on Jarrow, he couldn't offer much more in the way of hard news than they were seeing on TV. No; no more news of Mr. Deville, it was still a mystery as to where the video might have been shot. It looked like hilly, inhospitable country, didn't it? Snowdonia perhaps, the Cairngorms, the Mountains of Mourne?

He spent most of his time in the Fahr House basement idly drafting copy for *The Northern Sun*'s lead article in tomorrow's edition—the precise whereabouts of Shetland (essential, given that it was invariably stuck in a box top right), what North Sea oil activities remained (still going strong and, if oil provinces elsewhere were anything to go by, likely to remain so into the next century), what Baltasound looked like to the average Brit (about as familiar as the *Mare Tranquillitatis*), how many people lived there (not as many as sheep or Shetland ponies), gripping stuff like that—but until he had details of Max's assault on the place, he couldn't take it much further. He had no doubt at all that Max would succeed. The way he'd gone out to that chopper, Attila the Hun would have taken to his heels.

In the midst of this relative drudgery, Geordie had taken a call from Mr. Khalid Miah of all people, asking after Mr. Deville.

To whom am I speaking? Mr. Miah had begun, perhaps fearful of finding John Vaughan or Milan Petrov on the other end of the line.

To a colleague and family friend of long-standing.

Oh, ah...(silence)...they must be very worried.

No, just glad of the break. (Not half as worried as you must be, pal.) *This secession thing, taking over people's lives. Awful that people should stoop to petty crime because they don't agree with bits of it, isn't it?*

Quite dreadful, a failing of modern society, it is devoutly to be hoped there will be no backlash against the Muslim community...Of course, those people on TV may have been adopting a misleading disguise. Who is truly to know? They could have been anyone at all.

Oh? So you didn't think one of your sons might have been hidden under all those blankets? Does he own a sword? Not to be provocative, but is it a faint possibility?

(An intake of breath)...Absolutely not, quite out of the question, who could be thinking such a dreadful thing...I must be going, you will tell them I called?

Of course, have a nice day. Bye, bye.

That was a nice little shot in the arm for the article, Geordie thought. Denials were so much sexier than no comments, weren't they? Especially if they were lies. Nevertheless, he was vexed at himself for bringing the call to a premature end. He had been meaning to ask about social cohesion and the phrase in the Koran, *"Let not the believers take Unbelievers for friends."* How were moderate British Muslims managing to reconcile those two poles? And where exactly did this suicide bombing thing come from? If it was there, he'd missed it. So how had the ringing endorsement of terrorism, and specifically suicide bombing, in many Muslim societies—Lebanon, Nigeria, Jordan, Ivory Coast, Bangladesh, let alone Iran or Iraq—come about?

And did the moderate side of Islam have a view on co-existence these days? If so, how did they square it with the denigration dealt out to unbelievers in their Holy Book? Just to get a reaction, he would have liked to float the idea of some sort of world government at Mr. Miah, as Deville had once floated at him. In all truth, Geordie thought it idealistic to the point of fantasy. Besides, it would take forever to construct, it would probably take the United Nations as its model, and there was always the chance of Donald Rumsfeld clones being drafted in. Nevertheless, were moderate Muslims even permitted to contemplate such notions? Were they permitted to think at all beyond the confines of their religion?

As much as anything, he would have liked a considered Muslim view on the carefully drawn alternatives to the Christian versions of Mary and Jesus. He wondered how many Christians, *Post* readers included, knew that these beacons of Christianity featured in the Koran. Here was Mary, shorn of Joseph, stable, kings and shepherds, pregnant and alone in the desert. And here was Jesus, one of five revered prophets, a messenger shorn of disciples, trinity, crucifixion and resurrection, speaking from his cradle and making clay birds fly. Well, if you were into belief, it was as believable as loaves and fishes. He had debated whether the differences were attributable to the gossip or stereotypes of the age, the authors having had a few centuries to mull things over, incorporate what their audience would find palatable, get their own back on those who had chosen the Gospels, and feed some counter-intelligence into the system. In Geordie's mind, the whole thing had similarities to politicians today; point-scoring, spin, and gloss. When he had the chance, he should have asked, nicely.

On reflection, Geordie realised that he had been both provocative and foolish. Whether or not Mr. Miah's son was involved in the present nonsense, it couldn't be easy for people like Miah Senior to live such schizophrenic lives. As far as their brothers on the terrorist fringe were concerned, maybe moderate Muslims would become so fed-up with the suspicion and worse directed at them, that they would finally disown them. Follow the example of the Labour Party, and re-brand themselves New Islam. Or the whole thing might implode, courtesy of the internet or other uncharted technologies. Or was it possible that Islam's Achilles heel, looking far ahead, might be its women, some of whom, in less fundamentalist societies, were already living secular and relatively progressive lives? Friendly with Christian and Jewish mothers in nursery schools and courtyard cafés, and equally susceptible to the wares of Chanel and Gucci and Jimmy Choo?

But how likely was that, for instance, in Iran? What price feminism in societies where "*your wives are as a tilth unto you, so approach your tilth when or how ye will*"? Or where "*Men are in charge of women, because Allah hath made the one of them to excel the other*"?

Well, there was always science, Geordie thought gloomily. It might eventually cast some religious beliefs into outer darkness, but he wouldn't bank on it. After all, there were people who believed that *homo sapiens* began with Adam and Eve, that Darwin was evil, that Jesus Christ spoke English, that Joan of Arc was Noah's wife, and that the earth was flat. You could use up a lot of energy trying to change minds set in those moulds, or go nuts trying.

Anyway, it was too late now to ask the guy. And he didn't feel like calling back. What good would it do? Khalid Miah wasn't a Pope or a President or a holy Apostle. Like most people, he would just be getting on with whatever life he had.

Just before 6:40 p.m., Sarah came down to tell him that dinner was ready. She had made one of his favourites; lobster thermidor with rice, the lobster fresh out of the sea that morning, and there was plenty for Alistair, Rebecca, Daniel and whoever else might join them. Geordie asked if she'd mind another two minutes, got a shake of the head, and switched the television on to check Sky News.

They both started smiling at the same time. Jarrow's example had been spreading. Labour heartlands in Newcastle, Glasgow, Cardiff, Liverpool, and Blackburn, were among the places featured. The crowds weren't as big as Jarrow's and a few bystanders were looking in puzzlement at some of the placards. But sympathy protests were sparking everywhere. People had gathered in the streets, in the main city squares, outside City Halls, everywhere.

"Something's missing so far. Where's Trafalgar Square in all this?" Sarah asked.

"Patience. It'll be girding its loins."

Sarah grinned; the combination of public sympathy and Max's confidence had clearly reinforced Geordie's therapy. "Double speak? Would you like to do it again tonight?"

They had their dinner with Alistair and Rebecca, and then Alistair said he was going to prepare some data to e-mail through to Max. Rebecca looked at her Cartier and said she was going to take a nap for an hour.

Sarah and Geordie raised their eyebrows, smiled at each other and headed for the stairs, kissing each other on every other step, unhooking, unzipping, loosening. They couldn't wait, pulled their clothes off in a mad rush, fell together across Sarah's bed and joined together with incoherent noises, then after it was over and they found they could talk again sensibly, said "whew" and smiled again with relief.

As they lay recovering, Geordie started talking. He told her he couldn't lose her, not after the last two weeks, not after all this, it was unthinkable.

That seemed to cause, for both of them, the personal equivalent of the bursting of a dam.

"I wouldn't expect you to lose me," Sarah said, her face on the pillow next to his. "Or vice versa. You don't think it's just a physical thing, do you?" She slipped a hand under his neck and began tickling an ear.

"No, no, *no*," Geordie said, almost breaking her wrist with his vehemence. "God, no, it's much more than that. Oh, I'm sorry…did I—?"

Sarah smiled, retrieved her wrist, gave it a quick rub, then put it back.

"But what am I going to do about it?" Geordie asked. "What are *we* going to do?"

"In what way?" Sarah asked, stroking. "Isn't this good enough? Why do we have to do anything?" Not being in any way a fatalist, Sarah knew very well what George was getting at, but she was enjoying listening to his thought processes.

"Well, you know, Sarah darling, there's not a lot for me to do here. I mean, when all this is resolved, the secession I mean, what happens then?" He turned onto his front, put his arm around her and looked down at her. Having done so, he couldn't resist a dozen or so kisses, on her forehead, and eyes, and throat, and lips. Not that he would have dreamt of resisting.

"Oh, you never know, do you?" Sarah murmured. "Something might come up. If not, we'll just have to leave. I'll come with you, wherever, and we'll find somewhere nice. Maybe another island. Guernsey seems to be interesting, if you can find a way in."

"No, that wouldn't work," Geordie said. "How could I ask you to do that? It would be like tearing you up by the roots. I couldn't bear to do it. How could I?" More kisses. Skin like silk, he thought wonderingly; no, warmer and softer than silk. Better than silk in every way.

"Like a weed?" Sarah smiled in a short intermission. "You're comparing me to a weed?"

Geordie laughed. "Be serious. You know what I mean. You're umbilically tied to this island, and I'm hooked myself. How do we work our way around that? All your commitment to your home, to the secession, for nothing? Not a prayer. If I spoiled that, I'd never look at my face in a mirror again without feeling sick."

"I'd do it if necessary," Sarah said, wrapping her legs around his. "Leave the island, I mean. And you're being very unfair to the Romans, as well as to your face."

"The Romans? How did they get into this?" He saw a slight flush spreading from the hollow of her throat, close to where a pulse throbbed, and thought it was the most erotic sight he had ever seen in his life.

"Well," Sarah said, "if they couldn't build Rome in a day, what makes you think you can build our lives in half an hour? We have a bit more time than that, don't we?"

Geordie laughed again, and Sarah joined him. "A lot more time, I hope," Geordie said, easing himself down, squeezing, kissing her breasts. "There has to be a way out of this."

"You're sure you mean 'out?' Is that your best choice of word, reporter man?" Sarah asked, squeezing back, wrapping her legs around his. "We just have to think what we want and…work for it. You could still write for *The Northern Sun*…ummmm, George… freelance…write books…ohhhhhh…set up a paper here. Of course…there'll be a way…"

Their breathing quickened, and they lost interest in troublesome intangibles.

They'd find a way, they told each other. They made love again, and fell asleep.

They woke an hour later, realised the time, showered and dressed hurriedly. Rebecca hadn't stirred. They knocked on her door and got a sleepy reply. Alistair was still on one of the computers in the basement, and they could hear him pounding the keys. They smiled at each other. No convoluted explanations would be needed. They went down to join him.

Max phoned at nine, slightly later than expected. Alistair put him on the loudspeaker.

"Everyone's here," Alistair said. "They've all been catching up on their sleep," he said, grinning at Sarah and Geordie like the proverbial cat. "How're things with you, bro?"

"I'm sure everyone deserves some sleep," Max said. "Rebecca in particular. But thanks for the info, Ali. We've been looking at the lie of the land, and it looks as we thought from the photos. Wild, not a tree in sight. Stunted shrubs. The pilot says, between the salt and wind and sheep and rabbits, trees don't stand a chance. But it's a lot greener than some of the land we've flown over; the neighbouring island was a blanket of peat. It's a nice evening; bright, cool, a bit cloudy. And they put upturned boats to good use here, too. As sheep-houses."

"You're enjoying yourself already?"

"My kind of place. Nothing fancy. Scattered pebble-dash houses tucked into hillsides, crofts. Everywhere you look, water, birds I haven't seen before. Guy at the airport told us a bonxie, something like that. A great skua, bigger than the arctic ones we get later in the year."

"We've had them once or twice. What's first on the agenda?"

"Well, Daniel looks a bit conspicuous. I don't think they get many coloureds up here. We're going to wrap up a bit, go fishing. See if we can find a local to chat up."

"You're not heading for the hotel yet?"

"No, too early. Looking around, they must have gone there, even if they're not staying there. And believe me, any strangers here will stick out like sore thumbs. Us included. The hotel's over the far side of the Voe. We'll leave it an hour or two, nearer closing time."

"Voe?"

"A Shetland fjord, Ali. Local lingo. You've heard of Sullom Voe? It must have crept into the economics degree somewhere."

"Okay…right. You got the stuff on the other hotels?"

"Yeah. Guesthouses. One of them's near us. Another on the far side, Buness House, might be worth a look, but doesn't seem to have many rooms. Not as anonymous as the hotel, if it's possible to be anonymous anywhere here for more than ten seconds. Is George there?"

"Here," Geordie said.

"Any bother with the press?"

"No." Geordie told him about Miah's call and the spreading insurgency in British cities.

Max laughed. "The old man'll be pleased when we catch up with him," he said, as if they were all intending to go for a Sunday evening stroll. "Everything okay with you, sis?"

"Everything's fine. Just take care."

"Rebecca, Daniel would like a word," Max said. "Incidentally, that place Buness House might be owned by people related to your botanist. Edmonston, wasn't it? It sounds like he was some guy, a professor at twenty, dead not long after. Must have had as many brains as Alistair...he can let you see the paperwork. We'll touch base just after ten. Bye for now."

Alistair handed the phone to Rebecca, switched off the loudspeaker, and shrugged. "Not much more we can do for the time being, is there?"

"He sounds as excited as I've ever heard him," Sarah said. "A regular motormouth. I hope he catches a sea trout or something. Fishing, for heaven's sake. What does he think—?"

"Just so long as he catches the fish he's gone for," Alistair said. "We still don't know for sure they're in the place." He saw Rebecca putting the phone down, looking at him. "Okay, sorry, Rebecca. I mean I'm sure they were, but they might not be now."

"You think too much," Sarah told him. "Give the grey cells a rest."

"We've been told in no uncertain terms that we were fishing in the wrong place," Max said over the phone. "But the old feller who put us right was helpful in other ways."

It was a quarter after ten. Sarah, Geordie, Alistair and Rebecca had cracked open bottles of beer to give themselves a break from coffee. They had even tried a game of Scrabble, but no one could concentrate. Alistair, degrees up to his neck, refused to act as scorer.

"Other ways? Such as?" he asked his brother.

"Number one, our friends are on the island. So first, a big thank you to Rebecca for as good a piece of observation as I've seen. Anyway, they've gone to ground since early evening. They've been going about in jeans and sweaters, never more than one at a time, but they may as well have been in drag. Sticking out like sore thumbs was right. If they were looking for anonymity, they were out of their minds to come here. Anyway, we're reliably informed that one of them is suntanned, and the other is white."

"Any sign of Dad?"

"No, but they could hardly parade him on the streets bound and gagged, could they?"

"And no idea yet where they're staying?"

"That's number two. The old guy said they'd been seen at the Village Shop and on the north side of the Sound. Not over here. There are other tourists about, ornithologists, naturalists, but not many. The old guy said our boys didn't look the part; you can imagine, huh? So we're going to stash the rods and head over there. To give you all an idea, the hotel's a mile and a half from where we're standing. We can see it across the water. We still think it's looking good, and I like the sound of those cabins. They would be the logical place to go to ground. The other place, Buness House, is over there too, so we can have a look at both."

"Where are you?" Alistair asked, bringing up the Ordnance Survey map on screen, and a Google satellite image in another window.

"A place called Clingera. We're near the airfield again," Max said.

"We see it." Alistair pointed to the screen for the benefit of the others.

"Well, you'll see Buness is marked, and the hotel."

"They wouldn't be roughing it, holed up in a ruin or something?"

"I don't think so. Townies? It's open rolling country, working crofts, wooden telegraph poles. People in the fields. One or two, standing in doorways or looking through windows, have had their glasses on us. Not much moves around here that isn't seen, trust me. And if Miah's son is one of them, he's had no training camp background that Daniel's been able to discover. No, whoever supplied the BellRanger sure as hell won't baulk at putting them up in a wee hotel. Incidentally, the BellRanger's nowhere about. It must have headed back south, to Sumburgh maybe. It would have been too visible by half here."

"Okay. How long before you reach it? The hotel?"

"Fifteen minutes. The trouble is, it's still pretty light. That's number three. The old guy said there were only four hours of darkness now; he seemed quite proud of his 'simmer dim.' This time of year, they have more daylight than we do. We'll wait until the bar closes, if it ever does. I can imagine they'll have lock-ins here too, although we haven't seen any police to bother about it. But we'll let people get out of the way, then go in."

"What's the noise?" Alistair asked, as they all heard a clattering in the background.

"Another helo coming in. It's getting to be like Heathrow around here."

"Okay. Well, we'll sit it out here, then. Call when you can."

"Ciao. Is Rebecca still there?"

"Yes," Rebecca said.

"Over to Daniel."

"Just a second, Max," Sarah said. "What about the areas where Rebecca said the video would've been taken? The Keen? Or that hill…Colvadale? Could they be there?"

"Not likely. There are a few crofts along the road and towards the Keen, most of them working. Some modernised, some new. There's a big self-build tradition here, the old guy told us. But Colvadale is bare hillside and burns. We've had a look. The hotel's the best bet, trust me. Unless Rebecca would like us to pick some flowers as a souvenir?"

"Don't you dare," Rebecca said. "They're treasures. They couldn't take the home comforts down here."

Max laughed. "The old feller told us it *was* Treasure Island, or was used in writing it. Robert Louis Stevenson himself was here, in the 1860s, and his father and uncle built the lighthouse to the north, a place called Muckle Flugga. They're not easy on place names in these parts, are they?"

"I thought he modelled the island on Fidra. In the Firth of Forth," Alistair said.

"Oh hell, Ali, don't split hairs. Or spoil a good story. Here's Daniel."

Alistair switched the loudspeaker off, and Rebecca grabbed the phone.

CHAPTER TWENTY-THREE

They settled back as best they could, more long minutes having to be endured. Geordie, sitting at one of the basement's PCs, had already framed and discarded several attempts at an opening paragraph. There was no doubt in his mind that it was mission accomplished, that Max would be moving to the climax like the fabled irresistible force. But Geordie was floundering. He could only get so far with any sort of opener, and then he hit a blinking cursor and a more or less white screen. The details, he needed details...

The phone rang again half an hour later. Alistair, lost in research on Unst, went back to loudspeaker mode. He had been squinting increasingly at the satellite and map images, rubbing his eyes, and seemed relieved to be getting an enforced break from them.

Max *sotto voce*: "We're in. Dad's fine. Everything's cool. We're waiting. Get back to you a.s.a.p." The phone cut off. In its entirety, it had been a six-second call, obviously condensed by the circumstances.

Alistair thumped the desk, and did a high five with Rebecca.

"Oh, marvellous," Sarah said, eyes shining, jumping up to give Geordie a hug. "They have him. Heavens, that was quick. They must have decided just to go for it."

"They're waiting," Geordie repeated, detaching himself. "It must be for the controller."

"What?" Alistair asked.

"Who they're waiting for. *Número tres.* It must have been the helicopter we heard. Remember? It must have been bringing their controller. The Third Man, as it were."

"Of course, yes," Alistair said. "Brilliant, George, if I may say so."

"Broken promises, genius," Sarah said reprovingly.

"What?" Geordie asked.

"No more Spanish, remember?"

"Oh yes, sorry."

"You're forgiven. It helps that you could be right."

The four of them sat there, each thinking: what's going on up there? Each trying to picture it; Max and Daniel, now Deville, behind closed doors with whoever-they-were, waiting. Deepening evening gloom at that high latitude, 61°N, north of Oslo and Leningrad and Cape Farewell in Greenland, soft shafts of light still leaking through windows or cracks in curtains. Outside, gulls circling, the sound of the sea, the creak of rigging in the harbour, a boat engine chugging up the Sound, a car winding its way up the A968. Familiar homely sounds in an enveloping silence.

"I wonder if Max and Daniel had to hurt those people," Rebecca said.

"We'll soon know," Alistair said. "But really, in the circumstances, who cares?"

Geordie took out his mobile and phoned the offices of *The Northern Sun* in Newcastle. He was put straight through to the Editor, while Sarah, Alistair and Rebecca listened with mounting glee to one end of the conversation.

"Hello?" Geordie said. "Yes, it's me…yes, it's a cracker…you'll need to wait a bit…I can't help that, can I?…should be an hour or two…for God's sake, it'll be worth it, would I ask otherwise?…what, you don't trust what I'm saying?…no, I can't tell you yet…damn it, just hang on…yes, I know you'll have been there all bloody night…just as soon as I can…oh shit, have some patience…all right, some faith, you *fucking sceptic*!"

Sarah and Rebecca went off in peals of laughter.

"You may have talked your way out of a job there, George," Alistair said.

"Welcome to the ranks of the self-employed," Rebecca said.

More peals of laughter.

The clock blinked on towards 11:30.

They couldn't sit still; it was impossible. Like a slow-motion dance, they kept getting up, looking at the map on the screen, looking at the clock, walking around the room, sipping beer or coffee, sitting back down. Sarah twice had to go for a leak, and when she wasn't in the bathroom spent her most of her time playing with Geordie's hair. Alistair, between perambulations, zoomed in here, zoomed in there, and rubbed his eyes.

11:45.

What the hell was going on? The phones, all of them, sitting idle; useless, *dumb* lumps of plastic, red lights unblinking.

Once or twice, Alistair or Sarah ran their hands over the desk phone, pushing it this way and that across the surface. Everyone was on edge, strung out, impatient. Rebecca had a turn on the computer Geordie had been using, and took another look at Edmonston's chickweed.

"They'll have had to wait, of course," Alistair said, setting an empty bottle down.

Sarah groaned. "Tell us something we don't know, brother dear."

"Want to know my guess, folks?" Geordie asked.

They all looked at him; here was Revelation.

"What?" Sarah asked.

"They're on their way back to the chopper. They've got their hands full walking through the village. There are six of them, after all, and it's midnight. It won't be easy to be unobtrusive, especially if it's not fully dark. And even if Max and Daniel could do it in ten or fifteen minutes, civilians will need a lot longer."

Everyone's heads swivelled from time to time to look at the clock.

Finally, the digital glow showed midnight.

"You got that bit right," Sarah said. "Heaven knows about the rest."

The clock blinked on to 12:05...

Then 12:10...

The phone rang at 12:13. Alistair checked the loudspeaker was still on, and Geordie scrambled for his recorder.

"Hi, everybody," Max said. "All done and dusted. We're at the airfield. Should be with you between four and five."

"Hold on, hold on a minute. What's done and dusted?" Alistair said.

"Three prisoners. More business for the jail. Should keep old Daniel here out of trouble."

"Can we speak to Dad?" Sarah asked.

"Sure. Here he is."

"How are you, Sarah?" The familiar assured voice.

"Never mind me. How are you?"

"Oh, I'm fine. Hungry, a bit stiff with sitting, but the walk did us good. And what a nice place. Otters playing in the rocks. It's quite delightful, now I've had a chance to look around."

"What's been happening, for heaven's sake? Tell us something."

That's my girl, Geordie thought. If someone doesn't start talking turkey soon, there'll be no story at all for the old duffer, never mind fiddling around with a damn first paragraph.

"Well, Max and Daniel came through the door just before eleven, very abruptly I might add, immobilised two of our friends here, and untied me. We waited until the third of our friends arrived, Max immobilised him, asked him one or two questions, then we marched them back around the Voe to where we are now, waiting to board this handsome helicopter."

"Third?" Geordie asked. "Would you care to expand a bit on these people?"

"Hello, George, are you taking good care of my daughter?"

"I hope so. It's nice to know you're safe. Who are they? And who is the third?"

"Well, first there's young Miah. We know his father, you'll recall. The second...ah, is Rebecca there?"

"Rebecca? Yes, she's here," Geordie said. Jeez, he thought resignedly, now for the copious thanks; they have to be the next waste of time. Then he felt guilty for being churlish; of course Rebecca deserved thanks, the more copious the better. He sagged back in his chair.

"I'm sorry, Rebecca," Deville said. "I would have preferred to break this gently, face to face. But I'm afraid the second is your short-lived husband, one Charley Oakley. They were the two who jumped me at the house."

Geordie shot upright, almost overturning the table, empty beer bottles rolling around.

"Oh, no," Rebecca said. "Oh, no."

"Rebecca, this person no longer has any connection with you. It's a shock, I know, but he is nothing to do with you. Max tells me—"

"*Nothing to do with me*! Ohmigod, I *brought* him here. The absolute *son of a bitch*. I'm *mortified*. And I didn't even *recognise* him in all that kit! Let me speak with the—"

"Not a good plan, Rebecca. He is not...coherent. And we do have to leave shortly. You'll have a chance to speak with him when we get back. It's better that way, don't you think? You really mustn't—"

"Ohmigod, I'll kill him. How did he get to meet that *other* son of a bitch? It was just a couple of days ago I had him on the phone and he—"

"Calm down, Rebecca. This is in no way your fault. You are not responsible for his actions. He was introduced to young Miah through the third party, who met your disappearing husband in a pub. But of much greater importance—"

"Of course he did. In a pub, where else? Ohmigod, where else?" Rebecca sank to her knees, put her head on the table. "*Oh...my...God.*" Without lifting her head, she waved a hand at Geordie to get on with it.

"And the third party?" Geordie struggled to retrieve some focus, saw Sarah kneel at Rebecca's side, and felt doubly guilty.

"Hmm...a most interesting catch, George. Much more so than the others, I would say. You'll need to give him some prominence in your story. You are doing a story tonight?"

"Yes." For God's sake, what else would he be doing!

"It appears this gentleman, although he wasn't saying much, is in the employ of Britain's Security Service, otherwise known as MI5. As you know, this Service is not part of the Home Office, but is under the authority of the British Home Secretary. You'll recall I had a conversation with him, and Max a more recent one. I believe the Service is headquartered at Thames House, Millbank. The gentleman was imprecise about his job title there, and relied several times on the Security Service Act 1989 to avoid answering our perfectly civil questions. However, as far as we can establish, he is an Intelligence Officer or agent runner working in their security section. Or, perhaps it would be more accurate to say, the section charged with protecting the UK against, quote, militant separatism and threats to national security, unquote. I am not sure I care for the militant description. Have you seen any militancy on Holy Island, George?"

"Not so much as an Orange Walk. Do you have a name for this guy?"

Geordie asked, trying through Rebecca's groans to catch everything Deville was saying. "The Third Man?"

"Yes, but only because Daniel looked inside a brief case. The gentleman himself was unhelpfully silent on that point. And he was being called a variety of other names by his colleagues. None of them complimentary."

"And?"

"His name? His name is Brian Marjoribanks. I imagine it's pronounced Marshbanks. In his opinion, the good people of Holy Island have undermined parliamentary democracy by political means. That's from the MI5 Charter, I understand."

"Did you say immobilised earlier?" Geordie said. Not just a recorder, he needed a bloody stethoscope stuck into the phone, with Rebecca now shrieking a variety of imprecations between groans.

"Oh, you know, taken by surprise, overpowered, made to lie down, tied up and so on. First the two of them, then Marjoribanks when he joined us. There were no bones broken."

"Marched?"

"Well, everyone could still walk. They knew Max and Daniel had guns, so they weren't about to cause trouble. We were all back here in no time. Even with their luggage, the sword, and so on. Let's hope they remain docile during the flight. Our MI5 friend, by the way, was acquainted with young Miah previously, through his father. I understood young Miah to say they had met during some MI5-sponsored discussions. Something to do with keeping track of the more radical elements of his religion. Including the younger radical elements. As a result, I think he felt he had become an approximation of a civil servant himself. And Marjoribanks, as I said, met Oakley recently in a pub in Westminster. St. Stephen's Tavern, I believe."

Rebecca lifted her head. "That's where he was when I called him. The *manus*."

"Yes, but you weren't to know, Rebecca," Deville said, overhearing her. "In any event, he was apparently helpful to Marjoribanks in providing some local intelligence about Holy Island. I confess I was quite pleased to learn that MI5, clandestinely or otherwise, had been unable to find anyone else local to help them. Or so I was told by Oakley. He was actually quite proud of it, seemed to feel it gave him credibility. A purpose in life. Something beyond the compass of his waxwork colleagues, or so he seemed to be suggesting. He became quite garrulous on the subject after a visit to the hotel bar here."

Another prolonged groan from Rebecca, her hands bolted to the edges of the table.

"You're sure about his name?" Geordie asked. "This Marjoribanks?

His work?"

"Absolutely one hundred percent. Have no concern on that score. Documentary evidence, George, if not quite legally gathered."

"And did they say *why* they kidnapped you? What they were going to do with you?"

"Well, the three of them aren't exactly logical bedfellows, but they had managed to find common ground. Miah and Oakley had different but personal reasons, of course, but with revenge as the common denominator. Miah because I'd insulted his father, Oakley because I'd been insufficiently vigilant to prevent his own kidnapping. He doesn't like me or Holy Island at all, that young man. I think he felt it was what Francis Bacon—was it Bacon?—called a 'wild kind of justice'; revenge, a tit for tat, one kidnap for another. So he jumped at the chance. And all three believed my disappearance would cause disruption to the secession, if not its collapse, which was the aim of Mr. Marjoribanks. Who was, of course, the catalyst, the prime instigator. A fact you should make very clear."

"Did he have official sanction? Did anyone else know of this?"

"I think not, but he was cagey on that point. Maybe weighing up the advantages of claiming he did, against the certainty of dismissal if he was found out to have lied. If that isn't already a foregone conclusion."

"And where did they propose to go from there? Ransom wasn't on the cards, I take it?"

"No. Miah was all for the final solution, I believe. Oakley was having second thoughts, and I think hoped I would develop amnesia when it came to his involvement. Maybe he was suffering withdrawal symptoms by this morning, the shakes or whatever, but he'd lost enthusiasm for the venture. There was a serious falling-out between him and Miah when he expressed his longing for a restorative drink. That aside, the third and senior individual, Marjoribanks, intended to incarcerate me here in Unst, in a deserted croft he'd managed to find, until the secession was brought to an end. A safe house, as he called it. In fact, his return tonight was for the purpose of arranging my new lodgings. Although how he thought the other two were going to stick it out is beyond me. It wouldn't have been safe for anybody."

"And how were they proposing to end the secession? What did he have in mind after—?"

"I have no idea. And neither did he. I don't believe it had been thought through at all. I think he hoped his lords and masters would step in after he had shown them the way, and follow his good example with initiatives of their own...George, I hate to cut you off, but we really must be going. I see the pilot gesticulating. Is that enough for now?"

"Okay, it's fine, thanks. We'll look after Rebecca. Tell the boys not to forget their rods. Have a good trip back."

"Rods? Max?...Ah, you were fishing. Why not? How nice. I'm sure our journey will be fine. It looks to be an excellent aircraft...and with just the right number of seats. I must say I'm hoping the pilot has some sandwiches on board. And one or two of those miniature whiskies wouldn't go amiss."

"See you soon. Safe journey," Alistair and Sarah said.

"Indeed. And if Rebecca is still there...?"

"Still *here*? Ohmigod, I really can't begin—"

"Rebecca, you must try to put this brainstorm of Oakley's behind you. Draw a line. It was nothing to do with you. You have my unreserved gratitude. I understand it was you who identified this place."

"That's...no comfort at *all*."

"It should be. It was a much more important factor than your former spouse. I'm sure this escapade would have been attempted in some way without him. He was simply a handy tool. Your help and his interference don't bear comparison, I assure you. Well, see you soon, everyone. We're about to board."

Alistair carefully replaced the handset.

"It sounds as if it all went well," he said.

Rebecca laughed hysterically.

"If you can't face sleep, I'll stay up with you," Alistair said to her. "You have work to do, I suppose, George. Your job should be back on a secure footing, when this story breaks."

"Yes," Sarah said, ruffling Geordie's hair. "And I'm going to stay here with these two while you write it. Try not to be too long."

"I won't," Geordie said. It was in his head, just a matter of typing, but he picked up the recorder just in case and clicked it off. He didn't think there would be much sleep for any of them that night. Rebecca would need all the TLC available. If not Mogadon.

He went up to his room and opened his laptop. He seemed to have a third finger on the keys tonight, but didn't stop to check. However many there were, they were flying.

Holy Island First Minister Alex Deville Liberated

British MI5 Agent among the Kidnappers

Just before midnight Sunday, on Britain's northernmost island, an operation worthy of the highest traditions of the SAS was launched. Acting on the expert advice of botanist Rebecca Carter, Mr. Max Deville, eldest son of the First Minister, and Mr. Daniel Brigham, Holy Island's policeman, flew by helicopter to Unst...

At one point, he broke off to give the Home Office media department a call, trying to type with one hand and juggle his mobile with the other, both unsuccessfully.

Well, he thought mordantly a few seconds later, what else would you expect? A bloody answering machine; would you credit it? And unlike Fahr House last night, they had thousands of staff to man or woman the thing. Okay, well, it made things easier in a way; the Home Office media department, all the way up to the Home Secretary, would just have to choke on their breakfast cereal. He had no alternative left but to go with the simple truth:

"No one was available at the Home Office last night to confirm or deny these allegations…"

Thirty minutes later it was finished and e-mailed to Groat Market, with an abridged version winging its way to Washington.

He was just about to log off when he had another thought, and punched another set of numbers into his mobile. This time someone did answer. Still pissed at the lack of response from the Home Secretary's bailiwick—how did these people expect to catch all the damned paedophiles, illegal immigrants, foreign criminals at large, let alone keep up to speed with secessions, when they were asleep half the time?—he supposed it was because the office he was phoning now would *have* to be manned 24/7. There was no question, he told himself, that it could be said to represent global interests.

He asked for a number to fax or e-mail the story to, joked about it with the pleasant young lass on the other end, who was eager to chat, probably bored out of her skull with the still small hours, and sent another copy off. This time, he pasted in a compliments sheet from "The Office of the First Minister, The Althing, The Holy Island of Lindisfarne."

Having finished, he wondered if he had done the right thing. Was it outside his job description? He shrugged. It was too late now. What was it Deville had said? You had to seize the moment, *no*? The old man, bless his cotton socks, would have to live with it. If he ever found out. If Geordie ever got back to Groat Market to tell him.

He yawned, stretched, massaged his fingers, closed his laptop and made his way back downstairs, hoping Sarah hadn't fallen asleep over the conference table.

CHAPTER TWENTY-FOUR

Apart from the occupants of Fahr House, only half a dozen fishermen and a few hundred seabirds witnessed the homecoming. The helicopter put down on the front lawn at 4:20 a.m. Alistair, Sarah, Geordie and a jittery Rebecca waited on the front steps for the blades to slow and stop. Max was out first, giving the three prisoners a hand down, then Daniel, and lastly Deville. The pilot came around from the other side, carrying an overnight bag.

"You go ahead, Dad, Graham," they could hear Max saying. "Daniel and I will take this lot down to the jail."

"Congrats, brother," Alistair said. "You too, Daniel. Smooth job."

Daniel came over, moving as ever with feline grace, and gave Rebecca a hug. "That feels good," he said, smiling. "It's nice to be back. We might go on holiday up there one day if I can get a stand-in. It's an interesting place."

"Daniel, I need to talk about this," Rebecca said. "That specimen—" she pointed towards Charley, and then took a deep breath. "What?...that's *it*? Is that all you have to say? You come back...and you tell me we'd like a holiday up there?"

"Sure." Daniel meant it. Coming from a military family, a serving officer himself, he had seen enough of the world, some good, and some not so good. But he liked what he'd seen of Shetland. And Rebecca liked those flowers, so why not? Daniel's mind was as clear of Charley as it would have been of any miscreant. Charley was a tick in the "Done" column. "Neat place," he said. "Why not walk down with us?"

She looked over to where Max was shackling the prisoners, and received not so much as a glance from Game Boy. Surprise, surprise, she thought. So much for *him*. "Okay. That'd work fine," she said to Daniel.

"We don't need to hang around. It's just a matter of closing the door and turning the key," Daniel said. He nodded his head toward the captives. "Too long in that sort's company, and you realise why some species eat their young."

"Tell me about it," Rebecca said.

"Especially the spook," Daniel added, kindly.

Max came over briefly to say hello, in no mood to do more.

"It'd be good, sis, if you had breakfast going when we get back."

"What about them?" Sarah asked.

"Include Daniel and Rebecca, sure. The others'll be lucky if they get dry toast. Would you have a copy of this morning's story to show my father, George?"

"Yep, at least the e-mail version. Not a happy return journey, then? No sing-songs on the bus?"

"Comedian. See you soon."

He joined the others and they headed for the gates. There was no sign of any guns, Geordie noticed.

Deville meantime had his arm around Sarah. He seemed none the worse for his night in Unst, Geordie thought. Deville saw him looking and smiled.

"Expecting to see scars, George? To add a bit of piquancy to the tale?"

"Good grief," Geordie said, offended, "it *can't* have been a happy journey. We're just glad to see you back."

"We have some work to do today, you and me. The end game may be approaching, I think. But first, breakfast. Then a nap. Let's go inside."

Getting any more intel—Max's language—on last night's rescue was like drawing blood, Geordie thought. What annoyed him most was that Deville and Max, and then Daniel when he arrived, seemed to take it all for granted. It wasn't as if they were concealing things, just that things had been and gone. Didn't they realise the mileage in this? Like round-the-world above-the-fold mileage?

Whatever Daniel had said to Rebecca seemed to have worked. She almost had her smile back. And the breakfast, everyone agreed, was just what the doctor ordered.

The helicopter pilot, Graham Pearce, didn't take long over his. He excused himself, and took off to bed.

Deville spent several minutes reading Geordie's story. "This reads well, George. I do like the sub-heading. You must have been up half the night. I don't wonder you look a bit tired."

"That's the unexpurgated version. The subs, sub-editors that is, will have hacked it about a bit. They usually do," Geordie told him. Well, he would have to confess sometime why his beauty sleep was suffering, but it would keep for now.

Deville smiled. There were times when Geordie amused him. Did he seriously think that Deville, after decades reading and often featuring in *The Financial Times*, wouldn't know about sub-editors? "Maybe a word here or there," he said supportively. "They'll have found it hard to hack the substance, even if they wanted to. Did you send it across the water?"

"Something similar. Last night. They're what…six hours behind? They should have it in today's edition. Without all the fuss the old man kicked up."

"Good. Do I detect some rancour?"

"Just a difference of opinion on what was worth staying up for. So tell us what happened up there. How did Max and Daniel get to you?"

Eventually, egged on by Sarah, who had her own reasons for wanting to hear the details, Deville told Geordie the surprise had been complete. One minute, his two captors were sitting drinking tea, with silence outside except for the occasional cry of a gull, and the next minute the door was off its hinges and they were on the floor. It had been like watching something in fast forward, he said. If anything, the agent runner had been even more taken aback. Once the kidnappers were tied up, Max and Daniel had propped the door back into its jamb. It had simply flopped inwards when he knocked. He had watched it hit the deck, a bemused expression on his face, and the next second he'd been on the deck on top of it.

"Any injuries sustained?" Geordie asked.

Deville laughed. "Well, they were all stunned for a minute or two, but nothing serious. There was hurt pride, of course, and a convoluted post-mortem into why things had taken such a turn for the worse, and this regrettably occupied much of the journey back. The MI5 runner kept getting the blame from his protégés, which took a variety of forms. Oakley sounded off several times on the theme that he should never have chosen such a God-forsaken place, that he should have arrived earlier, and should have approached with more caution when he did. Miah Junior, although in agreement with much of this, added that he should have known these infidels were on their way, should have seen the door was hanging off its hinges, and was a pitiful advertisement for the British Security Service. At times, our two kidnappers seemed surprisingly in accord. In fact, if I may paraphrase the horse's mouth and ask Sarah and Rebecca to close their ears, the spook was unanimously condemned as an effing waste of space. Among other accolades of that nature."

"What had he to say for himself?" Geordie asked. "Or was he struck dumb?"

"To be frank, we learned more about him from his protégés and his briefcase than we were able to extract from him directly. I suppose he thought he was behaving in the best traditions of James Bond. The impression did grow with us however, and I think I speak for Max and Daniel too, that this was not only a black operation, but one that only Mr. Marjoribanks and one or two others had known about. By which I mean his pals at Millbank, acolytes, would-be assistants and so on. No one senior, I think."

"What about the BellRanger pilot?" Geordie asked. "Where was he in all this?"

"He was a courier, no more. Once he delivered us, he returned to the Sumburgh Hotel, awaiting further instructions. No doubt paid for through one of MI5's black budgets."

"And how did they treat you? Food, water, living conditions?"

"Not badly. It was more a case of neglect than aggression. The room was fine. The only tricky part, for them, was the video. They had a car laid on by their runner, which they picked up at the airport—there was no one about when we arrived except a chap called out on night duty—but they had to be careful in taking me up to the Keen of Hamar site, about which they had an illuminating linguistical discussion. I believe they were thinking hammer, as in fist of God. I should say this was at 6:30 a.m., before their breakfast, the sun high but quiet in the village. They simply bundled me into the back seat with Miah Junior for company, then set the camera on timer and took the sequence themselves. As I said to Max and Daniel on our journey back, I tried to give a hint on the video that Oakley was a known quantity, but was reduced to casting glances. The restraints, such as they were, made it difficult to do more. I might have managed to escape while they were setting it up, if my ankles hadn't been harnessed, although how far I'd have got is debatable. Maybe far enough to raise attention. In any case, the whole episode didn't take very long. Perhaps twenty minutes or so, there and back. Otherwise, I spent the time in the cabin tied to a chair, thinking how to get out."

"No food?"

Max interjected: "Not a bite. And that's exactly what they'll be getting down there today. Before they're force-fed road kill." Max was distracted, having an internal debate. Should he send one of the guys over, and institute a shift system to guard the house? On balance, he was disinclined; surely they wouldn't try again so quickly, after such a fiasco? But he would need to spend more time, more nights, here himself. Nothing predictable. One night in three, maybe. Random. And get some proper dogs. Dogs with fangs, who knew when to use them.

"What are you going to do with them all now?" Geordie asked.

"Try them," Deville said, looking surprised.

"All three?"

"Of course."

"Here?"

"Where else? Michael Cromarty or Elizabeth Swan will take the chair. I think I will have to recuse myself." Deville smiled. "Is that the term?"

"You have no concerns about jurisdiction?

" None. They committed their crimes, all but the initial conspiracy, here."

"Crimes plural?" Geordie asked.

"Certainly. Apart from conspiracy to commit a crime, there is trespass, criminal damage and kidnapping. There may be false imprisonment. Max has confirmed damage to property, and I have no doubt will make an exceptional witness. I would concede that trespass, being a debatable proposition at the best of times, is barely worth bothering with. In fact, on further thought, I won't."

"And Marjoribanks? Plural for him too?"

"Conspiracy and kidnapping, although his colleagues might prefer to include criminal negligence in the mix. The Unst hotel was paid in advance, or so we were told on the journey back, otherwise we might have added theft. But that would have been someone else's decision." Deville yawned. "Now you must excuse me, everyone. I need some sleep, and whatever the media want, or are saying, can wait an hour or two. George, would you make yourself available at, say, eight thirty? And Alistair, would you prepare me some notes on comparative penalties for the crimes of criminal damage, conspiracy and kidnapping? I think a day of negotiating, if not reckoning, may be approaching."

"Including the Shari'a penal code? If it recognises them as crimes?" Alistair asked.

"No. I'm sure we'll have Miah Senior on the telephone this morning, but frankly I regret discussing Shari'a law in previous conversations with him. It's the payback for losing one's temper. He is under no circumstances to gain the impression that the application of Shari'a law to a Muslim, one involved with lapsed Christians or not, is an option. We have the Dutch threatening to introduce it, and I gather it has been applied in unofficial 'court' rulings in Woolwich, Dewsbury and countless other hidden venues in what used to be English suburbs, but we'll have no such bifurcation here. Britain can do what it pleases, or what its government pleases, which appears to be to let people in and then let them do their own thing. Another case of Amy's plumbing leak. Not here. I want yardsticks, as before, from the western world; America, Canada, Australia and so on. Unlike our neighbouring state, Holy Island is not about to have a split legal system whereby one law applies for the indigenous population and others for religious minorities. We will have *our* law and *our* government. End of story. And thank you again, Rebecca, for spotting where we were."

That's him back to normality, Geordie thought. So that means us.

What Alex Deville had not elaborated on, out of consideration for Rebecca, was a snippet that Miah had divulged in one of his stormy exchanges with Marjoribanks on the flight back.

Apparently all the small but useful details—Holy Island's security arrangements, the approach to Fahr House, its occupants, its garden, its location near the public car park, the surrounding terrain, and the absence of Rottweilers—had been garnered by Marjoribanks in St. Stephen's Tavern, Westminster. Miah, who being teetotal had had to rely on his word, had complained that nowhere in this litany had there been any mention of carrying dead weights over walls and fences, far less the chance of someone taking pot-shots at them.

The other party in the Westminster bar had borne a serious grudge against Holy Island and Alex Deville. He had volunteered his services with alacrity if not sobriety. Deville knew that the chloroform he had been forced to inhale in his garden could cause short-term amnesia and unwelcome hallucinations. Like any other rich financier, he also knew how small the world really is. But even he had been surprised to wake up and find himself seated in a helicopter alongside an apparition who looked suspiciously like Charley Oakley.

"Some fresh air, sweetheart?" Sarah asked when they'd done the breakfast dishes.

"Great idea," Geordie said. "But...would you mind if I see whether the car can still start? Maybe drive along to the Snook? Have a walk over to the east side? I haven't seen that bit."

"And if the old heap doesn't start? As in upped and died?"

"Cheeky beggar. Well, if you put it like that...if it doesn't, it gets lifted by Max's next passing dump truck. And we do the usual, take a stroll around the harbour."

"Let's go."

The Clio coughed, wheezed as if it needed oxygen, but started.

"On the way past, let's see if Amy's up and about," Sarah suggested. "She's Dad's oldest friend and she'll have been worrying."

"Sure." He drove down Marygate. "Must have salt water in the tank," he mumbled. It was embarrassing, and a relief that the street was quiet. It was a case not so much of kangaroo fuel, as convulsions. The thing seemed bent on taking vertically to the air from a standing start, and join its zillion ancestors in obsolescence heaven.

Halfway there, after the turn on to Berwick Road, Sarah began a running commentary. "Salt *water*?...It sounds more like solid crystals...maybe a hundredweight of *sand*. Do you think it's going to get us all the way to Amy's? Where do you give a car the kiss of life? What was that thingamajig called...Heimlich...CPR?" Sarah asked. "At this rate, sweetie, we could be spending a lot of time at the roadside getting to know each other..."

Geordie had to stop the car while he howled with laughter and pain. On one of the Clio's attempted lift-offs, he'd banged his knee on the dashboard.

They made it to Amy's driveway at a quarter to six. She was around the back, giving George the Vietnamese potbellied pig his breakfast bowl.

"Oh, it has to be good news," Amy said when she saw them. They were still hanging onto each other in spasms of laughter, Geordie kicking the car.

They told her of the rescue. She nodded; even with her woeful hearing, which Geordie suspected was nowhere near as bad as she claimed, she'd heard the chopper's dawn arrival. He handed her a printed-off copy of *The Northern Sun* article.

"Spectacles, dratted spectacles," she muttered. "Come in when you're ready, George pet." She left the little pig's gate open and took them inside.

"Good writing, George," said Amy when she'd finished reading. "And they're not hurt?"

"Not at all," Sarah said.

"That Max. He's been raised with good habits, that boy."

"He did do rather well. And Daniel," Sarah said.

"Where are these people now?" Amy asked. "And how has Rebecca taken it? That fool of a man."

"She had a hard time at first," Geordie said. "But Daniel seems to be getting her back on track. The fool and his pals are in jail."

Amy clapped her hands.

"Where they should be, huh?" Geordie added.

"Oh, I'm not clapping about *them*," she said. "It's just nice to see young love."

"Well, damn…"

"Oh, the story's well enough written, George. Nearly as well as the other one's written. All over your face." Amy grinned. "And that young policeman won't mess around."

She insisted they had a cup of tea and asked Geordie straight out: did this mean he was going to be a Holy Islander? George the pig wandered in to listen and have his belly rubbed.

"Don't I need 'L' plates first?"

"Only after you decide to start lessons in earnest."

"To be advised," Geordie said.

"Ha!"

"Well, we can't let you in on every secret, can we?"

"As if you let me in on your romance. Sneaky pair."

Just as they were leaving, Geordie's attention was drawn by a flash of colour outside the window. He saw a handsomely-combed cockerel strutting his stuff in next door's back yard, clearly checking out his harem after their wake-up call, and was reminded of seeing similar plumes the day before.

"When do we start the Cochise treatment, Amy? The therapy you volunteered me for?"

"Oh, you have far more important things to do now. You'll remember that was when you were mooning about the harbour of a morning, and plucking up courage to ask Sarah out. Cochise'll keep anyway. He's just temporarily pixilated, and needs a good talking to. You leave him to me. You stick to your writing and helping Alex and looking after this young lady. You're not going anywhere in the foreseeable future, are you?"

He got out of the door while Sarah was giving Amy a hug, before things got any worse. George sent him on his way with a muted squeal. Even dumb animals were rubbing it in.

The Clio got them to the access road to Snook House and tower, relic of a nineteenth century attempt to mine ironstone and coal. It succeeded in negotiating the potholes without dying on its wheels, and seemed to be clearing the grunge from its system. Geordie was relieved. He didn't think his savings would run to a new car, especially as he seemed to be working for charity these days.

"Okay. The old heap sounds better," he said. "Where to now?"

At Sarah's suggestion, they turned back to the village and parked near St. Coombs Farm, at the junction of the Lonnens. She took his hand and told him they were in for a three-mile hike; that he would see his east side, plus a bit more. They headed up Crooked Lonnen, fields of sheep and lambs on either side, lapwings wheeling above, past a neat bungalow. As the land rose, they were treated to a different view, a view removed from the well-trodden tourist trail, of the north side of Lindisfarne Castle. And beyond it, across the shimmering water, they saw the solid bulk of Bamburgh Castle, Sir Lancelot's mythical Joyous Garde, looming over the marram-covered dunes and flaxen beach.

"What are they?" Geordie asked, pointing ahead at a pair of small birds. "Do you know?"

"Wheatears. Pretty, aren't they? You'll see a few."

The smell of seaweed was getting stronger. They came to the end of the track as it met a raised waggonway above a grass embankment, the shore below. They headed for a smart white triangle, brilliant in the morning sun, sitting on Emmanuel Head; a daytime warning, visible for miles north and south, of the reefs lurking offshore. The whole Farne Islands archipelago, from Inner Farne to Longstone, lay across the sea south-eastwards.

A flock of herring gulls and great black-backs were gathered in the shallows, and redshanks poked along the shore. Sarah pointed out gannets heading north, and one or two razorbills and puffins on fishing expeditions between the Farnes and the rich pickings of Berwick Bay. Two mute swans were swimming gracefully offshore, a nice foil for a two-masted yacht that could have set out earlier from Seahouses harbour.

They walked towards the beacon on Emmanuel Head and left the waggonway to cut through the marram grass, skylarks rising around them, taking care to stick to the narrow trampled paths, avoiding nests, small grey snails, and hairy caterpillars.

"Oh, my," Geordie said. "A beach all of our own."

"Happy childhood memories," Sarah said. "Hours of them."

They picked their way over the rocks down to Sandham beach, took off their shoes, and leaped over the necklace of seaweed along the tideline. A pair of eider ducks swam placidly in the shallows but a group of oyster-catchers didn't like the intrusion, flying in a clamour away to the north. Geordie and Sarah went hand-in-hand up to their knees in water before turning back.

Sarah shivered. "But not for skinny-dipping. Not in May."

"Roll on July," Geordie said, taking her hand through the kelp. "If that's any different."

"I'm just so glad it all worked out okay with Dad," Sarah said as they sat on the rocks with their arms round each other, letting their feet dry. "It was only a day, but felt longer."

"Are we going to tell him about us?" Geordie asked. "That a certain...commitment has crept in?"

"Commitment." Sarah laughed. "There's a word. We'll let him have his sleep first."

"What do you think his reaction will be?"

"Pleased. He likes you, George. He'll be thinking Daniel's committed too, so he's got a lawman. And, with Rebecca, someone who can help with the seaweed and horticultural ideas. Bonuses all over."

"Yes," Geordie said. "You know your father, all right."

They walked over the sand to the north end of the bay, climbed carefully through the grass and patches of pirri-pirri to the top of the dunes, skirted the old limestone quarry workings cut into the rock behind Coves Bay, and stopped again on top of the cliffs.

Geordie looked around him in astonishment. First, there was a ribbon of golden sand that seemed to stretch for miles north—he could see St. Abb's Head in the far distance—but what surprised him most were the cliffs themselves, steep and stratified, waves crashing at their foot. Castlehead Rocks, Sarah told him, pulling him back before he pitched over.

"This is Coves Haven. That's Snipe Point and Back Skerrs at the north end. Dramatic for a little island, huh?"

Geordie hadn't known the cliffs existed. Fulmars were nesting in them, circling above and below, looking as if they too resented the intrusion. The air was perfumed with their excrement, with warm sand, damp seaweed and marram grass.

"Jeez," he said, "it's like having your own private Nature Reserve."

Sarah laughed. "Well, it's a Nature Reserve all right, a Ramsar, but lots of people enjoy it. We've just beaten them to it this morning, that's all."

She pointed out the highest point of the dunes and they walked across an area of scrubby ground, a dune "slack," towards it. Geordie could identify not only thrift, forget-me-nots and may blossom on solitary hawthorn bushes, but sea campion as well. He told her that all of Rebecca's work hadn't been wasted.

"Ah, but what are these?" Sarah asked, pointing to some stalks of dense purple flower, like upturned ice-cream cones, that dotted the earth around them.

"Haven't a clue. Hey, I'm just learning."

"Marsh orchid. Another for your collection."

They enjoyed the view from the highest point, and walked back down towards open fields and a track leading to the village.

"What gets to me as much as anything," Geordie said, "what is really strange, we've heard nothing but the sea and birds since we set out."

"City boy," Sarah laughed. "Think you'll be able to sleep at night in all this silence?"

"Ummm…not too many problems so far. Nothing a book or two didn't cure."

"In future, I hope you won't have to rely on literature," Sarah said with a grin. "This is Straight Lonnen," she added, as they walked down a leafy track, hawthorn and elderflower on each side. "More wheatears, see? Pied wagtails? This is as near as we get to the archetypal Lover's Lane on Holy Island. I mean the seclusion, the greenery," she added hurriedly, "not that I have much personal experience."

"Much? Good thing I came along," Geordie said. "You'd have been an old maid before you knew it. On the shelf, never mind a rock."

He dodged a dig in the ribs.

"We missed out on the kissing gate back there," Sarah said, kissing him. "But otherwise it's been a lovely morning."

It was eight o'clock when they arrived back at the car. They had done the three miles, Sarah told him, perhaps a bit more with the detours. Had it been worth it? It had been great, Geordie said, an escape into timelessness. Sarah smiled. They felt invigorated, ready to take on the world. Provided the car behaved, Geordie reckoned, he'd have time for a shower before they hooked up with her father again.

He wasn't sure he was looking forward to it, but the walk had helped.

CHAPTER TWENTY-FIVE

For his next session with the man who in Sarah's words was "your official future father-in-law, and not too future at that," Geordie took more care than usual over his appearance. His laundry had been neglected over the last two days, but he managed to find an ironed shirt, and a pair of pants with creases in the right places. When he entered the basement war room, however, the first thing to catch his attention was not Deville but the television screen.

A Channel Four political correspondent, framed against a demonstration stretching along Whitehall, was saying that he expected "a story broken this morning by a regional newspaper in the north" (as if the city of Newcastle was somewhere under the disappearing Arctic ice-cap) would cause the resignation today of the British Home Secretary.

"Sit down, George," Deville said. "You may need to."

Sarah and Alistair were already there, answering calls. There was no Daniel or Rebecca, and Geordie guessed they were probably at the jail, or taking a walk of their own. He smiled to himself. If they had any sense, they'd be tucked up in bed, congratulating each other on being well away from a reinvigorated Alex Deville and any Fahr House action. There was no Max either; he'd be back on post at the security gate. Life goes on, Geordie thought.

The Northern Sun headline, his byline under it, flashed up on the screen. He could read the first paragraph. It was much as he had drafted it; the subs had either been satisfied or too weary to bother.

The TV showed pictures of Newcastle city centre, the familiar landmark of Grey's Monument, George Square in Glasgow, Lion Square in Nottingham, and then back to Whitehall. The expressions on peoples' faces were less angry than those in Jarrow yesterday, a brew of determination and disbelief. Geordie thought he could understand those expressions. It was one thing to bitch about your government's policies or actions; it was something else to discover your government was a collective criminal.

The camera cut to another sequence, this time of the British Home Secretary emerging from a limousine, scurrying towards Number Ten, microphones being thrust in his face, and voiceless questions being thrown. He brushed them off, ignored them, almost knocked one cameraman over, and gave a perfunctory wave as he disappeared inside. Among the waiting press corps, an anticipatory atmosphere was evident, much as would have prevailed among eighteenth-century Parisian gentlefolk winding their way to the Place de Grève to witness guillotine executions.

Back to the studio: *"We will of course follow that story, try to set up an interview...*"

Deville switched the television off.

"We've had an interesting morning already," he said. "Our friendly Scottish Nationalist MP was on the phone ten minutes ago. His party are not about to let this one slip through their fingers. They're thinking of going ahead on two fronts, and hoping to succeed with the first; an emergency debate that allows an MP to seek the adjournment of the House at the end of Question Time, about 3:30 p.m. today, if he or she wishes to discuss 'a specific and important matter that should have urgent consideration.' If the Speaker allows it, the debate is not held until the next day, but there is worse built-in delay for the other options. We're not dealing with anything streamlined here. Our friend thinks it might work. The Speaker isn't a fan of such debates, but he might be persuaded by the scenes we just saw on TV."

"And the second?" Geordie asked. Employed or not, it was difficult to break the investigative habit.

"To go for a private notice question. They can be taken at the end of Question Time, if the Speaker agrees in advance. But the Minister concerned has to be informed. In our case, which Minister? And he may not be available. Similarly, adjournment debates can be raised on matters of public concern, but need to be notified to the Speaker in writing. They are then subject to a ballot and debated the following week. A wonderfully efficient system, eh?"

"What about tabling a question?" Geordie asked. "Isn't that feasible?"

"Yes; *but*. Always the but. They could table an oral question today, for example, asking the Prime Minister in code whether he or any Cabinet member had a hand in kidnapping Holy Island's First Minister. *But*, the Prime Minister doesn't take oral questions except for half an hour on Wednesdays. When he's there that is, between trips abroad. And our friend can hardly table one for their Home Secretary to answer. He might not be there at all, come noon. Apart from that, a roster system operates between Departments, and the questions tabled are given a random computer shuffle. Oral and written questions aren't answered until at least three days later, supposedly to give Ministers and their advisors time to prepare a response. All that said, given that Ministers aren't supposed to lie to the House under any circumstances, our friend says he'll be fascinated to see what form of words they concoct to duck out of this one. He's actually quite upbeat about getting a debate, says it can't really be avoided. Bully for him. They should kick the whole mess into touch and start again."

"Too much protocol," Geordie said. "Inertia. But it would be beyond me to concoct a form of words if I were in their shoes. You'd need a special form of training for that."

Deville laughed. "Civil service-ese. You don't do yourself justice."

He poured coffee and handed Geordie a cup.

"I've also confirmed a decision of Max's yesterday and stood the pollsters down, until further notice. It seems a waste of time to ask people now if they've heard of Holy Island's secession. I've told them to submit their bill. We may get back to them if we need to quantify support. That it exists, and is alive and well, seems clear from the television screens and other media. Does that seem sensible?"

"Yes." Geordie wondered what he'd done to deserve consultation, even after the fact.

"But to get down to it, I have five other things to tell you," Deville said, smiling. "And don't bother with the props. They aren't, or most of them aren't, for publication."

"First, thank you for that," he said, nodding at the blank screen. "The cat seems to be well and truly among the pigeons. Two: I'm delighted Sarah has found someone to make her happy."

Geordie nearly fell off his chair. Wasn't he supposed to have lent a helping hand in this revelation? The relief almost took his breath away. He was conscious of Sarah smiling across the room, and Alistair drumming his fingers on the desk.

"I realise you may have some tricky decisions ahead," Deville continued. "If you need help, I'm here." He waved off Geordie's thanks. "I said help, not free jobs," he added.

"Three: I've had the expected call from Mr. Miah. I told him his son and friends were in jail here, and that they will be looked after. I've asked Daniel to relent on the food front, and they will be allowed visitors, but they will not be allowed bail, and they will be tried within the next two weeks. I have a recording of that conversation if you'd like to hear it. Miah wasn't happy, but neither did he argue the point. He seemed resigned, in fact. Wouldn't you say, Alistair?"

Alistair nodded, and gave Geordie a wink.

"Daniel tells me his Bulford friends were fairly sure that Mr. Miah knew what his son was doing. He may be worried about getting extradited here as an accessory before the fact." Deville smiled. "Four: I'm tempted to make a trip to London today. To strike while the iron is hot. The helicopter is due to return to home base in an hour or two and I may just beg a lift. We can talk about that in a moment.

"The fifth and final thing is something you may have gathered in our conversations about South Uist and the like. The halfway house I mentioned. I own this island, or most of it. The purchase was amicably agreed a year or so ago with the Lord of the Manor, in whose family it has been for some time. This is something I don't wish publicised or, unless it becomes necessary, known at Westminster. They seem to have missed it."

"You own Holy Island," Geordie said.

"I own most of it, is how I put it. It's my small ace in the hole. A safety net, as it were."

"Holy cow."

"Money and time can get you anything, George. Anything tangible, that is. Sometimes, it costs more or takes longer. Or it may need more or less diplomacy."

"Right. I must be deficient not to have thought of it."

"Not at all. Why should you? I don't publicise it. But you'll appreciate the benefits. As owner of a large part of Holy Island, I can stop not only speculation in land but also unwanted developments. The purchase was in fact agreed shortly after we kissed goodbye to a country club scheme. I understand Sarah told you the background. Plus, I can ensure that if plots of land or buildings which belong to the estate are sold, they are sold under the right conditions, in perpetuity or otherwise, to people I trust and who'll use them well. I can see to it that land is developed for community uses. I can have them developed myself. To borrow a catchphrase, these are helpful things to have in your locker." He smiled. "Okay so far?"

"Yes." Geordie was kicking himself for ignoring the Land Registry. What sort of investigative journalism was that? Bernstein, for God's sake? A cub reporter could have done better.

"You may take my word for it that I'll be a benevolent landlord to every Holy Islander, and a benevolent friend to every institution—English Nature, English Heritage and the National Trust come to mind—who either own part of the island themselves, or have its best interests at heart."

Deville poured himself and Geordie more coffee, and carried the pot over to Sarah and Alistair.

"Now...as I've said to you before, I don't wish to hold the position of First Minister for long. Not much beyond getting the Holy Island ship of state underway. Enoch Powell once said that all political careers inevitably lead to failure, and I don't want to risk that. Ownership is another matter. I've been working on a succession plan, on two succession plans in fact.

"The first concerns the government of Holy Island. Most of that is covered in the constitution, but I was worried that someone like Cochise, let us say, or George W. Bush, might railroad their way into pole position. With Amy's help, I drafted clauses to limit the First Minister's powers, and to ensure the people of Holy Island are able to confirm the post annually. If less than sixty percent are happy, there should be a leadership contest and vote. What do you think?"

"Shades of ancient Rome. Not quite as circumspect as the doges of Venice, and you could quibble about the sixty, but okay in principle. Not new, though. In principle."

Deville raised his eyebrows. "Ancient Rome? Venice? Have you been talking to him?" he asked, pointing at Alistair. "Have I got two of you to put up with now?"

"The old Republic. Divide power, hedge it, make sure no one gets too much of it, vote on it annually. Wasn't that the Roman idea?"

"Yes...well, it may not be a new one but it worked there for a time, before they choked themselves on too much of a good thing and the final dictator got himself killed. And it can be adjusted to work here. Hopefully, we can still learn from earlier models, and I would be seriously concerned if anyone thought I had ambitions towards dictatorship. Or dogeship, if that's a word. Now, on the other matter..."

"So you put yourself up for re-election next May, is that it?"

"Perhaps. More likely, I withdraw altogether. As I was saying, the other succession plan concerns ownership. In essence, when I depart this life, it divides the ownership of the island, with provisions for future progeny and indeed against any family disasters, between Max, Sarah and Alistair, with Max retaining the title. Having three children is fortuitous. I have no reason to suppose they will ever fall out, but the number three ensures that any one of them who goes deviant can be outvoted." Deville grinned across at his son and daughter. "It would have been trickier had there been only two, but that's by-the-by. Of course, either Sarah or Alistair may decide in future that the First Minister and landowner roles are as compatible for them as they have been for me, but that's for them to decide. I'm sure Max will have no interest in the political side." He stopped. "Is something the matter, George?"

Geordie was thinking: shit...Dear Bill. Parodies in *Private Eye* magazine. At the mercy of that satirical so-and-so Ian Hislop and *his* successors as editor. *Me*? Geordie Halloran, alias Dennis Thatcher, "Dear Bill" himself, the mercilessly lampooned husband, fan and faithful supporter of the former PM and Iron Lady? No, no, no, the whole bloody day's down the tubes. Day? More like his life. Sarah couldn't possibly contemplate...?

"No," he managed to articulate.

"Ah, I see. As a matter of interest, have you yet asked for my daughter's hand in marriage?"

"No." Better. Less strangled. More positive. If "no" can be positive. "In any case, I'd ask you first," Geordie added, recovering his voice and some of his poise.

"Excellent. That's how it should be. But there's still time to extricate yourself, you know."

"Dad, you're over-stepping the mark. That is *not* funny," Sarah said.

"Sorry, only having a bit of fun. I mean, it would be natural for any young man to have doubts in this situation. But you know you have my support however long it lasts…"

"*Dad!*"

"Oh, I know, I know, enough. I think George worries too much, but he's made of strong stuff. He's a Jarrow boy, after all. They're built to resist." Deville smiled, as Geordie wondered how in hell he knew about Jarrow.

"But, as I was saying, George, before I dragged us down this one-way street, I have worked hard for thirty years to ensure my family will be able to live, as I have done, in a decent, harmonious, democratic society. I have every intention of ensuring that Holy Island continues under a benevolent government as well as a benevolent ownership. As recent events have confirmed, if confirmation was needed, the British government are not to be trusted. It should go without saying that I do not intend to be benevolent to them. Unless, of course, they accept the inevitable.

"Now, with all that behind us, let us discuss the inevitable."

Geordie wondered what the inevitable might entail, but before he could speculate on possible answers the phone started clamouring again.

They looked at it. Surely, this time…Tension in the room built with each note. Deville reached over and picked it up.

"Oh, good morning, vicar. How nice of you to call…not at all…none the worse for wear, thank you…yes, those machines are noisy…I do hope you managed to get back to sleep…you have?…excellent…in eight days? That would make it the twenty-ninth?" (jotting down a note) "no, rest assured I'll be here…I'll look forward to meeting them…thank you for the call, it's always nice to start the day with good news…yes, indeed…and a good day to you."

"What?" he asked, looking at Geordie, Sarah and Alistair, mopping their brows and grinning.

"Well, we thought it might just be the Prime Minister," Sarah said.

"That was the vicar," Deville said. "And a damn sight more important he is to this parish than any Prime Minister. He tells me his cross-denominational visiting party is in place. We're to expect fifteen of them a week tomorrow. Does *The Northern Sun* cover ecumenical affairs, George?"

"Sometimes on page nine. Before the adverts," Geordie said, still in a jaundiced mood with the Editor. He'd phoned him earlier and received copious thanks for "a quite splendid scoop. All is forgiven, my boy, blah, blah, blah." Geordie was thinking that in this case, forgiveness was a one-way street.

"A sad commentary on the state of the world," Deville told him. "Well, you'll just have to live with the fact that for once you won't be on page one. It'll be a nice story, you know. Christian fellowship, promoting Christian unity, all that sort of thing."

"Oh, riveting stuff. Rest assured, I'm as convinced as you are. Might help if one of them broke ranks though..."

"Ridiculous. They'll be much too PC. Now..."

Another interruption.

Graham Pearce, the pilot, came down the stairs.

"Good morning again, all. I thought I'd pop down to thank you for the hospitality...much appreciated. Unfortunately, much as I'd like a quick look round, I'm going to have to leave you. Just had a call on the mobile. Lousy luck. I have to go to Edinburgh for a pick-up."

"Shame," Deville said, his eyes like Stone Age weapons.

Sarah got to her feet quickly, and said she would show Pearce out.

"And thank you for your help in bringing him back safely," they heard her say as she ushered him up the stairs.

"Damn," Deville said in vexation. "There goes one easy option. I should have been onto it earlier."

"It might not have been too good an idea, in any case," Alistair said.

"Oh? And why is that?"

"I was thinking how hot irons can work both ways. Get careless, and your own fingers get burnt just as easily."

"And how would you know? When did you last do any ironing?"

"No need to get huffy. You said, let's talk about it."

"Yes, well. Let's do that. And you can take over answering the phone again."

Interruptions three to six were media calls. *Was Mr. Deville back home? How had he been treated?* Points already covered in my article, Geordie thought disparagingly; didn't these dolts ever read anybody else's work? Did they think he'd been making it up?

Where were the kidnappers now? What was to be done with them? Could Alistair confirm that one had been a Security Service agent? Here we go again; it was the main point, you numpties; well, next to the return of...er...future father-in-law.

What implications did this latest blunder have for the secession, if any? Had Mr. Deville spoken this morning to the British PM? Did he expect to be doing so? Etcetera, etcetera.

Interruption seven was Sarah carrying the morning mail down the stairs. It was after nine o'clock, and the flats had been negotiable by Hummer for the last half hour. It had become standard practice in the last few days that mail from Berwick was dropped at the security gate, the limit of the British postal service's responsibilities. It was then brought over to the Holy Island Post Office as soon as the tide permitted. Fahr House was among the first properties in the village to receive its mail each day. Not because the First Minister asked for any special treatment, but because he lived not two hundred yards from the shop.

Sarah shuffled through the heap of envelopes and handed most of them to her father. He had a solid silver letter opener with a mother-of-pearl handle, a fiftieth birthday present from his late wife, and liked to wield it on them. He did it with gusto. Probably imagining he had the PM on an autopsy table, Geordie thought. Or Charley Oakley.

"One for you, sweetheart," Sarah said to Geordie in some surprise.

"Huh?" Geordie replied, equally surprised. This was a first.

"I hope it's not an old girlfriend chasing you up."

"Fat chance."

"Oh, dear. Didn't we have time for girlfriends? Too busy working? Clinging to a rock?"

Geordie didn't feel like gracing that one with a reply, and ripped the envelope open. A cheque, drawn on an American bank, fell out. Geordie looked at it, grunted with satisfaction, and pulled out its accompanying letter.

"Jeezo," he said, going pale. "I don't believe it."

"You got paid?"

"I got a lot more than that."

Deville smiled, but no one noticed. His children were looking at Geordie.

Daniel had been having a hard time in the jail. Relations between the Bigg Market Three, the Newcastle QC Haydon-Flint (now over halfway through his sentence, and hanging in there), and this morning's intake, were not going well.

The strife between the Bigg Market Three and the new arrivals had started when Daniel, as was his custom, had handed them mops and buckets to wipe down the floor of their cell.

This had caused comment from Mujaahid Miah, directed in particular at Abu Hashmi, whom he felt was not behaving in the best traditions of jihad. Demeaning himself before the infidels was not, in his opinion, the rightful flight path to Paradise. The infidels being David Bell, the Newcastle QC, the MI5 guy, Daniel Brigham, and possibly Shadrach Bunglawala (a question mark was hanging over Shad, there was a 50:50 chance he could be a believer). Given their recently shared experiences, Charley Oakley had so far escaped being bracketed with the rest, but only just.

Spurred on by Abu Hashmi—"suck on this, yah piece of piss" and similar poetic-cum-diplomatic overtures—the Bigg Market Three tried poking their brooms through the bars of the other cell into the nearest available eye. Miah ripped David Bell's broom out of his hand and broke it over his knee. Only the cell bars prevented full-scale hand-to-hand combat.

After carefully thinking his way through the options, Daniel had then kayoed David Bell and Abu Hashmi, thrown them unconscious on their bunks and strapped them down, making sure the buckles were out of reach beneath mattresses. For good measure, he handcuffed Shadrach Bunglawala to one of the cell bars. Until then, as their capture had been so quick and all-consuming, Mujaahid Miah and Charley Oakley had not appreciated the full extent of Daniel's capabilities. They began to look worried and back away to the far wall of their new home. Daniel shrugged, put human rights on the mental back-burner (he tended to think the whole human rights thing was taking on the character of a loose hyena anyway), kayoed them too, and repeated the manoeuvre with the straps and bunks.

"What you get if you step out of line," he said to his remaining audience. "A peaceful jail is a happy jail, I always think. Don't you?"

"Yes, indeed," said the MI5 agent runner, nodding enthusiastically.

"You'll pay for that broom, by the way," Daniel informed a semi-conscious Miah.

Then, with this minor fracas brought to a tidy conclusion, Daniel had been paid a call by Cochise, rigged out in new headdress, moccasins, deerskin waistcoat and leggings. Daniel had groaned inwardly, thinking this could well put the finishing touch to his morning, and that in all likelihood his new guest would be searching high and low for a war party to sign up with. But no, Cochise had brightly informed him that this was, "just a courtesy call, if it's okay with you, just checking on the old bivouac, right?" Daniel had decided to let that one pass. He was not about to start educating crackpots in the differences between jails and open encampments. But Cochise had other surprises up his sleeve.

Daniel thought the least he could do was offer the poor mutt a cup of tea. Cochise sat sipping his tea and began telling Daniel that, on doctor's orders, he had been laid off work since his "brief visit to this here wikiup." Daniel commiserated. Cochise waved it away. He said, as no money was coming in from his building job, he had found a new way of making some. He wished he'd thought of it years ago, when the island was much busier and white men were coming in herds. Much as buffalo used to roam the prairie.

Daniel learned that Cochise had taken to crouching behind the stone wall at the bend of the road where St. Cuthbert's Way became Chare Ends, jumping out when the time was right and bouncing himself off the bullbars of incoming SUVs. After a couple of experimental efforts, which had resulted in minor scrapes, he'd become expert in the act of bouncing off. So expert that when the driver, the loss of no-claims bonuses flashing before his eyes, emerged to find his victim lying on the road unharmed, his relief was such that he offered immediate damages. In full and final reparation, no strings attached.

When the going rate at first had been a measly twenty quid, Cochise decided to improvise. His latest and finest victim, "just this morning as white men came from across the sea," had donated one hundred pounds to the cause. It was simple, Cochise told Daniel. Instead of getting up and taking measly twenty pound notes when they were offered, all he had to do was lie there a bit longer, hold his ribs and groan. To demonstrate this newfound skill, he groaned at Daniel. He then thanked Daniel.

"Why thank me?" Daniel asked.

"Got the idea from a paperback right here," Cochise said. "Novel by a guy, G.M. Ford."

Daniel charged him, cautioned him, arrested him and threw him in the cell he'd had before. What else could he do? Tourists submitting themselves to highway robbery right, left and centre? He gave Cochise his half-consumed cup of tea, locked him in and looked around. Holy shit, at this rate he'd have to ask Mr. Deville to build an extension. He did a quick count of the occupants; three standing, four strapped down, and Cochise on his haunches rubbing two pieces of broom together, apparently trying to light a fire.

Eight in total. Five four-person cells, all now occupied. One by a threesome, one by a twosome, and three singles: Cochise, the spook and the QC. All being well, he'd lose the QC on Thursday.

Still, he thought he'd better phone Mr. Deville. Some additional shared occupancy might be called for, and Daniel didn't want the Holy Island jail getting the same reputation for overcrowding as its British counterparts. Nor did he want any cock-ups; Daniel abhorred cock-ups as much as he abhorred insincerity and sloppiness. And he was concerned about the volatile mix of cultures. He could keep knocking them out but, human rights or not, there was a limit on how much of that they'd be able to take.

Daniel didn't find it odd that he should be worried about integration in the jail, when he personally had found integration easy. He'd taken it for granted that no one would wish to upset him; and if they did, they only did it once. And he tried to take people as they were, one at a time. He had never understood how they could be defamed *en masse*—"money-grubbing Jews," "thick Irish," "lazy blacks," "stingy Scots"—when they were by and large decent, caring human beings. But he did remember his Mum telling him, "We could learn things from the animals. We may be more intelligent but that don't mean we're more comfortable. Cats and dogs weren't made to get along, were they?"

He didn't want to be a nuisance, and he could well imagine the level of activity up at Fahr House, but Daniel was a believer in flagging problems early, before they had a chance to take root. So he picked up the phone.

When this call was over, he'd also need to check out the paperbacks floating around the jail and warn Mrs. Donaldson, Amy, about loaning them out so generously. It would be embarrassing, and maybe upsetting for her, but there could be Le Carré novels lying around, Frederick Forsyth's, Stephen King's, anyone's, which this lot could find ways of corrupting to their own use.

Always provided they could read. Which, in the case of the Bigg Market Three, was doubtful.

CHAPTER TWENTY-SIX

Back in the basement of Fahr House, interruptions eight to eleven were more media calls.

Between them, this time to an enthralled audience, Geordie had been reading his letter, the first time word-for-word, and then picking out the best bits for another airing. Even reading it aloud, in whole or in part, he still found it difficult to believe. If he had been given a personal say in the content of his first letter as a resident of Holy Island, he couldn't in his wildest dreams have come up with anything better. He had to keep counting the zeroes and calculating exchange rates:

Dear Mr. Halloran

Please find enclosed our check for $6000 in payment for your recent articles.
You may not know it, but letters to our editorial staff indicate that your articles have generated great interest and a wide readership.
Our editor-in-chief has asked that you be approached with a suggestion.
As a younger man, he was a fan of Alistair Cooke's "Letter from America" which he enjoyed tuning into on the BBC's World Service and latterly on the internet. In the 1980s, he tells us he was greatly privileged to meet this phenomenal broadcaster at San Francisco Golf Club. He felt the man and his "Letters" captured the American spirit, indeed the spirit of broadcasting, in a way our own media aspired then, and aspire now, to emulate.
He finds the same quality in your articles, albeit in the reverse direction.
Our proposal is that you produce a weekly "Letter from Lindisfarne," by which we mean anywhere in GB and on any subject that would be of interest here. The editor-in-chief has suggested you start with a brief biography of King George III, set in his asylum. Castles always go down well here.
"Halloran's Letter from Lindisfarne" has a nice ring to it, I hope you agree?
For the exclusive rights to your "Letters," the Post *is prepared to pay the sum of $70000 per year. Our only condition is that a one-year trial period is agreed in order to ensure both parties are satisfied with this arrangement.*

Have a nice day.

Yours truly

"Holy cow," Geordie said. "It gets better every time. How about that? Can you believe it? Jeezo, what a turn-up."

"It doesn't mean," Deville said, "that you're aiming to hang around here indefinitely?"

"*Dad*! That's simply not on," Sarah said. "Let George make up his own mind. Without interference from you."

"I was going to add, if so, I'd be delighted," Deville said with a grin.

"Let me talk with Sarah about it," Geordie said. "Sarah? Kitchen?"

They shot up the stairs.

Alex Deville winked at his younger son. "This could work out fine, don't you think? It looks as though he's heading for permanent residency. You'll need to make him an ID card."

Then the phone rang again, interruption number twelve. It was Daniel.

"Not Cochise again?" Deville held his head in his hands. "Daniel, please tell me I'm not hearing this."

"Sorry, sir. You are."

"He's been doing *what*?"

Daniel repeated Cochise's scam.

"Oh Lord. So he's back in his own cell. I use the word 'own' loosely."

"Yes, sir. He seems quite at home. I think he likes it better than the doctor's surgery."

"Put him in with the MI5 person. That should be an education for both of them."

"Can't do that. Health and Safety, all that shit. Especially safety."

"Well, we haven't subscribed to its equivalent yet, but I take your point. I'll call the doctor and see if he'll put Cochise up again. Lodgings of choice apart, he does need medical help, after all. Although the last dose wouldn't appear to have been an unqualified success."

"It's worth a try. Thank you."

Deville sighed and put the phone down.

"Problems, Dad?" Alistair asked.

Deville told him.

"I'll phone the doc," Alistair said. "It'll give me a break from the press."

The doctor agreed to go down to the jail, and take Cochise into his care. However, he did say that he remained unpaid for Cochise's last treatment. He and his wife felt the stipend they received from the Althing's coffers, although generous, did not adequately recompense for the home care of raving loonies. His course in psychiatry, while excellent and wide-ranging, had not adequately prepared him for cases like Cochise. Furthermore, as Alistair would know, additional smaller payments were recoverable directly from patients, depending on the nature of their illness. He and his wife had not received a penny piece from Cochise, although he had been billed in the sum of one hundred and twenty-five pounds. Which, reflecting the seriousness of the case, was the biggest patient bill so far.

Alistair told the doctor that people could not be expected to pay for treatment that had patently failed, but he was sure, given the extraordinary circumstances, that his father would consider an *ex gratia* payment. The doctor thanked him.

Interruptions thirteen to fifteen were more media calls. Sixteen was a new variation.

Alistair grinned and put his hand over the mouthpiece. "Someone wanting to know if you need stress management therapy," he said to his father.

"Is that right? Do I look like it? Tell them to try Number Ten if they haven't already."

Deville shook his head and switched on Sky News to catch up with events in London. An electronic ticker-tape across the foot of the screen was announcing Breaking News. Not unexpectedly, the Home Secretary had been shown the door. By "mutual consent" and "with thanks for an outstanding term of office during which major advances have been made in making this important Department of State fit for purpose." Which, Deville thought, was one way of describing a sprawling, inefficient behemoth. Recently filleted, a chunk of its 75,000 staff finding shelter under a new "Department of Justice" umbrella, but still in his eyes a sprawling, inefficient behemoth. One that, among others, Lindisfarne would be better without.

After a couple of minutes, he switched the TV off again and checked the time. Ten fifteen. "Now," he said to Alistair, "if those two would just get back down here, we might just have that talk."

Meantime, Daniel was receiving yet another visitor. Malcolm Grant QC, bulging briefcase in hand, twenty-six week per year resident (and counting) of Holy Island, was knocking on the reinforced glass window and assessing the occupants.

His visit wasn't a long one.

First, Daniel was surprised to see him walk straight past his clients, all now awake but still fettered, and make a beeline for Miah Junior, Charley Oakley, and the spook. Glancing over his shoulder to check whether the competition, Haydon-Flint QC, was eavesdropping, Mr. Grant proceeded to tell them that he was the only available counsel on the island, that he was the only living expert on Holy Island law, and that they should consider themselves fortunate indeed to have fallen into such a safe pair of hands. Mujaahid Miah told him to stick his briefcase where the sun don't shine; no way was he going to be represented by an infidel on these trumped-up charges. Charley Oakley asked him if he had any beer in his briefcase. The spook was more economical with words. In fact, he said nothing at all. He simply looked at Malcolm Grant QC as if his shoe had picked up something nasty from the shore path.

Mr. Grant turned away, beginning to wonder if he had made the right decision in signing up for twenty-six weeks. It was beginning to feel like a life sentence. His wife missed the city centre shops and the MetroCentre. She was in a state of mild shock because there were so few places on Holy Island she could spend his money in. And because she blamed him for her enforced absence from large department stores, her libido, to put it mildly, was in a state of suspended animation.

Daniel watched Mr. Grant leave the jail and trudge back along the shore. At least, he thought, this visitor had come and gone without doing anything that warranted his detention. However, as the woebegone barrister passed the Popple Well, Daniel distinctly saw him kick the rusty iron standpipes that marked its site. Daniel was sure that this assault had caused something to fall off one of them. He debated going after Mr. Grant and arresting him for criminal damage, but on reflection decided not. Pointed in the right direction by Amy, he had read of a former Holy Island policeman whose nitpicking had reached such extremes that he'd been drummed off the island. The clear message being that the letter of the law had to be tempered with common sense, and Daniel was all in favour of that.

Besides, where the hell could he put the guy? In with his Newcastle competitor? In with clients he'd just cold-shouldered? In with guys who had given him the brush-off? Or in with Cochise? Daniel shuddered at the thought. Forget contempt, damage, robbery, conspiracy and kidnapping. Any way you cut it, that was a recipe for murder.

He looked at his watch and was tempted to call Rebecca, to see if she'd like lunch in The Ship. He wondered if he'd done enough to make her feel cherished after that business with her ex. He had told her to imagine Charley as a fungus spore, attaching itself to any available tree. Some of them were beautiful and full of life, like her. Some were felled and headed for the timber-yard, like the spook. She had seemed to enjoy the analogy, and he hoped she'd been able to embellish it in her own way.

Interruption seventeen was the front door bell, followed by the return downstairs of Sarah and Geordie. Rebecca was with them.

"Special delivery, Dad. A letter. Max brought the courier over."

Deville raised his eyebrows, and raised them higher when he saw the embossed seal. He opened the letter.

It was headed by a familiar ornate crest, beneath which was the two-word address of one of London's most famous landmarks. The body of the letter was typed, but it was topped and tailed in familiar handwriting and finished with an unmistakable insignia. It read:

Mr. Alexander Deville
First Minister, The Althing
c/o Fahr House
The Holy Island of Lindisfarne

Dear First Minister

I was delighted to hear this morning that your ordeal was over and you had been returned safely and uninjured to your home.

My husband and I have fond memories of your beautiful island, and find it difficult to believe that nearly fifty years have passed since our visit. It is my hope that we may do so again one day, but as you will know, public office has an unnerving habit of filling diaries.

Having suffered with you through your recent travails, by which we mean the regrettable bulldozer episode as well as your coerced absence from your responsibilities, my husband joins me in wishing you and all those who live on Holy Island well for the future.

(signed)

"Good God," Deville said. "How extraordinary. How on earth...?"

His son and daughter looked at him blankly.

"George? Did you have a hand in this?"

The former Home Secretary may have been surprised to hear that, for all his insistence on consultation, Deville had never been a great admirer of Britain's premier family. Indeed in terms of national degeneration, Deville viewed the mismanagement of their various divorces and disasters almost on a par with reality TV shows and joining the European Union. But being a pragmatic man and a believer in the philosophy that all good strategies should cover as many bases as possible, he could see the golden opportunity offered by this epistle.

"Well, I've sat here often enough when you've written to the lady yourself, or copied things," Geordie said. "I was just following protocol, you might say."

"Oh, don't get me wrong," Deville replied. "There are times, George, when your capacity for work reaches the heady heights of genius. Give the man a kiss, Sarah."

"Well, what the hell, I mean, I don't mind a kiss here or there, but..."

Sarah kissed him.

"Don't you see what you've done?" Deville asked.

Alistair twigged. Geordie and Sarah continued kissing each other. They'd decided upstairs, with Rebecca acting as a sounding board, that Geordie should accept the *Post*'s offer, and hand in a month's notice to *The Northern Sun*. They would then get a mortgage at reasonable rates (not preferential rates, nothing nepotistic) from the Holy Island Bank and Trust, and buy a nice house Sarah knew about along Sandham. From one of the second home people who had opted out of the twenty-six week commitment, she added.

Rebecca said it all seemed to fit together beautifully. She was in a much sunnier mood now that Charley was out of sight. In fact, following Daniel's cue, Game Boy was now in a timber-yard crawling with fleas, woodworms, spiders, beetles, rodents, and sundry other species of insect and animal life. She was enjoying the mental exercise of thinking up others; there were some particularly poisonous varieties in Australia. In fact, about eight of the ten most deadly creatures on earth lived in Australia...

She'd grinned at Geordie and told him he was stuck for life. And with luck, that she'd be joining him.

Finally, the British PM phoned, fresh from a farewell trip to Iraq and the loss of another Home Secretary. Deville switched on the loudspeaker:

PM: Good morning. I'm glad you're safe and well.

AD: Nice of you to call.

PM: However, you really can't detain British subjects. What you have done amounts to false imprisonment, which as you know is a first cousin to kidnapping. Two wrongs don't make a right.

AD: These individuals committed their alleged crimes here, Mr. Prime Minister. And we shall try them here.

PM: It is not quite as easy as that.

AD: Oh? Why?

PM: As you may have seen, the Home Secretary has just resigned. Part of the reason for his departure was that, unknown to him, his nephew and one or two junior colleagues had decided to do something about your illegal secession. Something wholly unauthorised, I should emphasize.

AD: What has this to do with these alleged crimes?

PM: You have falsely imprisoned his nephew. Let me spell it out...his nephew works, or used to work, for the British Security Service.

AD: Ah. So, let me think...this nephew's release is part of the deal you made in exchange for his resignation.

PM: No deal was made. He resigned by mutual agreement. No doubt he felt some embarrassment might ensue for the government when his nephew's involvement leaked out.

AD: In that case, nothing has changed. His nephew will be tried here on Holy Island for his alleged crime.

PM: Continue on that track and we will simply move to extradite him.

AD: In that case, Mr. Prime Minister, you are doing two things. First, you are recognising that this individual may stand accused of a crime committed in Britain and punishable under British law. Correct?

PM: Obviously.

AD: And second, by suggesting extradition, you are recognising the Holy Island of Lindisfarne as a nation state.

PM: Ridiculous.

AD: I think not. Indeed, over and above your earlier references to our status, which were duly recorded, I have this morning received a letter from our shared sovereign. Her letter also recognises the Holy Island of Lindisfarne as a state.

PM: It does *what*?

AD: You heard. I am not about to read you the whole letter since it is a matter of private correspondence, but it is clearly addressed to me as First Minister of the Althing of Holy Island. In good faith, however, I'll read you the last two sentences…(*reading them*)

PM: This is impossible…

AD: On the contrary. As has been said, Mr. Prime Minister, politics is the art of the possible. With that truth in mind, I'm happy to accede to your extradition request. In fact (*thinking of Daniel and Rebecca*), as a gesture of goodwill, you can have the other two as well. We can deal with the details later.

PM: Impossible…she was simply wishing you well…she would never begin to consider…it must have been a genuine mistake…

AD: Oh? Do you suppose Her Majesty doesn't keep abreast? Has no idea what's going on? Fifty-odd years of experience? Prime Minister after Prime Minister? I doubt if that suggestion would go down well.

PM: Out of the question…Her Majesty would never *dream* of allowing the break-up of…almost certainly, there has been a slip-up. Some unqualified secretary or other…

AD: Oh? I suspect that's a rare occurrence. For her anyway. And how do you propose to find out? Embarrass her by asking, on the off-chance it *was* a mistake? That wouldn't be good diplomacy, would it? Or embarrass your government by finding out it wasn't?

PM: (*After a pause for consultation.*) Perhaps it is time we had a meeting about your ambitions towards partial autonomy. If you would be willing to travel to London…

AD: It has been accomplished without a meeting, Prime Minister. And I should say it is pretty well complete. There is, however, one more thing you might reflect on.

PM: Which is?

AD: We are confident our friends in America will follow her example.

PM: Out of the question. They wouldn't. They have a hundred and one secessionist movements of their own. You think they would let that rabbit out of the hat? I can't think of anything more unlikely.

AD: Militants. Conspiracy theorists. Gun-toting rednecks, white supremacists and backwoodsmen. Very different breeds, and very different circumstances. I'm afraid you'll have to face up to it. It's going to happen. Good morning, sir.

"Champagne, everyone?" Alistair asked, moving to the fridge. "Our friends elsewhere will be delighted with this, father. They'll be popping the corks for sure when they hear of it."

"Friends in America? Friends elsewhere?" Geordie asked.

"Oh, Washington DC on the one hand," Deville said. "But Alistair was referring to other friends, whom the PM or his successor have yet to face. Not that they are yet aware of it, nor should they be. These are friends of ours, principally friends of mine, whose roots are firmly entrenched in other islands around the British coast. Islands like the Scillies, Great Cumbrae, Portland, and Walney. Along with some bigger examples, such as Lewis, Anglesey, Sheppey, and all being well the Isle of Wight. You see, George, although Holy Island is dear to my own heart, it is also a test case for others. Those others, the fraternity if you will, also have islands dear to their hearts.

"Now, I don't wish to come across as heavy-handed to future sons-in-law, not that I expect to have more than one, but no word of this is to leave this room. I should hate to think of Sarah's distress if you were placed in Daniel's care." Deville smiled, to soften the words.

"Point taken," Geordie said. "Ummm…how many of this 'fraternity' are there?"

Deville smiled again, thinly. "Fifteen, at the last count. In fact, Max could have called on one of them for help yesterday, a friend of mine who now lives back in his home town of Lerwick. They always have been rather ambiguous about their British connection up there. However, Max had the helicopter ready and, as a dutiful son who felt a sense of responsibility for his wayward father, decided to go solo. Or I should say, only with Daniel."

Well, shit, Geordie thought, I was handed all those clues and innuendoes and ignored them, or didn't follow them up. "Support," "damaged the model," "fraternity"...I missed the whole game plan. Friends United in the City, all brassed-off and with billions to spend. A cabal of islands...scoop after scoop. Still, he comforted himself, I wouldn't have been able to write about them then, and certainly can't now.

"In the circumstances, champagne is justified, Alistair," Deville said, looking at his watch. "But let's not forget how lucky we've been. You remember Henry Allison asking me at the public meeting a couple of weeks ago whether I thought the timing was right?"

Alistair nodded.

"Well, in that respect I don't imagine for an instant that our friends will have the same degree of fortune. The same juxtaposition of circumstances, as it were. I'll need to do some phoning around."

"It hasn't all been luck. You heard the PM. He's taken aback."

"True, but think about it. First, we have elections, national elections in Scotland and Wales, that make a serious dent in whatever confidence the British government had left. We have Scottish Labour politicians, after a close-run race which the SNP won by a short head, trying desperately to cling on to their fifty year-old monopoly of power...what they had come to think of as a divine right to dominate the Scottish people. In the wider British context, but still including Scotland, we have Labour MPs at Westminster running around lobbying for a new Leader, an unelected Prime Minister no less, instead of getting on with what they were elected to do. We have the swearing-in of a new Scottish Nationalist First Minister in their parliament in Edinburgh, which will hopefully also herald a new beginning for them. I believe these factors combined to give our own secession the status of a ball lost somewhere in the crowd. Then, with the Labour leadership business resolved, we had the *coup de grâce*, a duality of responsibility between a sitting and an incoming Prime Minister, one running around the world on a farewell tour, the other running around Britain on a hello tour, and neither with his eyes on the ball. Not to exaggerate, we are looking at a British government temporarily jellified because of the personal agendas of its two main players. Never again will there occur the same combination of circumstances. We have been very kindly treated indeed by Lady Luck. Our friends will know it, but it needs to be stressed."

"I think you're forgetting we made a lot of our own luck," Alistair said. "The work you've put in, the preparation, all the meetings, the cash, the interviews, and this latest thing with George. The PM knew the game was over. And if being jellified is the order of the day, how would they get back into the game in any case?"

"With difficulty. I'm not saying you're wrong, just that we've more or less been handed a winning streak," Deville said. "But we're there, bar dotting the i's. So pop the cork."

"Right," Alistair muttered, moving towards the fridge.

Alex Deville picked up from his desk the framed press cutting with the headline *"Hunger Drove Fasting Muslim to kill Eider: He and Boy Eat It Raw."*

"It's been a long road. Maybe I just can't believe it's finally over," he said, as though he were speaking to it. "All that work and talk and secrecy. But worth every step."

"What is that thing?" Geordie asked. He'd wondered about the cutting before too.

"A story from my childhood. Some paternal lessons. When I first became interested in the vagaries of justice, and tensions between different cultures and ways of life. You could call it a starting-point, a stimulus I suppose, but no more. It seems a long time ago now."

EPILOGUE

George Halloran and Sarah Courtney Deville were married four months later in a double ceremony with Daniel Brigham and Rebecca Carter at the Parish Church of St. Mary the Virgin. Their fathers, Alexander Beauregard Courtney Deville of Holy Island and Aidan Benedict Carter of Christchurch, New Zealand, gave the brides away.

Geordie found out what the Petting Stone was for that day. His new wife, supported by two fishermen, jumped over it, symbolic of a leap into a new phase of life. "Or into the unknown," Sarah told him when nerves were getting the better of her. It was a traditional wedding in other respects too; wildfowlers with shotguns forming a guard of honour, and more old fishermen barring the gate until they received their ransom for the bride's release. By then, Geordie knew them all, and was still humbled to reflect that many were able to trace their family histories not just by a few generations, but over several centuries.

Alex Deville's sisters and brother attended, with their spouses. His sisters flew over from St. Peter Port, Guernsey and St. John, Antigua respectively, and his brother from Washington DC. It was two years since any of them had seen their eldest brother, or their niece and nephews, so this was an additional cause for celebration. Geordie especially enjoyed talking with Deville's brother Sebastian. He wished his Mum and Dad could have met all these good people.

The double ceremony involved the entire population of Holy Island. Max Deville hired some lads from Seahouses to look after the border crossing for the day. This was for two reasons; to enable his friends to attend, and to ensure that the weddings, except for invited guests, were exclusively a Holy Island affair. And Max trusted the Seahouses boys more than British security firms.

Rebecca's mother Mary flew in from New Zealand with her husband and their son Michael. It was the first time Mary had been back to Lindisfarne since emigrating with her parents forty years before. She didn't think it had improved in her absence. The night before the weddings, she gave Alex Deville a ticking off, as though this state of affairs was his fault. She told him if he didn't get it back on track, and soon, he'd have been a disappointment to her twice over. She was appalled that pirri-pirri bur had been allowed to invade the island and distinctly underwhelmed to learn that the village hall was to be replaced.

Geordie's best man was Alistair Deville. Daniel's best man was Max Deville. Alistair gave a five hundred-word speech. At Daniel's request and following his own preferences, Max, who had treated himself to a new

Armani suit for the occasion, confined himself to fifty. He had invited a guest to the wedding, a buxom young reporter called Angela Dunn from Tyne Tees TV. Angela, who liked the sound of Max's voice more each time she heard it, was sorry he hadn't spoken longer.

Amy Donaldson had a front row seat in the church and George the Vietnamese potbelly lay on a blanket on the floor beside her. It was a cool September day, dry and bright but with a cutting east wind coming in from the sea. Amy refrained from heckling the vicar when he got confused and almost called Rebecca "Oakley." She had been tickled pink by the treatment dished out to Alex Deville by Mary Carter. Amy had forgotten she wasn't the only one capable of keeping the First Minister in line.

Over the summer Alex Deville had come to think of the new British PM as the latest in a long and inglorious line. Different in style from his predecessor, but another declared arch-unionist. Why was it that people held on so grimly to such concepts, at the same time contriving to undermine them with halfway measures? And furthermore, used only the most specious of arguments, an appeal to the fear of the unknown, to support their position? As far as this tortured individual's time in his new office was concerned, time would tell. As far as Holy Island was concerned, he had arrived too late to change anything. And thankfully, Holy Island no longer had to live under a regime where taxpayers' billions were hosed away on the trappings of the welfare state, all under the watchful eye of his *soi-disant* Prudence.

The financial deal eventually struck was that the British Exchequer retained 25 percent of the island's income tax revenue, in lieu of foreign affairs, defence and other high-flown matters, while the Althing took 75 percent for domestic use. This split, however, only applied if the individual concerned worked on the mainland. For those who lived and worked on the island, income tax was payable at 10p in the pound on income over £10,000 per year, and all of it went to the island's exchequer, ably administered by Alistair Deville. This was proving to be a good incentive for people to apply their skills locally. VAT was now only levied on cross-border goods and services. Local Council tax payments to the Berwick-upon-Tweed Borough Council had ceased in July.

With autonomy achieved, by Geordie's reckoning 85 percent financially and 95 percent morally, Alistair had turned his attention to the transfer of state pensions and social security benefits, and setting new quotas for those that would apply in future. The statistical challenge here was such that Geordie had retired hurt. As a conscientious husband-to-be, he had problems enough in researching options for his own pension arrangements, and harboured dark thoughts, still marinating in readiness for their appearance in a *Letter from Lindisfarne*, about (British) pension providers in general. Like banks, they seemed to have lost the art of customer service, if not the plot altogether. So far, to Geordie's regret, the Holy Island Bank and Trust was not a viable option, but he knew that Deville had ambitions in that direction and had talked of employing two or three investment specialists.

In any case, Alistair seemed to have had no problem with higher financial mathematics. At one point, he told Geordie that his job was a whole lot easier than the British Treasury's or Bank of England's. Imagine, he said, trying to manage an economy when you hadn't a clue about the true population. Or who was working, who was married (or its approximation), who was declaring their earnings, who could claim benefits, who was of school age, who needed hospital treatment, or who would be arriving in the back of the next cross-Channel lorry. At least on Holy Island, they had a verifiable count.

The two young men had become firm friends over the summer, although Geordie had constant difficulty pulling Alistair out of the house, his hard drive, and his advanced calculi. He had helped Alistair prepare for several "brainstorming" sessions, aimed at stimulating ideas for new industry and involving half-a-dozen other Holy Islanders. They had focused on high-tech lifestyle industries, those not dependent on proximity to markets, and had been successful in creating three ventures. A luxury second-hand watch and jewellery repairers, in which two local ladies had experience, was followed by a computer accessory mail-order company (suppliers in Taiwan and India) and SIFT. Initially, they had expected SIFT to make the most money and employ the least people. But, as a programme designed to reduce electronic spam, it had become clear over the summer that serious competition was afoot.

Nevertheless, by the time of the double wedding, these small businesses employed ten people. Deville and his fellow-Ministers were delighted. In August, Geordie and Alistair turned their attention to resource-based industries and, helped by Rebecca, were looking with interest at seaweeds. Against Amy's wishes, they had also begun working on ideas for a nascent Lindisfarne TV station. She had been only partly convinced when Geordie had told her it would be better than the BBC. At least, he added, it wouldn't announce a doubling of the British population within the next three generations and give the causes as the birth rate, increased longevity and, oh yes, immigration. As if this afterthought wouldn't account for nine-tenths of the total.

These initiatives aside, a further bonus for employment opportunities on Lindisfarne were the new jobs created in areas such as road and drainage maintenance, hitherto the preserve of the Borough Council of

Berwick-upon-Tweed. A few émigré Holy Islanders were returning home to fill them, and were enthusiastically buying "Houses for Sale."

Among the many presents received on their wedding day by both young couples, arguably the strangest was a stuffed short-eared owl given by Alex Deville to his daughter and her groom. It now sits on the mantelpiece of their house on Sandham Lane. Geordie is convinced it listens to their conversations and flies back to Fahr House each night to report.

Sarah still helps her father with his paperwork and cooks most of his and her brothers' meals, replenishing the freezer each time. Geordie drops in for a coffee, and to ask a few questions, at eleven most mornings. He has thought about trying to smuggle the short-eared owl back to its place on the oak-and-yew coffee table, but so far his courage has failed him.

He has also suggested once or twice to his father-in-law that letting go the ministerial reins might prove a harder proposition than expected, but has been told that as Sarah could be one of the potential successors, along with Michael Cromarty and Elizabeth Swan, he might be better advised to keep his own counsel. Come spring, Deville is determined to resign his position, retaining only the Chair of the Holy Island Bank and Trust.

Just before his wedding, Geordie had been intrigued to see that the village of East Stoke in Dorset had found an obscure provision in the 1972 Local Government Act empowering ten parishioners to call on their District Council for a poll on any issue. Some of the villagers had followed it up and the result, albeit after a low turnout, had been a vote in favour of an EU referendum. The mouse that roared, indeed.

Not that it made any difference, of course. The British government seemed to have decided against referenda in general, for fear of getting answers they couldn't handle. Geordie had debated taking Sarah on holiday to Dorset, but the wedding preparations had intervened and they were saving to go to Washington DC on honeymoon.

Towards year-end, rumours had also begun to circulate in Berwick of a poll-for-TV referendum on whether the town should revert to Scottish control. Before finally becoming English in 1482, ownership of the Border town had ping-ponged between Scotland and England no less than thirteen times. In the 1990s, a similar vote had resulted in a small majority wanting to stay English. But that was before Scottish devolution and different approaches to issues like the care of old people, education, and taxes on water consumption. Geordie expected the vote, due to take place in February, to swing in favour of Scottish control. And of course into a *Letter from Lindisfarne*.

In the latter half of the year too, driven by a growing unease in the opinion polls and some statistical howlers by the Home Office, the subject of immigration had clawed its way from obscurity onto the political agenda. Under the guise of government advisers and think tanks, a whole raft of talking heads had taken the opportunity to introduce a new slant, namely that a continued flow of immigrants was essential to Britain's economic well-being. Politicians of all hues had quickly taken up this seductive thesis. Ever on the lookout for *Letter* material, Geordie asked whether the economist in Alistair had a view.

Alistair said that if immigrants were the only people willing to take on jobs previously filled by what used to be called the working class, then the accessibility of unemployment benefits, as well as that of the country's borders, was in need of fundamental overhaul. What had happened was fairly simple; for the last several decades, Britain had rewarded laziness by calling it welfare and handing out benefits right, left and centre. It was one thing, he said, to bemoan the loss of Britain's manufacturing base, the state of Britain's roads and public transport systems, if you were prepared to be a welder or bus driver. It was quite another if you didn't know a hard hat from a haircut and chose simply to hold out your hands. The redistribution of wealth had gone badly wrong, Alistair thought, if innocent taxpayers' contributions were three steps away from a drug-runner's pocket. There wasn't any longer a working, middle and upper class, in his view. There was a sponging class, a victimised class, a bunch of Lotto winners and, as usual, a criminal class embedded variously in them all.

As autumn turns to winter, both Sarah Halloran and Rebecca Brigham are expecting their first child. Nothing further has been seen of Rebecca's first husband, whose name has been expunged from diaries and any other record books available to public view on Holy Island. Including the visitors' book of a guesthouse in which Charley Oakley once stayed a night. He is believed to have moved from a small abode in Balham to a very small one in Wandsworth.

The new Althing House was completed ahead of schedule and officially opened a week before the double wedding took place. It was built on land in the ownership of Alex Deville. Other projects are beginning to materialise around the village, also on sites in his ownership, including the construction of a new lifeboat station near the Heugh and a hostel for naturalists off Tripping Chare. Mary Carter was somewhat mollified at being shown these developments.

Elected Ministers to the Althing now stand at a total of seven. Michael Cromarty, Elizabeth Swan and Thomas Walker are still there, plus Deville himself. They have been joined by Trevor Patterson, Mary Selby and Dennis Cumming. Dennis's first contribution was to raise the question of joining NATO's Partnership for Peace programme. Led by Mrs. Swan, who had taken her summer holiday in Malta, the other Ministers were inclined to think the Maltese had been right to withdraw in order to avoid compromising their neutrality. Since Dennis was reluctant to let the matter drop and drew the meeting out to an unconscionable four hours, the First Minister has begun to suspect he may become a problem. Not as bad as the problem he once had with Jim "Cochise" Redman, but a problem.

Cochise has resigned his positions as Minister and Bank director, and his mental health is in good enough shape for him to act as Daniel Brigham's assistant jailer. Amy Donaldson was helpful to Cochise during his reincarnation as a white man. When she finished his therapy, she prevailed upon Daniel to try him out. In return, Cochise's help allows Daniel to get out and about more, and he is always a welcome sight patrolling the village. Especially if he is accompanied by his wife.

Cochise's usual charges are the Bigg Market Three. Every month or so, someone else arrives after a typical Saturday night in The Ship Inn or The Crown & Anchor, but they don't stay long. There was never much in the way of serious crime on Holy Island but now there is no serious crime at all. Visitors do sometimes drop litter but they always pick it up when asked nicely by Daniel Brigham.

The tides still roll in and out twice a day, bird life and flora are the same as ever, and English Nature, with the help of another New Zealand import, the former Rebecca Carter, continues to battle the pirri-pirri bur.

Nearing year end, Geordie had seen the four seasons come and go, all but the depths of winter; the pink carpets of thrift on the shore replaced by the white carpets of grass-of-parnassus in the dunes, the arrival of the flocks of wigeon, of barnacle and pale-bellied brent geese from the Arctic. He had seen the sheep-shearing, the barley being threshed and loaded for transport to the maltings, and had gone out with the fishermen a few times for crab, lobster, and most recently salmon. In short, he was as happy as a lark in his new life. And he fully expected that for the next few winter months Holy Island would take on the character of its past: a retreat almost empty of tourists, a place of wildlife, a place at peace. He was looking forward to the experience.

He worried sometimes about his unborn child, about the world that awaited him or her. But better Holy Island, he thought, than the streets of South Tyneside. He would no longer be able there to raise a child in the way he had himself been raised. Here on Lindisfarne, with Sarah, he had a chance.

He also wondered occasionally if he had been one hundred percent true to his calling, but didn't over-indulge such introspection. A beautiful vision of Sarah, lying beside him and talking about being unfair to Romans, tended to get in the way. And Sarah, their child, and the means he had found to support them, made the whole thing a no-brainer anyway. He spent more time wondering if he truly deserved this new life, and how it might all have been different had he not been working late at Groat Market that long ago night in May.

Since June, under his own name, the "Special UK Correspondent" tag behind him, Geordie has diligently written one *Letter from Lindisfarne* each week for the *Washington Post*, sometimes two. His column in that newspaper has a cult following across America.

He received an early edition of T. A. Coward's *The Birds of the British Isles* as his leaving present from *The Northern Sun* and even Old Smokey bade him farewell with a tear in his eye. But maybe it was from coughing.

One evening about a month after their wedding, a stormy October evening with showers sweeping in from the Cheviot, George and Sarah Halloran were sitting at the window of their house on Sandham. They were looking out over open views to the harbour, to Lindisfarne Castle, and to Bamburgh Castle and the Farne Islands in the mist and spindrift beyond.

"George," his wife said, "one day, in between all those American letters, you'll need to write it all down."

"All what, my love?" he asked.

"Those two weeks in May. The definitive book I think you once called it, remember?"

Geordie remembered the folk singer in The Ship and smiled.

"I wasn't here for the first day or so," he said, liking the idea. "But you and Rebecca might help out with that. You wouldn't mind if I locked myself away with my laptop some nights?"

"If it's a serious novel, no. Provided you don't tire yourself out. I'm sure Dad would like it if you wrote it all down, and it'll be a birthday present for the baby. Good enough?"

She smiled at her husband, ruffled his wavy brown hair, gave him a kiss and looked out over the harbour, watching the gulls in flight.

"If you don't," she said, "we'll forget what happened and we'll have lost something. So please write it down. Everything."

So Geordie did.

****

AUTHOR'S NOTE

Although set in real time and in a real place, this is a work of fiction—and apologies are due to the people of Lindisfarne for taking liberties with their beautiful island. In particular, there is no Fahr House or Deville family on Lindisfarne. In the interests of verisimilitude, the names of other residents of the island have been taken from old parish records. It is conceivable that some of those names may appear today, but all the characters to which they are attached in this book are fictitious.

Equally fictitious is the suggestion that Holy Islanders harbour a desire to secede from the UK. As far as the author knows, they have no such ambition. Neither is there a Northern Sun newspaper, although The Journal and sister newspapers are published from an address in Groat Market, Newcastle-upon-Tyne, England.

In other respects, the physical characteristics of the locale, and of Baltasound in Unst, have been portrayed as accurately as the story would allow, as have the weather and tides during the weeks in question. A rare plant known as Edmonston's chickweed or Shetland mouse-ear does indeed grow on only two sites in the world, although it seems to be struggling for survival on one of them. Both are near Baltasound.

The Scottish electorate voted on 3 May 2007 to make the Scottish National Party the biggest party in their parliament at Holyrood. A week later, in a statement that had been anticipated for some time, the British Prime Minister announced the date for his departure from office. Nearly two weeks later, the Leader of the SNP became Scotland's First Minister. References to these and other events in the first three weeks of May 2007 have been used as a backdrop but kept ambiguous.

The court case which the Prologue sets in September 1958 is based loosely on fact. However, the incident occurred in September 2006 in Llandudno in Wales, the bird in question was a swan, and the individual concerned acted alone. He was jailed for two months.

As usual, any mistakes or inaccuracies are the author's own.

ACKNOWLEDGEMENTS

With special thanks to my editor, Kenneth MacLean,
and to Lucy Overton and Isobelle Fenwick
for their encouragement and help with early drafts.